I0596185

The Haus Magic Built Publishing, LLC
Los Angeles, California
www.rosellatesta.com

Published by The Haus Magic Built

Copyright © 2020 Rosella Testa

9 8 7 6 5 4 3 2 1

The author asserts the moral right
to be defined as the author of this work.

ISBN 978 1 7357183 0 9

Printed in the United States of America

First Printing November, 2020

The Haus Magic Built and its logo are trademarks of
The Haus Magic Built Publishing, LLC

Cover Artwork Copyright © 2020 Lizz Lopez

Layout & design: T. Lacy *design@okdaimyo.com*

Editors: Dominika Ossowska, Michelle Footer, Tabita Padilla and Jennifer Ray

Proofreader: Holly Arete

THE LOST PLEIADES

SEVEN SISTERS AND THE SIBYLS

THE LOST PLEIADES

SEVEN SISTERS AND THE SIBYLS

ROSELLA TESTA

THE HAUS MAGIC BUILT

LOS ANGELES

Chapter 1

I WAS FIVE YEARS OLD when my journey from God's City to the City of Angels began. I remember sitting on a plane with my mother and father. I began to ask them a series of loaded questions they could never answer: "Mom, where is Jesus? You said He is in the sky above the clouds. We are above the clouds now, where is He? Can't see Him. Is He on the other side of the plane? Can I go over there and look?"

At that very tender age, I deeply believed that I would see Jesus once we were flying in the air. I'd seen so many paintings of Him sitting in a chair on top of the clouds, that I just assumed that's where He lived. How else could He see everyone and everything that's going on? My mind could not fathom believing in anyone or anything I couldn't see. From the way people spoke about Him, I was certain that almost everyone had seen or met Him while they were on a plane. Well, at the very least, the astronauts must have seen Him on their way to the moon, right? How else could they know how He looked, or know what He wanted us to do? I mean, the priest was always telling me how God wanted us to be, so how else could he know if they hadn't spoken?

Questions continued to swirl in my mind and pour out of my mouth, and my parents looked horrified.

I was so, SO excited to meet Jesus, that the night before our flight I barely closed my eyes. I remember dragging my father onto the plane, pulling at his large hand with all my might. To my mother's disapproval, I fidgeted the entire time with anxiousness and anticipation. Before I knew it, there I was high above the clouds . . . but no Jesus in sight. My child's mind could not accept this, and I cried as my heart broke. Despite their best efforts, my parents could not do anything to console me. They had limited answers to give me; every explanation they could come up with was *not* good enough to appease me. My mother did her very best to soothe me until I fell asleep. And as I lay in her arms, I remember thinking, *why didn't He want to meet me? Why could everyone else see Him, but not me?* I did not understand how I was able see my friends, whom everyone called "imaginary," but I could not see the only man everyone claimed to know. This moment would be a foreshadowing of the many difficult nights, when I'd stay awake thinking and wanting to know the truth about why life was such a mystery. Where did *it* all begin?

This very vivid memory replays in my mind over and over as I sit on almost the same plane I'd once traveled from Rome to Los Angeles, so many years ago. The only difference now being slightly better technology and worse service.

I can still recall every emotion my five-year-old self felt as I look at my mother sitting next to me. I reach over to hold her hand and she looks up, the sadness in her eyes overwhelming me. This trip is not for a vacation, but one to face a very difficult situation. Yesterday we received a call from her sister Silva. She told us that my grandmother had fallen ill, and it was serious. Without hesitation, my mother booked a flight for the both of us to go back to Italy, so that we could spend my grandmother's final days by her side. My father would soon join us as well. This will be a heavy trip for both my mother and me. I decide to give it my best attempt to distract her and make her smile, by retelling the Jesus story. She laughs out loud as she remembers the absurd details of that day and says, "Daddy and I knew we were in trouble! We could have never imagined that you were so aware and intuitive at such a young age. We had a lot of explaining to do, but no answers that would satisfy you. I never wanted to see a priest more than I did in that moment. We searched the entire plane to see if there was one on board!" We both have a good laugh about that. "We knew right then that we would have to be wiser and cleverer with a daughter like you, or else we'd never survive your teenage years!"

We reminisce a little about that formative time in my life. Although it was just a few years ago, it seems like another lifetime. At this moment, it occurs to me that this would be the perfect time to get my mother to open up about her childhood. She almost never talks about her youth; she is extremely private about the years before she married my father. She is always very good at changing the subject, or "dashing off to run an errand," whenever the conversation comes up. But I find myself on a thirteen-hour flight where she cannot escape me or deflect. I cannot let this moment slip from my grasp.

"Mom, what were you like as a young girl?" She pauses and locks her fingers tightly together. Good sign; typically, she has an annoyed look on her face when I ask this question. But today her face is soft, and her body language is calm. It does not have its usual uptight disposition.

"So different than you, Eli. You have always been an intellectual, and so far ahead of your years. I was a very simple girl. Being raised in Italy . . . well, it was a different life. I never questioned the way things were. I kept my head down and always did as I was told. I wasn't allowed to ask questions, or know a lot of things back then. We only spoke when we were spoken to. No dreaming big, just focused on working very hard for our family, to put food on the table."

My mom proceeds on with stories of her childhood adventures. I am desperately hoping to hear something new, but she goes on to tell the same stories I'd heard so many times. A moment before I start to lose interest and tune her out, she begins to speak in detail about my grandmother. *This is new*. I'm a bit taken aback. She is generally very protective and very private about her mother. Growing up, there were lots of extravagant rumors about my grandparents. All much too ostentatious to believe.

She proceeds to share with me that my grandmother's family is not really from Ceri, a small town outside of Rome.

"They are actually from Pretare," she says.

"What! Where is that? We've been visiting Ceri since I was born. How is it possible that no one has ever mentioned this before?!" I ask, irked and confused.

"Now don't be upset, there are lots of things you don't know. No one has lied to you love, it's just never come up."

My mother knows how sensitive I am about being lied to. *I'd better get used to this feeling,* I think to myself. For being Italian, we sure do have a lot of family secrets. This is the first time I can see that my mother *needs to* talk about my grandmother, Amelia. But as she goes deeper into details, so does her pain. I can see it all over her face.

"The eastern slopes down to the Adriatic Sea are steep, and it is in that area that your grandmothers were born," says my mother.

"Oh My God!!! You mean *both* my grandmothers are from there!" I yell in astonishment. I think my head just exploded.

"It's a small town called Pretare, and it's not too far from Umito," she continues.

I had occasionally heard of this town throughout the years, but I had never been, and sadly knew absolutely nothing about it. I turn to my mom who is trying to find a better position in her seat and ask, "Have you and Papa ever been to Pretare?"

She looks at me with a bit of hesitation and says, "No, we have never been. But we hear it is beautiful and filled with great history."

I proceed to ask, "Why do you think my grandparents never took either of you to visit?"

She sighs and says, "I think there are many sad memories for them there. It was much too difficult to return to that place; there was nothing left there for them."

Yes, I imagine that would be true. I knew almost nothing about my great grandparents on either my mother's or father's side. My mother, Elizabetta, daughter of Amelia, married Leonardo, son of Rosa. My grandmothers were quite determined to have at least one of their children marry the other's. They were best friends and it was their way of having the two families linked forever.

My mother continues, "Let me guess, you want to visit Pretare?"

She knows me all too well. I grab her hand, "YES, I would love to go there. Do you think it's possible?"

She looks down and says, "Let's see how your grandmother is doing, and we can talk about it once we know her condition."

I shouldn't push it, I think to myself, so I say, "Yes, of course."

In my mother's usual fashion, she shifts the conversation when it becomes too heavy.

"You know, your grandmother is going to be 95 years old this year," she mentions, casually changing the subject.

"Yes, I know. But how is it possible that she doesn't look a day over 45?" I ask.

"Good genes," she replies with a devilish grin.

"Since we're on that subject, can you please explain to me how *we* look the same age?" I ask.

"Don't be absurd!" she replies giggling, and obviously flattered.

"Why did those good genes skip my generation, Mom?"

"I don't think they did, Eli. Why would you say such a thing?"

"Well mostly because, well . . . I . . . "

Ding

Ding

"Ladies and gentlemen, we are ready for our final descent into Leonardo Da Vinci Airport. Please be sure your seat belts are fastened and that you are sitting in an upright position," says the robotic female voice over the intercom, interrupting me. It looks like for the first time, it was me who wanted to evade questions.

As we exit customs from our arrival at the airport, I see my grandmother's sister, my Great-Aunt Ersella, and her daughter Alessia—my second cousin. We're met with overzealous applause, countless hugs, and a million kisses. It's so good to see them, I've missed them *so* much. I haven't been back to visit for a few years now. I blame it entirely on my blood-sucking corporate job, and a boss that would rather eat glass than see me take a vacation.

"You look so exhausted, Eli. Your mother tells me that you work for Lucifer's kin!" Aunt Ersella says with disapproval, yet with a humorous undertone. I swear this is another woman in my family that never ages, she has hardly any wrinkles and the most flawless complexion.

"Yes, if you squint, you'll be able to see his horns," I reply sarcastically.

"Well, I have a lot to say about that! Eli, are you really going to let a washed out, insignificant man, who is trying to take all of your ideas because he's too stupid to have any of his own, AND not give you credit or proper pay, ruin your life?" She continues, "You're going to hear it from your grandmother too, she's very upset about this." Ouch, that stung. Geez, I forgot how fast she talks. And how awkward it is standing in the middle of the airport, holding my suitcases and being lectured.

"Wonderful! A deathbed lecture to look forward to! What every girl lives for," I reply playfully.

My mother shoots me a scowling look.

I smile, "Too soon?"

My dark sense of humor seems to get me in trouble every time. Alessia saves me from any further scowling as she grabs my hand and pulls me away.

"I miss you so much cousin, your hair is so long now!" she says ecstatically.

It reaches right below my shoulders—not as long as I'm used to wearing it, but to be fair, it's the longest it's been in some time. Last year I suffered hair loss because of stress.

"It's finally growing back," she says with so much joy and hope in her eyes.

"Yes," I answer, "let's hope the worst is over."

The last few years I've had some unexpected health problems. Something I hope to leave far behind me.

"Your skin is still flawless too! Why aren't you aging either?! What secret are you and Aunt Ersella hiding?" I ask Alessia. "How is it that you still look 15?"

"Olive oil!" she exclaims, and we both laugh hysterically. This is the answer every woman in my family gives.

Alessia is my favorite cousin; she is incredibly smart, funny, well-spoken, and drop-dead gorgeous. She is a 27-year-old restaurant entrepreneur. She and her brothers inherited the business from my Aunt Ersella and Uncle Adolfo, and she's consistently trying to find her place in the family business, as she stands in partnership with her two dominant brothers. But if you ask me, she's always been the boss, just like her mother. Standing perfectly at 5' 8" with long, full brown hair and almond-shaped eyes, she's exactly what you'd imagine a Roman goddess to look like. As far as her brothers, well . . . let's just say they are not only the kindest of men, but they resemble warriors from the Trojan War. I can't imagine my stunning aunt and uncle could have made anything other than perfect specimens. The food at their restaurant—Osteria D'Ugo—is divine. 'Food of the Gods' is its famous moniker, given to them by acclaimed food critics worldwide. It is said to be one of the best restaurants internationally, and like nothing else in all of Italy. But I'm convinced that people also go there to get a glimpse of this beautiful family.

I ask Alessia about her brothers, and we small talk about the rest of our family. As she catches me up on all the latest details of her love life, my aunt interrupts to ask, "Are you hungry? You're both so thin, don't they have good food in America?" There is laughter, then a pause.

"I think it's just the stress of the last few years with Eli's health," my mom says, "but we are ok now. And we intend to make up the weight loss while we're here!"

My cousin winks at me with optimism. There must be something in the earth here, because the food—in my opinion—is the best in the world. I haven't had an appetite in so long. But with only 20 steps into this country, all my hunger seems to have returned full force. I desperately want to go to their restaurant for lunch; I dream about that place every day! There is a kind of magic in my aunt's tomato sauce that makes people from all over the world come to try it. My mother says that absolutely no one can replicate it. Try as they may to learn from her, there is dexterity in her hands that no one else can replicate. Everyone swears they watch her and take careful notes, but as my mother puts it,

"It's like the moment you blink, she adds a secret ingredient."

Although my aunt and cousin are very insistent on stopping by the restaurant before going to my grandmother's house, my mother politely declines the invitation. It is nearly a three-hour drive to Umito from Rome. It's not ideal to drive straight there, directly after a 13-hour flight, but it's clear to all of us from my mother's face that she is very anxious to get to my grandmother.

We load everything into my great-aunt's brand-new van, which she often uses to transport things to and from the restaurant. I notice additional bags in the back.

"Ále!" my nickname for Alessia. "Are you staying in Umito?" I ask with excitement.

"Yes my love, we'll be staying in town for a bit," she replies.

I scream out, "YESSS!!!" as I jump on her and she spins me around.

My mother turns to look at her aunt and says, "I am so happy that we will be together. How long will you be staying?"

"I don't know, Elizabetta. However long it takes," my great aunt replies to my mother.

A moment of silence falls on us all as we realize the meaning of those words.

"Well, this car isn't going to drive itself!" Aunt Ersella yells out. "Come on, everyone in!"

I sit in the front passenger seat and Alessia drives. I must admit, the van is very comfortable and spacious—which is a great thing because it's a long drive. Before I settle into my seat, a wave of the hot and humid August weather hits me. I take off my jacket and turn on the air conditioning to full blast.

"Did you fly in stilettos, Eli?" Alessia gushes, looking down at my feet, while I take my shoes off. Every woman in our family has a shoe fetish.

"Just on and off the plane; I changed into socks for the flight," I reply.

"You have to let me try those on later!" she says.

Before I can respond, my mother chimes in, "She's got a suit-case full! Shoes are the only thing she really spends any money on. But those are so darn uncomfortable! I think they made the bottoms red so people don't notice when your feet bleed from the pain. Eli, I don't know how you wear those!"

We laugh because we all know she's right, but they are so gorgeous!

There is an electricity in the air that I feel every time I come to Italy. It enraptures your soul with its incredible history, a sense of the unknown, and a yearning for exploration. But there is also a renewed feeling of life, as if you are born again as your better self, a more authentic self. Somehow your core values are re-stored, and you are no longer afraid to believe in the things you cannot see. But also, somehow believe in things you *feel* with the same conviction.

This kind of freedom is something I never feel in Los Angeles, or anywhere else, really. But here, I can feel it deep in my bones. This kind of freedom makes me want to forget everything I know. It pulls me in to learn about things that I normally have no interest in, and to do things I've never done before. I know under the circumstances of this trip I should not feel this way, but I do. It's stronger than me, and it happens every time I place my foot on this soil. It's like an electrical message automatically sent to my neurons, reminding me that Mother Nature knows her citizen has returned home.

The drive to Umito is so beautiful. It weaves in and out through green plush hills and mountains; a storybook-like ter-rain. Driving past all the lovely small towns, I wonder what all those people and their lives must be like. I can't help but think that this would have been my life if we hadn't moved to America. I wonder, do they know that they live on some of the most exquisite land in the world, that many could not even imagine in a dream? Or have they felt trapped by its smallness? Do they appreciate its simplicity, or are they bored by its predictability? I've had the privilege of traveling a lot in my short life, but nothing quite compares to Italy—its history, landscapes, art, food, but most importantly, its people. They are some of the kindest and most generous the world offers; true salt-of-the earth souls. I know God isn't supposed to have favorites, but I dare say that Italy is some of His finest work.

We continue to talk over each other about family gossip and the latest news—who's dating whom, who got married, who got divorced, and it wouldn't be an Italian conversation without talking about who died. And it's certainly not a complete conversation until someone asks, "Eli, when are you going to get married and give your mother some grandchildren?" This time it's Aunt Ersella who is demanding. Oh boy, here we go again . . .

"I don't know Auntie; I think I'm still too young. Besides, why don't you lecture Alessia? She's older than me and not married." Alessia punches me hard in the leg and I let out a scream.

"That's gonna leave a bruise, you beast!" I squeal at my cousin, as I rub the sting out of my leg.

"Good! She's on me every day about it. For once, I was glad the conversation wasn't about me!" she answers back. She has one hell of a right hook; she must have learned that from her brothers.

My aunt then addresses us with a tone that insinuates we've both said the stupidest thing in the world, "Well, I know that the television insists we are all living longer, but I don't believe that we have the same amount of time we once did." We stare at her puzzled. I can't wait to see where this is going.

"What? Uhm . . . how do mean Auntie?" I ask with a chuckle, excited to hear what crazy thing would drop from her mouth.

"Well, I mean everyone is so busy these days. No one seems to have time for anything anymore! In my day, you'd be almost dead by now with at least three grown children," she says adamantly.

"Auntie, when was 'your day' exactly? Was that in Jesus' time?" I ask teasingly, "I know you claim to be 4,200 'Earth' years old, but things aren't that way anymore."

She gives me a smug look and says, "Now you listen Eli . . . my day, your day, whatever! It's all the same and so are men's attitudes. And I'm much older than Jesus, I mean really, don't insult me." Alessia and I can't help but laugh at Aunt Ersella's eccentric and exaggerated story telling. She has been this way as far back as I can remember. She's completely mad, and I love it!

"Now, I know you are meant to marry for love and not for money, as you should of course," she continues. "But, let me advise you on that path." Alessia and I lock eyes as we listen closely.

"When you marry for love, you will either suffer of a broken heart or suffer from disappointment. And by the time your husband will appreciate you and have the money to buy you a proper gift, you will be too old to care. Let me explain," she presses on, and Alessia and I do our best to hold our laughter.

"Let's say you've always wanted a fur coat, but by the time he can afford it, you'll be in menopause and sweating like a pig, and all you'll think about is where you're going to hide it. Maybe you've always wanted a big diamond ring. By the time he can afford that three-plus carat, your dainty, beautiful, youthful hands will be wrinkly and swollen from all the years of working and raising his children. Suddenly, that diamond ring brings more attention to your hands than you want, because you fear that it will give your age away."

I'm starting to see where I get my dark sense of humor from. My aunt proceeds without missing a beat.

"Then there's that perfect two-story house that you dreamt of your entire life. Well, you finally get it, but by the time you do, you will have arthritis and you can't climb the damn stairs anymore!" Aunt Ersella finishes triumphantly as my mother and her high five each other. They break out in uncontrollable, hysterical laughter. It becomes contagious and we all can't stop.

Aunt Ersella is quite a character. She is 5' 7" with a statuesque build. Her hair is short and she has, as we say in America, "Big Texas Hair!" Everyone compares her to the magnificent Sophia Loren, which she flutters her long eyelashes at every time she hears the comparison. What I love most about her is her grand style, and her non-politically correct ways that are brutally honest, almost to the point of being offensive. Her condescending attitude adds to a bewitching charm that only she can get away with. She's perfect in my eyes, and I hope to be just like her someday. But I'd never have the guts to say what she does. She is, without a doubt, the most authentic and unapologetic person I have ever met. I love that she *doesn't* want to change, for fear of losing who she really is. She claims that she does not want to conform to this "new world." She doesn't waste time caring about what anyone thinks of her, because she insists, "They would never understand." When she looks at you with her big eyes that sit perfectly framed by her huge, black, oval-shaped eyeglasses, it's as if she can see into your soul. She knows exactly who you are and loves you anyway.

In regard to her style, she'll wear more jewelry in one day than I own. Liberace had nothing on her. There are several layered necklaces of different lengths on her at all times, and many with various stones. She loves her bracelets to line up perfectly, going up half her forearms on both sides. Her earrings are always long and grand. And of course, her rings—I die for them; she actually wears multiple rings on each finger, and I am forever mesmerized by them. I remember as a child I would beg to try them on, but I was never permitted to. All of her clothes and shoes are designed by a well-known fashion designer in Rome. When she visits him about twice a year, excluding special events, she is greeted with air kisses in private meetings with personalized sketches. She then chooses what she wants, and the garments are made precisely to her body shape—which is incredible for her age. To no surprise, she refuses to tell anyone her real age; I honestly don't think her kids even know. Any time we've asked she says, "Roughly 4,200 'Earth' years old, but who's counting darling!" Which only lends to the insanity that I love about her. Her specialty is creating "beauty potions," as she calls them. You can see the effects of these "potions" in her hair, skin, and nails, but she will not share the secrets of the ingredients when she's asked, not even with her only daughter.

Aunt Ersella is now a widow. Alessia and her brothers have very few memories of their father, that they can recall. Although I never met my great-uncle Adolfo, I feel like I know him through the stories everyone tells. I am told he was a very interesting man, but layered and complicated.

In the car, Aunt Ersella starts to sing an old Roman song about the long suffering of a wife and her cheating husband. This is yet another thing I love about my aunt. She knows songs and stories that no one has ever heard of. She likes to sing them in a way that gives them a theatrical feel. She's absolutely fascinating and exciting! Her voice is so beautiful; the sound is romantic, but also a bit raspy and rough. There is so much pain and joy, and a lifetime of lessons in her singing. I ask her if she ever thought about singing professionally when she was younger, and she laughs at my question. She proceeds to ask my cousin and I what we think of various current pop stars. We're shocked she knows anyone on the radio, let alone their songs! She tells us that singers are storytellers, and if we listen closely, we can hear prophecy being told. She says that music is the manifestation of the hopes, dreams, and changes we want to see in the world, that's why the world can connect through music regardless of race or age. She starts to sing to the song on the radio. My cousin Alessia pulls the car over, stops, looks at me, then looks at her mother and says, "Who are you?"

"Your timing couldn't be more perfect Alessia," my mother says as she unbuckles her seatbelt, "I really need to use the restroom."

As I look up, I notice that she has pulled into a gas station. "I think I'll just fill up while we're here," Alessia replies.

I get out of the car to stretch, and it feels *SO* good to inhale that pure, perfect mountain air. They all go inside to either use the restroom, or purchase water and snacks. I stand outside the car door and tilt my head back to the sky and yawn. I stretch out my arms as wide as I can, and I notice a sign that says Aquasanta Terme 100km, which is approximately 62 miles. We had traveled more than I realized. It must have been all of my aunt's singing that distracted me, because usually this drive feels like it never ends. Aquasanta is a small city at the bottom of the mountain where my mother is from. The small town where she was born is called Umito. It is actually the last town at the very top of the mountain, and approximately 25 minutes from the bottom.

As I'm staring at the road sign, I suddenly realize that there is a man smiling back at me. Maybe because of my exhaustion, I don't realize that he is directly in eyeshot of the sign. I am instantly flustered and embarrassed, because it dawns on me that he must think I am staring at him.

"Real smooth, Eli," I mumble to myself, as I look down and away from him. After a moment, I turn back to see if he's still there.

"Flying can be exhausting; I don't blame you," the stranger

says, startling me as we lock eyes. He's somehow directly in front of me.

"H-how do you know I've been flying?" I manage to ask, stumbling over my words.

"The hair on the back of your head. I recognize that look, I fly a lot myself. It must have been a long flight. Where did you come in from?"

"Los Angeles," I reply, as I start to fix the back of my hair, embarrassed once again. I can feel my face getting hot.

"It's a tragically beautiful place," he comments.

"Have you been?" I ask.

"Yes, on a few occasions."

I look over my shoulder as I hear my family walking towards us. When I look back, he's already at his car; he nods his head knowingly, gets in, and drives away.

"Whoa! Who is *that*?" Alessia yells out.

"I have no idea. Someone I just made myself look very stupid in front of. He thought I was staring at him and decided to add to my awkwardness by making small talk about my airplane hair," I reply, my cheeks still burning.

"Well, I don't blame you for staring! He's gorgeous! And SO hot—he doesn't even look real! Those perfect blue eyes, wavy dirty-blonde hair, high cheekbones, full lips, and oooh, that jawline that could cut you . . . what about that body, holy shit!" She says raising her eyebrows and squinting her eyes as she gushes.

"I *wasn't* staring! I was looking at the sign and he was in my way," I reply defensively.

"I wish he was in *my way*," Alessia blurts out.

"Eli likes to pretend that she doesn't care or pay attention to those kinds of things," my mother says smirking.

"WOW! That car, though! Mom, is this what you meant by marrying for money and not love?" Alessia asks while laughing.

"Now Ále, I never said to marry for money. I just want to let you girls know what you're walking into when you marry for love," Aunt Ersella replies. "But if I were a measly 40 years younger, I would marry that nice young man for both!"

"Me too!" my mother adds.

"MOM!" I yell out, as I put my head in my hands and everyone begins to laugh.

As we pull out of the gas station, my boy-crazy cousin continues to talk about the handsome stranger and how familiar he seemed. They all start to chime in about who he could have possibly been, but everyone agrees not a model or actor, because no one recognizes him. Ále goes on and on about his car and what he was wearing. I don't have a clue about anything she is saying; I must have been too embarrassed to notice.

I ask my cousin what kind of car it was and why it is a big deal anyway? She looks at me with extreme disappointment for not knowing, like at a child that forgets how to tie their shoes. She then proceeds to tell me it's a limited-edition sports car that's impossible to get, something about it not being out yet. They go on about him being someone of influence in order to obtain a car of that caliber. I don't even know why I asked, it's not like I care. Usually strangers don't speak to me, so when they do, I'm always caught off guard and typically don't notice details. He seems more like the kind of guy that Alessia turns down on a Tuesday. Men like that throw themselves at her feet and pledge their life to her every day. I could never imagine someone like that ever taking an interest in me. I'm sure he thought I was gawking at him and was just trying to be polite to my airplane-head.

I suppose I have a love-hate relationship with myself. And a full-on hate relationship with love. Some people just *love* love. I'm just broken by it. You can't love something that doesn't love you back—love doesn't love me, and so I don't love *it*. Even though I'm still very young, it becomes more and more complicated as I get older.

I've also become quite sensitive about my skin, hair, and my overall physical appearance over the last few years. It's amazing how vain we become when we have no control over the way our body is changing. I've become sensitive to aging—well, more so to *how* I age. Sometimes I don't recognize myself. I've questioned whether it's my eyesight or my self-esteem that is going bad. I see differences and notice changes in my appearance every day, and I wonder how this is possible. I've spoken with doctors, psychologists, and my family several times. No one is ever able to give me a straight answer, and they often look at me like I'm making it up. At first it seemed minor, like my face seemed less childlike. But recently, my features and body are changing so much, that I've been accused of having cosmetic surgery more times than I can count. Not that I have anything against plastic surgery. Typically people do it to improve their features, but I find that the response I tend to receive is "you just look different." Not bad, not good, just *different*. Ugh, that would be my luck. It has only led me to become more aggrieved. I suppose with all of the good genes in my family, it was only a matter of time before I became insecure. I am the only one on both sides of my family that doesn't look like I belong on either side. On several occasions, I've joked around with my parents about them bringing home the wrong child. I'm convinced there is another family somewhere in Italy, wondering why their child doesn't look anything like them.

On my mother's side, everyone is Mediterranean-looking: olive-toned skin, brown eyes, brown hair, and curvy bodies. On my father's side, they are all mostly fair-skinned with light hair, light eyes, and thin, long figures. Between both of my grandmothers' uncommon and extraordinary looks, and the modest yet handsome features of my grandfathers, all of their children and grandchildren turned out above average. I look like the "milkman's grandchild," as one of my obnoxious cousins once said. Although that comment really hurt, I couldn't have said it better myself. My skin is very pale, *too* pale—I make the English look tan. My dad nicknamed me "Ghost" growing up. I tried many times to tan throughout the years, but the best I ever got was a warm, sun-kissed version of pale-on-pale. Indoors, my hair and eyes are brown, but when I'm in the sun, they shift color. My hair turns into auburn red with a honey-gold hue, and my eyes turn hazel with the same honey glow that is in my hair. My body is a shape that is unidentifiable to me; it is neither long and lean, nor sexy and curvy. My nose is not thin and perfectly pointed, and my eyes are round, not almond-shaped like on either side of the family. My face shape is between round and square, so far from everyone else's chiseled cheekbones, with jawlines aligned in perfect symmetry. Even in LA, the land of the famous, my parents are gawked at. I've learned to walk behind them. I often hear that I have an old soul and an Old-World look to go with it—well too bad I wasn't born one hundred years ago.

Once, I took a human anatomy drawing class in college. The assignment was to draw an organic and free-flowing portrait of a couple. I didn't have the courage to ask anyone else I knew to sit for that long, so I asked my parents. I received a low grade on that assignment because my art teacher told me that I did not draw the portrait "organically." He insisted that "no one's face has perfect symmetry," and if they did, they would be "very unattractive."

Sometimes it's just exhausting being their kid. It's not just the way they look. It's like they are perfect at everything they do, and everything they touch turns to gold. Anything they build, make, cook, or grow turns out perfect. And they are so smart;

they know everything about everything, except how to give a five-year-old an explanation of why Jesus isn't above the clouds. Most people call that being a well-rounded person. I call it being annoying. I would give anything just to have an ounce of that, but I just seem to fall short, whereas they are brilliant. To the rest of the world being Italian seems to mean having a killer fashion style, a gourmet food palate, and an excellent taste in cars. My style on the other hand is basic; straight lines and plain clothes. But, I am obsessed with shoes. This is the one area of my life I *may* have my family beat. I suppose aside from comparing myself to them, part of my insecurity is having to live in a city convoluted with so many beautiful people; everyone from celebrities to models, and a whole social media world that has created an impossible expectation to live up to. Looking ordinary is something I can actually appreciate, because it's taken the pressure off, and I am able to get lost in the crowd.

The chatty voices in the van become muffled as my eyes grow heavy. The more they talk about the handsome stranger, and relationships and love in general, the more I find myself starting to daydream as their voices move further and further away from my thoughts. I close my eyes for what seems like a second, when I'm startled awake by Alessia shaking my arm. We have almost arrived at my grandmother's house.

"Hey Airplane-Head, we're almost there."

"Very funny. Is that going to be my new nickname?" I reply to Alessia, clearing my throat.

"There's a good chance," she nods and winks.

Trying hard to get out of a sleepy haze, I drink some water, powder my face, and reapply my lipstick. I know there will be tons of family and friends there to greet us that I haven't seen in years, and I want to look my best, even if my best is a third of what the rest of my family's best actually is—believe me, this was a hard life lesson of acceptance within myself. Good thing I've got my sense of humor.

Chapter 2

As we drive up the hill and pull in front of the house, every-one starts to run outside. That's the thing about these small towns, everyone can see or hear your car coming from a mile away, because there's only one road in and one road out. And of course, everyone knows everybody and their business. NO such thing as privacy or a surprise visit. I haven't even removed my seatbelt, when my door flings open and my uncle is pulling me out of the car, like he used to do when I was a little girl.

"My beautiful Eli!" my Uncle Giovanni says, as he holds my face in his hands. He is emotional and trying to fight back his tears. I throw my arms around his neck and fill his face with kisses. He is my mother's older brother, and absolutely the most compassionate and wonderful man I know, outside of my own father. He is a handsome man with very masculine features. He has a warm smile, and a mole on his cheek that I love to kiss. His deep brown eyes and brown hair, along with his lightly grown beard, give him a kind of mysterious look. He stands at about 5' 10" and has a little belly; he's by no means overweight, he just loves pasta. Uncle Giovanni is a bit shy by nature but can turn on the charm when he needs to.

"God has heard our prayers; you are finally home. We have all been waiting for you. We've missed you so much," he says. Uncle Giovanni—we call him Uncle Gianni—always tells me I'm his favorite niece, but says it's a secret, because he doesn't want the others to get jealous. Then anytime he introduces me to someone, he tells them I'm his favorite, so I'm pretty sure the word is out, Uncle Gianni. To be the favorite *anything* in our family is a great honor, because there are so many of us on both of my parents' sides. But it's especially an honor to be *his* favorite, because he is such a special person.

My mother comes from a family of ten children, and my father comes from a family of seven. It feels like I have hundreds of cousins, second cousins, and third cousins. All I know is that at every wedding we have a minimum guest count of four hundred.

It takes nearly thirty minutes to say hello to everyone. I become overjoyed and I can't help but feel emotional from the love and happiness I am feeling. I want to cherish this moment forever; it feels like a gift. Everyone is so lovely and so excited to make plans with me. They want to catch up, go out, and maybe even get into a little trouble.

Uncle Gianni leans in and says, "Don't let Elizabetta hear that, she won't like it. My sister is a glutton for suffering and pain during sad times. She won't want anyone making plans and having fun!"

"Uncle, you know her so well. Why is she like that?" I ask.

"Well, we had a difficult childhood and we were taught in times of sorrow there is no joy. But now we know that without laughter, we will never get through this. Right, Eli?"

"Yes, that's so true. I would've never made it through last year without it. No help from my mom!" We have a good laugh about my mom's occasional strict and uptight ways.

"Your father must be anxious; he hasn't been back since the passing of his mother. When is he going to arrive?" Uncle Gianni asks. My uncle and my father are best friends; they have been since birth. They have a bond that my father never even had with his own brothers.

"Well, he's on standby for now. Just depends on how Nonna is doing," I reply.

"Speaking of, I think it's time you go in to see her," he says to me. My mother and Aunt Ersella went into my grandmother's bedroom within minutes of arriving, but I was still trying to muster up the courage to go upstairs. I know I finally have to see her.

I hug my uncle and begin to walk through the hallway and toward the stairs. In that moment, I look around and realize that there is one person that I would never see again, and my heart begins to ache as a pain pierces through my soul. It is my Nonna Rosa, my father's mother. She was the most spectacular creature. Even in her old age she was divine. She was absolutely the most striking and glamourous woman I've ever seen; stunning was the word that came to everyone's lips when they met her. If I'm being honest, both of my grandmothers were quite striking. If you'd ever laid eyes on either of them, you'd realize they didn't look like anyone you'd ever seen; breathtakingly beautiful in a way that you would imagine an angel to be, rendering one almost speechless at first glance. Not that I've seen a real angel in my life, but they are the closest thing I can imagine to that kind of beauty and enchantment.

My grandmothers, Amelia and Rosa, were best friends since infancy. They were completely inseparable; so much so that I've always had this strange suspicion they could read each other's minds. They were both easy going by nature and free spirits in every sense—not much could upset them. There wasn't anything they couldn't do: fix, cook, heal, or create. They were dedicated wives and devout mothers. They participated in community service, and were the first people to arrive and give a lending hand. They had the capacity for knowing when you needed help— they were the doctors, nurses, and mid-wives when there was no one else around. I often wondered how they were able to do so much—I can barely work, pick up my dry cleaning, and cook for myself.

Growing up there was never a shortage of stories and laughter between them. And definitely never a shortage of learning. They were masters of nature; they knew every plant and what it was to be used for. They knew the name of every star in the sky and the myths among astrology. They could name every kind of animal in the Apennine Mountains, which is a mountain range extending 1,207 kilometers across the Italian Peninsula. My grandmothers would share countless stories and imaginative anecdotes, which I now lovingly refer to as "faerie tales," about their parents, their siblings, the trying times of war and famine, and even joyfully recall how they met my grandfathers. I questioned who or what to believe and wondered if they were just making up these intricate tales as they went along. They would speak as if they had lived a thousand lifetimes and I would incessantly tease them about it. And one of them would always turn to me with the same mischievous look and magical smile, and say, "How do you know we haven't?" I would think to myself, *sure Nonna, time to put the vino down.*

At the time of my Nonna Rosa's passing, I was too sick to travel and unable to make the flight. I never had a chance to say goodbye—her death seemed so sudden. She was a true hero in my life. Both of my grandmothers were always the greatest heroes in my eyes. I'm so proud to come from a legacy of such women—I would give anything to have the courage and strength they had. As I looked around while greeting my family earlier, it was strange not to see my Nonna Rosa there. It felt unreal. In my mind, she was just running late and would be walking into the room any moment . . . but the pain in my heart reminded me that that was not going to happen. I am still in denial of her passing. My mother thinks it's because I didn't have the closure I needed. But the truth is, I just don't know how to face the reality of being abandoned by both of my heroes, because of their death. I feel paralyzed by the idea of walking into Nonna Amelia's room, and having to face dealing with two losses so close to each other.

I take a deep breath and with every ounce of courage inside me, I walk up the stairs. I drop my purse and stand outside my grandmother's door—I'm terrified to walk in. I can hear my mom and her sisters talking to my grandmother. I have missed her voice, it's just not the same over the phone. My hand is on the doorknob when suddenly an emptiness washes over me as I think about seeing her. I pull my hand away and the door suddenly opens. My Aunt Silva is standing there—of all my mother's sisters, she is the one I feel the closest to. She's the vixen of all the sisters and has that Marilyn Monroe sex appeal. She's blonde and wears her hair like she's a housewife from the 1950's, has brown eyes, and a very full and curvaceous figure. She has big natural lips, full breasts, a tiny waist and Lombard street hips. She is fun and full of life with a sarcastic wit and an amazing sense of humor. For people that don't know her, she may come across as if she's a bit of an airhead, but in truth she is the smartest person in the room, and nothing escapes her. There really is no one in this world that has Aunt Silva's uniqueness.

"Eli!" she screams as she throws her arms around me, "your grandmother was insisting that you were standing outside the door and asked me to open it. Well come in my love, she's been expecting you."

She silently mouths, "It's ok" to me and hugs me again. She

lets me go and steps out of the way to let me in. As I turn the corner, I see my grandmother laying in her bed with my aunts and her sister by her side. Her bedroom looks exactly as it did the last time I was here—books everywhere, her perfumes on her dresser, a photo of my grandfather on her nightstand. She is wearing the white robe that he gave her when they were first married. Her hair is down; I've never seen it down. It is very long, shiny, and straight with some waves at the end, and a perfectly white and silver hue. As I get closer, I notice something has changed. I've never seen her look this way, she looks *different*.

Then it hits me like a lightning bolt—I can't believe my eyes . . . is this really possible? In a shock, I realize *her* different is *my* different. Her features have changed, the same way mine have. We look *alike*. I look like her, but a *different* her; she does not have the face I have known all my life. How is this possible? I can't think clearly. I rush to her side and tears begin to pour down my face. My legs go numb and I fall to my knees by her bedside. I hold her hand tightly.

"Hello, my love," she says gently, in that beautiful voice I'd so longed for. I can't help but to be overwhelmed.

"Hello Nonna," I manage to mutter, as I close my eyes and place my head by her bed. I can smell her sheets; they're the same scent they've always been. And they have the same effect on me today as they did so long ago; they make me feel calm and safe. She puts her hand on my head, and I ask her how she is feeling.

"Well, by the looks of things, better than you all," she jokes. We all giggle a bit.

"I can't believe you're joking, Nonna," I say.

"Someone's got to. It's just death—it's not like it's forever," she says, as if it were fact.

"Well I'm glad to see you haven't lost your sense of humor."

"That wasn't a joke," she replies. I've long known that my grandmothers always had their own unique way of seeing things, and we've learned never to question it, as the answers would only further confuse us.

"It's so good to see you," I say, as I lift up my head to look closely at her. Once again, I'm shocked at the resemblance between us, but wonder if it's all in my mind, or if I'm having one of my hallucinations that my doctors insist aren't really happening. I look around the room and notice my mom and aunts holding one another watching us, or to put it more accurately, staring. In that moment it becomes clear everyone is thinking the same thing, and my grandmother knows it.

"Darling, why don't you go and get some food. You must be famished; I remember how traveling makes you hungry," says Nonna, breaking the awkward silence.

"I don't want to leave your side," I reply.

"I don't know what you've heard, but I'm not going to die today, or even this week. We have a little more time together, Eli. Please ease your mind." And with those words, she soothes me, and I reluctantly get up and start to head downstairs. As I get halfway to the bottom, I realize I've left my purse at the top of the stairs. I'd dropped it on the floor outside Nonna's bedroom before I walked in. I run back up quickly; I hear increasingly loud voices. I can't help but to walk closer to the bedroom door and listen.

"Elizabetta, the change has happened much faster than you suggested. Why didn't you tell me?" I hear Nonna say reproachfully at my mother. I'm relieved to know I'm not going mad, but I feel perplexed and lost. Everyone seems to know something I'm being excluded from.

"I didn't realize it myself, until I saw you side by side," my mom answers defensively.

"Do not lie to me," Nonna hisses angrily.

"I just want to protect her. Knowing the truth about this family will only shake her to the core. And she will be furious with us! She will never trust me again." I hear my mom's voice breaking and rising with emotion.

"I understand that, and you have done a good job protecting her all her life. But doing so now will only do damage," Nonna retorts with a gentler tone.

"SSHHHH!" I hear someone say. I get a feeling that they know I'm eavesdropping. I become very nervous, quickly grab my purse, and run down the stairs. A guilty-looking Alessia is waiting for me as she fidgets nervously.

"You ok?" she asks, as I am sure I look completely flustered.

"Yes, fine. Just hungry." I grab her hand and walk towards the living room where everyone else is eating and drinking.

"You're shaking Eli, what's wrong?"

"Alessia we talk all the time and you've never lied to me. But now it seems you're one of the many who are keeping secrets from me. Are you really going to tell me that you haven't seen *her* like *that* before today?" I reply frustrated, pointing to Nonna's room. "So, unless you're going to come clean about what the hell is going on, I suggest we go eat."

With her big perfect eyes filling with anxiety, she replies, "Okay." We head to the dining room in silence where we socialize with our family and friends. The dining room has a very long table, it seats twenty people and each chair is filled. I look over at my grandmother's china cabinet; I see that it has only become more cluttered with various items she's collected over the years. On the other side of the room there is an old hutch where she keeps all her silverware and special table linens. She displays various framed photos taken throughout the years on its countertop. I see a new frame—it's a photograph of my grandmother and me. I remember the day it was taken vividly, but I don't remember taking that photograph. It was the night before we left for America. I am sitting on her lap and we are embraced. It is a very tender moment between us—my eyes look hopeful and bright, as you would imagine any child who's filled with excitement for a new adventure. My grandmother's eyes are the opposite—they are filled with great melancholy. She is smiling but I can see the pain. I cannot imagine what it cost her to let us go that day.

My thoughts are making it hard to concentrate and keep conversations going. I blame it on jet lag, and everyone seems to give me a pass. But my mind can't help replaying what I heard. What could they have possibly meant? What is my mother not telling me? I have more questions now than ever. I keep on replaying my mother and aunts staring and whispering to each other. I excuse myself and thank everyone for coming to see us. My uncle tells me that my bags have already been taken to my old room and kisses me goodnight. I can see the worry in his eyes too; my mother must have told him. Now I'm just feeling paranoid.

Once again, I go upstairs and knock on my grandmother's door.

"I just wanted to say goodnight," I say, as I walk towards her.

"It's so good to have you home. I feel like I can finally sleep tonight," she says with her beautiful smile.

"I love you so much Nonna."

"I love you. I know you must have a lot of questions, and I will answer them all very soon. I promise we will have just enough time, okay?" she says to reassure me.

"Okay then, tonight we sleep and tomorrow we talk," I reply.

"First, I need to have a long conversation with your mom. Give me a couple of days. Then we can talk," she says. "I know you don't like that, but please try to be patient. I know I've asked a lot of you."

"Why do I feel like you will be asking so much more?" I ask hesitantly.

"Because you have very good intuition, my love," she responds as she winks at me. I smile at her and walk over to kiss her on the forehead. I sit next to her on the bed. "You were a quick-witted and smart child. Nothing could get past you. Even now, always keenly aware of everything that surrounds you. *Always* listen to that intuition of yours Eli, you will need to trust it."

"I don't know if I trust anything anymore, Nonna. Especially when it comes to myself, I can never seem to get things right," I reply skeptically at her advice.

"I have watched you run circles around yourself your entire life. Never truly being sure of who you are and what you are capable of." She puts her hand on mine. "Do you remember the first time you wanted to make bread with me?"

I shake my head no. My grandmother is known for her bread, everyone is obsessed with the softness and flavor. When it bakes, you can smell it a mile away.

"Well, you were just a tiny little thing and you insisted on helping. I had to prop you up on a chair and your tiny hands and arms could still hardly reach. We worked hard at making it just right." Nonna giggles.

"Wait . . . the apples . . . " The memory begins to surface in my mind. "I remember you would put apples in the wood oven, and depending on how quickly they would become soft, you knew if the oven was at exactly the perfect temperature to put the dough in. Oooh the sweet scent of the apples would make the entire house smell so delicious!"

"That's right!" Nonna smiles happily at my recollection. "And once the bread was finished baking, I took it out of the wood oven and cut a warm slice for you, but you chose to eat the apple sauce instead of the bread. Do you remember that, Eli?"

"Yes." I put my head down. "I thought because I helped you make it . . . I-I was afraid it wasn't going to be good enough. I didn't eat it because I didn't want to face my failure."

"Eli, you only thought that because you did not trust yourself."

"Looks like some things never change," I mumble.

"But they need to, and soon." Nonna takes a deep breath. "You know, that was the best loaf of bread I ever made. Even your grandfather said so. And I believe it was because of your hands. You are of my blood. What I can do, you can do . . . Do you trust *me*?"

"YES! Of course, with my life! You are probably the person I trust the most!" I jerk my head up in dismay to her question. Nonna Amelia is the most humble, loving and caring person I've ever met. I've never heard her lie, or seen an unkind gesture or word come out of her. She is without a doubt the most selfless and self-sacrificing woman; sometimes I wonder how she didn't make sainthood with all the people she's saved. I would never have been able to make sense of the cruelty and injustice of the world, without her love to guide me.

"Then please trust me when I say that you will see and experience many things in your life that do not align with your truth. When that time comes, you will undoubtedly question *everything*. You must, without fail, trust your instinct, it is the only way to survive this world. Believing in yourself is the *only way* to keep your mind intact."

"I will work on it," I say to her with a gentle smile. Ugh, if she only knew just how long I've been trying to work on it. "I've kept you up long enough. Good night Nonna."

"Good night my beautiful girl, it's so wonderful to have you under this roof again." Nonna says as I kiss her hand and see myself out.

I go to my old room and sit on the lumpy bed where I slept

many nights during my childhood. I'm too tired to unpack. It hits me that I'm absolutely exhausted, both mentally and physically. It takes all the strength I have just to get myself ready for bed. As I lay down, I notice that the candle next to the window is lit, as it was every time I slept in this room growing up. It occurs to me that I have no idea who lights it. I always assumed it was my grandmother, but I know for certain it wasn't her tonight. I hear a knock at my door, and it's my mother.

"Hey, are you ok?" she asks, as she comes in and sits in the bed across from mine. She bounces on the bed a little.

"What is 'ok'?" I am so tired my voice cracks. "I can't believe Nonna made these mattresses. They literally give me the best sleep of my life."

"One of her many talents. I think she made every mattress in this town until the 1970s," my mom says proudly. "Did you know in the very olden days, they would use corn husk to fill the mattresses?"

"No I didn't, that's interesting. But these are made from sheep's wool, right?" I ask.

"Yes. Your Nonna, with a small group of women, would shave the sheep when it got too hot. Then they'd wash the wool very, very well multiple times in the nearby river, because it has the cleanest and purest water. They would then dry it out in the sun. Once it was dry, they would fluff it by gently pulling it apart until it looked like tiny clouds. It was a long and tedious process. And then your talented grandmother used a specialized technique to make each individual mattress. They do require upkeep, but it's well worth it. It takes incredible physical strength and sewing skills. It's a lost art."

"Can you imagine what these mattresses would be worth to all those farmhouse chic artisans back home? Nonna would have had the most successful business if she had been born into this generation. She'd probably have her own TV show!" We both chuckle.

"Yes, I have the same thought when I watch the ones about food or décor. The fans would have devoured her!"

"Mom, you know I think you are just as brilliant as she is—and in some ways even better."

"How is that even possible, Eli? You worship her."

"Maybe I do. But I idolize you. You're like everything every girl wants to be—mom, you are such a badass! Domestically you are every person's dream, and such a feminist! You don't let any-one tell you what to do, if anything, *you* are the influencer. You can farm during the day, then dress up in a ball gown that same night and enjoy an evening with aristocrats. Seriously, who can do that? I really admire and respect that you always stand up for what's right, no matter what or who it costs you. And you're so damn brave, you walk into any situation so fearlessly. It's not easy being your kid, it's a lot to live up to."

"Well, you do it effortlessly Eli. You have your own ideas and you've absolutely made your own way in life. You are all the parts of your dad and I that we were afraid to be—you are not held down by tradition or stifled by obligation. You are *free* because *your mind* is free. I've watched you escape into your thoughts and create a reality that belongs to you alone. You are unapologeti-cally unbound to anyone's ideals and expectations. You have cre-ated your own rules of what it means to be a woman—a person in this world. Do you have any idea how hard that will be for your child to live up to one day? We must all be who we can live with, and nothing else will do."

"You always say the right thing, mom," I reply. She proves once again how incredibly incomparable she is.

"Your eyes look like they are getting very heavy—good night love," she says, getting off the bed she is sitting on. She leans down to kiss my head.

"Who lights the candle in the window?" I ask abruptly.

"What?"

"Since I was a child, every time I've slept here that candle has been lit. I always assumed Nonna did it because I was afraid of the dark. But it couldn't have been her tonight. And what would be the purpose? I'm no longer afraid of the dark. It also occurred to me that I've never seen that candle wear down or be replaced . . ."

Mid-sentence my mother interrupts me and calmly says, "Good night Eli, I love you," and closes the door behind her.

Chapter 3

I WAKE UP to the birds chirping outside, a big change from the sounds of the 101 freeway. I sit up and stretch my arms as wide and as hard as I can. I look to the window and notice that the candle is still burning and it isn't any shorter. I look at my watch and realize I've been sleeping for twelve hours! I haven't slept that long, *ever*. I put on my robe, try to shake off everything I'd heard the night before, and walk downstairs, as I'm desperately in need of coffee.

"Buongiorno principessa!" says my Aunt Silva joyfully, as I walk into the kitchen. It means good morning princess in Italian. She would say that to me every morning when I was little as she woke me up, so now it's become a tradition between us.

I miss my grandmother's kitchen. She taught me to make some of the most delicious food right on this table. Everything in my grandmother's home, except for her refrigerator and stove, is a little rustic and antique. Some of her herbs are spread throughout the kitchen. The rest are stored in the cantina with the various meats, cheeses and homemade wine. Every piece of furniture, painting on the wall or tile laid on the floor in her home, has a story about a place, an artist, a builder or a friend. It is a special home because of the love and stories built into these walls. Only someone like my grandmother could create such a beautiful place.

"I made you an American breakfast today! Pancakes, eggs, pancetta, and toast!"

"This is amazing Auntie! Thank you, I'm starving!"

"I noticed you barely touched your meal last night; I figured you would need a hearty start today," she says, as she hands me the most delicious cup of espresso latte.

"I'm sorry, you know I love your food. I hope I didn't offend you, I was just very tired from the flight," I reply, in my best attempt to cover up the real reason for my loss of appetite.

In the Italian culture, not eating the food that the hostess offers is probably the worst, and absolute rudest thing you can do in someone else's home. Italians believe that hospitality and food are one and the same. It is their way of showing love and friendship. They believe it's an act of kindness that can mend bridges in difficult circumstances, as well as the best way to catch up on gossip with your old friends and make new ones in the process. They are convinced that over a good meal and a proper glass of wine, we can achieve world peace. I think they are probably right about that. As an experiment, we may want to schedule the next world conference in Umito, Italy. It can't hurt to try, nothing else seems to be working.

"We both know that is not completely true," my aunt empathizes as she sits next to me, interrupting my thoughts. "I know you must have a lot of questions, Eli. I don't blame you for possibly being a bit confused."

"A bit!" I say with my mouth half full of pancakes. She glares at me for speaking with my mouth full. "Sorry," I mutter, with my mouth still full.

"Your grandmother's spirits are up since you and your mother have arrived, she may even get out of bed today!" Aunt Silva says hopefully.

"How long has it been since she's left her bed?" I ask.

"This has been the longest stretch, about two weeks. Before that she would at least make her way over to the window and sit in her rocking chair to read, or just look out," she continues, "She hasn't recovered since the death of your Nonna Rosa. We thought she would die of a broken heart," she stops to sigh, "It's been a . . . complicated two years, love."

Before I can ask any questions, she annoys me by holding her hand up, "Please don't. I know what you're going to ask, but I can't. It's not my place Eli, please don't put me in that position. You know I would do anything for you, but this has to be between you and your grandmother. And don't be angry with your mom, it wasn't her place either."

I sigh with frustration. "These evasive conversations are really messing with my head, and I'm starting to feel like everyone is a liar," I say to my aunt. "All I want is to know more about our family history, so I get to the bottom of my . . . changes."

"I understand why you feel that way, Eli," says my mother, as she enters the room and stands behind me. I turn around to look at her and my uncle Gianni follows her in. They look as if they've been hiking. My mother and uncle are both wearing quilted vests, button-up shirts, fitted dark denim jeans, and hunter boots.

"Did you seriously coordinate your outfits? I mean, I know you're siblings, but really?" I say, and then proceed to mumble "so weird" under my breath.

"How was your walk?" Aunt Silva asks the matching-outfit-duo, before my mom pokes me with her walking stick.

"Very good! Nothing like fresh mountain air to clear the mind and open the lungs!" my uncle Gianni says, briskly rubbing his hands together with his usual upbeat demeanor. He looks over at the table and his eyes light up.

"Silva! American breakfast, my favorite!" exclaims Uncle Gianni. "You are the best sister!" He smiles, then looks at my mother and winks. As he sits next to me, I can smell that delicious sweet smell that can only be found here in this beautiful place. It is the smell of my childhood and the fruit I most covet: blackberries. If Eve knew about these blackberries, she would have never handed Adam the apple. She would have just eaten the blackberries herself and walked away as an independent woman. And for the rest of time, a woman would never be blamed for the original sin. That story still pisses me off.

"Uncle you didn't!" I say excitedly, as he opens a handkerchief he is holding in his hands. It's filled with perfect blackberries.

"Do you think I wouldn't pick them for my favorite girl?" he says as he hands them to me.

"I forgot that it's the season, how amazing! Thank you so much!" I jump up and give him a big kiss on cheek. He hands them to me, and I walk over to the sink to wash these coveted blackberries. I can recognize that scent anywhere; they are my absolute favorite. There is something about this mountain that makes them grow so exquisitely. My mouth is salivating.

"Luca!" I hear my uncle say, as someone walks into the kitchen. My grandmother's home has always been a place where everyone is welcome. She used to say, "In my home, any stranger will become a friend with a plate of pasta and a glass of wine." It is a place where everyone stops to say hello. It has always been a place of joy and love for all who enter.

I also hear Alessia and Aunt Ersella walk into the kitchen. As I turn around, I see my uncle speaking to a young man that looks familiar. I look over at my cousin who looks like she's just woken up and is battling a bad hangover. I notice her eyes get very big, and she quickly opens the refrigerator door to hide behind it. She starts freaking out, pointing and jumping, and proceeds to point and mouth things to me I can't understand. I'm shaking my head and shrugging my shoulders at her, but what I'm mostly focused on is the bird's nest shape her hair has made, and the mascara coming down her eyes.

"What!" I whisper to her, but before she can reply, I hear my Aunt Ersella exclaim, "Gas station boy! Well, I was wondering when you'd get here." I feel myself freeze and I'm unable to move my legs.

"Aunt Ersella, do you know Luca?" Uncle Gianni asks her.

"No, but we've been expecting you," she says to Luca, as she extends her hand to shake his.

His face looks confused, but he politely extends his hand to shake hers and says, "So nice to meet you, madam."

"Handsome AND well mannered. That's new," she replies.

"Luca is Stefano's best friend. He is here visiting family near-by, and I invited him to over," Uncle Gianni says to everyone.

Of course you did, I think to myself. Stefano is Uncle Gianni's son; he also has a daughter named Sophia. They are both some of the most wonderful cousins a girl can have.

"Hello Luca, it's nice to meet you. Thank you for stopping by," says my mother as she shakes his hand. "Are Stefano and Sophia coming today?" she asks my uncle.

"Not today. Stefano is on a business trip, and Sophia is study-ing for exams. But they will both be here by the weekend," re-plies my uncle.

"Will *you* be returning this weekend?" Aunt Ersella asks Luca in her usual nosy fashion with one eyebrow up.

"I'm not sure yet. I'll be speaking to Stefano today," he replies. I didn't realize what a soothing voice he has. I suppose it would be hard to tell at a gas station. I also detect a slight accent, but I can't make it out. It doesn't sound like it's from around these parts.

"Luca and I are going to have a beer at the pub. I'll be back later," says Uncle Gianni, as he waves goodbye.

"Nice to meet everyone. Good day," says Luca, as they both walk out.

"Alessia, if that refrigerator door doesn't stop beeping, I'm going to lock you up in it!" yells Aunt Ersella. Alessia steps away and closes the refrigerator door.

Aunt Ersella then looks over at me and says, "Do you plan on making jam with those now?" I look down and notice that I squeezed the blackberries so tightly in my hands, that not only have I ruined them, but it looks like my hand is bleeding.

"Shit!" I quickly toss them into the sink and rinse my hands.

"What a mess you girls are. No wonder you can't find husbands!" states Aunt Ersella, as she opens up her fan and begins to cool herself off. Then she, Aunt Silva, and my mother make their way out of the kitchen laughing hysterically.

"Oh my God, that was disgraceful!" says Alessia, exasperated.

"No kidding. *I'm* used to being a mess, but what happened to you? Isn't this the kind of guy you usually eat for breakfast?" I ask, surprised by her reaction while Luca was here.

"Yes! Literally it is. But look at me!!! I mean . . . You cannot utter a word of this to *anyone!*" she says, pointing her finger at me.

"Ále, your mom was here. Everyone will know this story before dinner!" I reply, trying to hold back my laughter. Aunt Ersella, God love her, she just can't keep something this good to herself—even if it would mean saving us from embarrassment. Alessia and I start to mock one another and then begin to laugh uncontrollably.

"I haven't heard a laugh that beautiful in years," says a familiar voice behind us.

"NONNA!" both Alessia and I rush over to my grandmother as she is being escorted into the kitchen by her nurse.

"What are you doing down here!" Alessia asks in shock. At the same time, I ask the nurse if it is it okay for her to come down the stairs.

"Well, if I wanted to be harassed, I would have come down when your mothers were here," Nonna replies. "Please fix my chair next to the fireplace girls, I'd like to sit there."

We quickly fluff the pillows and pull out a blanket. She continues, "You know how much I love to have the fireplace on and look out the window."

"Ms. Amelia, it is still much too warm to turn the fireplace on, it's not even the end of summer," says the nurse.

"Yes, but not for long. Fall will come early this year, and it will be quite chilly soon," my grandmother replies to the nurse.

"How do you *do that*, Nonna?" I ask. "You always know the weather and the perfect timing of each season. If our weather people got it right half as often as you do, I'd actually wear the right outfits to work."

"Those silly people, they do try their best. The answers are always in the stars," she says to us.

"Well, the stars don't seem to speak to us the way they do to you," Alessia says to my grandmother, then she turns to me and taunts, "What do you know about seasons anyway? Isn't it always around 70 degrees in LA? Doesn't everyone wear their winter coats the moment it gets into the 60s?"

"Alessia, you stop being jealous," the nurse teases, as I give Alessia a dirty look and hit her in the arm.

"It seems like you two are just what your grandmother needed. I'm going to let you have some time together. I'll be in the sitting room if you need me," says the nurse, walking out.

"When was the last time you were in the kitchen, Nonna?" I ask, as we take a seat next to her.

She smiles and says, "It feels like just yesterday I was baking that loaf of bread," she pauses to reflect. "I suppose that was three months ago now."

"You've been in your room for three months?" Alessia asks as she holds her hand.

"Oh, it's not so bad, it was my choice after all."

"I don't understand, mother said it was the doctor's orders?" Alessia proceeds.

"What do they know?" Nonna replies dismissively. "I knew I was dying; everyone knew. And I couldn't bear to see the way people looked at me. I decided it was time to withdraw."

I become sick to my stomach at the thought of her dying. I can't take her speaking this way. I would do anything to save her, spare her life. I would gladly give up my life for her to have more time. She is one of those people who literally makes the world a better place. I just can't imagine the universe without her. She is the kind of person who in her life has created change, actually saved people's lives, and helped the planet. I'm just another compliant person who does nothing but wakes up, goes to work, and sits in traffic most of my days. I donate to charities because I have no time to actually help others. I walk my friends' dogs because I can't commit to having one of my own. The idea of taking care of anything for fifteen years terrifies me. The only exploring I do is walking from the valet to the latest trendy restaurant. I'm not sure what kind of life that is, but one I would happily surrender to give her more time. My eyes fill up with tears as I have this thought.

"How much time could I possibly have left?" she asks, as she looks directly into my eyes.

"What?" I say softly. Did I say those thoughts out loud?

"My husband and friends are all gone now Eli, my time is done," she says gently.

"Your children and grandchildren are here, and we need you!" I say with desperation in my voice.

"And you are all so precious to me. You are my legacy. Others will know me because of you. Once there was a time when I thought all I have now was impossible. I never thought I could have a family. This lifetime has been a miracle. But now I can no longer be selfish, it's time to let it go," she says to the both of us, never losing her gentle smile.

"Mama always said that you both would live forever," Alessia says as tears come running down her face.

"My sweet girl," Nonna says as she leans down and touches Alessia's face, "I know this moment is making you think of your own mother. But my sister Ersella is much younger than I am. She still has many years left; you must enjoy every moment with her. Not to worry, she still has much work to do here." Alessia nods her head, I can see that these words give her comfort.

"Is it true that you are seven sisters?" I ask.

"Yes, there are seven of us," Nonna replies.

"Then why have we only known Aunt Ersella? Where are the other five?" I continue. All my life I've thought it was so strange that we have never really known any members of our extended family.

Alessia turns to me and says, "Good luck trying to get an answer, I've been asking my mom that question all my life."

Nonna responds, "Yes, I suppose you deserve to know. But not today. Your mothers will be back in fifteen minutes. It will take me at least that long to get up the stairs. Let this be our little secret, I don't want them bothering me about coming downstairs."

We joyfully agree, as long as she promises to do it again.

"Yes, I promise," she says in agreement. "Alessia, be a dear and get the nurse please."

As Alessia walks out of the room, my grandmother turns to me and whispers, "Eli, we need to speak privately. But before we do, please take a few days to rest. Even take a long walk to clear your mind. Can you do that for me?"

"Yes of course, Nonna," I reply, trying to hide my rising excitement in hopefully resolving some of our family mysteries.

My cousin and the nurse enter the room just at that moment. We help my grandmother back to her bed, and as usual, she is correct about the timing of my mom and aunts' return. I just don't know how she does that. That gift would have helped me a lot in high school.

The next several days are a mixture of sleeping off the jet lag and a parade of visitors coming to see us. It is wonderful to catch up and hear about all the things I had missed. In moments like this I wonder why we ever left Italy; most of our family is still here. Neither of my parents had any of their siblings follow them to the U.S. But we do have some family in the states from my father's paternal side. I thank God for them, without them we would have been completely alone. My parents were so courageous taking on such a big move, with a five-year-old child and being so young themselves. They wanted a better life and believed in the American Dream. I am so proud of who they are and all they've accomplished. Any child of an immigrant can tell you how many sacrifices are made, and how hard a parent has to work in order to give their child the opportunity of a better life, even if it's in a country they do not know, with a language they do not speak. Immigrant parents give up their dreams so their children will have a chance to live their own. There is a special bond, an unbreakable loyalty that blossoms in immigrant families. It's a journey that only the people that have lived it can understand. It is beautiful, but it can often be a bittersweet journey.

Countries like Italy have an "it takes a village" kind of outlook. Everyone helps each other out, everyone raises the kids together, and everyone has each other's backs in good times and bad. It's not uncommon to find many households of multi-generations living together. I was raised more independent and with a great deal of freedom. My parents were protective, but not overbearing, which is almost unheard of for Italians. They have always allowed me space to live my life on my terms. So, the times when I return to Italy, it takes a little adjusting because everyone seems so invasive, especially my mom, which is in complete contrast to who she is in LA. There is no such thing as personal space here. But before I know it, I'm right back in there with them like I had never left.

Chapter 4

"MOM what day is it today?" I ask as I finish getting dressed, while my mom is standing at my vanity, looking for an elastic band for her hair.

"Friday. Can you believe it's been nearly a week since we arrived?"

"No, wow that went by fast . . . When is dad coming?"

"I don't know yet; we are just playing it by ear at the moment." She quickly changes the subject. "Eli, have you decided if you're going to give your job notice? I really wish you would leave that horrible place."

"No, I haven't decided yet. I keep trying to weigh out the pros and cons. Maybe I'll go for a walk today to stretch my legs and give it some serious thought."

"I think that's a really good idea," she says encouragingly. "If you do go, remember to stay on the trail up the mountain, I don't want you to get lost."

As I watch my mother brush her long dark brown hair, I admire her dark brown eyes, lovely olive-toned skin, her perfect nose—except for the tiniest (and barely noticeable) bump from when one of my uncles elbowed her as a child and broke it. If I remember clearly, they were fighting over a doll. She is not very tall, but she has the personality of a giant. In true Goto form, she has a flawless hourglass shape. In this moment I take her in and remind myself how lucky I am to have her as a mom. She always has my best interests at heart. She is by far the most beautiful woman in the world to me and my father, but who she is as a person far exceeds her external beauty. She has been the best example of a woman, wife, daughter, and mother to me. My mother is both a gentle and tough woman; and the least selfish person on earth. She's the kind of person that will give you the shirt off her back and the last piece of bread in her home. She makes no mind of your background or stature in life. I don't claim that she is without her flaws, but in this moment, I can only appreciate her strengths.

"Thanks mom," I say as I lean over to kiss her.

"Be careful!" she says, as I head down the hallway to my grandmother's room. I peek in and see that she is still asleep. I close her bedroom door; I feel a chill in the breeze from the window and I shiver. I grab my hoodie and head out for my walk.

I forgot how picturesque this place is. The greens are so lush and magnificent. Everything from the chirping of the birds, to the colors of their wings, is bright and so alive. I call it the "Umito color palette" because, as far as I know, these vibrant colors only exist here. As I begin my walk up the hiking trail, I see a lot of the locals picking porcini mushrooms; which, by the way, are the best in the world, in my opinion. I love the smell of the mushrooms as they are pulled out of the dirt. These mountains are a part of the National Forest and protected by law. People are not meant to pick mushrooms, truffles, or any plants without permits, but it's hard not to when they are growing right under your feet. As I walk a little further, I see my blackberries and I rush to them and start picking them off the branches. I don't even care about being poked by the thorns! I pour some water from my bottle over them to rinse them and shove a handful into my mouth. Heaven . . . finally! And no Luca to ruin the moment for me. I don't even sit to enjoy my blackberry feast because I'm always worried about snakes that linger about. It's also the reason everyone takes a walking stick with them; it is easier to hit or scare a snake off, if need be.

The further up the trail I go, the more I begin to see people that travel in from out of town to hike. They are quite serious with their gear. They arrive very early to get as much hiking in a day as possible. There are no campsites on the mountain, so rangers expect everyone to be out by sunset. Also, the higher up you go, the colder it gets. There it is again, that chill. I put on my hoodie and veer off to an area of the forest very few people know about. It's a cliff-side filled with beautiful yellow flowers. It's also very dangerous. It is several kilometers above any roads or signs of civilization, and there are no safety rails to keep a person from falling off. Should something go wrong, no one would ever be able to find you. That's why my mom insists I stay on the trail, but it's just so easy to get lost in such a beautiful place. This forest is like a second home to me. Growing up, I used to play and spend endless days exploring it with my cousins and friends. I have always felt safe here.

I make my way through the deep forest filled with magnificent trees, that are taller than many skyscrapers and old as time itself. I walk about a kilometer west of the hiking trail when I begin to see familiar yellow flowers on the ground. That was always my indication that I was in the right place, getting very close to the cliff. Another sign is how incredibly quiet the forest becomes, but not in an eerie kind of way. My grandmothers told us the silence was a gift from the forest so that we could know what true peace feels like, and they were right. I feel excitement settling in and start to walk faster through the trees. I finally break through the last of the branches and here I am. Paradise.

I look around and walk slowly through the field, taking in its breathtaking views. It is mighty. In every sense of the word. The flowers are more yellow than I remember, and the fragrance is almost overwhelming. It smells like a mixture of milk, honey, lavender, and moss, if there ever was such a scent. The sun's rays beam down and glisten on every flower, every leaf, each piece of grass, and every surrounding tree that my eyes can see. The sky is a crystal baby blue, without a cloud in sight. The air is so clean it gives my lungs a sharp sensation when I breathe. As I make my way closer to the edge of the cliff, my hands start to sweat. I always feel a little nervous when I'm on the edge—I can't make out if it feels like the end of the world, or where it all began. I pick a flower from the edge and put it in my hair. My grandmothers told me that if I did this each time I visited, the flowers would heal me. Not sure if it's true, but I always do it.

"You are one of the great wonders of the world," I say out loud to this magnificent place. It is without a doubt the world's best kept secret. Nonna has always said that this place was special, and the forest wouldn't allow just anyone to find it. I giggle at the thought of how gullible we were as children, believing all those silly stories.

I walk to the center of the cliff and lay on the flowers and grass. It feels *soooo* good. It is the only place on the mountain where I can ease my mind about snake bites. My grandmothers told me that snakes, and other animals that attack, are not permitted to enter here; the flowers repel them away. Although I'm sure that's a myth, I must say in all the years I've been coming here, I've never seen anything but butterflies in the flowers.

I feel the cool grass settle under me—my body and mind start to relax, and I begin to reflect on my life. I first begin to think about my job and if I should stay or resign. Should I move out of LA? Will I ever find someone I love forever? My continuous inner rambling goes on for a while with nonsense, and my endless need to question everything. I'm starting to exhaust myself with this chatter. My eyes feel heavy and I slowly fall asleep.

A few moments later, I feel a shadow over me and someone blocking the sun from my face. The figure kneels down and says, "My love, you must wake up. It will be dark soon."

I blink and try to focus my vision in the direction of the voice. The pixels come together, and I see a woman that seems so familiar to me. Could it be? It looks like her, but it can't be her . . . this girl is young and vibrant. She looks exactly like my grandmother Rosa, as she did in her wedding photos sixty years ago. For a moment, I question if the flowers are hallucinogenic. She smirks, and in this moment, I know it's HER!

I jump up and throw my arms around her, "Nonna!!! I miss you so much! What are you doing here? How did you get here?"

"Always so inquisitive, my beautiful Eli," she replies in her gentle voice. "It will be dark soon and you must get to the bottom of the mountain before sunset. You will have everyone frightened sick if you don't."

"It's hardly noon, the sun is still shinning so bright. I've only been here a short time. Wait, how did you know I was here?" I respond.

"Eli, you are still sleeping. You need to wake up!" she says with urgency. Before I can get another word out of my mouth, she pinches my arm with all her might and I am startled awake yelling, "Ouch!!! Shit!!!"

I sit up and rub my shoulder aggressively, I can still feel the sting.

"Okay crazy, that was just a dream. Calm down," I say to myself. I look up and see that the sun is actually starting to set.

"Oh my God, how long have I been here?" I blurt out.

I look at my watch, it is nearly 7:30 pm.

"How is that possible?" I say to myself once again, still in disbelief.

I get up quickly and continue to rub my arm as I dart back into the forest. I try to shake the fog from my mind as I begin jogging. I don't have any time to lose—it will be fifteen, twenty minutes tops before it's completely dark, and it usually takes thirty minutes to get down the mountain from where I am. I hope to find some straggling hikers to walk down the mountain with, once I get back to the trail. I don't have a flashlight and it will be safer that way, should it get dark before I make it back.

I need to stop. I've been jogging for ten minutes but find myself a bit turned around. I don't recognize where I am; this is unusual because I know these woods like the back of my hand. I try to refocus and get my sense of direction back by reconfiguring where my north, south, east, and west are. Once I am confident, I proceed. About five minutes later I see a small cabin. The lights are on and there is smoke coming from the chimney. I feel so relieved to see a sign of life. I walk up to the cabin and see an older gentleman sweeping the front porch. There is a sign above the open front door that reads:

LIVE WELL. LOVE WITH A PURE HEART.

He is a curious looking man; short in height with a small frame, and silver hair long enough to cover his ears. As I get closer, I notice he has gray-brown eyes and soft pale skin with flushed cheeks. By the look of things, it seems like he's lived here all his life, but I've never seen him before. Come to think of it, I've never seen this cabin either.

"Good evening," he addresses me with a pleasant disposition.

"Good evening. I'm so sorry to bother you, but I think I've gotten myself mixed up and I could use some help finding my way back to the hiking trail."

I look around and I see several plants in vases with odd items attached to them. I can't quite make out what they are, but I can't help and take notice of all the different variations of gnomes he has spread throughout his porch and garden. I am completely distracted by them. I hear him tap his broom and I realize that I am being rude, and I make eye contact with him.

"It's been known to happen my dear," he replies. "If you follow the direction right through those two large elm trees, you'll find a short cut and your way home in no time."

"Elm trees? I didn't know they grew in this part of the mountain," I reply, trying hard not to look at all of the clutter and madness in his garden.

"You best hurry, it will be dark soon. And I don't have a telephone for you to call your family," he says, as he urges me along. I thank him and wish him a good evening. I turn to wave at him as I jog through the elm trees. I look back around, and in front of me is the hiking trail. He wasn't joking when he said short cut—I'm already at the bottom of the mountain. How did I never know about this short cut? I'll have to tell my family about it, it saves so much time. I pick up my pace and run to my grandmother's house as quickly as I can. I walk into the house just as the sun is setting.

There are about a dozen people in the sitting room as I walk in.

"Thank God!" I hear someone say, as well as sighs of relief all around.

"ELI! You had us worried sick!" my mother exclaims with both anger and joy in her voice, as she smothers me with an embrace. "Do you have any idea how long you've been gone? We were about to send out a search team!"

"I'm so sorry, I lost track of time. I didn't mean to worry any-one," I say, feeling very embarrassed.

"Did you get lost, cousin? Are you hurt?" Alessia asks, as she examines me.

"No, I'm fine, really," I can feel myself turning red. "I'm so sorry again, everyone. But I could really use a shower."

"Yes, of course darling," says Aunt Ersella, "and please see your grandmother as soon as you're finished showering. In the meantime, I will let her know you are home and safe. And we'll want to hear about your day when you come down."

"Nonna had the worst anxiety spell I've ever seen. We could not get her to calm down while you were missing. Mother had to give her blue vervain for her nerves," Alessia whispers to me.

"Anxiety? She's never had anxiety," I respond, in a confused tone.

"I know," she says, as she locks eyes with me.

"And I wasn't missing, I'm just late," I reply, as I shrug her off and head upstairs to shower.

There is a knot in my stomach when I think about Alessia's words. Anxiety? Nonna has always been so calm and *very* in con-trol. Why would this have upset her so much? I will speak to her and show her she has nothing to worry about. Maybe because she is in such a fragile state now, she may feel things differently. Maybe it makes her worry more.

As these thoughts run through my mind, I turn on the water and begin to undress. I take off my shirt and in the corner of my eye I see something. I look closer in the mirror, and I see a welt and a large bruise. *That's not possible, I must be seeing things*, I mumble to myself. I just need to wash my face with cold water, and I'll be fine. I get into the shower, grab the bar of soap, and wash my face. But I can feel the pressure of the water hurt my arm. I look down at it again. I can't deny it this time. I start to breathe heavy as I slide down the shower wall. I'm unable to move—the water falls down on my body. The pressure in my heart feels like it's going to cave my chest in. Without any control of my body, I begin to cry, and I can't stop.

I hear a knock on the door. Alessia rushes her way into the bathroom, opens the shower door and turns off the water. She grabs the towel off the rod and covers my body with it.

"What the hell happened out there today, Eli?" she asks, as she lifts me up and helps me walk to the bedroom. She sits me down on the bed and helps me put my robe on. She hands me a cup of tea that she brought up for me and tells me to drink.

"Mother said you would need a cup of blue vervain tea," she says, as she gently puts lotion on my face and hands.

"How did you get that mark on your arm?" she asks me.

"I don't know. It was there when I woke up from my nap on the yellow cliff," I tell her.

"We haven't been able to find that cliff in years! How did you find it?" she asks surprised.

"I went to the area we always go to," I reply, and then we both sit in silence for a moment, unsure of what to say. We had once heard of a legend that the yellow field was a gateway to "the other side." If you could find it, you could speak to someone who died. She shakes her head lost in her own thoughts, then starts to brush my hair. The candle catches my eye, I become entranced by it.

"Ále, did you light the candle in the window?"

"No," she replies softly.

"Do you know who does?" I ask, as I turn to her and grab the hand she is holding the brush in.

"Mother says it's our guardian angel," she says, as she sits next to me, "Who knows, Eli. Maybe the housekeeper?"

"The candle is always lit, three hundred and sixty-five days a year. It never goes down or changes shape. I have never seen it replaced. Please Ále, I'm begging you, tell me what you know," I plead with her.

"Eli, I only know slightly more than you do. And what I do know, only has to do with my own parents. Mother swore that Aunt Amelia was ready to tell us about our family history. I am as anxious as you are to know . . . Doing our family tree in fifth grade was so embarrassing." We both smile. "There are too many missing pieces, too many unexplained circumstances and far too many questions. I know you pretty well and I can see something has done your head in. I promise we will start looking for answers to the black hole that is our ancestry."

"You do know me well. If I could just have some knowledge of our lineage, I could start doing research on our medical history and maybe better understand my own health. I swear Alessia, today was the worst hallucination I've had yet. I thought it was a dream but . . . but Ále, I swear to God I'm losing my mind!" I start to shake and cry once again.

"Hey, hey, look at me," Alessia says grabbing my face. "You are NOT losing your mind. We are gonna get to the bottom of this—together! Let's get your robe on, everyone has left, and your mom has warmed up some food for you. Come, let's go downstairs."

"I need to show Nonna that I'm okay first," I reply, as I slip my arms into the robe. Alessia's words give me comfort, and I'm glad not to be doing this alone, as I have done almost everything else for most all my life.

"She knows. She is resting now. Today really shook her up. You can see her after you eat." Alessia grabs me by the hand and we go downstairs. I am starting to get feeling back in my body again, but my arm is still killing me.

As we go into the kitchen, my mom is steeping tea and Aunt Ersella is sitting in my grandmother's chair next to the lit fireplace. "Is it already that time of year?" I ask.

"There was quite a chill today, wouldn't you say Eli?" Aunt Ersella asks.

"Yes, Nonna is right. Fall must be coming early this year," I reply, as I sit at the table stirring the soup my mom has placed in front of me.

"Well, I'm so happy you're home safe and sound. Your father was about to get on the next flight," my mother says as she sits next to me.

"Mom, I don't think it was that serious. I was just a little late."

"Eli, you were gone for over twelve hours!" I was shocked by her response. I didn't realize it had been that long.

"You were alone and without your cell phone, we didn't know what to think!"

"Really, I am so sorry . . . and I'm so embarrassed. I fell asleep in the yellow field and I totally lost track of time."

"You did what!" Aunt Ersella exclaims. "Did you say you fell asleep on the yellow cliff?"

"Yes, I know it was so silly. I closed my eyes and it felt like I was only sleeping for five minutes. Thank God for the little old man in the cabin that I ran into on the way back. He showed me a short cut to get back down the mountain before sunset. Mom, do you know him? I don't ever remember seeing him there before." I eat a big spoonful of soup and then look up. My mom is as white as a ghost, and my aunt is no longer in the room.

"I've never seen my mother move that fast," Alessia says teasingly.

"Where did she go?" I ask.

"I don't know," Alessia answers, furrowing her brow.

"Excuse me girls, I'm going to go check on your grandmother," says my mother as she gets up from the table and nearly runs out of the room.

"You know how to clear a room," Alessia jokes.

"No kidding," I agree. "Why is this family *so weird*?"

"I don't know, but I think it's time we find out. Finish your soup, Eli."

For the first time, I see my cousin is as frustrated as I am. And she has that look in her eye.

"We are either going to get some answers once and for all, or we are going to start playing detective," Alessia says decisively. I eat that soup as fast as I can.

Alessia and I march upstairs. Without knocking, she opens my grandmother's bedroom door. Sitting around my grandmother are my Aunt Silva, whom they clearly woke out of bed, Aunt Ersella, and my mother.

"Come in," Nonna Amelia says to us.

"We want some answers," Alessia demands. I love it when she gets so feisty! I just hate it when it's towards me, good thing it's working to my benefit today.

"Oh Eli, I love your robe," says my Aunt Silva, "those American robes are so soft and plush. I've only ever seen them on American TV shows. Let me have a feel, Eli," she says as she calls me over with her hand.

"Elizabetta, why haven't you ever brought me one?"

I start to walk over and Alessia pulls my arm back to stop me. "Ouch!!!" I yell out.

"I mean really Alessia, must you be so rough?" Aunt Ersella chastises her daughter.

"Show them," Alessia demands.

"Alessia . . . " I say nervously. As I look over, they are all staring at me with inquisitive looks.

"We are going to get the ball rolling, starting with what happened to you today, Eli. Tell us what really happened. It's the only way you will force their hand," says Alessia.

She is right. They will only manipulate us and change the conversation to questions about American robes or some other nonsense, like they always do.

"Fine," I say, as I push her hand off my arm. I drop the robe off my shoulder to show them the welt and bruise. Before I can get a word out, Nonna Amelia gets out of her chair and touches my arm. Her eyes well up with tears and she says choking up, "She saved you."

"Who saved her?" Alessia yells out.

"Rosa," my grandmother replies.

"What! Eli, what is she talking about? You saw your dead grandmother today?" I never said Alessia was diplomatic.

"Of sorts," I reluctantly answer.

"You might have NOT left that out of the story when I asked you earlier!" she yells back.

"I'm sorry Ále, I don't know what I saw myself. It was all so confusing. She looked so young; I never knew her that way. I thought it was just a dream. But when I woke up with this on my arm, I didn't know what to make of it." My answer seems to quiet her down.

"Please everyone, calm down," says my mother, as she escorts my grandmother back to the chair.

"Nonna, how did you know it was her?" I ask, wanting to quell my curiosity.

"Because that's how she used to wake me up when we were . . . *young*. She thought she was so funny, and my arms would be black and blue. I would recognize that mark anywhere."

"You need to tell us exactly what happened today, Eli. Please do not leave anything out," Aunt Ersella says to me in a slow and steady manner.

Alessia and I pull up the bench my Nonna Amelia has placed at the edge of her bed. We insert ourselves into their circle. This is the first time I feel like I belong in my family. I tell them the story about my day, describing each moment and doing my best not to leave out any details. They each ask so many questions that by the end of this two-hour conversation I am completely drained. I can't stop yawning.

"Today has been a long day for us all. How about we sleep on this and pick things up tomorrow?" Aunt Silva suggests.

"Per usual, you haven't given us any information as previously agreed," Alessia says in her lawyer-like tone. To be honest, I don't mind since I am so tired, I can barely keep my eyes open.

"Must you always be so difficult Alessia?" snaps my Aunt Ersella.

"Well if you must know, we are from a magical Celestial bloodline, but also faerie-affiliated. That means your grandmother Rosa, our mother Amelia, and Aunt Ersella, are Celestial Beings . . . It's a bit complicated, you see," Aunt Silva says, fidgeting with her fingers and shrugging her shoulders. "Your grandfathers are human. But *your* dad," pointing at Alessia, "and *your* great-uncle Adolfo," pointing to me, "was not human. It's all quite a romantic story, really. That makes Elizabetta and I half Celestial Beings, and half-mortal. Except that most of us children managed to not attain any kind of special powers—which mostly just makes us boring!" She rolls her eyes in disappointment, then continues, "Alessia, you're a one-hundred percent magical breed, we call that a *mage*. But, Eli . . . hmm, I'm not sure about you . . . Mama, what percentage magic would you say she is?" My ears aren't sure what they just heard, as my mind rushes to process Aunt Silva's nonsensical explanation.

As I look around the room, no one blinks. Aunt Ersella's eyes look like they might pop out of her head, while my grandmother raises her eyebrows at Aunt Silva. Everyone is sitting very still, waiting for our response.

"Are you drunk?" Alessia breaks the silence and chastises Aunt Silva. "We aren't children anymore! We aren't just going to believe every silly story you come up with like we did when we were little. Give us some credit! All we want is the truth. But it's clear that you have *no* intention of ever giving it to us! How bad could it possibly be? I mean, it's got to be better than these outrageous stories!"

It feels like my head is going to explode. All this build up for nothing. I need to get out of this room, the walls feel like they're closing in on me. I excuse myself and walk straight to my bedroom. I get into bed and put the sheets over my head, defeated. A few moments later Alessia comes in and gets into bed with me.

"I'm sorry, Eli," she says in a whisper.

"Me too," I whisper back.

*   *   *

The next morning, I open my eyes to the sound of running water from the nearby fountain. The house is very quiet, then I remember that my grandmother has a doctor's appointment today. My insane aunts and mother must have all gone with her. Wherever Alessia is, I'm sure she will be home soon to wreak havoc. This is nice; lovely actually. I finally have the house to myself. I make myself a fresh cup of coffee with toast. I even take my time getting ready. I don't know what to wear since I have no idea what I'm doing today. Maybe I'll take Aunt Silva's car and go into the main city, Ascoli Piceno, to do a little shopping. Retail therapy is much needed after last night's drama. I decide to wear my skinny black pants and fitted long sleeve black shirt. As I put it on, I notice the bruise on my arm is now black and huge, but at least it doesn't hurt anymore. I put on a scarf I received as a birthday gift last year, to keep my neck warm from this cool chill that keeps coming through. Speaking of birthdays, I think I have another one coming up soon. Has it already been a year? And now, for the most important item of my outfit, which shoes? My new flats will be perfect to walk around in. I look in my jewelry pouch for a pair of earrings, and I notice my Nonna Rosa's ruby ring. I inherited it after her passing. I don't wear it often because it makes me cry every time I look at it. My grandmother wore this ring every time she dressed up, it was her pride and joy. I can't recall one special occasion, including every Sunday, that she did not wear it. Somehow, today it feels right, and I slip it onto my right-hand ring finger. I spray on a little perfume and head downstairs.

As I am looking for the keys to the car, I hear Alessia walk in but she's not alone. My cousin Stefano and his sister Sophia are with her. I can't believe it, what a wonderful surprise! We run to each other and hug in a triangle formation, as we jump up and down.

"I remember Uncle Gianni mentioning that you might be coming, but he wasn't sure about your schedules," I say to them.

"We told him to say that because we wanted to surprise you!" Stefano responds.

"Well done! I'm very surprised! But you nearly missed me, I was about to go to Ascoli to do some shopping."

"We just came from there. We had coffee and pastries at Caffe Meletti, Luca treated us," Alessia says, as she winks at me. With all the excitement, I didn't notice that Luca had entered with them.

"Hello Eli, it's a pleasure to finally meet you," Luca says, as he extends his hand to shake mine. There is a static shock as we touch.

"Thank you, likewise. I'm just happy to look presentable to-day," I say laughing. Everyone laughs and it occurs to me that they've let Stefano and Sophia in on the embarrassing details of our last two encounters.

"We heard you ladies had a long night of reminiscing and we didn't have the heart to wake you up this morning. I hope that's okay Eli; we didn't mean to leave you out," Sophia says looking at me with her big doll eyes, and a face you could never be angry at.

"Yes, lots of reminiscing . . . " I say as I look over at Alessia, "No, of course not, it was much needed sleep. And it was won-derful to wake up to a bit of peace."

"Well, don't get used to the quiet, we will be staying here for the next week to spend some time with you," says Stefano. I squeeze Sophia's hand with excitement.

"Not me, cousin. I have to get back to school. I wish I could stay, but my semester is just beginning and I can't miss any days, I'll be dropped from class if I do. I leave tomorrow," Sophia says with disappointment. My stomach sinks.

"We, as in Luca and me!" Stefano says with excitement.

"Surprise!" Alessia says as she waves her hands side to side. I give her a darting look and she responds with an *I had no idea* shrug.

In some ways, Stefano is your typical guy—zero common sense and is oblivious to most things. But the world—and our family—lets him get away with every annoying thing he does, because he has the looks of a model and the IQ of Einstein. Stefano is a thirty-year-old lawyer that specializes in global art appraisal and sales. He graduated top of his class at the University of Bologna, which happens to be the same school Sophia is now attending. He spends most of his time in Milan, but travels all over the world for his clients. It's no wonder he has friends like Luca.

Sophia is twenty-one years old and sharp as a whip. She is

quite clever but has to work much harder in school than her brother. She is a very sensitive girl. Her innocence and vulnerability are written all over her awkward stance and shy demeanor. It makes the family very protective, and constantly questioning the motives of those around her. Which is a good thing, until that person happens to be a boy she likes. I'm not sure she's ever had a boyfriend. Alessia, Stefano, Sophia, and I are the closest of all our cousins. We spent every summer together in Umito. I would fly in from LA, Alessia would drive in from Rome, as would Stefano and Sophia from Ascoli. For most kids, not being in school was the best part of the summer, but for us, it was being together, enjoying simple adventures in a small town at the top of a mountain.

"So, did you uncover any more family secrets last night?" Stefano asks sarcastically. "Can you believe that Nonna is not actually from Ceri but from Pretare? Who *are* we?"

"My mother told me on the flight here," I reply.

"Why do you think they are telling us now?" Sophia asks.

"Guilt," I reply, "there must be some kind of implication. Or why not take it to the grave?"

"You're right Eli, I've never thought of that," Alessia says, as she taps her fingers on her lips. Her face suddenly lights up, as she scrambles to get her phone out of her jacket.

"I totally forgot! I found a letter a few years ago from Aunt Amelia to my mother. There were many parts of the letter that didn't make any sense, one in particular. I took a picture of it because it was the only letter my mother ever read in secret. Let me see . . . " she says excitedly, as she slides, swipes, and taps her phone until she finds it. "Wait, wait, here it is!" She proceeds to read it aloud:

> *I know now that the very farcical decisions we made carried momentous weight. The profound effect it has had in our*

*lives is like a command without clout. Our sovereignty has
become our powerlessness and our ultimate weakness. Sister,
what is one to do when she realizes that being important
is no longer significant? Our mastery is impetus, as is our
dominion. Our antecedent will find us soon. The mark is
upon us.*

My knees feel weak and I recede into a chair. There is a daunting feeling in my heart.

"I don't know what half those words mean!" Sophia exclaims.

"Me neither, well at least not initially. I had to look a few of them up," Alessia replies, "but it makes sense now, it must be guilt over bad choices."

"Yes, but it also sounds like something is coming, like some kind of consequence," Stefano says.

"Like Nonna's death?" Sophia asks.

"No, more like something bigger than both of them," Alessia says, reflecting.

"If you'd like, we can visit Pretare. I'd be happy to drive us there today," Luca chimes in, eager to offer.

"Today?" I ask with uncertainty.

"Well, it's Pretare's town festival this weekend. It will be a fun time to visit and learn about its history. You may be able to find some information about your family. You know how these small towns are, everyone knows each other."

"YES!" Alessia shouts, with a mischievous look in her eyes. "Let's go, get your coat!"

"How far is it from here?" Sophia asks Luca.

"It's about 20 kilometers, I would say less than a thirty-minute drive," he responds. "If we leave now, we can be there in time for lunch."

I can't believe it. All these years, she was just thirty minutes away from her hometown. The place she was born was right there, and we just never knew. I suddenly feel a strong urge in my gut to go. I want to see this place that she's been running from all these years.

"Yes," I say, as I get up. I grab my handbag and jacket and quickly walk outside before I lose my courage.

Moments later Luca follows me out, "You okay, Eli?"

"Yes, fine, thank you. Just a bit of family frustration, I'm sorry," I respond.

"No, that's okay, we've all got it."

"I suppose that's true," I say. And then there is that awkward silence.

"What is taking them so long?" I ask.

"Stefano and Sophia are freshening up, and Alessia is writing your mothers a note as to our whereabouts today."

"Thank you for doing this, it was very kind of you to offer." I point to his car, "I suppose that fancy thing is yours?" He smiles. It is the first time I see him really smile, with his lips parted and his mouth slightly open. And I begin to see what all the fuss is about.

"I take it you're not a car enthusiast?" he asks, through those perfect white teeth.

"No, I couldn't care less," I say arrogantly. I realize how rude that sounded, but only after it comes out of my imperfect mouth.

"Sorry!" I say, closing my eyes and rubbing my forehead, "That was horribly rude. I don't mean to undermine your interests. It's very luxurious and I'm sure it does lots of fancy tricks."

Foot in mouth Eli, stop talking! I keep repeating internally to myself.

"Well, it's not a horse," he says laughing, "but the pedigree is good."

Finally! Everyone walks out to meet us at the car. Luca opens the car door to let me in, and then steps away for a phone call. I realize my hands are sweating, but why am I nervous? This guy is Alessia's and Sophia's, and maybe every woman's dream. But not mine. I mean, what has this guy ever done to change the world for the better. Besides, it doesn't seem right that any man should be this distinguished and handsome. Guys like this are too dangerous. Mostly because they lure you in with their charm, only for you to discover that they either suffer from narcissism or lack the ability to stay monogamous. Or both. In full disclosure, a man like Luca has never looked in my direction, let alone spoken to me. I can see why girls like it, it's good for one's self-esteem. I can't help but wonder how Stefano would feel if he knew that every woman in our family is falling over themselves over his best friend.

Alessia makes herself comfortable in the front seat next to Luca. Somehow, I find myself sitting between 5' 10" Sophia and 6' 4" Stefano in the back. The car is surprisingly very spacious, even with two sets of legs that never end on each side of me. My cousins each tilt and adjust their seats to the perfect position. They clearly know what they're doing, and I am feeling very out of my element. The back seats remind me of those overpriced first-class seats I walk by to get to coach on the airplane. As I look for buttons to adjust my seat, I am distracted by the softest leather I've ever touched.

"I apologize, the center seat doesn't adjust. You're actually sitting on the mini fridge," Luca says, as he adjusts his rearview mirror to make eye contact with me.

"The what?" I reply dumbfounded. The only time I've had a mini fridge was in my college dorm room.

"That reminds me cousin, do you want a soda, champagne, wine?" Stefano says, as he pulls me off my seat and onto his lap like a rag doll. He pushes a button and the center seat opens and lifts up for access to the beverages. My eyes nearly fall out of my head. I've never seen anything like it. I feel like I'm on a spaceship. Everyone speaks over each other to request beverages from Stefano.

"Anything for you, Eli?" Stefano asks.

"Umm . . . uhh . . . water," I stutter; he hands me a bottle of Pellegrino. I watch him push another button to close the compartment. He then tosses me back into my seat like this is all very normal. Sophia and Stefano proceed to pull out trays that fold out from in between the seats. They set their drinks down and pull out their phones while having a conversation. I am in dismay and my mouth has dropped open. I can see Luca looking at me and laughing under his breath. How embarrassing, I feel myself turning red. He must think I'm a vagabond that's never been anywhere nice.

Ring

Ring

Everyone checks their phone—it's mine.

"Hi mom," I answer, but the line is cutting out and I can barely hear a word she's saying, "Mom, did you get our note?" I yell louder, as if that will clear the line. "I can't hear you. We're going down the mountain. I'll call you later," and hang up.

"What did she say?" Alessia asks.

"I couldn't make anything out, but she seems mad."

"Dad has been sending me messages to turn around and come home. Ignore them, Eli. Just turn off your phone. Actually, everyone turn off your phones!" Stefano says rebelliously. "Today will be a cell phone free day. Let's just enjoy ourselves and deal with our controlling parents later." We toast to that and put our phones away.

Chapter 5

T HE DRIVE to Pretare is very smooth and fast. I usually love the journey from city to city when I'm in Italy, because the scenery is always so stunning. But the way Luca drives leaves little to enjoy. He is an efficient driver; I will give him that.

We slow down and find ourselves in a bit of traffic as we start to drive down the main road. There are so many people out walking towards the center of the festival. The streets are lined up with vendors everywhere. There is so much food, and so many games and toys. You can feel the joy and excitement in the air from all of the visitors. Luca pulls off the main street to a private road. He parks in an open spot, directly in front of what appears to be an apartment building.

"This looks like private property, Luca. I don't think we can park here," Alessia says, turning to him. Not that she needed to move her head much, she barely took her eyes off him the entire way.

"Yes, it is. It's mine," he says, as he turns off the engine.

"FRIEND! Why am I not surprised you have a home here too?" Stefano exclaims, as he pats Luca on the shoulder from the back seat. What does he mean "too," how many houses does this guy have?

"Wait, are you saying this building isn't apartments? It's like *one* house? Like, *your* house?" Alessia says astonished. I don't think any of us have ever seen anything so grand.

"Actually, this home has belonged to my family for several generations. My father spent many years here. He never had the heart to sell it, so he restored it and kept it as a family home. No one ever comes here anymore."

We get out of the car and he offers us a tour of the house. Alessia does not turn down the offer, she probably wants to see what could potentially be "one" of *her* homes someday. He takes us through a back-service door that leads directly into the kitchen. There, we find an older couple cooking a meal that smells incredible. I suddenly feel famished.

"Signore Luca!" exclaims the older gentleman, as he cleans his hands on his apron. He smiles big and throws his hands in the air like they are old friends. The gentleman then places one hand on Luca's shoulder and with the other, he shakes his hand, "We did not expect you to walk in through this entrance!"

"Gian Carlo, it's so good to see you! Please, let me introduce you to my friends," Luca says, as he introduces us one by one. Luca then walks over to the older woman and embraces her with all his might.

"Julia, I've missed you so much!" and he kisses her on the cheek.

"Signore Luca, it's been too long this time," Julia replies, and touches his face gently. In his usual gentlemanly manner, Luca introduces Julia as his second mother. You can see the pride in her eyes for him.

"Lunch will be ready very soon!" she says to us.

"I will give them a tour of the house while you finish preparing. We'll return shortly," Luca says to Gian Carlo.

"Where shall we set the table, the formal dining room?" Gian Carlo asks.

"No, I think we will all be more comfortable in the usual place."

"The kitchen table it is, Signore," Gian Carlo happily abides.

"Luca, I wouldn't want to put them out. We can eat at one of the vendors. Really, it's not a big deal," I say to him.

"I called before we left, they are preparing lunch for us. It would be rude not to stay," he says, with that smile again.

Luca explains to us that Julia and Gian Carlo are the keepers of the residence. They have been residing there for many years and have done a wonderful job at taking care and protecting the home. Luca goes on to say that he sees them as mother and father figures, as his were often not present in his childhood. The tone in his voice has no sadness about their absence. Instead, any disappointment seems to be replaced with love and respect for Julia and Gian Carlo.

"Well in that case, we wouldn't want to be rude," Sophia says coyly, as she grabs my hand and we walk through the hallway to the main part of the house.

"I suppose we . . . " I'm speechless. I find myself standing in the foyer of the house. "House" is an understatement, it's more like a museum. We are all astonished at what we see. The incredibly tall ceilings are covered with beautifully painted frescos—marble floors and double stairways lead to the second floor, with paintings and sculptures displayed throughout. The windows are so large and so long, they create a panoramic view of the Apennine Mountains.

"Luca, it's nice to finally see where you've put all that artwork I acquired for you. It looks magnificent here," Stefano says, pleased with himself.

"They are safe here. No one would think to look for such pieces in such a small town. For liability purposes, we feel like it was the right choice."

As I look around, I begin to recognize some of the work I've only ever seen such a collection in museums. I did not know that any one person would ever have the ability to collect this kind of historical art. This really makes the mini fridge look frivolous.

"How sad to hide such beautiful work," I say, still in shock as I look around, "to keep something so beautiful from the world is an offense."

"I agree. We often lend our pieces to museums and galleries around the world. We share them as often as we can," Luca says reassuringly, as he escorts us into the formal sitting room. I notice an intricate painting that takes up the entire side wall of the far room. It's a tree. I walk closer. I feel as if it's almost drawing me to it. I've never seen anything like it. The canvas is a fabric I cannot identify, it looks like it may have been woven with gold thread, but I'm not sure. The brush strokes have a kind of vibration running through them. As I look closer, I can see that there are images painted into every branch of the painting. There are layers upon layers, it is captivating. I look for a name on the canvas—no name.

"ELI!" I feel someone grabbing my arm. "Are you okay? I've been calling your name for five minutes," Stefano says to me.

"Sorry . . . Luca, who is the artist? I don't see a signature anywhere," I ask, stepping away from my cousin.

"It's a family heirloom, I'm not sure. It's been around forever," he responds.

"It's captivating, I've never seen anything like it. Stefano, don't those brush strokes look familiar, but also so unique, and one of a kind?" I ask, as I put my face up to it. There it is . . . the vibration again. It's intoxicating, I can feel it on the back of my neck.

"Some water, Eli?" Luca asks, as he hands me a glass of water. As I look at it, I realize how dry my throat is.

"Yes, thank you." I turn around and make my way back to the group.

"How big is this house?" Sophia asks with excitement, as she steps out onto the balcony.

"This home used to be quite small, until my father commissioned this villa to be built forty years ago and it became all of this. He used the best architects and builders to create a home that would be worthy of hosting such art."

"Well done Mr. Vinci, bravo!" Stefano clapped. "Your father is a genius!"

"Don't remind him. He hasn't been back here for twenty-six years now . . . " Luca replies, with a condescending tone. "The house can be intimidating. I hope you understand why I brought you in through the back."

I look over at Alessia, who has been quiet much too long, and even she looks like she might be in over her head. She may know everything about food, but art is not her métier. She thinks museum benches are for nap time. I smile at her and she gestures at me for a glass of wine.

"Yes of course, a glass of wine, you'll have to excuse me I'm not a natural host," Luca says, noticing her gesture. "The wine cellar is in the basement. I know a little about wine, but I am no sommelier. How about we all go down for a tour, and maybe Alessia would be so kind as to pick out a bottle of wine for lunch?"

"Now we're talking!" Alessia says, as she jumps out of that eighteenth-century sofa that may have been owned by Marie Antoinette herself. We take an elevator down to the basement. The moment the doors open, cold air hits our faces and we all shiver.

"The basement is actually made up of underground caves that

run underneath the house," Luca says, leading us off the elevator. "These caves are quite cold. They were built in the early 1500s. But they are the perfect temperature for wine, cheese, cured meats, and of course, preserving art," Luca says, as he looks for the key to the cellar. I look around and notice that there are five doors, four with a sign above them that state either: *Wine, Meat, Cheese, or Art.* There is one door that is not labeled. I hear him unlock the *Wine* door and let the others in.

"Luca, what's in there? It's the only door without a sign," I ask.

"You are quite perceptive. I believe it's storage," he replies nonchalantly, as we walk into what looks like my father's idea of heaven.

"Holy shit!" Alessia blurts out. The cellar must be at least ten thousand square feet filled top to bottom with different wines, champagnes, and liquors from all over the world.

"I'm not certain I can choose just one," Alessia says, as her almond shaped eyes become round and huge, "This is my dream for the restaurant, wow . . . "

"Please choose as many as you like. It will be a pleasure to finally enjoy these."

"Ále, don't take too long, I'm starving," Sophia says in a child-like voice. Thank God for this kid always being hungry. My stomach is beginning to growl.

"How about we fill a case with different kinds of wine, that way we can enjoy them this week," Luca offers.

"Marvelous idea!" Alessia happily agrees.

"Let's just stick to looking at the first few sections Ále, or else we'll be here all day," Stefano says, knowing our cousin so well.

Without any shame, Alessia recognizes several bottles and fills up most of the crate. As she ponders about which last two she has room for, Luca walks up from the back with three bottles in his arms.

"Alessia this is for you," and hands her a bottle. Her hands start to shake with excitement.

"This is a 1947 Maison de Atienne! I didn't even know this bottle still existed. I can't accept this," she tries to hand him the bottle back. It must have been a big deal if *she*, of all people, said she couldn't accept it. "How do you even have this?"

"I didn't know I had it until five minutes ago. Must not be that important," he replies, pushing the bottle back to her.

"Are you mad! This has to be worth over $300,000!" She is yelling now.

"Oh f—," Sophia begins to say as Stefano covers her mouth.

"All the more reason it shouldn't be sitting in the back of a wine cellar," Luca replies kindly. This guy is starting to get on my nerves. Can anyone really be this hot and generous? Maybe he's just trying to win her over. Well, I think it's working.

He then hands Stefano a bottle, "It's not a 1947 Maison de Atienne, but in my opinion, it's better. It's wine from our vineyard in France, enjoy friend." He and my cousin share a brotherly half handshake, half hug. I mean, seriously? They have vineyards that make wine for them in France? A gross example of misguided, exuberant wealth. Who are these people? Why don't they put their money to good use instead of buying vineyards in France? We have perfectly wonderful vineyards here in Italy. Show-off. I have mentally checked out and look at my watch—it's noon. Now I'm just annoyed and want to eat. What time are we getting to this festival anyway, isn't that why we're here?

"This one is for you."

I see a dirty green bottle with no label being handed to me.

"Me?" I ask with an attitude, "Oh, I'm not really a wine drinker. The only wine I ever enjoyed was my grandfather's wine. He had vineyards here. In Italy. In Venarotta," I say, hoping he gets the hint.

He half smirks and says, "His name was Giuseppe? Giuseppe Tesani? Your paternal grandfather."

"Yes, how did you know that?"

"Turn the bottle over." I do as he says. There it is, my grandfather's signature:

Giuseppe Tesani 1943

My eyes well up with tears instantly. I brush my finger over his signature, I can feel the ridges from the inscription he had done by hand.

"How . . . " my voice cracks and I clear my throat, "How do you have this?"

"My family knew him, they said your grandfather was the best wine maker in all of Italy, maybe even the world. They would buy cases from him each year. It is said 1943 was his best, they bought his entire stock that year."

"Ah yes, the infamous 1943 wine . . . " I fight back the tears as my voice trails off. Luca looks at me with pain in his eyes. He knows the real story.

"Thank you, Luca. This is extremely generous of you. I think we should open this for lunch. I'm missing him very much and I would love to drink this."

Stefano reassuringly wraps his arm around my neck and kisses my head, as we head back towards the elevator.

*　　*　　*

"The food is going to get cold! Everyone to the table!" Julia says, hurrying us to sit.

"It smells wonderful," compliments Sophia, as we all ravenously take our seats.

Gian Carlo brings a huge bowl of pasta to the table, made with tomato sauce and fresh ground parmesan cheese sprinkled on top, "Well it's not like the food at *someone's* famous restaurant," he says as he winks at Alessia, "but we hope you enjoy."

We all applaud the chefs and thank them for the wonderful presentation. During lunch, Gian Carlo and Julia entertain us with many stories of Luca's childhood. They consider Luca like a son because they never had children of their own. They have lived in this home most of their lives. The Vinci family pays them to look over the grounds and home. These days, Luca's family splits most their time between Rome and Milan. Julia said that Luca is the only one that will come to visit once or twice a year. She hasn't seen Luca's parents since they left Pretare.

What was just a plate of pasta turns into a three-course meal. I'm so full I can hardly move.

Luca pours the last drop of my grandfather's wine in my glass, "It seems only right that you get the last sip. To your health," and we toast.

"Eli, what is the story of the infamous 1943 wine?" Sophia asks. Gian Carlo and Julia shift in their chairs, and Gian Carlo gently places his hand over Julia's.

"Did you know him?" I ask. They both look like they are younger, but close to my grandparents' age.

"I was a boy when I first met both your grandfathers, Giuseppe and Alfredo. We later fought in World War II side by side. They were great soldiers, but even greater men."

"Thank you, you're very kind. I'm sure they were very fond of you as well," I reply to Gian Carlo.

"So? What's the story?" Sophia asks.

"Well, for the sake of time, since I really do want to make it to the festival today, I'll give you the Cliffs Notes version," I say casually, keeping my emotions in. The truth is, that the details are too painful and excruciating, and I could never say them out loud without completely losing my composure. "In the dead of winter in 1944 my grandmother Rosa and grandfather Giuseppe had no food and no money. My father was only a few months old. They sold everything they could that had any monetary value, but it was still not enough. The only thing my grandfather had left was the wine he had made the year before. The problem was that no one would buy it from them. They had become very thin and ill from not eating. My grandmother was boiling ice from the snow over the fire just so they could drink warm water to fill their stomachs. On the fourth day of not eating, my grandmother had no milk left to give to my father. She said her last prayer was that they would all perish at the same time to prevent the other from suffering. On that day, an "angel" appeared, that's what my Nonna Rosa called him. He heard that my grandfather had wine to sell and wanted to buy the entire lot. When I saw this bottle today, I realized that it must have been someone in Luca's family that purchased the wine," I pause. "The money they received from the sale lasted them far past the end of the war. They were able to build a proper home and life for their growing family."

Gian Carlo's knuckles are white from how tightly he is clenching Julia's hand. I know from the look in their eyes, they know how much I have dignified the story.

"So today, let's drink to this wine and the Vinci family "angel"—without either of which I would not be here today," I raise my glass and we silently toast.

"Thank God for that Eli," Stefano says. "Luca, looks like we owe your family one on behalf of Eli's grandparents."

"No Stefano, it's quite the opposite," he replies. Even I don't catch what he means by that.

"Well, I think it's time to liven things up a bit!" Alessia shouts out as she stands up, throws her arms in the air, and snaps her fingers. Leave it to Alessia to bring the party back into any situation. In this moment, I'm very grateful for it. We get our things together and thank Gian Carlo and Julia for the wonderful meal and amazing hospitality. I lean in to kiss Julia's cheek and I notice how lovely her skin is, and that the color of her eyes is gray brown. I realize I've seen these eyes before. They're just like the old man in the mountains. I look over at Gian Carlo and notice that his are the same gray-brown color too. Huh, what are the chances, three people in two days.

"Come closer, darling," Julia says to me. As I bend down closer to her, she says softly, "Please be careful today. Do not get separated from the group."

"Is it a dangerous festival?" I ask.

"No, it's quite lovely. But it doesn't mean there aren't dangerous people."

"Yes, please don't worry, I will be careful," I assure her, and kiss her goodbye on the cheek.

We walk to the festival from Luca's house. It's a beautiful August day, but it feels more like September/October. The sun is out but there is a cool breeze in the air. The temperature is changing all over the world now. The seasons seem to be confused and the weather is unpredictable, no matter where I go.

"Excuse me!" I hear a tiny voice trying to push through us. I look down and there's a group of little girls of different ages all dressed up in costumes.

"Well, aren't you beautiful. Are you all butterflies?" I ask.

"No!" they giggle, "we're faeries!"

"Are you going to come watch our play?" asks the older one.

"There's a play?"

"Yes, right over there," she says as she points to the main stage. "It's going to start in a little bit."

"Ok good luck! I'll be watching." I wave at them as they scurry off. As I take a moment to look around, I notice that there are children dressed as faeries everywhere I look. They are wearing long white flowy dresses, flowers in their hair, and faerie wings. Even teenagers and some adults are wearing faerie wings, almost every vendor is selling them.

We make our way down to the main stage and find a place to stand. There are hundreds of people waiting around to watch the performance.

"This is the best part of the festival; you're going to love these kids!" Luca shouts. It's hard to hear over the music and people talking.

"How about a beer?" Stefano suggests. He and Luca walk down to the vendor to get us beers.

"Yummm, can you smell the peanuts and cotton candy?" says Sophia, "Can we get some?"

"Sure, but take Alessia with you, I don't want you to go alone," I suggest to her. Her brother is overprotective, and the last thing I want is to be responsible if anything happens to her. You know, like a cut on her knee. "I'll wait here to hold our spots."

I look around at all the little girls in their whimsical faerie outfits and my mind starts to replay Aunt Silva's words. Could there be truth to what she said? But that would be absolutely inconceivable. I don't think my mind has the ability to expand to that capacity. It's too out of reach even for someone like me, who believes anything is possible. I suppose somewhere deep inside of me, I always suspected that magical creatures could have been real at some point in history. And like dinosaurs, they just became extinct over time. The indisputable difference is that we have fossils proving dinosaurs once roamed the earth. There is no evidence that magical people ever did. There is also no evidence that they didn't. Once again, I am standing at that impasse—how do I believe in something I cannot see? It's been nineteen years

since that day on the plane. And it bothers me to my core that
I've made no progress on this dichotomy.

"Signore! Signora! Signorina! Please take one!" My thoughts
are interrupted by a shouting teenage boy wearing a vintage her-
ringbone Jaxon hat, long-sleeved white shirt, charcoal grey vest,
and black trousers. He hands out brochures out of an old newspaper satchel. As he passes one to me, he tips his hat and winks
flirtatiously. I take the brochure and gently tap him over the head
with it. We both laugh and he moves onto the next pretty face.
These Italian boys, they really are charismatic. The men pass it
on to their boys every generation, and some things never change.
I should know, my very first heartbreak was at the hands of one
of these charmers. I open the brochure, on the left is the weekend's line up of various local bands and times for the theatrical
performances. On the right is a brief description of the festival,
it reads:

> *Welcome to Faerieland! August 15th and 16th will be filled*
> *with entertainment and magic, as we evoke the Legend of*
> *Faeries on the Feast Day of San Rocco, our patron saint.*
> *Please join us for the beautiful and original theatrical pre-*
> *sentation that recalls the story of Sibyl and her faeries. The*
> *reenactment will bring us inside Sibyl's cave as Guerrian*
> *Meschino goes on a quest to find his brother . . .*

My reading is interrupted by a familiar scent. Milk, honey, lavender, and moss. I look up and notice a very well-dressed woman
standing next to me. She is holding a delicate umbrella made of
silk and lace, just big enough to keep the sun out of her face.

"Excuse me madam, what is that perfume you're wearing?" I
politely ask, as I lean in to take another inhalation of this intoxicating scent. She gently moves the umbrella from her left to her
right shoulder as she turns to address me. I freeze as she looks

at me. She is the most STUNNING woman I have ever seen. I am at a loss for words. I've met a lot of beautiful people in my life, but no one has come close to this. She is magnificent. She looks like a painting—she doesn't seem real. Her skin is smooth and flawless. Her eyes are both tender and dangerous. They are brown and hazel green, the color of moss. I notice she has a small freckle in her left eye. She is tall, slender, and very feminine. Her lips have a natural lining with just the right amount of fullness. Her nose is small and thin, with a slight point at the tip; I bet those Beverly Hills doctors would do anything to get results like that. Everything about her looks delicate and refined. It takes, utterly, all of me not to touch her to see if she is real, or if I'm hallucinating again.

"It's my own blend. I mix the oils myself," this divine creature says to me with a soft and slightly smoky voice.

I stand there like a fool, overwhelmed by her presence, and unsure of what to say. I have never been so intimidated in all my life.

"Are you well, dear?" she asks, as she looks at me, a bit concerned. She has a strange accent. I can't really make it out, maybe a bit of Italian mixed with Middle Eastern and British?

"Y—," I clear my throat a few times, "Yes, fine thank you," I manage to stutter out, "It's a lovely scent."

"Thank you, I love your scarf," she says, and I feel flattered. "Is it your first time here?"

"Yes. Yours?"

"No, I come every year. I live nearby, it's a favored festival in these parts."

"Are you from here? I couldn't help but notice your accent," I can't resist asking.

"No. I was born very far from here. Then raised in Jerusalem. I came to Italy as a young woman and I've never left," she replies in her sultry voice.

"I hear an English accent as well." I know I'm pushing my luck, but I can't resist, she is fascinating.

She smiles an enchanting smile—it reminds me so much of my grandmother—and says, "You have a very good ear. Many of my teachers were either British, Latin, French, or Greek, it must have stayed with me along the way. I can hear that you have a slight accent of your own. American?"

"Yes. Well, I was born here, but we moved to America when I was a little girl. I live there now, I'm just here on vacation," I reply politely.

"How long will you be staying?"

"I'm not sure."

"Hmm . . . " she ponders, "Are you enjoying your stay?"

"Yes, I forget how much I miss being here," I reply. I put out my hand to introduce myself. "I'm Eli, by the way."

She slowly raises hers and embraces mine. The vibration of her touch is exhilarating. It is like two circuits that come together to create a surge of pure energy. It is as if I can feel the beginning of life traveling through my veins. It frightens me immensely; it is both beautiful and terrifying. I pull my hand away quickly but calmly, trying to regain my composure.

"Enjoy the show, it's very entertaining," she says, as she gestures to the stage with her closed fan that had been hanging from her wrist, "You'll learn a lot about this place. They mostly have it wrong, but it's still enchanting."

I look up in the direction she has pointed to. The show is about to begin. I look back to thank her, but she is gone. Her scent lingers, I can still smell her. And apparently so can Luca.

I hear Sophia and Alessia behind me, walking up the hill, when Luca grabs my arm and pulls me off to the side, out of the earshot of the others. He's so worked up he nearly spills his beer all over me and himself.

"Eli, why were you here alone? Did someone speak to you? Are you ok?" he asks, almost out of his mind.

"Luca, what's wrong?" I ask. He's usually so in control and poised.

"Please answer my questions," he says with about all the nerve he's got to keep himself calm. I can see Alessia looking over at us with a tinge of jealousy in her eyes.

"Yes Luca, I'm fine." I try to calm him down, but he maintains his agitated state. He doesn't pay any mind to Alessia or anyone else for that matter.

"What is this about?" I ask, annoyed.

He takes a deep breath, waits a moment and says, "You answer my questions first."

"Yes, I spoke to a lovely local woman. I loved the scent of her perfume and asked what she was wearing. We had a small conversation and she left," I say, trying to reassure him, so he will leave me alone.

"That's all? Nothing else?" he presses.

"That's all." I sigh and continue, "She was captivating. I wish I had an ounce of her beauty. Maybe if I did, I wouldn't be so . . . "

"So, what?" he looks angry now.

"Invisible," I say softy. I can't believe I said that out loud, especially to him. Why am I feeling so vulnerable? He shakes his head in disbelief and still looks angry.

"Eli, I'm not about to get into that with you right now," he replies sharply, "I need to know if anything else happened. Did she ask you any questions? Did she touch you?"

"We shook hands when we . . . actually, I never got her name." Huh, that just occurred to me, I was so enthralled with her, I didn't even ask her name. I look back at Luca annoyed at all the questioning. "Listen, I'm not playing this game with you, Luca. What the hell is your problem? And just so you know, this is not a good look for you. Alessia has been glaring at us this entire time. You're going to ruin your chances with her."

Luca looks me dead in the eyes and takes another long deep breath. He then takes a step into my personal space and hands me one of the drinks. As I take it from him, he carefully places his hand over part of mine. Before he says a word, I feel it *again* . . . the surge, the electricity. This time it starts in the core of my spine, and slowly, I feel it spread throughout *every* ounce of my body. The electricity is increasingly stimulating, and my body feels like it's on fire. This is very different than the last one. I GASP. I am trying pull my hand away, but I literally cannot move. It's as if he has a complete hold on me. I look down and see his hand is just barely touching mine.

"Eli, we need to leave. I can't explain why right now, but you need to trust me. Let's go," Luca orders. Despite his warning, I can't contain my defiance to his demands. Here it is again, another man in my life that wants to control me. This one isn't even my boyfriend. What is it with almost every man in this world thinking they can just dictate orders at women, and we're just supposed to obey and follow commands. I'm done with this, no more!

I feel anger rise from my navel to my throat and just like that, the hold he has on me vanishes. I pull my hand away. Luca looks more astonished than I do, that I am able to break free of whatever nonsense that was.

"Enough. I've had enough of this. If you want to leave be my guest, I'll find my own way home. I am going to stay, enjoy the show, drink a beer, and eat peanuts. I'm sorry if that doesn't work with your commands. I've come here to learn something about the place I just learned my grandmothers are from. Like it or don't like it, it's all the same to me." For the first time in my life I push back, and it feels *SO* good.

I walk back to the group, who are focused on the show that has just started. I wedge myself between Alessia and Sophia.

"What was that about?" Alessia asks, in a very aggravated tone.

"Keep your boyfriend in check Ále. I'm not in the mood," I reply, with disdain for her tone.

"He's not my boyfriend. Even if he did give me a $300,000 bottle of wine, I can barely get the guy to look at me. Maybe he did it to impress you," she says with a sigh. "I can't believe I'm going to say this, but I think he likes *you!*" She is half smiling as she sticks out her tongue at me.

"You're insane!" I reply, and the three of us have a good laugh. We put our arms around each other and continue to watch the show. The cast is mostly children, teens, and a few young adults. The details in all the props and in their ethereal costumes are so beautiful. The colors are various shades of soft pastels. And there is an abundance of glitter and sparkle to catch the light just perfectly.

The play of "Il Guerrino Meschino" (Wretched Guerrino) is based on a book written by Andrea da Barberino in 1410. The story itself takes place in the year 842. Guerrino is a slave-born hero who emerges from his circumstances strong and unshaken. After several dangerous adventures, he discovers he is of a royal bloodline. He seeks out to find his parents. As he crosses the mountain pass above a small village called Norica, he encounters the devil who's playing the role of a pimp. The devil tells him to find Sibyl, because she is the only one who knows his parents' true location.

According to folklore, Sibyl, also known as The Eleventh Sibyl, is a virgin prophetess who can read the future and see the past. Guerrino seeks her out in hopes that she will give him answers. Sibyl was once God's favored oracle, but after a falling out, He condemned her to live in the Apennine mountains until the end of time. To find her, Guerrino must locate the bowel of the mountain known as the "Mouth of Inferno," in order to get access to the grotto. There, he discovers her kingdom with the help of a talking serpent called Macco. It is a paradise protected by dragons and surrounded by the "Sibyl gold," as well as precious jewelry, various treasures, and Sibyl's faeries. The faeries would capture all of the knights, promising them immortality and a salacious life.

Sibyl welcomes Guerrino in, listens to his requests, and endeavors to tempt him into corrupting, sinful acts. She is described as the "inaccessible virgin who became seductive, impious, and greedy." But the brave and chivalrous Guerrino spends a year resisting all temptation. He has to find a way out, because no one can stay more than three hundred and sixty-five days. If he were to, he would lose his soul and become a prisoner in her kingdom forever. Instead, he manages to escape and find his parents, securing their release from prison where they were being held captive. He then marries a Persian princess and lives happily ever after.

The end.

At the end of the performance everyone applauds with an endless amount of enthusiasm, while shouting and tossing flowers onstage.

"That must be one of the only stories in history, where a man is the main character of a happily ever after faerie tale," Sophia says.

"It's like he was both the damsel in distress *and* the hero of his own story. Seems both sexist and empowering. I have mixed emotions about it," Stefano expresses.

"You get that it's not a modern story, right?" Alessia teases him.

"It was during a time when men had to literally fight for their lives to overcome the adversity of their nascency. Has this not fundamentally carried into modern times?" Stefano confidently states.

"One point for my brother and zero points for you, cousin," Sophia high fives him.

I look over at Luca, he's doing the same thing he's been doing for the last hour—looking around obsessively. It's like having an agent from the secret service around. I want to ask him what's going on, but I'm still much too angry. Sophia sees me looking over at him.

"Stefano, what's going on with Luca? Why is he acting paranoid?" she asks.

"I've been trying to get it out of him, but he won't budge," he replies, and tries to act like we're not talking about it. "He mentioned that he saw an old foe earlier. It got him wound up pretty tight, there must be some bad blood."

"A wealthy family like that must have a few enemies," Alessia muses.

"They are very careful with their affiliations. His father runs a very tight, exclusive group. And they are an even tighter family. Mr. Vinci has always treated me like a son, but even I only know about one percent of their dealings. Our family may have secrets, but his family is very private," Stefano admits.

"Is there a difference between secrets and privacy in our family?" I ask him.

"No, not anymore," says Alessia.

"Look at that sunset!" We all look as Sophia points to the west. It is breathtaking. It looks like a million orange, yellow, gold, red, and blue crystals piercing into the sky and through the heavens. It's descending behind a marvelous mountain top. The entire mountain is a blanket of bright and beautiful flowers all around it. It is by far the most magical thing I've ever seen.

There is a part of me that is in disbelief the world does not yet know that such an enchanting place truly does exist. And there is an even greater part of me that is terrified that they will. I pull out my phone to photograph it for my own memory, when I feel someone behind me.

"It won't translate well in photographs. If you take a picture it will just look like any other sunset with pretty flowers. They only bloom from early June to August. There are over 1,800 different kinds of flowers that grow here. It's best to enjoy it, it will only last a few moments," Luca says. Well, well . . . looks like someone is thawing out and returning to his old self.

"What is that mountain called? It looks like a dream," I ask Luca, wanting to forget our little "episode."

"Monte Vettore, also known as the 'King of Sibillini.' It is the most striking mountain of all the Apennine mountain range; maybe even in the world. Just below the peak there is a small enclosed valley with a lake called Lago di Pilato. Legend has it that the body of Pontius Pilate was buried in those waters after he was sentenced to death by Tiberius," he says, as he now has our full attention for the geography and history lesson.

"Who or what is Sibillini? I've always wondered why the national park was named that." Sophia asks curiously.

"Sibillini is the area of the mountain group that borders Umbria and Marche. Those mountains are mostly composed of limestone. They formed fifty to one hundred million years ago at the bottom of what is now an extinct sea. The land itself emerged about twenty million years ago. The highest peak can be reached at Monte Vettore, over eight thousand feet up. Making it the King of Sibillini," Luca says so proudly of his historic and beautiful town.

"Sibillini sounds a great deal like Sibilla, which translates to Sibyl. Luca, is this terrain actually named after the legend in the play?" I ask, then like a train, it hits me, "If the mountain is the king, then she is the queen."

Oh my God, how did I not see it sooner, this entire festival is in honor of her! Alessia and I lock eyes. This must be why my mother demanded we turn around and go back. There's clearly something about this story she doesn't want us to know. What would Celestial Beings have in common with Sibyl and her faeries, anyway?

"Is it possible, by any stretch of the imagination, that Aunt Silva wasn't joking about being magical ?" I ask her.

"Of course she's joking!" shouts Alessia. "I'm a *mage*? I mean, I would know if that were true! Such BS!"

"Does someone want to fill us in, we're feeling left out?" Stefano asks, throwing his hands up.

I shift my attention to Luca and demand to know, "Why did you bring us here today?"

"Eli don't be rude to him. He has been nothing but hospitable and generous with his home and time. What has gotten into the two of you today! I've never seen you act so . . . strange," Stefano says to us, in a very upset tone.

"Maybe he's been *too* nice," I reply, as I step into Luca's personal space.

"What are you suggesting anyway? Luca is not someone who has ulterior motives," Stefano says this time defensively. "Is someone going to tell us what's going on?"

"Yes, I'd love to know that too," Luca says, while never taking his eyes off mine. "Let's not do this here. How about we go back to my house?"

"Losers, are you kidding me! Why are you all so much drama? The music is so good, and everyone is finally dancing and having fun! That's what we are supposed to do at a festival: F-U-N!" Sophia is starting to have a slight meltdown. "Do you even know what that is anymore? It's not even late, and there's like five guys I want to talk to!"

I don't know what it is about this place, but it gives the women in our family the strength to speak our minds. Even the sweet, shy ones. We all stand in silence for a moment. Sophia is not an outspoken person and we're all taken aback.

"She's found her voice," chimes in Alessia. Thanks for the obvious news flash.

"I choose dancing too. Come on, Sophia!" I say and I grab her hand, as she jumps around with excitement and we waste no time sashaying to the dancefloor. I don't know what's come over me. I can't explain why I'm feeling so rebellious. But I let Sophia and Alessia lead the cavalry tonight.

We dance. We drink. We talk to boys. We drink more and more and more. And we even dance together to the very last song. Before I know it, Luca and Stefano have come to whisk us up off the dancefloor. I kind of forgot about them, I hadn't seen them all night. But I'm sure they had used their secret service agent skills to spy on us.

"What time is it?" I ask, as I stare at my own watch. "I can't see where the hands are. They keep moving. Time doesn't work like that, right? Or did it change? It's too hard to tell time this way. I'm sure you k-know the president of clocks or something . . . can you ask him to umm . . . change it back."

Luca can't help but laugh. Stupid, gorgeous, beautiful white teeth smile. *Why does he bother wasting it on me anyway*, I think as I squint at him.

He leans in to catch me when I move away. "Don't touch me. That thing. I don't want that thing. Happen again."

"You're swaying, I just don't want you to fall," he says, trying so hard to hold his laugh in.

"Alessia will hel-pp me. Where is she?" I ask him, as I look around. At a near distance, I can see her throwing up behind a tree. Next to her is Sophia—also throwing up. And above them is Stefano holding back both of their hair. "Oh damn! Are they-y-y drunk?" I ask and begin laughing.

"Frankly, I don't know how any of you are still standing," Luca replies.

"Frankkkly," I mock him, as I wag my finger at him, "Why are you so p-perfect? It annoys the shit out of me!"

"You think I'm perfect?"

"No. I never said that."

"You just did."

"I hate that you're so rich, you know? It's gross. What does one person or f-family do with all that money? And you're so beautiful. It should be illegal that any man be that beautif—," I pause a moment because my stomach feels queasy.

"You ok?" he asks.

"Fine," I say as I move my wrist around to keep him at a distance, "I mean . . . in allll the books and alllll the movies and the other stuff too, why does the girl *always* fall for the rich, good-looking guy? It's, umm, so cliché. So *stupid*. Why does he always have to bbe rich and handsome? And like SO cool," I ramble on, as I roll my eyes. "Why can't he be like . . . average and average? Right!" I say, with absolute conviction.

"You think I'm cool?" he asks, unable to hold back his chuckle.

"No," I say shaking my head, "Oh. I shouldn't do that."

"Do you want to sit down?"

"That's another thing! Why are you alwayyyys soooo polite? Is it real? I just don't believe anyone stays . . . mannered so well. Like that. For-ever."

"Eli, how about we get back to the house. Stefano and the girls have already started walking back."

"Finally you said. Something. Smart."

"Yes, finally," Luca shakes his head laughing.

With each step we take to his house, my stomach gets more and more upset. I start to sweat and begin to feel so sick.

"How much longer?" I ask, "It's undignified to be sick . . . out. Here."

"Uh-huh, and I'm the snob," he says taunting me. "We're standing at the door." We walk in and I can't hold it anymore. He rushes me into the nearest bathroom and holds my hair back. I'm sick for what feels like an eternity. And I can't stop crying. I cry uncontrollably every time I throw up. I don't know why, but I've always been this way.

"Did I just throw up in a gold toilet?"

"You did."

He gets me up to the sink where I rinse out my mouth a few times, and then he helps me lay down on the cold marble bathroom floor. I'm trying to soothe myself and stop crying. The cold floor feels good and it's helping.

"Why do you have a gold toilet? There are children starving in the world. That toilet can feed at least a trillion of them," I say, blubbering through my tears.

"A trillion only?" Luca asks, as he puts one towel under my head and hands me the other.

"Yes, at a minimum."

He sits behind me with his back against the wall as I do my best to calm myself. I hear a soft tap on the door and my cousin Stefano's concerned voice.

"How's she doing?" he asks Luca.

"It might be a long night. How are the girls?"

"Knocked out. Gian Carlo and Julia helped me put them to bed. Good thing they were there to meet us at the door as we arrived. Or else it would have been a whole different scene when you walked up. Julia just gave them some Potiodamus. She said it would help," he sighs. "You know, those two are really strong for their age. They lifted up those girls like they were light as a feather."

"How about we get this one up to bed," Luca suggests. Stefano offers to help, but Luca tells him he can handle it himself.

"I'll meet you in the drawing room for a drink in ten minutes. Don't worry, I'll have Julia take care of her."

Stefano seems pleased with the plan. He tells Luca that in the meantime, he is going to call our family and let them know we will be spending the night here, and not to wait up. I hear him walk out of the bathroom as Luca shuffles his arms underneath my body. He places one arm under my knees and the other holding my back. He lifts me up and holds me tightly against his chest. We enter the elevator and he presses 3. How many floors does this bloody place have?

My thoughts are interrupted, and my mind goes vacant. And before the elevator doors close, the center of my spine feels as if it is on fire. There it is again . . . that sensation . . . but this time it's stronger and deeper. I can feel it in the core of my soul. I have no strength inside of me to fight it. I let the electricity flow through my body like water running down a violent stream. I have no control, so I surrender. I feel a vibration in the blood of my veins, the same way I did when I was standing in front of the painting. I can hear my heartbeat so loudly in my ears—then I hear two. I can feel it happening to him too. I wrap my arms tightly around his neck and my legs around his waist. I can feel my body melting into his. He has his arms around me so tightly, it feels as if he might crush every bone in my body. And it feels *so good.*

I close my eyes and lay my forehead against his. I can hear our heartbeats gently slow. One beat at a time they move closer together until our heartbeats are perfectly in sync. I can no longer tell where I end and he begins. There is no skin, bones, or blood between us. A singular thread of electricity flows through us as one entity.

The euphoric cord is injected with erratic flashes. Events of history, different spectrums of time, people and places from all over the world. Then a flash of blinding light. I feel Luca kiss me with a passion and rage that should have frightened me. But I welcome it. As our lips touch over and over, more erratic flashes fill my head. This time with people and places that seem immi-nent. It looks like . . . the future? Once again, there is a bright flash.

"Young man, have you gone mad!" Gian Carlo yells at Luca, as I find myself being torn from his arms by Julia. We are standing in a bedroom. I have no recollection of how we got here. The last memory I have is of going into the elevator.

"What have you done, Luca? You know there will be severe consequences!" Julia panics, as she has me sit.

"I KNOW!" Luca shouts, "I'm sorry—I know. I don't know how it happened. I was just carrying her to bed. I-I . . . "

They begin to whisper—it sounds like some kind of plan. Gian Carlo and Luca leave the room abruptly. I cannot keep my eyes open. I am totally drained and can no longer feel any part of my body.

Chapter 6

I WAKE UP the next morning feeling better than I deserve. My head is heavy and I'm very thirsty. I look around feeling confused. "Where the hell am I?" I say out loud. I sit up and rub my eyes. I notice a bottle of water on the nightstand and I drink all of it. I kick the heavy comforter off me and notice I'm in my shirt and underwear. I walk over to the window and open the curtain. Big mistake—too bright. I suddenly have a flashback of a bright light. Were we playing with flashlights last night? My head is very fuzzy and I can't really think. I need coffee. I see a robe draped across the lounge chair with a note. It reads:

Good Morning Miss Eli,
Please make your way down to the kitchen when you wake.
I will have fresh coffee and pastries waiting for you.
-Julia

I put on the robe and slippers and look at my watch to see the time. Why was I wearing it upside down? I take it off my wrist, it reads 9:30. I pull out my cell phone from my purse to text my mom, but the battery is dead. Great, she's going to kill me. I might as well enjoy the last few hours of my life. I push the drapes all the way open and see that instead of a window, there are French doors that lead out to a balcony. I step out to a warm, clear, and sunny day. The balcony overlooks beautiful green knolls, with scattered sheep all around eating grass. I step back in and nearly fall over. I hadn't realized how enormous this bedroom is. It must be close to two thousand square feet. It is decorated like a bedroom out of Versailles. The opulence and grandeur are only fitting for such a home. I've never stayed anywhere like this before. It's no wonder I got the best sleep of my life, the mattress must be made out of golden geese feathers. Speaking of golden, was I hugging a gold toilet last night?

I take the elevator down to the first floor and make my way into the kitchen. I see Julia standing near the stove pouring a cup of coffee.

"Good morning Miss Eli, how did you sleep?" she asks.

"Good thank you," I reply, as I take a seat on the stool at the kitchen island. "Who helped me get to bed last night? I don't remember a thing."

"It was a group effort by Signore Luca and Gian Carlo. But I was the one to undress you and tuck you in. As I did with Miss Alessia and Miss Sophia," she replies, as she hands me coffee.

"Thank you for your kindness and hospitality. I feel humiliated about last night. I never drink, it's not like me."

"That is evident my dear, but you have nothing to be ashamed of. You were perfectly fine," she says to comfort me.

"Thank you for lying to me," I say, as I take her hand and she smiles at me. "I'm horribly embarrassed, I remember very little about last night," I sigh and take a big sip of coffee. "Where is everyone?"

"Well, Alessia and Sophia are still sleeping. Stefano and Luca have gone for a morning hike. And Gian Carlo went to the grocery store to pick up some items for lunch," she says, as she pulls out fresh croissants from the oven. I see a charger on one of the counters and I walk over to charge my phone.

"My mother is going to be so upset with me. Not only did I not respect her wishes by coming here yesterday, but I also never returned any of her calls. And now my phone is dead, and I'm going to be dead too when she gets her hands on me," I say, as I plug it in and walk back over to my seat.

"You can't blame a mother for worrying," she answers sadly. I remember that she and Gian Carlo never had children. I want so badly to ask her about it but think it would be much too invasive.

"Your mother is Elizabetta Goto and your father is Leonardo Tesani?"

"Yes, do you know them?" I ask, with my mouth half full of delicious, buttery croissant.

"I've never had the pleasure. I knew your grandparents, they're truly exquisite people. I'm sorry to hear Amelia is not well."

"Thank you. How did you know them?" Julia suddenly becomes tense as I ask this question.

"Our husbands fought in the war together, as you know. And during that time, we women had to stick together to help the children and the elderly," she says carefully.

"I'm sorry, that must have been a very difficult time for you all."

"Yes, very." It is obvious the memories are still very painful.

"I've just recently learned that my grandmothers are from Pretare. Were you all childhood friends?" I ask in order to change the subject. But it only makes her all the more tense.

"Yes, we were good friends until they married, then Amelia moved to Umito and Rosa to Venarotta," she replies with a heavy heart. "Of course, I was very happy for them. But things were never the same around here after they left. Their presence has been missed."

"It's very strange to me that they live thirty minutes away and never returned. You wouldn't happen to know why?" I ask.

"You're a clever enough girl to know that I cannot answer such a personal question. You must ask Amelia," she says, with a genuine and sweet smile.

"Believe me, I've been trying."

Alessia and Sophia walk into the kitchen looking as if they have been hit by a train. I can't imagine I must look much better. They are wearing similar robes and slippers.

"Coffee, coffee, coffee pleeeease!!!" Sophia says, sitting down next to me and putting her head on my shoulder, "How is my head not pounding this morning?"

"I asked myself the same thing!" I reply.

"Before you went to sleep, I had you take Potiodamus drops, which I make with my own mix of herbs," Julia says. "I created them for healing various ailments and well . . . *conditions*. I started giving them to the Vinci men many moons ago. As you can imagine, from time to time they can be heavy drinkers. They're much easier to deal with the next day if I give them drops the night before."

"Many moons ago? How old are you, Julia?" Sophia asks.

"Much too ancient to mention," she says jokingly.

"You're starting to sound like my mother," Alessia says, as she finishes her second cup of water.

"How is Ersella? Feisty as always?" Julia asks.

"Worse," Alessia replies. "I didn't realize that you two knew each other."

"We were just talking about that as you walked into the kitchen," I mention.

"How do we find out about our lineage? Is there anyone around here that knows our family? Maybe they can tell us something that might help," Alessia asks.

"Our best option is to go to city hall or the local church. They must have records somewhere." Sophia's brain seems to be waking up faster than ours.

"It's Sunday, you'll find everything closed. It's best to speak to your mothers, I'm sure they will be able to tell you everything you need to know." There Julia goes again, getting tense.

"That's the problem, everything is on a need-to-know basis. We're very frustrated Julia, and we want to know everything," Alessia replies.

"The truth can be hard to speak, but hearing it can be odious," Julia says, as I get a chill up my spine.

Speaking of which, why do my back and lips hurt so bad? Did I fall last night?

"Then it's settled," Sophia says, as she taps her hand on the table, "No one will have to say anything. It will be fun to do our own research! We're going tomorrow!"

"Going where?" Stefano asks, as he and Luca walk in the door with Gian Carlo entering right after. "Last time you used the word F-U-N, it ended in anything *but* that for me." We all can't help but have a good laugh about that.

"Sorry brother," Sophia says, as she embraces him.

"We love you," Alessia adds, as he walks by and she gives him a big kiss on the cheek.

"Eli, don't you think you owe Luca a thank you?" Stefano says to me and points at Luca.

"Luca took care of me?" I ask, with no recollection.

"Well, there was only so much hair I could hold back at once," Stefano teases.

I turn to Luca and feel my cheeks getting hot, "I'm so sorry. Please forgive anything I might have done or said last night. I have very little recollection of the evening. And thank you. For taking care of me."

"You really don't remember anything?" he asks, smiling.

"No, nothing. Maybe hugging a gold toilet. Please forgive me." All I feel is humiliation that the person I have to apologize to is the one I've been judging.

"It's not confession Eli, nothing to forgive you for. Don't even give it a second thought."

I know in my gut he is just being polite, as usual. I can hear the girls laugh.

"I don't know why you two are laughing. You were both a disaster last night," Stefano says. "No more 'fun,' not for a long time! Thank God you're going back to school, Sophia!"

"Actually, we were thinking about going to look for family records at city hall and the church. I know everything is closed today, but we can go on Monday," Sophia answers.

"Sophia, you have to get back to Bologna tonight. Your classes start tomorrow," Stefano says to her in a parental tone.

"Well, I'm not going. I don't want to take that class anyway. I only registered for it because I couldn't get into the one I really want."

"Sophia, what has gotten into you? There's no way mom and dad are going to go for that. You've been so rebellious the last few days, this isn't like you."

"Maybe it is now! And maybe everyone should get used to it!" she replies to her brother.

"Have you spoken to our parents?" I ask Stefano to interrupt their argument.

"Yes, both last night and this morning."

"Is my mom angry?" I fear the answer.

"Yes, she was very upset. But both Luca and I spoke with her and she seems to be fine now. You should call her."

I get up to take the phone off the charger and Sophia and Stefano continue to argue. My distraction did no good. I turn on my phone and it starts to go crazy with social media alerts, text messages, emails, missed calls, and voicemails. Half of them are from my mother. I decide to call her before I look through them. I'm not in the mood to feel overwhelmed.

"I'm sure Luca won't mind if we stay another night! Right Luca?" Sophia shouts.

"I'm sure he does. He got a call this morning, his father is coming in tonight!" Stefano shouts back. I can feel the entire room get tense. Gian Carlo and Julia look at one another, then at Luca.

"Yes, it's true, my father is arriving for dinner tonight," Luca confirms, "but I know he would love to meet all of you."

"Didn't you say he hasn't been here in twenty-six years?" Alessia asks.

"Yes, but he is coming at my request to help me with some family matters."

"Well, I'm staying. It makes it all the sweeter to be able to meet the alluring Mr. Vinci." Sophia sits and crosses her arms.

"Yeah, I'm with her on this one." Alessia raises her eyebrows at Stefano.

"Eli, please tell me that you will be the voice of reason here," Stefano pleads with me. I am standing there with my phone in my hand unsure of what to do. I am shamelessly curious about Mr. Vinci, as I tried looking him up online yesterday. The only photo I was able to find is a grainy, black and white photo in a newspaper from the 1970s. But I also know that my mom will lose her mind if I stay another day.

"I need to call my mom. Give me a moment," I answer, and make my way to the small library—not to be confused with the formal library—to make my call. I dial the number and my mom picks up immediately.

"Eli, I've been so worried. Are you ok?" her voice is shaking.

"Yes mom, fine. We had a lot of fun yesterday. We drank too much and Luca was kind enough to host us."

"Why are you drinking? That's not like you."

"Mom, what's wrong? You're acting crazy, even for you."

"There are just a lot of things we need to discuss. In person. And your grandmother and I would like you to come home right away."

"Mom, you have been saying that since we landed. I know it's just a ploy to get me home."

"What do you mean? Are you planning on staying there?" I can hear my grandmother's voice and commotion in the background. "Your grandmother wants to speak with you," and I hear her hand Nonna the phone.

"Darling, hello," says Nonna Amelia, in that perfect tone that can fix any problem.

"Hello Nonna, I'm sorry if we had you worried yesterday."

"I'm an old woman, you mustn't do that. I heard you had an eventful day yesterday."

"Yes, we had a great time. You come from the most extraordinary place. I can't believe you've been hiding this all these years. I've never seen anything like it, it's like one of the great wonders of the world."

"In more ways than you know. I'm sorry I never told you about it, I promise to tell you everything when you get home."

"*Everything?*" I ask.

"Yes, no more secrets." I'm not sure what brought on this change, but I'm relieved. "Have a lovely time at dinner tonight, Eli, be sure you ask the right questions. Here's your mother." How did she know?

"Mom, I just want to let you know that I'm going to stay another night."

"Why? I don't want you there!"

"We were invited to have dinner with Mr. Vinci tonight. And well, I kind of want to meet him. He's so mysterious."

"Alessandro is coming to Pretare? Tonight?"

"Oh wow, I didn't know you were on a first name basis with *Alessandro*. Do you know him?"

"I met him when I was younger, we were even friends for a brief time. How does Luca know him?"

"It's his father. I heard that he hasn't been back in these parts for twenty-six years." There's a lingering pause. "Mom?"

"His son?"

"Mama, you didn't know?" I hear her question my grandmother and then cover the speaker—the rest is muffled. A few minutes later she returns to our call.

"I didn't realize who he was, the last time I saw Luca he was just a child. Eli, it's best you stay another night. I need to have a long talk with your grandmother and my brother." It's never a good sign when she doesn't address people by their first names. "Please be on your best behavior. We'll continue this conversation when you get home tomorrow."

"Ok mom, I love you."

"I love you too. Eli, you are the greatest love of my life. I thank God for you every day. I'm sorry if I can be overbearing at times. I know how much that kind of fuss upsets you."

"I know mama-stalker."

"Have a good time, my love."

As we get off the phone, I have a strange feeling in the pit of my stomach. She had an unsettling tone in her voice. I'm accustomed to her being assured and decisive. By the sound of things, it looks like I'm not the only one who's been having information withheld. It's a terrible feeling to be in the dark. Although I don't wish it on her, I am glad she's getting a sense of what it feels like.

I walk back to the kitchen and quietly reinsert myself into the group. It's nice to see that the bickering has ended. Everyone has moved onto what will be on tonight's menu.

"How did my aunt take the news?" Stefano asks.

"Better than expected. Apparently, my mother knows Mr. Vinci, or as she called him, *Alessandro*. Actually, all of our parents do, they used to be *friends*."

"What!" Alessia and Stefano say at the same time.

"This family is *so* drama," Sophia responds, as she rolls her eyes and takes a bite of her apple.

"I hope we are not somehow related, like most people in these towns. That would be weird," Alessia says with a vile look on her face.

"And gross," Sophia adds. Geez, this kid really has found her voice.

"Not to worry, there is no blood relations among your families. Julia and I have lived here all of our lives, if there was, we would know," Gian Carlo comforts us with his words. Alessia lets out a sigh of relief.

"I don't know about you all, but I think I still might have some vomit in my hair. I'd love a shower," Sophia reminds us of how bad we might actually smell.

"My sister sends clothes here that she doesn't wear. She thinks this place is her personal fashion storage. Let me show you where they are. Please feel free to take anything you like, she'll never know it's gone," Luca kindly offers. "Stefano, you and I are about the same size. What's mine is yours, feel free to wear anything you want."

"I purchased toiletries for everyone at the store today. You'll find them all in your bathrooms," Gian Carlo adds.

Luca walks us to the second floor. At the end of a long corridor to the right, are double doors. He opens them and the angels sing. We think we have died and gone to heaven. It is a room larger than the one I slept in last night, filled with racks and racks of clothing of all types. The walls have built-in shelves with ladders that store shoes from floor to ceiling. Did I mention they are on every wall? I cannot believe my eyes. I can feel my mouth salivating.

"This is insane, Luca!!! You guys, how crazy is this! It's like our very own department store!" Sophia shouts out with more joy than I've ever seen her express.

"In all fairness, it's both my sister's and mother's. But mostly my sister's."

"I don't think I'll ever leave this room. Why would I? Are you kidding? Most of these clothes still have the tags on them, they've never been worn!" Alessia says excitedly, as she begins to look through the garments. You can see that they are perfectly organized by color and style. And they're endless.

"This is better than Christmas!" Sophia exclaims, as she is trying on more shoes than she has feet for.

"You may have lost us forever," I say to him, as I pull my hair back in a ponytail.

"Is that your game face?"

"Oh, hell yeah," I reply, as I pull up the sleeves of my robe and get to looking. We spend an hour and a half in there before we notice that we've only browsed through a handful of racks and a few shoe shelves. Alessia is right, we could spend all day in here.

"Ladies, I really need a shower. I can't take the smell anymore," I say to them, as I hold a few items of clothing in one arm, and a pair of shoes in the other.

"What did you pick out, cousin?" Sophia asks, as she continues to put mounds of clothing together.

"Sophia, are you really taking ALL that?"

"What? It's not like anyone will notice." Looks like the girl has found her voice AND her balls.

"Well, show us!" Alessia says, as she sits on the sofa to the side of a rack. I pull out a pair of jeans and simple top to change into after my shower. And a vintage dress I found in the very back of the room for dinner tonight. They both gasp as I show them the dress.

"Where did you find that, Eli? It's spectacular!" Alessia says, applauding.

"It is, isn't it . . . I hope it fits, it looks so tiny."

"Of course it will fit!" she reassures me, "What about those shoes?"

"I found them in the same garment bag as the dress. I figured they're a set and they are my size, so why not!"

"I thought for sure you'd pick out one of these custom shoes, considering your fetish," Alessia says.

"How do you know they're custom?"

"Because half the shoes in here are from couture designer houses, but I've never seen them on any runway or in any store."

"I confess, if I had this kind of money, I might splurge a little on custom shoes too," I say.

"What do you say we take a walk around the grounds before dinner?" Alessia suggests.

"Please do, so I can get a nap in before we have to get ready for dinner," Sophia gripes.

Alessia and I agree to meet in the sitting room at three o'clock. I take the stairs to the third floor and look around for the room I came out of this morning. I must have been in a haze, because I don't realize that there are only two rooms on the third floor. One to the left, and one to the right. I take a 50-50 chance and enter the double doors to the left. I peek in, I see my pants hanging over a chair and my shoes on the floor, and I know I'm in the right room. I walk in and put the garments down on the lounge chair I found my robe on this morning. I find my bed made and fresh towels with the toiletries Gian Carlo promised. I hear shuffling coming from what sounds like a nearby room. But there are no adjacent rooms.

"Hello?" I yell out.

"Hi!" Luca jumps out from behind of what looks like a wall and scares me half to death.

"What are you doing in here? You scared me!" I reply, clenching onto the collar of my plush robe.

"Sorry, I was just in my closet getting a few things. I thought you were still downstairs looking at clothes."

"Is this your bedroom?"

"It is. I thought you'd be most comfortable here. The temperature is always perfect, not too hot or too cold."

"That's very thoughtful."

"Is that a compliment, Miss Tesani?" he says, walking towards me. "That would be new for our friendship. I'll be sure not to get used to it." I notice his shirt is completely unbuttoned. I must have walked in as he was dressing.

I can't look away; I find myself staring at his body. I can see his chest peeking through his unbuttoned shirt. Michelangelo himself could not have sculpted a more perfect man. The way he was standing in the light, shows me what I'm most afraid of—he has no imperfections. Not one scar, pimple, mark, or discoloration. His eyes are more blue than the morning sky. His hair is a light brown color, nearly blonde. Lips that are strong and masculine. And a jawline that looks like it could be made from the same fifty-million-year-old limestone in the Sibillini mountains. I didn't notice any of these things about him yesterday or the day before. What's changed? How am I able to see him this way now?

"Is that all you picked out?" Luca asks, as he notices the clothes I've brought in. "I thought for sure you would have chosen a dozen pairs of shoes."

"I didn't want to be rude or acquisitive. But I can't say the same for my cousins. We may need a truck to bring back the things they've picked out."

"I'm happy they did, seems like such a waste to have so much here with no one to enjoy it."

"I'm very grateful for the clothes, thank you."

He looks at me with a bit of confusion, "Eli, if you keep being this nice, I might get used to it."

He's right, why am I being so nice? "I need to meet Alessia downstairs shortly. Can you leave so I can shower?" I say, with one eyebrow up.

Luca looks down, smiles and says, "Yes, of course." He looks back at me for one second, turns, and walks out. This time it did not feel right.

*　　*　　*

I pour myself a glass of water as I'm waiting for Alessia in the sitting room, and Stefano walks in. I notice that he has also changed and is looking very smart.

"Have you seen Luca? I'm supposed to meet him in the sitting room to review some contracts. I figured we should get some business done while we're here and review it with his father tonight."

"I'm excited to finally see my amazing cousin in action. I hear you're a monster."

"I wouldn't go that far."

"I think he probably meant the formal sitting room," I clarify for him, "that one is in the west wing." He looks confused so I continue, "The one with all the paintings. The huge tree painting?" Meanwhile Alessia walks in.

"Oh yes!" he says, tapping his leather binder on his head, "I can't keep up with all the names of each room. What are you ladies up to?"

"We are going to take a lovely stroll on the grounds. Why don't you join us?" Alessia offers.

"That sounds nice. Once we've finished our meeting, and if it's not too late, we'll try to catch up with you."

Alessia and I head out arm-in-arm. Once we are far from the villa, I confide in her about my awkward encounter in the bedroom with Luca. And as of today, how bad I feel any time I'm being even slightly rude to him.

"Maybe we shouldn't have stayed, Àle. I just don't feel like myself, I don't know what's going on with me."

"You can't be serious? You really don't know?" she says to me, with pity all over her face.

"No, what are you talking about?"

"Well if you don't know, then I won't say. You'll figure it out, doll. In the meantime, try to be polite. You really are hard on the guy. It's not his fault that he's tall, rich, gorgeous, well-mannered, impeccably dressed, smart, and has an amazing taste in cars, art, and women." We both have a much-needed laugh.

"I think that's the problem, he's too perfect. I can't find a flaw and that unnerves me. It means that whatever the flaw really is, it's worse than anything we can imagine."

"That's what I love about you Eli, you always have such a unique perspective. You are able to see things that no one else can see. You think of options and possibilities that most of us just do not have the ability to," she says as she caresses my hair. "Well, if he's got one, I'm sure you'll find it!"

We reach the top of the hill. From here you can see the entire Vinci Villa and its land, which seems never-ending. As well as the beautiful town where people continue to celebrate and enjoy the festival. Today, it looks like there is double the amount of people that were there yesterday. Luca mentioned that it isn't just the locals; people come from all over to experience the festival.

We find a very large tree with lots of shade to sit under. There is a cluster of crows loudly singing their mixture of caws, clicks, and rattle sounds in the nearby trees. Crows scare me. Between Edgar Allen Poe and the image of Tippi Hedren being attacked by these birds, they never had a chance at symbolizing a good omen.

"Ále, is this an elm tree?"

"It is, I think."

"I didn't know that they grew here. I found two beautiful ones when I was hiking the other day."

"Yes, let's talk about the other day, Eli. Is there anything else you may have left out? Maybe because you didn't want to worry Nonna or your mom."

"No, I told you everything."

"Everything except where you were for twelve hours. You barely sleep six hours a night, and now you just want me to believe that you happened to fall asleep in a forest all day?"

"Yes, I-I swear. I don't remember anything else." It just sinks in now that I have had two blackouts in one week. One I blamed on sleep, the other on drinking. This is not a detail I wish to share with her or anyone else at the moment.

"I don't think you're lying. I'm just worried about you. There's so much going on, and any time things get complicated, you have a tendency to become introverted."

"I'm sorry, I don't mean to do that. I'm not trying to shut you out. It's just hard when there are so many people in our family that are so opinionated and so loud. Sometimes it's just easier to not fight. It's not like my thoughts will make an impact, everyone is too set in their ways."

"But that's the thing Eli, they do. You have such a unique way of translating other people's intentions, and giving insight in a way that solves problems as opposed to fueling them," she grabs my hand. "I think our family could use more of that. It's also time we both take a little more control. Nonna Amelia's heart can give in any day now. I think we need to become more aggressive with our agenda."

I know she's right, but how do I tell her that I don't know if I really want to know. All of this feels so dark and convoluted. Maybe some things are just meant to remain unknown. I've never seen a secret buried this long have a positive after-effect. I thought I came here to say goodbye to my last grandparent. Instead, we seem to be playing an investigator's role in a Hitchcock film. I mean that literally, with the sound of the crows around us.

"Ále, why does it feel like every conversation is a labyrinth of words on a downward spiral?"

"See, that's exactly the type of perspective I'm talking about! Even though I don't know how, what you just said helps."

"It doesn't, it's just the truth. Are we sure we want to do this? We need to consider the consequences."

"I'm not sure we have a choice. Eli, have you looked at yourself lately? Your face is changing! Like, A LOT. And I don't know if it's even possible, but overnight your features have shifted even more. You look more like young Amelia than she does. That's some weird shit!"

This explains why everyone was staring this morning. I thought it was because I had last night's mascara all over my face from crying.

"I want to desperately ignore what you're saying," I say insecurely, and touch my face.

"Well you can't, even if you try."

"Maybe this is what happens right before you turn twenty-five?"

"I've been twenty-five, that's NOT what happens. It's your

face for goodness sake!" she replies, thoroughly annoyed with me. "Even though I think she's completely batty, Silva tells us that my mom, and *both* of your grandmothers are magical beings. We get here and everyone is worshiping some Queen Faerie, virgin Oracle. That has to be more than a coincidence!"

"Again, are you really suggesting that we are part magical? You were just saying how it's BS!"

"No, of course not! But I am suggesting that maybe our ancestors are! Maybe they don't exist now, but who says they never existed. And before you say it—yes, I think all magical creatures once existed," Alessia responds.

I can't help but reflect on my own similar thoughts as I lie on my back to get her out of my sight. I don't want to talk about this yet, especially with Ále who can read me so well.

"I have no doubt we are facing a ripple effect by instigating this. But has it occurred to you that the ramifications of not knowing could be worse? The foundation of our lives could rest on this. And if the implication of knowing the truth means that we have to be someone other than who we are comfortable with, then so be it," Alessia continues.

"I'm slightly impressed with your argument. I mean, it is a bit state of the union-ish . . . " I say laughing. "Aunt Ersella is right, you should have become a lawyer."

"Maybe in my next life. This one is too enigmatic; we have a lot to unravel."

"You might have a good point. Fate has brought us this far." I sigh, as I know I am almost defeated by her logic. As usual, she's using her "voodoo" to influence me. That's what we nicknamed her manipulation skills as children.

"Are you *in*?" she asks me and puts out her hand for me to shake.

I sigh and sit up, "I hope I'm not making a deal with the devil," and we shake on it.

"YES!" she shouts, "Now, no more being a wallflower!"

"One thing at a time, Ále. Let's get through dinner tonight. What do you think Luca's father is really like? And why do you think he disappeared from the public eye all those years ago?"

"Well, if anyone can figure it out, it will be you tonight, Eli," she stops and is distracted by something she sees. "Are you serious?" she smiles and gestures for me to look. "Looks like your knight in shining armor has arrived."

There he is at the bottom of the hill, standing between two horses: one black, one brown. I cannot decide which of the three is the most beautiful.

"Now that's what I call a stallion," Alessia says, as she taps my arm to get up.

I see Stefano is waiting with two horses as well—this gives me instant relief. The last thing I want to do is be alone with Luca today. I can't quite sort out my thoughts of him. It feels like he's hiding something and that he knows more than he's showing. Something inside tells me to keep my distance until I can figure out what that is.

Alessia and I walk towards the bottom of the hill. I get more and more nervous the closer we get.

"Ále, I'm terrified of horses," I confess.

"Oh, I forgot!"

"What do I do?"

"Eli, suck it up. You need to get over that, it was years ago. The horse was just playing, it didn't mean to almost roll over on you," she says, partly trying to encourage me, and partly laughing as she recalls the memory. "You need to face your fears my darling, and today is that day!"

"Hi," Luca says, "did you enjoy your walk?"

"We only managed to get to the top of the hill. It is very peaceful here; you are so fortunate to have such an exquisite place to come to."

"Now you do too. You are always welcome here whether I am here or not. Gian Carlo and Julia have taken quite a liking to you. They may enjoy your company more than they do mine," Luca replies.

"I'm sure that is far from the truth."

"Stop procrastinating Eli and get on that horse!" Stefano says impatiently. He and Alessia have already straddled their horses and are latching their helmets.

"She's afraid of horses," Alessia says. I wish I had a riding crop to smack her with.

"Would you like to ride on the back of mine?" Luca offers.

"NO. No," I clear my throat and politely decline, "I'm fine."

"He gave you the best horse to ride, Eli; he's the Ferrari of horses. You're in good hands," Stefano tries to reassure me. But he doesn't, because Ferraris are fast.

"They are all Arabian horses, that means they are all Ferraris. And they are each special in their own way. You should know better than to say that in front of the other horses, Stefano. You're just looking to get thrown off! They are smarter than you think," Luca states, as everyone but Stefano laughs. "This is Wasi, it means 'Guardian' in Arabic. He can sense that you're afraid, so it's best to get comfortable with him before we ride."

"Do you have any Valium?" I ask.

"I don't," he laughs. "Calmly and slowly get close to him, let him get a sense of you. I will stand next to you if it helps."

"Yes please." He hands Stefano the reins of his horse and proceeds to gently guide me through the process.

Wasi is divine. The color of his entire coat is a jet black. He is radiant and soft. I gently touch his body with the tips of my fingers. He is a big horse in stature and his muscles are tight and strong; actually, the strongest I've ever felt. His mane is long and luxurious. And his eyes are black as night—at first, they intimidate me. But as I look closer, I can see that he is tender and just as afraid as I am. I can feel my anxiety calm as we are eye to eye. I step closer to him and place one hand to caress his face and the other close to his mouth. I feel spellbound by him.

"Must you be *everyone's* favorite?" Luca says in a whisper, as he stands behind me. The bond between Wasi and I feels safe, and I am ready to ride. Luca assists me with getting on the horse. I notice he is very careful not to touch any part of my body where my skin is exposed. Maybe it wasn't just me that felt that sensation at the festival. No time to examine that now; we only have a few hours before we will need to get ready for dinner. And I'm going to take advantage of every second, because this is the first time in my life, I feel excited to ride a horse.

We start slowly. Luca is watching me carefully to see my reaction. I smile at him to let him know I am okay, and he seems to relax. He and Stefano talk about the land, some details of its known history, and the weather. After almost an hour of this, Alessia and I become a bit bored with the conversation. I can tell Wasi is too; I get a sense he wants to stretch his legs. I hint at her to do something.

"Ok boys, so this conversation is very stimulating. But I think it's time we take it up a level." If I didn't know any better, it looks like Wasi and Alessia's horse, Hamia, just nodded yes dramatically at each other. "How about we do some real riding in this beautiful place?" she says, with a very tempting tone.

"I'm always up for a little competition," Stefano says taking the bait, "what do you have in mind?"

"I say we ride to the top of that hill and back," she says, as she points at a nearby area under Monte Vettore.

"You're on!" Stefano takes off giving himself the lead. We all charge behind him. We ride and ride hard, and before I know it, I have passed them all up.

Wasi does not disappoint. He is as fast as he is strong, and definitively the Alpha. The rumble of his legs with every stomp of his hooves makes the earth shake under me. The faster we go, the deeper I feel connected to his power. And as that power grows, I begin to feel the *rise* of the Alpha in *me*.

I close my eyes and lean down to the center of Wasi's neck, and I place my hands on each side. I listen closely for his heartbeat and in turn he allows my eyesight to penetrate through his own eyes. I don't know how this is scientifically possible, and I'm shocked at how calm I am. It's like a burst of freedom, it is the most alive I have ever felt. My visibility is larger and better. Everything is an enhanced clarity; I can see every detail. The depth of my perception is far and wide. I can detect the slightest motion from an extensive and wide angle. This extends further than I have ever been able to see, and it is exhilarating. I see us passing through the trees onto the grassy knoll and gazing through the beautiful flowers that I was only able to see at a distance yesterday. They are brighter and more beautiful than I had the imagination to visualize, all of the various shades of colors and different species side-by-side, growing together to create utter harmony. I can feel the tears coming down my face.

"It's okay, they're tears of joy," I whisper to Wasi. He picks up the pace as we finish crossing the field. We cross a crystal blue stream with one leap, and as we do, he looks down for me so I can see all the fish swimming upstream. "You're brilliant," I say aloud to him as I kiss his neck. We continue on until we reach the bottom of Monte Vettore. We have far surpassed the hill we were meant to stop at. I see an area surrounded by trees, bushes, and flowers. In the middle of nowhere, there are small, stand-alone square structures made of brick, scattered throughout. They look almost like giant fireplaces. They are approximately six feet high and five feet wide. I can't make out what they are, they're very peculiar. It looks like there's layered stone in between the brick but I can't be sure. Wasi begins to slow down; he shows me a small stream of water that is coming down from the top of the mountain.

"Ah, you're thirsty. You deserve it, my friend. Thank you for giving me the greatest gift of my life," I say to him. I sit up and open my eyes. The scenery is breathtaking, even through my human eyes. I climb down from him and he walks over to the stream. I hadn't realized how far we rode until I look for the Vinci Villa in the horizon. It looks very small from here.

"It must be amazing water to ride all this way for." I kneel down and cup both of my hands into the stream—it is ice cold. I drink and drink it. It is the purest and most amazing water I've ever had. "I can see what all the fuss is about, Wasi," I say.

"There's nothing as thirst quenching as fresh spring water," I hear a familiar voice say. It's *her*. Wasi nudges me with his face to get up, and places himself adjacent to me. I put my arm under his face and touch his mane softly to comfort him—he seems agitated. She is sitting high on a spectacular white horse. Very similar to Wasi's shape and size, but just a bit smaller. She is wearing a full equestrian outfit head to toe, complete with a riding top hat and red lips. The fit is impeccable. She looks like she just stepped out of Vogue magazine. Once again, I'm in awe.

"Hello, it's nice to see you again," I say nervously.

"Did you enjoy yourself yesterday?"

"I did, thank you. Your horse is beautiful. I've never seen such an illuminating color; the coat looks almost iridescent."

"This is Malak, she is very special," she lovingly caresses her, "and Wasi is quite the stallion."

Wasi starts to pick up and kick with his hind leg. He seems agitated by her presence.

"They are both masterpieces, don't you think?" she asks. I agree.

"Malak and Wasi are from the same . . . breeder. Her name means 'Angel' in Arabic. Since you're riding Wasi, I assume you're staying with the Vincis."

I can't help but think these Arabic names have some kind of special significance.

"I am. Do you know them?" I ask inquisitively.

"Yes, we're old friends," she says, as she looks out to the villa. "Nearly neighbors, I live just over the hill."

"Pretare is such a heavenly place, I can see why you choose to live here."

"Heavenly . . . " she ponders, "I once thought this was hell. And I wouldn't say I chose to live here. But it has grown on me. And it's certainly become more beautiful over the years. What I enjoy most about it is all of its . . . convoluted history."

"Would you happen to know what these peculiar scattered walls are?" I ask.

"They are barricades built for the soldiers during the medieval years. The soldiers would use them to block the winds during the hard seasons. They would build a bonfire in the center to keep themselves warm. This area, in particular, was a favorite because it was a perfect place to rest and hydrate their horses. As you can see, it's quite revitalizing for them," she says, as she looks down at Wasi. It makes me feel protective and wonder why she felt the need to do that. Maybe she's bitter she didn't get him too.

"It's amazing that anything can survive that long. A brick and stone barricade fireplace, how smart and resourceful," I say.

"Resourceful yes, but smart is not a word I would use to describe medieval soldiers. You would be surprised by how many things can last forever."

I'm not sure I like her tone.

"It was nice to see you again, but I need to get back. I lost track of my friends en route, and should probably find them."

"I don't think that should take long," she says, as she stares intensely behind me. There they are, horses in full stride riding to reach me.

"Enjoy your evening, Miss Eli," she says with a glance, then looks back intently at Luca. There is something about that look that gives me the chills. She smiles at him, tilts her hat forward, and pulls on her reins and rides away in the most elegant manner, just moments before he arrives.

"I wish I was half of that, Wasi," I say out loud. He shakes his head and flares his nostrils forcefully. The group reaches us and Luca nearly flies off his horse.

"HAVE YOU LOST YOUR MIND TO RIDE OFF THAT WAY?" Luca shouts at me.

"Excuse me?" I reply, caught off guard by his tone.

"Seriously Eli, you scared the living daylights out of us. Why did you take off like that?" Alessia asks, getting off her horse, "We were worried that something happened."

"You're lucky that Luca is a good tracker and we were able to locate you. This mountain range is endless." Stefano seems just as irritated as the others.

"I'm sorry, I thought you were behind me the entire time," I reply. I know I'm lying, but how can I ever explain that I completely forgot about them.

"DID YOU EVEN BOTHER TO LOOK? YOU WOULD HAVE NOTICED WE WEREN'T THERE!" Luca is still shouting, "AND YOU, WASI, ARE IN BIG TROUBLE. YOU KNOW BETTER THAN TO DO THAT. I'LL DEAL WITH YOU LATER."

As Luca is yelling at me, I notice his horse seems to be shaking her head at Wasi. "Luca, is your horse shaking her head at my horse?" I ask, ignoring whatever else he might be saying.

"What? No, that's . . . so now he's *your* horse?" He's still spouting.

"Who was that woman you were speaking with? She's sensational!" Stefano interrupts.

"She's the lady I spoke to at the festival yesterday. The one with the lovely perfume. I can't believe I keep forgetting to ask her name. She said she lives around here."

"Who's her fashion stylist? Did you get the name of that red lipstick?" Alessia asks.

"I should have, it was the perfect shade," I reply.

"If she looks that good, I can't wait to see what she smells like," Stefano adds.

"It's pretty amazing," I answer.

"You're all joking, right? We just spent over an hour worried sick and looking for YOU. And you guys are talking about lipstick and perfume as if nothing happened?" Luca says, with a very stern tone.

"That's how we are, Luca," Alessia says, "no matter how mad we get, once we see each other, it's like it never happened."

"Well, it *did* happen. And this could have ended very badly," he's lashing out again.

"She said she knows you and is an old friend of your family, Luca," I mention, to change the conversation and keep him from getting worked up again. "Who is she?"

"I'd rather not speak of it. And I would appreciate it if you, actually any of you, wouldn't speak to her again in my presence."

Whatever it is between them, it must be very bad. It does not seem like him to show so much disdain for any person. I notice that, for the first time, Luca will not make eye contact with me. He's hiding something.

Chapter 7

L UCA DOES NOT SPEAK or look at me the entire ride back. As we arrive at the stables, Stefano takes Wasi's reins from me as I kiss and thank Wasi for the most amazing day. I promise to say goodbye to him before I leave tomorrow.

"Don't worry about Luca, he didn't mean it. He's just nervous about his father's arrival," Alessia whispers to me.

"I don't know if I should feel sorry for him or slap him," I reply.

"I suppose when we meet Mr. Vinci, you'll have your answer," she says.

Alessia and I walk into the villa through the kitchen's entrance, as it feels less formal and more at our own comfort level. I notice the staff has multiplied, and they are running around swiftly. There are nearly a dozen faces I didn't see before. There are maids, cooks, a butler, and a few others I can't make out. In addition, there are security guards in every corner that I can see. Standing between the kitchen and the hall is a tall woman, taking notes on a leather-bound notepad with two greyhounds at her feet.

I walk into the kitchen and pull Julia by the arm, "Who is arriving, the king of Italy?" She smiles back at me.

"I thought I would never see this house come alive again. Isn't this wonderful! I suspect we owe it to you, Signorina," Julia replies.

"Me? Why?"

"You don't worry about all of that now. You should be off getting ready for dinner."

"Has Mr. Vinci arrived?"

"No, he should be arriving a little after eight o'clock."

"Who's the femmebot dictator?" Alessia asks, pointing to the tall woman in the very tight knee-length dress, stilettos, and glasses.

"That is Donatella. She is Mr. Vinci's right hand and personal assistant. She and the staff have come early to prep the house and ensure everything is to his liking," she says with excitement. "I hope he is pleased. If he is, he may even stay a little longer, and that would be very good for his relationship with Luca."

"How long is he scheduled to stay?" I ask.

"Until tomorrow afternoon."

"*All this* for less than twenty–four hours!" I say in shock.

"Now hush! You hurry along. I'm sure Donatella will expect you to be on time."

Alessia and I walk past Donatella as she inspects us carefully. Her demeanor is strong and unfriendly. There's a good chance a riding crop is tucked into her garter belt. And I have no doubt she will use it if we get out of line tonight.

"I think fashion week lost one of their models," Alessia says under her breath, as we get into the elevator.

"Did you expect anything less from the Vinci men?" I say with a sigh as I push the elevator buttons. "I'm more uneasy with all of the security. Why is it necessary? It's insane Ále."

"Whatever it is, I'm so glad we stayed today. I have a feeling things are about to get *very* interesting," Alessia says rubbing her hands together. "I've never been around anything like this. You know Elizabetta and Ersella are going to want every detail!"

"Yes, by all means, let's take notes," I say beyond annoyed, as she walks out of the elevator onto the second floor. I continue on to the third floor. When the doors open, I notice that there is activity happening in the bedroom across from mine. I peek in and see several maids changing sheets, dusting and scrubbing frantically.

"Will someone be sleeping in this room tonight?" I ask. One of the maids walks up to me, smiles and slams the door in my face. I am as horrified as I am embarrassed. I put my head down, turn around and charge back towards my room. I just want a hot shower. As I reach the door, I see Luca's shoes. I look up.

"Do you want me to fire her?" he asks kindly. "That was completely unprofessional."

"It's okay. She did it because she can see I don't belong here. She probably thinks I'm another one of your . . . lady friends . . . looking for a climb up."

"It doesn't matter who you are. You are a guest in this house, and I will not tolerate that."

"I'm sure she has a family and really needs this job. I am not that important—please don't say anything."

"May I come into your room?"

"It's your room Luca, of course. Do you need to get clothes for tonight?" I ask, as I open the door. He follows me in and we both have a seat on the antique sofa that is worth more than anything I own. He's got an intense look in his eyes again.

"It takes everything inside of me to stay calm when you say things like that. You are the most important person any one of us will ever have the honor of knowing."

"I appreciate the flattery, but—"

"Please let me finish," he says, as he interrupts me. I stay quiet.

"I know there are a lot of things that remain unexplained. And I know you came here to find answers. I can feel that you are angry with me because you can sense that I am withholding information. You are right. I suggested to bring you here because I thought we would just be able to have a day of fun. You'd hear a few silly folktales and it would be over. I thought if I was here, I'd be able to keep things in control while appeasing some curiosity," he pauses as he leans into his hands.

I can't help but to jump in at the pause, "You treat me as if I'm a child. It's like a deceptive tactic parents use with their children, when they give them a lollipop to distract them from the cake!"

"I know, I'm sorry. I'm just trying to protect you until your family—" he stops himself. "It is unequivocally not my place to tell you your grandmother's story. But I will give you mine. I beg of you, please let's get through tonight. It will be very difficult to have my father here. And I need to be able to deal with him with a clear mind. I know you're upset with me, it's all over your face. I'm *so* sorry," there was a desperation in his voice, "this is the best I can do tonight. There are boundaries and agreements that cannot be broken. Not even for you, Eli. Please try to understand that."

My head is spinning, and I don't know what to make of his words.

"I know I was hard on you today—" he continues to say, but it's my turn to cut him off.

"'Hard on me? That's not the right description, Luca; you are controlling and slightly paranoid! For the love of God, why is everyone in my life so controlling?"

"There's a reason for that too," he replies.

"Let me guess, you know what *that* is too . . . "

"This is not a game, Eli," he says with that stern voice I hate.

"Really? Because it feels like a really *wicked* one to me. You have twenty-four hours, Luca." There is an anger inside me, brewing.

Knock. Knock. The door opens.

"Excuse me Lu—, Mr. Vinci. I didn't realize you had company," says the femmebot.

"Hello Donatella. I am actually Miss Tesani's guest. She is occupying this room for her stay."

"Please pardon me Miss Tesani, I work for Mr. Vinci Senior. How do you do?" she says, as she shakes my hand with her long, boney, yet extremely soft hands. "We ask that everyone be in the foyer this evening at 8:05pm. Mr. Vinci will be arriving at 8:10 pm, he expects to be greeted by his guests. I have informed the others."

"Thank you Donatella, we will all be there," Luca replies. She politely smiles, adjusts her glasses, and walks out with—what seems like—a runway strut.

"Why all the formalities?" I ask.

"My father prefers that some traditions don't change."

"I'm not comfortable with this Luca, it's *too* much. *You're* too much. The traditions. This house. Your father. The secrets. The lies. Your lovers—you don't think I can see the way that woman looks at you? This life is not normal," I say, as I frantically get up and start to grab my things, "I think it's time for me to go home. I shouldn't have stayed. Why don't I listen to my mother when I should . . . I will call someone to pick me up."

Luca steps in front of me and holds me so tightly in his grasp I can't move. In that second there is an instantaneous flash in my mind of Luca and me. We are in an elevator. I am straddled on him and he is holding me with the same force. I don't know what this is. It can't be a memory. Possibly a dream?

He lets go.

"I won't stay here without you, Eli. If you go, I go." I can see I've made him feel out of sorts. "There is a driver downstairs that can take you anywhere you want to go, day or night. Just know that I will be in the car behind you."

I can see that he is serious. I don't really know how to respond, other than my nerves have settled with his words.

"You can come down anytime. And you can meet him in any room. Forget what Donatella said, do as you please. Please just stay."

"O . . . Okay," I hesitantly agree to his terms.

He leaves the room and I feel very grateful to have some time to myself. I take off my clothes and get into a shower in a bathroom that is bigger than my entire apartment. I let the water pour over me, and once again I feel so lost. How does this place make me feel both like the strongest and the weakest person in the world? The only people I can really trust know less than I do. What could Luca's story possibly be? I thought he was just my cousin's best friend. Does Stefano know? Would he keep it from us? So many questions, thoughts, and scenarios run through my mind. Each one is worse than the last. Whatever the truth is, it already seems inconceivable.

*   *   *

As I finish blow drying my hair, I receive a text from Sophia. She is coming up to see me. I realize just then that I've forgotten to respond to any of the text messages from my friends in LA. I miss them so much; it feels like they are a world away. This last week might as well have been a year, I've completely lost track of time. Sometimes I don't even know if I'm in the same dimension.

"What an awesome room, cousin!" I hear Sophia say as she

closes the door behind her. "I think this place is closer to a palace than it is a villa."

I turn around to see that my little Sophia is no longer so little. She is wearing a fully fitted white lace gown. It has a high neck and long sleeves. It seems demure, until I realize that it is totally see-through. The lace is sitting just right on her nipple to keep it from showing, and there is heavier detail covering her below the waist. She is wearing no underwear or bra. It's something that only someone with her body shape can pull off. She has grown up so much the last few years, I almost can't believe it. She is now a sensational, strong young woman with her own mind and a beautiful spirit.

"Ohhhh Sophia, you are breathtaking!" I exclaim and hug her tightly.

"Thank you! Not bad, right?" she says as she does a spin.

"Not at all!" I feel a little emotional inside. It must be all the crying I'm doing lately. I must have opened some emotional dam. "When did you grow up?" I ask.

"I don't know! But I love this place, I feel so free! I wish we never had to leave."

"I can't *wait* to leave," I reply.

"Why, Eli? Did something happen on the ride today?" she asks protectively, as she sits next to me.

"No, not at all, on the contrary," I lay my head on her shoulder, "this has all just been a bit much. I'm feeling overwhelmed."

"Sometimes I forget how much you feel, Eli. It's your greatest strength and your greatest curse." She couldn't be more right.

"I'm sorry, I don't want to ruin the mood for you. I know you want to have F-U-N tonight!" And we both start laughing.

"Let me do your makeup! I know how much you hate doing it, and it will relax you," Sophia offers. We are lucky Alessia never parts with her makeup bag, and she lets us borrow it tonight.

"Yes, I would love that." I am so grateful for her in this moment. Sophia tells me funny stories about the Vinci staff arriving today. She knows how to help me clear my mind and take all this pomp and circumstance less seriously. By the time she finishes my makeup, I forget what I'm even getting ready for.

"Lipstick is done!" she says with excitement. "Okay, my enchanting Eli, I don't want you to see the makeup just yet. If you do, you're going to think it's too much, but it's not! You just need to see it all together. The waves in your hair are perfect for this look. Come on, get dressed!" I can't believe doing makeup on me can make this girl so happy.

"Ok, sounds fair," I reply. She helps me step into my dress. It's a vintage gown with no tag; but whoever designed this dress must have had my measurements, because it fits me like a glove. It is black with light sequins throughout. Low in the black, and in the front, and cut deeply into the sides. It has an ethereal cape attached to the sleeveless shoulders. The cape is the same fabric as the dress, just without the lining. It is transparent with a beautiful design throughout the bottom. It almost looks like moons, but I can't quite make it out. The shoes are stilettos; black silk with a crescent moon shape that sits near the ankle.

"Eli. You. Are. Captivating . . . " she says, holding her chest. I walk to the mirror and I have no idea who's staring back at me. I don't recognize that girl in the mirror. I can really see it more than ever now—I look like them. Both of them. I look like my grandmothers. I touch my face in dismay.

"Sophia, how is this possible?"

"Eli, don't be mad, but Alessia told us about your . . . transformation, when you first arrived. Stefano and I have been talking about it for days trying to figure it out. We've been doing extensive research online, trying to get our hands on rare books, and talking to genetic specialists. Stefano has even used his connections to reach out to spiritual tribes in different places around the world, trying to get answers. But we haven't been successful," she says. "I know your hair and eyes have always changed in the sun. We thought this might have been connected somehow, but there seems to be no correlation."

"Thank you for your efforts," I reply, with a deep sigh. Once again, I'm disappointed and a little frustrated they've been talking behind my back. It's been one dead end after another.

There's another knock at the door. It's Alessia. She walks in and gasps. She doesn't know which one of us to look at first.

"We clean up nice, ladies!" she says, running in with her arms up. Her dress is a mermaid style pink strapless gown. It is extremely tight at the knees and she can barely walk. Sophia and I can't stop laughing. We fuss over one another with joy, before Stefano walks in to escort us downstairs. He nearly faints when he sees us standing together. He looks so handsome in his navy suit.

"I could not be prouder; you all look stunning. You are clearly related to me!" he says jokingly, and Sophia smacks him on the head.

"It's time to head downstairs before Donatella comes in here with her riding crop!" Alessia says.

"Eli, I know Luca said you can come down at any time, but it would give me immense joy to walk together. You have nothing to be afraid of, we will not leave your side," Stefano says to me as we are all holding hands. I believe him, and I know it is the right thing to do. It is Mr. Vinci's home after all.

We hurry down the stairs. I don't know if we are late or he is early, but as we arrive almost to the bottom of the stairs, we see the butler and Donatella, who is dressed in a very sexy, gray, off-the-shoulder dress. To the right are four maids, and Gian Carlo and Julia are to the left. In between them is Luca greeting and shaking his father's hand. Mr. Vinci hands the butler his coat and hat as he steps further into the house. He stops midway and looks directly at me; he looks as if he's seen a ghost.

I look away and see a woman standing at the door, draped in a silk red, deep cut gown, with a slit that starts nearly at her hip, where her bone protrudes. Her breasts sit perfectly on her chest, her collar bone curves exactly to her wide shoulders. The dress hugs her body perfectly. The fabric is so thin, it's like a second layer of skin. She has platinum hair down to the curve of her back. It's wavy, in the way it looks when you unbraid your hair. She still has one braid laying softly across the front of her head, and it looks like a crown. Her eyes are sharp and dark brown. The shape is both round and almond-like, and her black eyelashes that surround her eyes, look like feathers. Her skin is pale with dainty freckles scattered under her eyes. She has high cheek bones, but delicate and soft features; she is regal and resembles a goddess. My eyes are drawn to her long neck by a beautiful gold necklace. At least I think it's gold; I've never seen a similar metal. It seems as if glitter is mixed in with the gold—it illuminates across the room. The necklace is U-shaped, in the design of a twig or a small branch. It sits gently at the base of her neck with the opening gap in the front. She glides as she walks from the doorway into the room. She kisses Luca hello and continues to walk past his father. I find her standing directly before me as I try to hide my awe.

"You must be Eli. I'm Micella, Luca's sister." Still in shock, and trying to maintain my composure, I politely greet her. A lingering moment of silence follows. She doesn't let it phase her.

"Well, to be fair, we have different mothers. He always was the better looking one," she turns to wink at him. Her voice is soft and very soothing.

Luca steps forward to introduce her to the others. He seems

genuinely surprised by her visit, leading me to believe she wasn't expected. As I glance at Stefano, I see his mouth slightly ajar. He is smitten. By the look in his eyes, you'd think he's going to ask her to marry him on the spot. I've never seen him so enamored. The world's most distinguished bachelor is turning into melting wax before my eyes. I must admit, it gives me pleasure to see him this way. It shows that there is no exception; *everyone* has someone they'd break all the rules for.

I notice Mr. Vinci has not moved from the place he has been standing since he first entered. Donatella is trying to say something to him, but he immediately dismisses her. I decide to greet him; his staring is starting to become awkward. I can't believe that this is the man I was terrified to meet. The same one everyone is walking on eggshells for. He seems lovely and unassuming. Like Luca, he is about 6' 5", if not taller, with a slender build. His head is covered in thick salt and pepper hair. He has big, deep brown eyes like Micella. He is an older looking man, even older than my father. There is a heaviness in the lines of his face, suggesting he has lived a difficult life. He is wearing a charcoal grey suit, with a darling black silk tie that has tiny stars all over it. His handkerchief is made of the same fabric. It has an image of an ouroboros with seven stars in the center.

"Good evening Mr. Vinci, it is such an honor to meet you," I say, as I extend my hand.

"The honor is all mine," he accepts my hand, but instead of shaking it, he kisses the back of it gently. It's the first time anyone has ever done that to me. It's no wonder women love chivalry. I feel myself blush a little.

"Thank you for hosting us in such a magnificent place."

"I hope my son and staff have treated you well, and that you've been able to enjoy yourself. You know, I haven't been here in many years; this town is much smaller than I remembered," he says gracefully. The tone of his voice is deep and kind.

"Yes, Luca mentioned it," I pause, as he takes a moment to reflect on what I've said, "I apologize for not arriving on time to greet you at the door."

"Your timing is exactly perfect, my dear," he says and smiles. I can see where Luca gets his charm from.

"You will have to pardon me besetting my gaze on you," he continues on, "that dress . . . it belonged to my wife, Victoria. The last time I saw her wearing it was our wedding day. I was besieged by memories when I saw you standing there. Please forgive my rudeness. It is not becoming for a gentleman to behave in such a manner."

"I am so sorry Mr. Vinci, I had no idea—" I begin to apologize profusely, when he calmly touches my shoulder and says, "I am so pleased to see you wearing it. It could not have gone to a more exquisite person."

I smile politely, unsure of how to feel. Under my obvious embarrassment is gratitude for his understanding about this faux pas. I know very little about Mr. Vinci and even less about his wife. The only thing I've learned recently about her, is that for many years she lived in England, which explains Luca's mixed accent. Victoria left when Luca and his little brother, Dante, were much younger. The reasons for her departure are unknown, but she and Mr. Vinci never divorced. From what Julia said, the boys only see her once or twice a year. I could never fathom such a distant relationship with my mom. I would feel so lost without her guidance; just as I do at this moment.

The butler calls us to the formal sitting room where drinks will be served before dinner. Luca makes his way next to me as we walk.

"How did I do?" I ask him.

"You're a natural," he looks pleased.

"Did you know this was his wife's wedding dress? Is that your mother?"

He smiles, "She is not my mother, she is my step-mother. And I did not—it's beautiful. You look ravishing, truly."

"Should I change my dress? I don't want to make your father feel uncomfortable tonight."

"She *is* a smart one . . . " he muses out loud, dismissing my question and continuing to smile and nod his head. "She certainly wanted her presence known. She wouldn't have allowed you to see it, unless she approved of you wearing it."

"I have no idea what that riddle is about, and I'm not sure I want to," I say perturbed by his response. I quickly change the subject and nod towards Micella, "Hey, you might want to watch out for your best friend. He may become your brother-in-law by the end of night."

Luca laughs, "If only I could be so lucky. I would lay out the red carpet for any man that would dare to win my sister's affection."

"She's never been in love?"

"No. She's very . . . focused on her goals. She's never been the marrying type."

"So, she's career driven?"

"Sure, let's go with that."

If he keeps up these annoying and indirect responses, it's going to be a very long twenty-two more hours.

In the formal sitting room, we are served a glass of chilled Prosecco. The room itself feels very different at night—there is soft lighting from the wall sconces and spot lighting above the paintings. There are candles glowing all around the room, giving the feel of a different time and era. I love it so much more this way, I only wish it was cold enough for the fireplace to be on. I could never imagine owning a home like this and not visiting, let alone not even living in it. Once I am able to see past the opulence of it all, I'm able to appreciate the history, architecture, and décor. And to think, I've only seen a third of the property.

Stefano and Mr. Vinci get straight to business regarding various pieces of art and properties. Luca and Micella are in a corner having, what looks like, a very deep and personal conversation. Alessia, Sophia, and I are trying our best not to look as out of place as we feel. We make ourselves comfortable on the very uncomfortable antique furniture and begin discussing a plan for tomorrow's pursuit and quest for answers. Our day will begin at city hall, and then we will make our way to the local church, library, and cemeteries. I hope to be able to make some kind of connection to our family history.

A few moments later, Luca and Micella step into our conversation. We update Micella on our intended search, while Luca's expression exhibits disapproval. She seems genuinely interested in our adventure. Our conversations switch seamlessly from one subject to another; she has a lovely and curious nature. She is as refined, as she is fortified. Brilliant, as she is beautiful. She speaks over a dozen languages and is an extremely good listener; she seems to absorb every detail. Unfortunately for her brother, she also has a very good memory, and she loves teasing him about his antics over the years.

"Luca, can we trade you in for your sister? She's way more awesome!" Sophia jokes.

"I wouldn't blame you if you did, she's the best," Luca gloats, "I'm so happy you are able to meet her tonight."

I become distracted from the remaining part of the conversation, as the candlelight captures the brilliance of Micella's necklace. And just then, I remember that I have seen that gold before. It is the same color that is in the painting of the tree. Even the lines in the design of the branches and twigs are exactly alike. Since the blackouts, my memory hasn't been quite the same.

I step away with the excuse of refreshing my drink, but what I truly want is to see the painting close up to see if I am right. My back was to the painting as I was seated, and I didn't want to make it obvious. I replace my glass and attempt to make polite conversation with the server as I subtly position myself to look over. There is no doubt, it is exactly the same. Micella is sitting directly in front of the painting, but to the side of the tree. She looks like she belongs *in* the painting. Or maybe it looks like the tree is part of *her*. I see an illuminating glow come off them both as if they are one, like some kind of optical illusion. I can't tell them apart, and I don't know what I'm looking at anymore. I think my mind is playing tricks on me, when I suddenly feel the vibrations again. This time they are a million times stronger than the last. Their powerful sensation is not just in my veins, it's in my bones, my muscle, my tissue, my heart, and in my mind. My heart starts to beat hard like it did when I was riding Wasi, and there is a white noise in my ears. My vision starts to blur as a figure walks towards me—I can barely make out that it's Micella. She touches my arm and I hear her soft voice asking me if I'm okay.

There is a white blinding light and a flash: I see Micella running through a forest at the speed of light. She is hunting a dark shadow. I see her jumping into the air and shooting an arrow. I feel her immediately take her hand off my arm, and suddenly we are back in the safety of the beautiful room.

She is staring at me, speechless. I blink my eyes to refocus my eyesight and try to catch my breath without attracting attention. I put my drink down and excuse myself to use the restroom. Micella follows me intently, looking concerned.

"Eli, are you ok?" she asks softly.

"Yes, fine. I'm so sorry, it must be my anxiety getting the best of me. I hope I haven't made you feel uncomfortable," I reply, as

I soak a towel in cold water to pat on my neck.

"Not at all, don't worry yourself with that. How can I help?"

"There's nothing, thank you. I seem to be having blackouts, but I'm not sure. I've never had them before. It started last week, shortly after I arrived."

"What do you feel when they happen?"

"It's a strange sensation, like a surge of electricity all through-out my body. It sometimes feels euphoric and other times just powerful. After that comes a flash, and then nothing. Darkness. When I come back to, I can't recall anything that happened the moment before. Tonight has been the strongest I've ever felt it."

"You don't remember anything?" she sounds surprised.

"No, nothing, it's like a blackout of some kind. Please don't tell anyone, I feel like I'm losing my mind." I can feel my eyes welling up with tears.

"No, of course not," she says, taking the towel from my hands and handing me a tissue. "Julia has wonderful Nervitus Liberus drops to calm the nerves. I will be sure to have her put a few in your water at dinner." I nod yes in agreement.

She points her finger up. "They are ringing the bell now, that means it's time to be seated for dinner. I'll be by your side should you need anything. Just tug at your ear anytime you want to leave. I'll create a distraction, if need be."

"Thank you." I couldn't have asked for a better plan. We walk out of the bathroom side by side and into the hallway. I can hear Stefano and Luca making silly comments about why girls are always going to the restroom in twos. Micella gently pulls at her father's hand and they lovingly walk arm and arm. She quietly says to him, "Father, please arrange the cognac and grappa to be served in the small library after dinner. It is best we do not return to the sitting room." He nods in approval, as he looks at her with one eyebrow lifted.

The servants open the double doors into the formal dining

area as we approach. In theme with the grandeur of this home, the dining room is no exception. My eyes take in the high ceilings, stunning crown molding, and beautiful artwork that adorns every wall. There must be over a dozen chandeliers hanging from the mural covered ceiling, their crystals illuminating every inch of the room. The table is set for a king; only the finest china, crystal, and silverware are on display. Down the center of a long table are countless candlesticks and an entire garden's worth of seasonal flowers. Only in my imagination could I have dreamed up such exquisiteness, and yet here it is, in physical manifestation. I've only ever seen this kind of luxury in movies, or in photos taken at Buckingham palace. All this serves as a grand distraction, and I've almost forgotten about my incident a few moments earlier.

Like me, the girls are absolutely in awe, while Stefano is acting like he's right at home. Of course, I forget that he's been working for people of this stature for quite some time. He must be accustomed to all of this by now. The only thing new about him tonight is the way he cannot take his eyes off of Micella. I can't tell if she's interested in him as well, but she does seem amused.

We take our seats and as promised, Micella is sitting directly across from me. Her father stands and gives a lovely speech to welcome us. I notice that Micella has the water glass instead of the wine glass in her hand, as a reminder for me to drink the water first. I smile at her in gratitude. We toast and as I take a big sip, I feel the effects almost immediately. Julia really does have a way with herbs. I feel relaxed, and I happily enjoy the conversation through what feels like a twenty-course meal. Everyone is in a joyful and pleasant mood, sharing stories of their very different lives and adventures. Once we finish dessert, we are invited to the small library for a nightcap. As we make our way over, I see Julia peeking through from behind a wall. I rush over to her.

"Julia, you saved my life tonight, thank you so much! I don't know what I would have done without your drops," I say, as I embrace her.

"Miss Eli, it was my pleasure. I just wanted to check in on you and see how you're feeling," she says, holding one of my hands in between hers. She takes a moment to look at me in the gown and says, "If I'm being honest, I wanted to get a glimpse of you in this dress again. It looks like it was made for you. You're so beautiful."

"Oh Julia, I had no idea it was Luca's stepmother's wedding dress! I'm so embarrassed. I didn't know people actually wore sparkly black dresses on their wedding day!"

She giggles earnestly, "Black is not just for mourning, as people say. It also symbolizes the end of one cycle and the beginning of another. Such as the phases of the moon at the bottom of your dress. And you are the center star among them." So they *are* moons.

"Thank you for being so good to me," I say with the utmost love in my heart.

"You should go in before Micella thinks you've had another episode," she taps my hand gently, "but remember to ask the right questions." That reminds me of what my grandmother said.

"Thank you, Julia," and I kiss her on the forehead.

I walk into the small library and Alessia hands me a glass of cognac. It is quite strong, but delicious and very smooth.

"That's quite a fancy bottle. I love the strange design with the silver and gold tones. Oh, and I love the crystals! I want to take that back to school, my friends would love it," Sophia says to us.

"Well little sister, that will never happen," Stefano says to her. "Those 'tones' are 24-karat gold and dipped sterling platinum. Although the bottle itself is crystal, those things you see set in it are 6,500 certified diamonds. Each bottle originally sold for two million dollars. Since Mr. Vinci purchased a dozen, I negotiated the deal."

"What the f—!" Sophia silently screams; this time it's me who covers her mouth.

"Henri IV Dudognon Heritage cognac. It might be the most expensive, but arguably the best. Depends on your taste," Luca says, as if it somehow makes it conceivable that I'm holding hundreds of thousands of dollars in liquor—in a glass, in my hand. Sophia, Alessia, and Stefano drink without hesitation. They act as if this is the most amazing thing that has ever happened to them. I hand my glass back to Luca.

"I saw that coming," he says to me under his breath.

"I just don't understand what it is with your family spending this kind of money on things you digest. It's going to come right out of you in thirty minutes anyway."

"I don't think that's the point."

"What *is* the point Luca? Do you have any idea what this kind of money can do for millions of people?"

"I'm certain you've already lectured me about it."

"I have?" I have no recollection of what he's talking about. It must have been something I said while I was drunk. I'm afraid of what else may have come out of my mouth.

"I see that you are not enjoying my cognac," says Mr. Vinci as he walks over with Micella under his arm. "How about we try something else?"

"I'm fine, sir. Just a glass of water will do." It is in my hand before I finish the sentence.

"Please, make yourselves at home," he gestures for us to have a seat in the large, soft-leather sofas and lounge chairs.

"Thank you for tonight, it has been one of the best evenings ever. My best friend and my family together, I can't imagine anything better," Stefano says graciously. I can see Micella likes what he said.

"It really has, Stefano. If I knew your family was so charming, I might have come sooner!" Mr. Vinci teasingly replies.

"My mother says she knows you. She mentioned you were childhood friends. Who else do you know in our family?" I ask.

"Yes, that is true. I know almost all your family, primarily the older generation. But your generation is even more impressive!" Hmmm, charming and illusive. This is not going to be easy.

"What brings you to town after nearly twenty-six years?" Alessia courageously asks. Stefano jumps in, insinuating that the question might be too invasive.

"No, that's alright Stefano. It's a fair question after all. I'm sure everyone is thinking it," Mr. Vinci replies kindly. "As you all know, my wife Victoria left when my boys were younger. The day she left, this home was never the same. I built this home for our family, but I simply could not bear to live in it any longer. There was nothing in my power that I could do to make her return. I packed up our things and moved to Rome, and eventually Milano. I never looked back, as it was much too painful. So, I turned it into a museum of sorts. It tells the story of our lives, and of the worlds."

I clinch my dress and want to bury my head in it.

"Oh, don't do that dear, it looks striking on you," he says, as if he's reading my mind, "but back to Alessia's question. I am here because my children asked me to come. They have called on my services for a family situation. And it is only at their will that I would ever return to this place," he pauses, "but having you all here has brought life back into this home. You have each brought me great joy tonight. Thank you for that." He holds out his glass, and we toast to his words.

"You're so cool, Mr. Vinci!" Sophia gushes. She's made quite a connection with him tonight. He seems to have taken a liking to our little Sophia.

"As are you, my dear!"

We all have a laugh.

"Now, I know you mentioned that you have a fascination with literature and world history. Have you ever heard of the Mason Library, dearest Sophia?" Mr. Vinci asks, as he takes a sip of his cognac.

"Yes, we all search for it on campus but can never find it, so it's always been more like a myth."

"What's the Mason library?" Alessia asks.

"Only the most exclusive library in Italy. Other than the Vatican, it stores *the* rarest and most unique books in all of the world," Sophia replies. Mr. Vinci smiles wide.

"How about I make a call to my good friends at the University to let them know we have a new member?" he says joyfully.

"REALLY? So, it's like a REAL place! I mean, no one has ever really seen it. You would really do that for me?" she screams with excitement, as she nearly knocks over her million-dollar drink.

"Yes, we'll have it done first thing in the morning," he assures her.

"There are only one hundred members in all of the world. Now there's one hundred and one. Looks like the *boss* has made an exception. I don't think I've seen that happen in a millennium," Micella says, as she winks at Sophia. "Typically, someone has to pass away before that membership can be given to someone new."

"What an honor, I-I don't know what to say! I am too selfish to act humble and turn it down," she says with a gracious-like tone. We can't help but laugh at her honesty.

"You're just our kind of girl!" Mr. Vinci says laughing, "Also, please let Donatella know what your preferential classes are for this year. I'll make sure you get into them without any trouble. *And* that they don't give you any problems about starting the semester late."

Sophia jumps out of her chair and throws her arms around him.

"Luca! If I'd only met you ten years sooner!" Stefano says with light-hearted disappointment. "I could have used this when I was in school."

"Hopefully we are doing right by you now, Mr. Goto," Micella says, with a slight undertone of seduction in her voice. She's caught him off guard. She's so sexy that everything about her can be seductive. I *almost* feel sorry for the guy.

"Yes, quite," he replies, with a slight undertone of wanting to be seduced. Sophia pays no mind, it's her moment.

"I'm going to be the envy of the school. Never mind the school, the world!" and throws her arms up in the air.

"It's actually quite an exclusive membership, Sophia. You will not be able to tell anyone outside of this room," Luca interjects seriously, but with a slight smile. "There is a contract and very strict rules that you will be required to follow. One of the many benefits is that your entire educational tuition will be paid for until you finish school." He turns to the servant and asks him to call Donatella into the room. Sophia is now spinning in circles. There is no getting her down from this cloud.

"Hello Donatella, my father will be adding an additional member to the Mason Library. Please draft the contract for member 101," Luca says sternly.

"101? I don't understand . . . " she replies, with an irritated tone.

"Nothing to understand," Mr. Vinci says loudly, "I built the place, they're all my books as much as my wife's. I can do as I please. Please draft the contract. I will need Stefano to review it with his sister first thing in the morning."

"Yes, sir." And off she goes with her tail between her legs.

Stefano hugs his sister and lifts her off the ground. I'm sure he is beyond relieved for himself and his family that she will be taken care of. This will give her the guidance that he so wishes for her. After such an incredible gesture, it will be difficult for me to be inquisitive, but I have so many questions and such limited time.

Everyone is in such a celebratory mood; the drinks and toasts keep coming. Luca is playing vintage albums on the phonograph, and everyone is dancing. I limit myself to just a few glasses of champagne; I don't want a repeat of last night. But Alessia and Sophia are well on their way, and Stefano has joined them. No matter how much Mr. Vinci, Luca, and Micella drink, their state does not alter. It's almost as if they're immune to alcohol. Which confuses me all the more as to why they have so much of it.

After a few hours of dancing and singing, things start to unwind a bit. Micella walks over and lounges next to me on the sofa.

"I haven't seen my father this happy since my mother was alive," she confesses.

"When were he and your mother together? You look so much younger than Luca."

"Aren't you sweet. No, I am much older. It took my father many years to remarry after she passed."

"Well, you look like you're twenty," I say, and briefly pause before asking, "What was her name?"

"Tariess."

"What was she like?"

"She was elegant, intelligent, kind, and very strong," Micella breathily says with nostalgia in her eyes.

"Did you look like her? The only thing you seem to have in common with your father is his eye color."

"Don't let him hear you say that!" she laughs and says, "Yes, I look a lot like her. I'm grateful for it." She goes on to tell me lovely stories about her mother and shares her fondest memories. She sounds like she was an exceptional woman, and some-one who did a lot of good for so many people. Someone I would have liked a great deal.

"If you don't mind my asking, how did she die?" I inquire gently.

"She died fighting for a cause she believed in. She died for her people," I can hear the sadness in her voice. "I don't want to speak on this anymore, if that's ok. It's very difficult."

I want to ask so badly who her people are, but I need to re-spect her wishes. I can't imagine how hard it would be for me to talk about the way my mother died, especially if it wasn't from natural causes.

"I'm sorry, she sounds like someone I would have liked to know."

"Yes, I believe she would have liked you very much."

"Who are we speaking of?" Mr. Vinci asks, as he sits near us.

"Mother, as if you did not already know," Micella replies.

"Fascinating woman. Brave. Filled with great knowledge and brilliance. She was the love of my life," he says with great sorrow. "I was so lucky to have been able to share my life with her. She gave me many wonderful gifts, but by far Micella is the greatest." He kisses her hand. Their bond is strong; you can see it by how they interact with one another. I don't know if it comes from the loss they share or simply the affinity they have for each other. But there is great love and respect in this family. And from what I gather, no secrets. I'm very envious of that.

Luca comes and joins us. I turn around to see all three of my cousins have fallen asleep.

"How embarrassing. I'd be happy to pour water over their heads and drag them to bed," I say, partially teasing, but mostly sincere.

"Let them be. I've had many moments like that in my life. Some of the best times in my life ended in that same position," Mr. Vinci chuckles. He seems humored by it.

"Thank you for being so understanding," I say, apologizing on their behalf, "after such a wonderful night, it's not very becoming."

Luca pours us all another drink. There is a moment of silence followed by a toast to my Sleeping Beauty cousins. And I know in that instant that there is no better time than now to ask my questions.

"Mr. Vinci, may I ask you a personal question?" My stomach is turning with anticipation.

"I'm intrigued. No one's asked me that in centuries."

"Well . . . who are you? And what exactly do you do?"

Luca and Micella look at one another completely amused. Luca then turns to his father and says, "Don't say I didn't warn you."

"You certainly did, son," he replies to Luca. He then turns to me, "You are much more direct than I expected."

"I'm sorry if that was too forward. I didn't mean to be rude. You must be one of the most interesting people I've ever heard of. But there's nearly nothing about you in the press. And yet, you are one of the wealthiest and most affluent men in the world." I have to take a breath; I can feel myself getting excited. It dawns on me that he may actually answer my questions. "I managed to find one small clipping of you from the 1970s. And for it being like 50 years ago, well, you look almost the same as you do now. I can't help but be curious."

"What have your mother and grandmother told you about me?"

"Nothing. I didn't even know they knew you until this morning."

"It's a small province, quite normal for families to know one another," he says in her defense. "Your mother was once very good friends with my wife, Victoria. Did she mention that?"

"No, she did not."

"Well, it might be a sore subject. I take full responsibility. I introduced them when I brought Victoria here on her first visit from England. She and your mother hit it off right away and became very good friends almost immediately," he takes a moment to look down and reminisce. "You see, when Victoria left, she didn't just leave us. She left her friends too, including your mother. Elizabetta was deeply affected by this. As we all were."

Oh. This would explain why my mother has a difficult time creating new friendships and building attachments.

"There are no secrets in my house. But that doesn't mean your grandmother was wrong to keep hers for so long. I would have done the same."

"So, you know her story?"

"I helped write it," he says reluctantly, "but it is not mine to tell."

"That's the second time I've heard that today," I shoot Luca a glance, as his father smiles.

"If that's the case, then it must be true." Mr. Vinci clearly agrees with his son. He then clears his throat to continue, "So . . . to answer your question . . . most call me *the Magician*, although I prefer the modern term of 'philanthropist.' I am someone that is able to manifest peoples' dreams, and often change the course of history, current events, and public opinion. I don't always get to everything on time, but I certainly do my best to fix things once they go awry. This wealth that you are not fond of, it helps billions of people every year. My family and I have acquired it over centuries. And it takes legitimate money, especially in the era of mainstream press and social media, to help others. Otherwise, we would be breaking the rules and setting off too many alarms." He clears his throat once more. "Considering I participated in creating those things too, I cannot be upset with the outcome as such. I make a global income in many different ways, and many different means, even within this house."

"I did not mean to offend you!" I hastily apologize for my insensitive comments about their financial status.

"No need! That's how I knew I liked you, you judged me for the right reasons, my dear," he says lovingly, to comfort me. "You see, the difference between me and the other 'philanthropists' in this world, is that I do not ask for recognition. My family is *always* anonymous. I'm sure you've heard the phrase, 'it was like magic.' Well, that's me."

I feel dumbfounded and stupid. I don't know what to say. Once again, I find myself wanting to bury myself and hide. Here is this nice family that just wants to help others, and I'm the jerk that judged them for wanting discretion. There isn't enough champagne in that entire cellar to numb this feeling of humiliation. Who cares if he thinks of himself as some sort of magician or anonymous superhero who thinks he can save the world— maybe he actually might be able to with that kind of money. All the same, I find it endearing.

"No Eli don't do that," Micella leans in closely sensing my utter embarrassment. "You did nothing wrong. You trusted your eyes, just as you have been taught to. But maybe now it is time to trust the things you cannot see and instead *know* them to be true." I feel her empathetic words burrow deep into my soul.

It's like she knows my secret, and the one question I've been asking all my life. I can feel some part of her has crawled down into that deep, dark place inside me. That place with no light and no sound. That place where I don't trust anyone or anything; not myself and sometimes not even God. It's the place that five–year-old created to compact her feelings of things that could not be explained. A place to run away to, one that looks for no acceptance and no explanations from either side of life or death. It's the place between worlds, words, and breaths. It's the place I am most *free*. There, in this place, I do not wish to know myself, nor my demons or divinity. A place where love has not yet broken me or confronted me with impenetrable pain. Innocence cannot be taken nor damnation awarded, because they do not exist here. Maybe it's the place I was born. It may possibly be the place where I will die. But I am certain it is the only place inside my being that is real. And in this moment, I feel as if Micella has somehow witnessed this sacred space.

Mr. Vinci glances at Luca and Micella, and then looks down at his feet before looking back up at me. "Eli, would you be so kind to follow us back into the sitting room?" he asks.

I happily oblige, relieved to be tempted away from my thoughts.

Mr. Vinci escorts us back to the room with the painting, and we stop and stand before it. Luca is to my left, Mr. Vinci to my right, and Micella next to him. I'm unsure why he's brought us back here, but I feel uneasy about being so close to the painting. Every time I'm in this proximity, it unravels some part of me. We are standing in silence. It seems like Mr. Vinci is waiting for something to happen. I look up at Luca and he gently shrugs his shoulders.

"Father?" Micella asks softly, as she places her hand on his shoulder. He takes a deep sigh.

"Eli, ask your questions," he says to me.

"Father is that really a good idea? The timing—" Luca jumps in.

"Son, you asked for my help. This is the best way." Luca is reluctant to agree.

"Please ask," Mr. Vinci says motioning forward to come out with it.

I take a deep breath. There are so many questions, I don't want to ask the wrong one. Or worse, sound like a silly child speaking nonsense. I'm searching for the right words in my mind.

"How many can I ask?"

"I'm not a genie, you don't only get three. Although, I must say they are one of my better creations," he seems delighted with himself. "You can ask as many as you like, as long as they do not have to do with your family. I cannot break that agreement."

That just eliminated about ninety percent of the questions in my mind. It's really what I want to know most. Maybe I should begin with what is directly in front of me.

"What is this painting?" I finally ask. There, that wasn't so bad.

"It is the Tree of Life."

I give Mr. Vinci the "AND?" look. It sounds like an interesting title but it still does not tell me what it is. I'm trying to be mindful of my follow up question. I don't want him to change his mind.

"And," he smiles, "it is the root of all life. All existence. The beginning and end to all things. And . . . " he smiles again, "the original holds the only entrance to the Underworld and the Asbgahs."

"What's an Asbgah?" I ask inquisitively.

"Well, I suppose the closest definition would be a realm . . . or a dimension of some kind," he pauses and takes a sip of his drink—I can see him trying to choose his next words carefully. "There are fourteen official Asbgahs. The first being the space where God himself exists, and we do not count that one. So, I suppose if you leave that out, there are thirteen Asbgahs. And before you ask any more questions, please bear in mind, that I will not be able to answer anything further on this topic."

With nowhere else to go on that topic, I revert my attention back to the tree.

"So, this is not an original painting?" I ask, confused by his words. "Who made it?"

"Well, the tree itself is made by God, of course. The painting *is* an original, and it was a 'gift' from people who are very special to the both of us."

"Who?" I ask abruptly. But he shakes his finger. That must mean the answer is connected to my family, and he won't answer it. Ok, I'm starting to understand how this game works.

"What is it made of?"

"The canvas is tightly woven Celestial hair. Extraordinary, isn't it? Simply a painter's dream." He stops himself, as he realizes he's gone off subject. "There is also faerie gold in the painting, better known as Sibyl's gold."

"Faerie? Is that a homonym for something?"

"No. I mean quite literally, the magical creatures," he pauses. "Well . . . not exactly the same. The fictional ones you have seen in animation or cinema are not quite right. Loads of silliness with those."

"Silliness," I mumble to myself, as I try and let his words absorb into my mind. He is starting to sound about as batty as my Aunt Silva. Maybe they all did the same kind of acid together when they were young. A million new questions start running through my mind. But there is one that I need to ask above all.

"Mr. Vinci, I've been feeling strange vibrations . . . randomly," I say as I look at Luca, "ever since I laid eyes on this painting. And I always feel them when it's nearby."

"Do you feel them now?"

"Well, there is always *something*. But no, not like usual. Is it because you're here? Because you're standing so close to me?"

"Yes. You are a smart girl. Why don't you trust your intuition?"

"Mostly because it's broken." They all chuckle.

"We'll have to see about fixing that." He turns gently to take a seat and looks as if his worries have settled.

"The vibrations, the blackouts . . . what is *IT*?" I ask desperately, pleading for an answer.

"My darling girl, give me your hand. Let me have a peek," he says, as he reaches for my hand.

My chest goes into a one-beat convulsion. Our bodies connect, we are standing face to face. My heart starts to beat in sync with his. We hold hands tightly as if we cannot break free from one another even if we try.

There is utter silence.
No oxygen.

There is only light that surrounds us. It is not blinding, like the one before. This one is soft and peaceful. I can see every fiber and particle in the air as I look around.

"Where are we?" I ask unafraid, surprising even myself.

"This can *NOT* be possible," Mr. Vinci replies with strain in his voice and fear in his eyes. "Do not let go of my hand, Eli!"

Then like lightning, there are flashes tearing through my mind. The most unimaginable images I've ever seen. Things I recognize and things I do not—The Tree of Life, Heaven, Hell, magical worlds, angels, demons, strange creatures, constellations, planets, Micella, the lady at the festival, my grandmothers, Zeus, Greece, magic, stars, angels, Egypt, Cleopatra, kings and queens of all times throughout history, the Middle East, Jesus, Mary, Rome, Vikings, the Medieval Ages, Asia, Africa, India, the Americas, North Pole, South Pole, sporadic islands, Di Medici, Leonardo Da Vinci, Michelangelo, Nostradamus, Napoleon,

Freemasons, Native Americans, Washington, slaves, Lincoln, Edison, Einstein, WWI, poverty, hunger, Churchill, WWII, war after war, dictators, presidents, prime ministers, current leaders, future leaders, many religious leaders throughout the globe, my family, Luca, mythical creatures, *ENDLESS* faces and places I do not know or recognize. Then suddenly, a single child, infinite space, war and peace, followed by images I cannot identify.

I can feel my chest begin to choke for air and then,

Darkness.

Chapter 8

"GOOD MORNING sleepy head!" I feel Alessia caressing my hair. I squint, trying to get my eyes open; it is far too bright. My throat is so dry, I can barely speak.

"So much for not wanting to drink last night. My head is pounding," I reply with a raspy voice, trying to sit up. She hands me a glass of water.

"Julia put her famous Potiodamus drops in the water. She said you'll recover in no time."

"How did I get to bed?" I look to see if I have any clothes on. I do not.

"How did any of us get to bed? Who knows!" she says laughing.

"What an embarrassment we must be to our family!" I say, as I put a pillow over my face.

"Oh, come on. Mr. Vinci seemed to be totally amused by us. He doesn't seem mad at all!"

"Is Luca? This is the second night in a row he's had to look out for us," I ask, as the pillow is still covering my face.

"Nope! Saw the entire Vinci clan this morning at breakfast. They were having a great time teasing us," she laughs again. "By the way you missed an exceptional breakfast. These chefs are five stars, I'll have you know."

"Great," I reply with a dry tone, still trying to wake up.

"Drink the rest of your water," Alessia orders me. "There's coffee and toast on the table. Oh, and Micella had me bring up clothes for you to wear today."

"How are these people so nice and we are such degenerates?"

"Well, if we're lucky, we might learn a thing or two from them," she says shaking me. "Anyway, it's eight o'clock. We have to be at city hall at nine. Hurry up!"

She leaves the room and I get out of bed to pour myself a cup of coffee and grab a bite of toast. I find myself standing in the sunlight. It feels so good on my skin, it gives me goosebumps. I'm never naked other than when getting into the shower. I'm too self-conscious about my body. Even during rare moments of intimacy, I always seem to hide under the sheets.

As I put the coffee cup down, I notice that I have some bruising on both my hands and wrists. There is one in the shape of a thumb on my right wrist.

"Oh God," I say out loud to myself, "please tell me I didn't do anything stupid last night." That's all I need today, hearing stories of how I was jumping off furniture or hanging from chandeliers. I smack myself on the forehead; bad idea, it's still pounding.

I take a hot shower, get ready quickly, and head downstairs. The entire way down I am praying that I did not break anything last night. Even my entire life's savings would not be enough to replace a single vase in this house. I hear voices in the sitting room. I walk in, and it looks like I am the last to arrive.

"Good morning!" I hear everyone shout their salutations at me.

"Good morning, everyone." I don't have the courage to make eye contact with anyone. I walk over to Micella and thank her for the clothes. She, of course, looks divine and fresh as a daisy.

"How are you feeling this morning, my dear?" Mr. Vinci asks.

"Once again, better than I deserve. I'm very grateful for Julia's drops, the pounding in my head is finally subsiding."

"Julia is very knowledgeable with natural remedies, she's saved me on more occasions than I can count," Micella says, praising Julia.

"I'm horribly sorry if I did anything or said anything or broke anything I shouldn't have," I say looking down, ashamed.

"You don't remember anything?" Micella asks curiously.

"No, nothing. The last thing I remember is Luca pouring us a drink. I'm so sorry again . . . "

"You and us all, cousin," Stefano says. "I think we celebrated Sophia's membership to the Mason Library a little too much."

"Definitely, but it was so worth it." Sophia is still smiling from ear to ear.

"Sophia and I will be staying behind today; we need to officiate her contract. And I need to finalize other business with Luca and Mr. Vinci," Stefano says in his lawyer tone.

"Luca has been kind enough to offer us his chauffeur," Alessia says as she widely opens her eyes.

"NO. No, please that won't be necessary," I reply feeling uncomfortable with his generous offer. "You have all been too kind and we have taken more than enough. We'd be happy to walk; it isn't that far. It will be good for us to stretch our legs." I can see Alessia giving me a dirty look from the corner of my eye.

"Now come along, I insist that you at least take one of the cars," Mr. Vinci replies back. "I would be more at ease if you did. You are our guests after all, your comfort and safety are our priority." Spoken like a true gentleman. Mr. Vinci may be the last one left.

"As would I," Luca says.

Alessia raises her eyebrows at me.

"Only if it doesn't inconvenience anyone," I reply.

"Are you kidding? My brother is dying to show off his new toys," Micella says winking at me. "Well, this is my cue. I must be off to my responsibilities. It was nice meeting you all." She gives Stefano a very sensual glare; it nearly melts me, so I can't imagine what it's doing to him. "I'm sure we'll be seeing each other again very soon," she says departing, and glides away.

Alessia looks at the time and tells me that it's late, and that we must leave too. Luca escorts us out and we follow him to the garage. As we make our way through the foyer, I just barely catch a glimpse of Micella as she gets into the elevator. As we pass it, I see that it stops at the bottom level. That's strange. The bottom level is where they keep the wine, meat, cheese, and art. She said she was leaving. There is no exit on that floor, could I have missed one? No, I remember clearly only five doors. My mind goes directly to the fifth door with no label. But Luca said it's just storage. I need to mind my own business and not overthink it, maybe she needs to retrieve something before she leaves.

We walk through the kitchen to get to the garage, where I see Julia and Gian Carlo. I give them several kisses on the cheek and thank them. They ask about our plans for the day. We give them a general overview and tell them they shouldn't expect us for lunch; we'll be eating in town. Julia looks surprised that Luca won't be joining us. Actually, I am too. He says he has pressing business to attend to and has complete confidence that we will be fine. He tells them that I won't be chauffeured because I am anti-elitist. And that driving ourselves was the only way to keep us from walking. Julia tells me she's proud of me, and to always be true to myself. Luca doesn't seem pleased that Julia doesn't side with him. I don't think that happens often, or ever.

As he opens the door to one garage, six more doors follow. Every luxury car known to man is at our disposal. Alessia is freaking out so bad she's singing Queen in acapella. She high fives him about ten times. And he is clearly thrilled to be showing them off.

"You two are a match made in heaven. You really do belong together," I say to the both of them. Luca's face changes from joy to utter disappointment in me.

"That's gross, Eli! He's like my other brother now," Alessia says, clearly annoyed with me.

"Really? Sorry, I missed the memo. When did this happen?"

Alessia proceeds to tell me about a deal that was made last night. She, Sophia, Stefano, and Luca made a pact to be close and love each other like siblings. She insists that because it happened before they were drunk, that it's real and it counts.

"Why did I get left out of this pact? I'm the one with no siblings," I ask. Alessia shakes her head at me like I'm the stupidest person alive. Luca walks away to get keys.

"What?" I mouth to her in confusion and she flips me off. Luca walks back with two sets of keys.

"Here are your options ladies. Rolls Royce or Mercedes Maybach." This guy hasn't listened to a word I've said.

"Damn!" Alessia shouts, "I'm not one to ever turn something like this down, but don't you think they are too big for these small roads? They are so small, there isn't even a line to divide them."

"Safety," is all he says.

"Not for the people behind the wheel of the opposing cars," I state.

"You might have a point." I'm shocked Luca agrees. Alessia tries to coax him into taking one of the sports cars; she seems to be salivating over the Lamborghini. He tells her that they are too dangerous in these areas. She argues that his comments are sexist and that women are better and safer drivers. He then argues back that she's discriminating against men. This goes on at least for five minutes. They really have become brother and sister overnight.

"What about that Fiat? Can't we drive that one?" I point at a darling Fiat 500 sitting in the parking lot.

"That is Julia's car. I don't think she would appreciate you taking it," Luca replies back snippily.

"Oh, on the contrary, I don't think she would mind at all," I smile, as I walk back into the kitchen. A moment later, I come out swinging the keys, and quickly jump into the driver's seat.

"You've got to be kidding me!" Alessia shouts out, exasperated. Luca is shaking his head, but at least he's laughing.

"You have thirty seconds to get in, or I'm leaving without you!" I shout back. She stands there hesitating, so I pull out of the parking spot. She dives in through the open passenger window, and we drive off.

Once in town, we find ourselves driving in circles, only to realize we've passed Pretare City Hall several times. Since the town only has a population of a few hundred occupants, city hall is just a small office with a small sign that's on the door, which is inside of a hallway.

Most of the local businesses here thrive off tourism. It's the perfect place to plan a relaxing vacation. The larger cities are only a thirty-minute drive, and the ocean is less than an hour away. For something more accessible by foot, there are local waterfalls and lakes to swim in, and streams for fishing. Late spring, summer, and early fall are reserved for hiking expeditions. And during the winter, there's lots of skiing. For those not involved in the town's hospitality, food, or tourism business, it's a short commute to Ascoli for work each day.

We walk into the office and it's completely empty, other than a middle-aged woman sitting at a desk. She has short brown hair and is wearing reading glasses. She is aggressively chewing on a piece of gum and indulging in gossip magazines.

She looks up. "How can I help you, girls?" she asks, as we walk up to the counter. Her voice is nasally.

"Good morning, we'd like to inquire about some family birth records. Specifically, my mother and both her grandmothers," Alessia answers.

"Were they born here or in the outskirts?"

"We're not sure, but we believe here in Pretare," I answer.

"Do you know what year they were each born?" she asks.

"No," we answer simultaneously. She seems to think that's strange because she frowns and shakes her head at us.

"Do you know the names and surnames of their parents?"

"Um, no . . . " Alessia answers, pouting her lips and scrunching her nose.

"Do you know their maiden names?" she is now looking at us sideways.

"Yes!" we both answer simultaneously, feeling confident that we are able to answer at least one question.

"Please print their first and last name, and the first and last name of the person they married on this paper." She hands us a blank paper and a pen.

Alessia receives a call from her brothers. There's drama at the restaurant and they need her assistance; she steps out to take the call. I fill out the paperwork quickly and hand it back to the woman.

While the woman is reviewing the records, I check my phone. Of course, my mother has already texted me half a dozen times. I decide to reply before her texts double:

> *Hi Mom, everything went great. They are a lovely family and very gracious. Tell you all the details later. We'll be home sometime this afternoon, maybe late afternoon. I'll text when we're on our way. XOXOX*

A few moments later, the lady walks over to me with a smug look on her face.

"I've lived here all of my life, and I have never heard those last names. But as a courtesy, I wanted to check them for you anyway. And as I suspected, no one by the names of Rosa Taygeta, or Amelia Maia, or Ersella Maia, were born here. Are these women even Italian? The last names don't sound Italian."

"Of course they were born here," I say defensively, as I take the sheet with their information back.

"I'm sorry lovely, but they were not. Those names aren't from around here," she says insisting.

In a slightly irritated tone, I thank her for her time and walk outside. I stare at the paper in my hand. I hate to admit it, but she is right. Those are not Italian last names.

Alessia walks up to me as I am standing like an idiot on the sidewalk.

"Oh God, what is it? Is it bad? Were they orphans? Oh, they're not really Catholic!! But they made us suffer in church every Sunday anyway. And they forced us to do our first Holy Communion and Confirmation anyway? Wait . . . Norway! They're really from Norway and that's why they're so tall! No, I know, they were married before! OR they weren't married before and lived in sin, and we have another family somewhere!?!"

"Ále, SHUT UP!" I shout out, while I smack the paper on her chest. I start rummaging through my purse to find the keys. But I'm so flustered, I don't realize I've had them in my hand the entire time. She pulls the keys out of my hand and has me take a seat on the sidewalk curb.

"Eli, Maia is not my mother's last name. It says here Ersella Maia," she points across my writing. "My mother's maiden name is Celaeno, Ersella Celaeno." We both pause in confusion. "Your grandmother and my mother are full blooded sisters, why would they have different last names? How are we just now seeing this?" Alessia asks dumbfounded.

"I don't know, maybe for the same reason they don't have a record of them?" I suggest and she looks at me with total disbelief. "Deception? Camouflaging the truth? Hiding from someone? I don't know," I continue on, baffled. "How did we not notice it all these years, Ále? That lady is right, these last names don't even sound Italian."

"I suppose you're right," she says, pondering the options in her head. "This isn't good Eli, we have no idea who they really are."

We get in the car and drive over to the church located close to the town's cemetery. We hope to have a bit more success with their records than we did at city hall. As we enter the church, it feels so nice and cool. I love churches, I always have. There is a feeling of tranquility and love that transcends in every church all over the world, regardless of race or creed. Both of my grandmothers went to church religiously. There was always so much peace for me in that. I spent a lot of time in similar pews praying and asking for forgiveness. But today, I'm going to pray for answers.

We walk over to the woman who's cleaning the church and ask her where we can find the priest of this congregation. She offers to walk us over to the building he resides in. It's a small house, just off to the side. She knocks on the door, then lets us in behind her. She asks us to sit in the waiting area as she retrieves him. Shortly, she returns to tell us it's just going to be a few minutes, but she must return to her work at the church.

"This room looks familiar to me," I mention to Alessia, "I think it's where my grandparents took their wedding photo."

"Which ones?" she asks.

"Both actually. Look at this wall," I point to the crack on the wall, "that's in the photo, as well as the same curved stairway and statue of an angel. That has to be a sign that we are in the right place."

"Let's hope so, because things are going to get really weird if we're not," she replies.

A very energetic priest comes out to greet us. He looks like he is in his late seventies, and he's wearing his collared uniform with the sleeves rolled up. There is a kitchen towel over his shoulder that he's wiping his hands on. Before we can get proper introductions in, he says, "Girls, come with me into the kitchen. I am making fresh tomato sauce for lunch, and I don't want it to burn!"

We scurry in after him. The house is quaint and very old. The furniture is simple, minimal, and worn. Everything other than the appliances looks handmade. I would give anything to live in a storybook home like this in LA. But this kind of building could never exist in the New World.

We take a seat at his kitchen table, and he pours us a glass of water. "I'm Father Gabriel, how may I help you today?" he asks with a big warm smile across his face. Ále and I introduce ourselves, and we get right to it.

"My grandmothers were born here in Pretare, and we're hoping to get some information on our family history," I say.

"Oh, that is wonderful! It's great to see such young people wanting to learn about their family tree."

"We just came from city hall, but they don't seem to have any documentation on them. We were wondering if the church still has any birth and death records on file?" Alessia asks.

"Ah, so you met Barbara. She is quite informed about all things Pretare. Was she able to recognize the names at least?" he asks, while he stirs his sauce slowly.

"No, she wasn't," I reply scornfully.

Alessia becomes easily distracted around food. "That smells incredible!" she says, complimenting his cooking skills. "I own a restaurant near Rome, and I know what good food smells like."

"Do you really! What's it called?"

"Osteria D' Ugo, have you ever heard of it?"

"As a matter of fact, I've eaten there. Many years ago, of course. Do you know your restaurant is famous?" he asks her, and we both start laughing. He goes on to talk about what a wonderful experience he had there, and how much he loved the people.

"Actually, this sauce is a recipe from the original owner herself, Ersella."

"She's my mother!" Alessia bursts out.

"Yes, I figured as much. I can see it by the striking resemblance."

He invites her over to try his sauce; she seems genuinely impressed.

"Well, only your mother has the magic touch. No one can make it the way she does!"

"I'm shocked she gave you the recipe!" Alessia says. I am too; even my own mother doesn't have it.

"It was a thank you gift for traveling with her to Ceri; for whatever reason, her husband was unable to travel with her. So, she asked me; she had no one else. You see, back then a woman could not travel without her father, brother, husband, or her priest," he says, as he adds a dash more of salt. "It was a time when we had nothing to give. No money to buy gifts. So, we showed our gratitude by sharing the things that we loved most," he smiles nostalgically, "and then of course, your mother threatened me with kingdom come if I *ever* thought about giving her secret recipe away!" We start laughing again—that sounds exactly like Aunt Ersella.

"She's actually here, in Umito. I can call her if you'd like to speak with her," Alessia offers.

"What brings her here?" he asks, with a more serious tone.

"My grandmother Amelia is dying. She's come to spend whatever final time she has left with her," I answer.

He sits in a chair slowly. A wave of sadness comes over his face.

"Please forgive me, I did not expect that news."

"Did you know my other grandmother as well, Rosa?"

"Oh goodness . . . you must be Elita," he says, closing his eyes for a moment.

"I am." I ask, as my heart starts to beat faster. This is so much better than any paperwork or City Hall records.

"I knew Rosa and Amelia shared one grandchild. It was very significant for them; for us all."

"Why?" I ask, anxious for more answers.

"Because there was always a special bond between them. And sharing a grandchild meant it would last forever, from bloodline to bloodline."

"That's beautiful," Alessia says as she chokes up a bit, "Just like us, we'll share a bloodline forever."

"Actually, you don't," he corrects her. "Amelia and Ersella are not blood sisters. Ersella was the youngest of the girls, and Amelia took her under her wing. But they told everyone that they were sisters. And they meant it."

"W H A T!" Alessia looks like she's about to blow a fuse, as the lovely family moment is over. "She lied about that too?!"

"Oh, you didn't know?" he says with an "oops" expression.

"NO, I most certainly did not! Please, enlighten us!" she says furiously, crossing her arms.

"I wouldn't say she lied," he says shaking his head. "Would you consider children who are adopted not to be 'real' siblings? Or will the fact that you are not blood with Eli, make you any less of cousins?"

"No, of course not!" she snaps back.

"Then how is this any different? She may have withheld details, but she didn't lie," he says to her calmly.

"Father, for being a Catholic priest, you really walk a *distinct tightrope* about what a 'lie' is," Alessia says squinting at him.

"You inherited her expressions, I see," he says smiling.

"Well, you don't have to be my cousin anymore, you can officially be my sister." I hold her hand as tears start streaming down her face. I've never seen her so emotional. The news of us not being blood cousins must be more distressing to her than I thought. She puts her arms around me and whispers "forever" in my ear.

Father Gabriel invites us to stay for lunch. We enjoy a glass of wine and a marvelous plate of pasta together. During lunch he shares stories—many of which we've already heard—but we don't have the heart to tell him. We ask him several questions about our family. He does everything he can to answer diplomatically, without giving away too much detail. Based on the way he is able to dodge and turn questions around, I have a suspicion that he may have once worked for the Italian AISE, the equivalent of the CIA in the US. But we are able to confirm that he did in fact marry both my Nonna Amelia and Nonna Rosa at this church. And he also was the priest who married Aunt Ersella in Ceri.

Once we finish lunch, he sets out a plate of cookies and makes us a cup of much needed espresso. He changes the subject and tells us a little history about Pretare but does not mention the "faeries" once. He then pulls out a brochure from his kitchen drawer and lays it on the table for us to take. He tells us about this particular tour he thinks we would enjoy. The brochure has various dates and times listed for the tour of the Seven Churches Dedicated to Mary. The tour is from Montegallo to Montemonaco. Each church has its own story. He encourages us to go, by telling us it's a wonderful way to see the country and learn the local history. Father Gabriel can read me well, as this is right up my alley. I also feel like it's a good way to distract us from speaking further on the topic of our family. But I'm not quite ready to let this go, so I decide to give it my best shot and circle around once more.

"Father, I need to ask you something. And I need you to not 'withhold details.'" He grins as I speak to him. "In all your stories, much like my grandmothers' and mother's, there is never mention of my great-grandparents," I state pressing on, "and the only sibling or great aunt I know of is Alessia's mother. Who and where are my grandmothers and my Aunt Ersella from? What is the *real* story?"

"Yeah," Alessia echoes my sentiments.

"Girls, it is not my story to tell." Before he can even finish his sentence, Alessia and I are throwing our hands up and fussing up a storm, talking over each other with exacerbated remarks. It takes everything we have in us not to cuss in front of the good priest.

"Now, now, calm down . . . I assume you've heard that already," he says as he gestures to relax.

"Like a million times," I say, as I press the palm of my hand against my forehead, "and please don't add 'there must be a reason'." He goes silent, so I must have taken the words right out of his mouth.

"Eli, what are those bruises on your wrist? Did someone hurt you?" Father Gabriel looks horrified.

"ELI! Oh, my G—," Alessia stops herself. "How did I not notice those? That looks terrible! Does it hurt?" she asks, pulling both my hands to her.

"No, not at all. Actually, I have no idea how it happened. When I woke up they were there," I say looking down at them.

They've gotten darker since this morning. And it's not looking as minor as I had originally thought.

"Please Father, don't worry. We drank too much last night and I must have fallen," I try to reassure him. "Or maybe we were playing around too rough? I tend to bruise easily."

"Geez Eli, I feel so bad. I was so out of it. I don't remember anything either." Alessia has a bit of panic all over her face.

"No, please don't worry! I would know if anything bad had happened." I'm not doing a good job of even convincing myself.

"I had assumed you drove in this morning. But it sounds like you're staying in town. Were you here for the festival?" Father Gabriel asks.

"Yes, we came in on Saturday. We are staying with the Vincis," Alessia says. Father Gabriel suddenly goes quiet. His entire demeanor changes. He looks serious, and very displeased with this discovery.

"Does your grandmother know?" he asks directly.

"Yes, I spoke to her yesterday. I told my mother that we were staying to have dinner with Luca and Mr. Vinci. And Luca's sister, Micella, joined us as well," I reply.

Father Gabriel's face turns ghost white.

"Father are you okay? Ále, get him some water."

"I'm fine, fine," he shoos us away. "They are all here? At the same time?" he asks in disbelief.

I answer "yes," and then suggest we all go outside for some fresh air. He looks like he is in terrible need of it, and he complies.

The garden outside is very peaceful and tranquil. There are beautiful old oak trees all around, giving us just the right amount of shade. Alessia and I decide to change the conversation since it seems to have upset the Father so much. So we make small talk about the weather, and the wonderful seasons I miss out on by living in LA. We continue on with pleasantries until Father

Gabriel's color returns to his face. But he does not return to being himself; he still seems troubled.

I look out beyond the garden and see the cemetery. It reminds me that I have one more person to visit before we leave. Father Gabriel sees me looking and offers to come along. I pick a few flowers as we are walking out of the garden. Father leads the way to help me find him. My understanding is that Nonna Amelia's first child, Mauro, was buried here.

Before I know it, we are standing at the grave site of my uncle Mauro. The plaque is nearly completely covered in vines. I would have never been able to find it without Father Gabriel's assistance. He died when he was an infant, just a few days old. She gave birth to ten children; nine survived. Technically, my Uncle Gianni and mother are her second and third child. I was told they chose to lay him to rest here, because he died here. My grandfather could not bear my grandmother's grief and decided to "bury him with the angels where he was born," as he liked to say. As far as I know, she and my grandfather never returned to the grave site since it happened. It's possible that this is the reason why she won't talk about this town or claim it as the place where she was born. She may loathe it for taking her first child.

"I was fortunate enough to have baptized Mauro before he died," Father Gabriel says, "He was a strong little lad . . . may his soul rest in peace."

"How did he die?" Alessia asks.

"No one knows for sure. My grandmother said she heard him let out one single cry in the middle of the night, and then he was gone."

"Yes, that is as they say. It happened here," Father Gabriel says sadly, as he gestures to his home. "It was one of the worst nights of my life. I'd never heard such pain and tears come from any being, Amelia was in pieces," he pauses a moment as he deeply recalls that memory. "There was nothing we could do. We each took turns watching him to make sure he was well and safe. I don't understand how it happened right under our noses."

"It's not your fault Father, it sounds like it was an occurrence of nature," I say, touching his shoulder.

"Nature? No, I would not call it that," he replies, as his thoughts seem to drift to a dark place.

"Father, is there something we should know?" I ask.

"By your very presence alone here, it tells me that Amelia has broken her vow, and you will soon know everything," Father Gabriel says. "She knew you would find your way to me, so I need you to give her a message, Eli."

"Of course, anything."

"Please tell her that everything is as planned."

"I would ask you what that means, but I know you won't tell me." He nods his head in agreement.

"It's time for me to get back to her, I've been away too long. Thank you for today, Father Gabriel. We really appreciate your kindness and generosity." I embrace him.

"You gave us more than we thought we would find," Alessia says, as she pauses for a moment to ask. "There isn't anyone else in our family buried here by any chance, is there?"

"You have my word," he replies, holding us each under his arms.

We say our goodbyes. Alessia leaves Father Gabriel her mother's cell phone number, in case he'd like to reach her. He invites us to come to mass the following Sunday and reminds us to sign up for the tour.

As we get in the car, we nearly jump on each other discussing Father's horrified reaction to the Vincis.

"What the hell was that about?" Alessia says out loud, vocalizing my own thoughts.

"I don't know, but it feels like they all have some deep history together."

"It's so crazy, I literally thought he was going to faint."

"Ále, he would have warned us if we were in danger with the Vincis, right? He wouldn't just let us walk back into the lion's den?" I ask, feeling worried about returning to their home.

She furrows her eyebrows together. "No, he would never. It would totally be against his sworn morality with God. He's a priest, for God's sakes!"

"Yeah, he did seem okay once we told him our family knew."

"Not really," she disagreed. "What about that cryptic message for Aunt Amelia?"

"I know! Okay, well, we're back here now. Let's stop talking about it," I say, pulling up to the back of the Vinci house. "Let's get our things and leave. It's nearly two o'clock, everyone will be waiting for us to be home soon. Okay, sister?"

"Eli about that . . . " Alessia looks like she's sick to her stomach.

"About *nothing* babe. It stays here. That's between you and your mom. I will take your lead, if you want to say something. If not, it dies here. Okay?"

"Okay, sister." She smiles, relieved.

We walk into the kitchen. The staff seem happy to see us; they must have had an uneventful morning. We walk over to Julia, and she's making fresh bread. I slide her car keys into the pocket of her apron and thank her. She politely asks about our day and we ask about hers. I see her staring up at something above my head. I turn around and its Donatella, the Femmebot.

"Hello Donatella, how are you today?" I ask.

"You have returned much later than we expected. Everyone is waiting in the formal sitting room, please join them."

I suppose there's nothing like a girl who can dictate orders. "I'll be back in a bit to say my goodbyes," I whisper to Julia, and hurry along to catch up with Alessia and the Femmebot.

"Hey, what's up with the suits?" Alessia says with a squint. We walk into what looks like a boardroom meeting. All the men are in suits, including the Femmebot. Sophia on the other hand, looks like a very refined young lady. Her hair is pulled back in a tight ponytail. Which is strange, because she's only ever had two styles: messy, or fancy-messy. She is wearing a dark navy, long-sleeved, silk knee-length dress. It bow-ties at the neck, and buttons all the way down. It's fitted at the top and flares out past her waist. She has it paired with killer stilettos and a handbag.

"Lady, who are you!" Alessia points up and down at Sophia's outfit.

"You look hot!" I add, really excited. As I look around the room, no one is humored or smiling. There is a very uptight and uncomfortable feeling in the atmosphere.

"Did somebody die?" Alessia asks Stefano.

"No of course not, thank you for the compliments," Sophia says formally. "Mr. Vinci has offered to give me a ride back to school on his private plane. Stefano will be coming along. But I didn't want to leave without saying goodbye first."

I'm taken aback; what did we miss? She walks over to hug us. She tells us she loves us and will miss us, but she will try to visit soon. Before she lets me go, I feel her slip something into the back pocket of my jeans.

"Luca will drive you home and ensure you both arrive safely. I've notified my parents that Sophia and I are going directly to Bologna with Mr. Vinci," Stefano says, with slight sadness in his eyes. "Thank you for understanding cousin." He kisses us both on the head as they walk out.

Mr. Vinci approaches us. "It was an honor to meet you both. I've told Luca that I will return soon. I hope to see you both again for another splendid evening," he says, in his most charming voice. I begin to extend my hand to say goodbye, when I notice him partially bowing as he quickly leaves the room.

"Your personal items have been sent in advance. No need to get them. They have been delivered to your home in Umito," Donatella snaps, and then follows Mr. Vinci out.

"Luca?" I turn to him in disbelief of what I just saw.

"Not here," he replies under his breath. Just then, one of the servants enters to notify him that the car has been pulled around. I tell him I cannot leave without saying goodbye to Gian Carlo and Julia. He insists we don't have time, but I dismiss him and go anyway.

I find them in the kitchen and embrace them tightly.

"Oh, we'll miss you too Miss Eli!" Gian Carlo says in his jolly voice, as I squeeze them. I pull back and place my hands on each of their faces. "I hope to see you again someday," I say.

"Now, why wouldn't we? We're just a thirty-minute drive. Come visit us anytime," Gian Carlo winks. As I lean in to kiss them, I move my hand further back towards their ears. I only now notice that they don't feel like normal ears, they're . . . very . . . long . . . Maybe that's why they're always covering them up. Luca walks in and they pull away from me quickly.

"It's time to go, Eli," Luca insists. I wave goodbye to all the workers and thank them, as Luca rushes me out.

"What's the hurry?" I say to him, as we clear the hallway.

"Eli, please. Don't give me a hard time. Alessia is already waiting in the car." He's annoyed and not making eye contact with me; that's never a good sign.

Luca hits the road like a bat out of hell and accelerates far past anything close to a speed limit. He really must be in a rush to get us out of his way.

"I didn't see this Range Rover in the garage yesterday. It feels strong and heavy like a tank," Alessia says, trying to make small talk while bracing herself. I sense her trying to give us both some comfort in knowing that we are in a safe car, that may save our lives.

"It arrived this morning, it's custom. I had some special features added," Luca replies.

"Anything in your life not tailor-made to your silver-spoon specifications?" I say harshly, as I stare out the window. But in the reflection, I can see him squeezing the steering wheel so tightly that his knuckles turn white. He bites his tongue and doesn't respond. I don't know if I should be happy or insulted that he won't even take the time to reply. Somewhere between 9am and 2pm I must have become a real waste of time for him.

"Hey Luca, not to add to whatever is going on with you today, but I thought my cousin said you'd be getting us home safely?" Alessia says angrily, as she's being tossed around in the back seat. His driving is erratic and dangerous—these mountains have sharp curves and this behavior seems out of character for him.

"Yes Ále, I know you're right. Give me just a few more minutes." I see him looking at every road sign we pass. Just ahead there are two signs, one that indicates we are leaving Pretare with a peculiar quote I hadn't seen anywhere else. It says, "A Place Lost in Time." The other, just beyond it, has the name of the next town. The moment we clear the "Leaving Pretare" sign, he takes one last look in the rearview mirror and lets his foot off the gas pedal. The look on his face is instant relief. I can see the muscles in his face begin to relax. We all let out a deep sigh.

"Thank you Baby Jesus!" Alessia does the sign of the cross on herself. Then without hesitation she lays into him.

"WHAT was that about Luca! Do you plan on racing this thing in Formula One? Believe me, we are not the right passengers to try that out on! Seriously, that was so scary! What were you thinking! Why did you do that? Are you insane? PULL

OVER!" She has a tendency to rage on people when she keeps her anger in for too long. Alessia repeatedly yells at him to pull over, until he finally does at the nearest gas station.

She gets out of the car and slams the door. I watch her walk into the restaurant nearby and see her order a beer. I would have followed her in, but I know her, and I know she wants to be very far from the both of us at this moment. The restaurant is al fresco; I am able to see in and have a direct view of her sitting at the bar. Luca and I slouch in silence as we watch her slam down the first beer in sixty seconds. She then orders another. And another.

"Are you going to tell me what this is about? Your twenty-four hours are up," I finally ask.

"The silver spoon in my mouth doesn't seem to permit me to," he replies sharply, looking away. I must admit I did not think he was the kind of man to go back on his word. Looks like he is typical after all.

Silence. Again.

More silence.

After nearly an hour of watching her drink beer, eat an appetizer and flirt with the bartender, Alessia finally gets back in the car. She is calmer, more relaxed and a bit drunk.

"So, did you guys work out this gnarly shit between the two of you? Because I can cut the tension with a knife," she pauses, licks the tip of her finger and holds it up in the air. "Nope. Still there!" then kicks the back of the seats. "Ugh, you assholes didn't speak at all did you!?!"

Luca shifts his body to face her. "Ále, I'm so sorry I scared you. I would never do it intentionally, please accept my apology."

"IDIOTS," she slurs back at both of us. "I mean seriously, can't the two of you just figure it out already?" What does she mean? Figure what out?

"Dang, did you see that eyebrow go up?" she points at Luca to look in my direction. "Now we're both in trouble!"

"Yes, that eyebrow has been glaring at me for an hour," he replies to humor her.

"See, now you're funny! I like it when you're funny. But I don't think you should wear suits anymore. They make you all . . . Jason Statham, like, serious Transporter and shit—you know?" she laughs and taps him on the head. "It's not sexy . . . well it is sexy when he does it. And it's sexy when you do it too, but you're my brother now so, it's just weird—you know? Just don't do it."

They have both just stepped on my nerves. I get out of the car and I hear them both start up with, "where is *she* going now!" and "aw you effed up boy, she's gonna let you have it now!" I walk around to the driver's side, open the door, and start shoving and kicking Luca to the passenger's side. I admit he's completely solid; it is not an easy task.

"How are you so freakishly strong?" he asks me, astonished. I don't bother to reply. I strap on my seatbelt, start the car and drive nonstop until we are home. In silence.

*   *   *

As we walk into the house, I notice that per usual, several people and other family are visiting. I'm just not in the mood for this today. My mom sees me and runs to hold me tightly; it feels like she's never going to let go.

"It was only two days mom, take it easy," I say to her, trying to get some space. "I'm going upstairs to see Nonna."

I hear my mother speaking to Alessia and Luca, asking them why I'm upset and what happened. She quickly realizes Alessia is drunk. As I walk upstairs, I see her pulling Luca outside from the corner of my eye. But I'm just too drained to even care what that's about.

I knock softly on my grandmother's bedroom door and let myself in. I see the nurse putting a small pillow behind my grandmother's back to make her comfortable in her chair. She is a sight for sore eyes.

"Hello, my love, I saw the car coming up the hill and I thought it would be nice to get out of bed and have a cup of tea together," she says to me. It's that beautiful voice that makes me feel like I'm home. She has her favorite tea pot and teacups out just waiting to be poured. I kiss her hand.

"Too many people downstairs for you?" she asks.

"Yes, you know me well. Don't get me wrong, I love that they come to visit you. I'm just so drained and exhausted, it's hard for me to be social and function when I feel this way. But this, here with you, is perfect and exactly what I need."

I can see the nurse has been staring at me obsessively since I walked in. It's so obvious my grandmother asks her to step out, she can see it's making me uncomfortable.

"I'm sorry about that," she says to me with a gentle smile.

"It's okay, I've been getting it a lot these last few days. That's another reason I don't want to see anyone. They'll all think I changed my face at a plastic surgeon's office in Beverly Hills," I take a sip of tea. "I'm keenly aware that somehow, I've managed to look exactly like you. And her." We both take a moment to look at a photograph she has on the dresser of her and Nonna Rosa. They were so young.

"I don't know how this is possible, Nonna. There is no scientific explanation. But I also don't know if I'm ready to hear the reason from you today. It's been a very long weekend."

"Do you want to tell me about it?" she asks.

"Yes, I'd love to. But only if you promise to tell me *your* entire story. And no leaving out details." She smiles knowing exactly what I mean. "You don't have to do it tonight, but you have to do it soon. Very soon."

"That sounds like a fair trade," she agrees.

The next four hours are filled with every detail of my weekend over tea and cookies. As I'm telling her about my adventure, I notice a light in her eyes I haven't seen in years. It gives me the energy I need to tell her everything, and not to leave anything out. She laughs, cries, worries, and laughs again. By the end of the four hours, I hardly have a voice left to speak with.

"You get that from Rosa. When she was exhausted or stressed, she would lose her voice," she says softly. "Let's call it a night. We'll talk more about these blackouts of yours tomorrow."

I agree, I don't know how much longer I can keep my eyes open. I thank her for the tea, kiss her goodnight and tell her I love her. But before I walk out, I remember Father Gabriel's message. She remains quiet and nods her head in understanding. She looks pleased by his message.

I call the nurse back in, and as she enters the room, she continues to stare. I go into my bedroom, kick off my shoes and lay down in bed. I don't even have the energy to put my pajamas on. I focus on the burning wick of the strange candle as I fall asleep.

Chapter 9

6:00 AM—the clock reads as I open my eyes. I get out of bed and stretch, I'm still in yesterday's clothes. I put on my robe, make myself a cup of coffee, and get ready for the day. Everyone is still asleep; it's so nice to have peace and quiet in the morning here. The serenity of Umito is very healing and rejuvenating. Knowing my family, I'm sure no one got any rest while we were out. It's good to know they got some last night.

I think I want to surprise everyone with fresh pastries this morning. It will be my way of making up for my terrible mood yesterday. I go into the pockets of the pants I was wearing yesterday for cash, and I remember Sophia slipping something in my pocket. I open the tightly folded paper—there is a phone number I don't recognize written in Sophia's penmanship. I take the cash and my cell phone and head out the door. The moment I turn the corner at the bottom of the hill—where I'm sure no one will hear me—I dial the number and someone picks up.

"Eli."

"Sophia?"

"Perfect timing."

"How are you even awake? Do you have an early class?"

"No, I haven't gone to bed yet."

"What's going on with the secret number and no sleeping? What are you up to?" I ask, not knowing whether I should be worried.

"Look, I don't have too much time to answer all your questions right now, but I will," she says, as I hear her walking through the city. "This is a burner phone I got last year to use with my ex-boyfriend."

"What? You had a boyfriend?"

"Not really the point Eli, but yes, I didn't want my family to know, so I got a separate line just for him."

"Who was this guy?"

"*Not* important."

"Okay, so what is it? You're freaking me out. Why can't we talk on your regular cell phone?"

"Because it's being tapped. It's part of my contract. But I think it's only a matter of time before yours is too, maybe even today. Have you heard any clicking and tapping during this call?"

"No, I don't think so."

"I need you to get a burner phone and then call me back on this line. *Hurry.* I'll explain everything in detail then. Just trust me."

Dial tone.

"Okay then . . . " I say out loud to myself in disbelief. A few minutes later I arrive at the pastry shop and run a few other errands while I am in the area, including purchasing a burner cell. I call Sophia back as I shove a fresh croissant in my mouth. I've been craving them for days; I can't even wait to get home. The crème beignets are next. There is nothing like Italian pastries, they're heavenly!

"You took long enough," Sophia answers.

"Are you kidding, that was so fast! You're lucky they even had any phones!" I reply with a full mouth.

"It's a little after seven am, hmm . . . let me guess, beignets?!" she's laughing.

"Croissant. Those are next," I say, still chomping away.

"Leave some for Nonna, you know how much she loves those."

"Yeah," I reply as I take another bite. "Well? Do you want me to die in suspense?"

"Eli, walk down to the stream that we used to go to as kids." She's back to her serious tone. "Do not reply to anything I'm saying until you are there and alone. And turn off your regular cell phone."

"Why?"

"It has a microphone." She's not typically a paranoid person, so this level of discretion surprises me.

"Okay, walking there now." The stream is just a few blocks from my grandmother's house. It was once used for fishing, but no one goes there anymore.

"Eli, I need you to stay calm. Promise me," she says.

"I promise. But you're making me nervous."

"I'm sorry, but there's no other way. I wish I could do this in person."

"I'm off the main street now, Sophia. No one can see or hear me now. I'll be at the stream in ten minutes," I reassure her.

"I don't know if I just made a deal with a god or the devil," she begins. "Everything that I'm telling you cannot be repeated. There are severe consequences for me, should it come out that I've shared this with anyone. Tell me you understand."

"Yes, completely."

"Eli, I've just become a member of the Masonry." I nearly choke on my croissant and spit out whatever is left in my mouth. Not my most graceful moment.

"As in the *Freemasons?*" I shout, "I thought that was only a fraternity? How is that possible?"

"Well, there is a public sector that is. That's the one you know about, the one most people have heard of. And from what I gather, they serve their purpose." She takes a deep breath, "I am an apprentice for the Masons that . . . have only been known as a myth. Like the ones that hold secrets and stuff."

"And stuff? They are not real!"

"They are, and so much more than you can imagine," she gives me a moment to take that in. "The Mason Library is where all the world's treasures and universal secrets are kept. There are both men and women members, but mostly men. Are you ready for the biggest surprise of all? The leader of the organization is *Victoria*. As in Victoria Vinci, who is actually VICTORIA MASON!"

"Victoria . . . as in Luca's stepmom?!" A light bulb goes off in my mind.

"Yes! It's ALL named after Victoria and her family. Actually, the entire organization serves her! Eli, there are millions of members worldwide, and all these men just serve her. So badass!" She squeaks and continues, "I guess that's where the fraternity part comes in, something about men serve and women create. I'm not totally sure about the details, I'm still learning. I've only been here twenty-four hours. But there are several degrees and levels here. It's quite complicated."

I want to ask more questions about the organization, but my mind wanders to Luca's stepmom.

"Did you meet her? What is she like?"

"Yes, and she's everything I want to be. She's totally brilliant! I can't even put her into words!" I could hear the excitement in her voice. "She knew exactly who I was, she said she chose me! Mr. Vinci made it sound like it was him doing me the favor, but it was actually her making the decision all along. Eli, do you remember how Micella said they haven't added a new member to the library in a millennium?"

"Yes."

"Well it wasn't just a figure of speech. I signed a guest book when I entered the library yesterday. Member one-hundred signed and dated the book over a thousand years ago! I am signature one-hundred-and-one. Anyone 'new' is not really a new member; it's just inherited from one generation to the next."

"So, you're literally the only new, non-inherited member in a thousand years. How did she . . . they, decide who's worthy?"

"That's a very good question. I'll put that on my list of things to ask. Here's the weird thing . . . "

"It gets weirder?" I can't imagine.

"Well, yes. Some of the exclusive one hundred members I am a part of are . . . they're, umm, different."

"How?"

"They are . . . ancient . . . several of them . . . we may have seen them in our history books . . . "

"May have seen them in our history books? What the hell are you talking about, Sophia!"

"Yeah, I'm still trying to figure all that out," she stops herself. "My point is, if I can figure out what's happening to you, it is *here*, Eli! I have all the resources I need to find out why, and how, it's even possible for you to physically change."

"I suppose that makes sense. I mean, if it's possible for any of this to make sense."

"Have you had any new symptoms or changes since I saw you yesterday?"

"Nothing dramatic, just minor changes every day."

"I don't know why or how I got chosen for this, but I feel like it's connected to you somehow, Eli. And I'm going to get to the bottom of it."

"Thank you, Sophia. But if these people are really this power-ful and this connected, there's a good chance they are also dan-gerous. DO NOT put yourself in jeopardy for me."

"Stefano is here with me, I'm not alone. I feel safe with him around," she assures me.

"Does he know?"

"Yes, the organization has hired him on as their legal advisor and council. They needed someone new to oversee their con-tracts and deals. I'm pretty sure he's going to be a billionaire by next year. You would die if you knew who some of these members actually are," she says squeamishly. "Anyway, they said because of who our family is, we are best suited for these positions."

"Who *is* our family, Sophia?" I ask, slightly afraid to know.

"I'll need you to figure that out, Eli. They are really tight lipped about those details around here."

"Ok, I'll do my best."

"I won't be able to speak often. They expect Stefano and I to catch up quickly. I'll call you, same time a week from today. If you have an emergency, text me. I'll be checking the phone periodically." She adds hurriedly, "Eli, they know and hear ev-erything. Watch what you say and who you say it to. If you need to have a personal conversation, go out into an open field. Be careful. I love you."

"I love you too."

Click.

I don't know how I'm supposed to go on with my day knowing what I just found out and acting like everything is normal. I turn my burner cell off and my regular phone back on. There's al-ready a text message from my mom wondering where I am. And all the pastries are now cold. I make my way back up to the main road. At a near distance, I see someone hiking; he looks familiar. Ah yes, it's the man from the cabin that showed me the short cut down the mountain.

"Good morning sir, nice to see you again," I say, as he walks towards me. He is wearing jeans, a hat, and a red flannel shirt. He's using a tall walking stick with several different stones and rocks around the head of it.

"Good morning to you as well! How do you do?" he says, as we shake hands.

"We didn't have a chance for introductions the other day; I'm Eli."

"Nice to meet you Eli, I'm Dwintra."

"That's a unique name, I've never heard it before."

"It means 'Walkers in the Trees'."

"Then it suits you perfectly, Mr. Dwintra."

"I suppose I know my way around a forest," he replies humbly. We proceed on with polite conversation about his love of nature and many expeditions over the years. As he's speaking, I notice one of the stones in his walking stick looks familiar. It's the same color gold in the painting, and on Micella's necklace.

"Sorry, where did you say you were from?" I interrupt him. I can see I've caught him off guard.

"Oh, it's a town quite far from here. I'm sure you've never heard of it, very small really. But I like to think of myself as a citizen of the world." I can tell he's trying to avoid answering the question, and I don't want to pry. "I've had my cabin here since I can remember, it's one of my favorite places. I've known your grandmother Amelia almost all of my life. I hear she's taken a turn for the worse, I am sorry to hear that."

"How do you know Amelia is my grandmother?" I ask, taken aback.

"The resemblance is utterly undeniable," he says smiling. "I'd heard through town gossip that Amelia and Rosa's granddaughter is here visiting. They also mentioned that you are a spitting image of them, and I can see with my own eyes that certainly is true. Please accept it as my highest compliment, they've always been exceptional women."

"Thank you." I'm not surprised to hear that he's known them. They're beloved by everyone. And at one point or another, they helped heal and serve most people in this province.

"Actually, I should be getting back to Nonna. I've been out longer than I expected this morning."

"Yes, I understand," he says, "but before you go, allow me to give you something." I watch him remove a stone off his walking stick. As he holds it in the palm of his hand, I can see the small stone's vibrant shades of purples, greens, and blues.

"Please accept this as a gift." As he places it in my hand, there's a kind of warmth to it. "It's called a Halledrite crystal. The ancient people used it both for communication and to block it. If you hold it tightly and think of someone, they will come to you. But if you simply wear it on your body, it causes interference. Blocking others from hearing your thoughts or listening to what you are saying."

"If it does all that, are you sure you want to give it to me? I'm sure you can make a lot of money selling it on the black market," I respond, feeling humored by this stone. Dwintra on the other hand, does not find me funny; he stands there looking at me quite seriously.

"Sorry," I reply, realizing that he was kind enough to give me a gift and I made fun of it. "It is very beautiful, thank you. I didn't mean to come across as ungrateful. All my life I've heard of crystals and stones having special powers, but I've never seen them accomplish anything."

"You are cynical?" he asks, shocked.

"If you mean that . . . I think magic and faerie tales are nonsense and a ridiculous waste of time, then yes, I'm cynical."

"Well, that is quite the irony!" He leans back and lets out a boisterous laugh. "The grandchild of Rosa and Amelia does not believe in magic."

"I'm not sure how that's ironic." I've suddenly become the serious one. "But no, I do not. I don't read silly books about magical creatures in magical realms or watch sci-fi films. I prefer historical facts and non-fictional stories about real people that did extraordinary things."

"Ha! Isn't that the kicker!" He seems very humored with himself. "What does your mother say about this?"

"She seems pleased about my lack of imagination," I reply sarcastically as I put the stone in my pocket. "I really must go."

"Yes of course. Your pastries must be cold; here, let me warm those up for you." Before I can reply, he takes another stone off his stick and lays it on top of the box. Within a moment, I can feel the warmth of the pastries in the palm of my hand that's holding the box. I stand there in shock, not knowing what to say. He puts the stone back on his stick and tilts his hat slightly forward in gesture of his leaving.

"Good day Miss Eli, say hello to Amelia for me. I'm sure we'll meet again," he says, as he walks past and away from where I'm standing. I look back at him. "Better get back, before they get cold again!" he shouts.

I stare down at the box, but I can't deny it; I feel the warmth in my hands. I replay the image over and over again in my mind the entire way back to the house. I don't know what to make of him, his gift, or what just happened.

*   *   *

I walk into the house at half past eight. Everyone is awake and in their robes having coffee. They are all delighted to have fresh pastries. My mother kisses me and thanks me for my thoughtfulness. I'll take that as a sign that she's forgiven my rudeness from the day before. I look over at Alessia; she's sitting in my grandfather's old lazy chair, wearing dark sunglasses with a blanket over most of her body. She is directing me not to speak to her with flaccid hand gestures. And she looks exactly as you'd imagine someone would after three days of being drunk—a total mess. Aunt Silva, in between bites, brings to our attention all of the clothes, shoes, handbags, and accessories delivered yesterday by a moving truck, just as Donatella mentioned. In my exhaustion, I'd completely forgotten about it. Apparently Micella was so generous with the number of things she sent over, they had to move items into the shed just to get everything to fit. Aunt Silva not so subtly hints that it would be a total waste if they are not enjoyed. Which translates to the fact that she's already picked out items she wants for herself. She says the racks are divided and separated by our names. This surprises me; I can't imagine any of those items are for me. I hadn't picked anything out. Although I still have the outfit she let me borrow yesterday, I had every intention of returning it.

Alessia threatens Aunt Silva's life from underneath the blankets, if she touches anything on the racks with her name. I, on the other hand, have no interest, and tell Aunt Silva she is welcome to take anything that has my name on it. Her eyes sparkle, and just for that moment I can imagine what she was like as a child. She throws her arms around me and shouts out that I am her favorite niece; which I'm sure she's only saying out of spite for Alessia's rudeness. She doesn't waste one moment, possibly for fear that I might change my mind. She kisses me on the forehead, and rushes into the garage to retrieve her coveted items.

My mother later tells me she had hoped I'd say that, because Silva had things picked out from the day before. Everyone is in awe of Micella's generosity and kindness. They ask lots of questions about her, and what she is like. Alessia and I gush about her, and all her magnanimousness.

Uncle Gianni changes the conversation in order to boast about his children. He says he is thrilled that Sophia is back at school, and how proud he is about Stefano's new position with the "Mason Group." I can't help but wonder if he knows the truth; I'm not sure I even know what that is these days. By the way he's speaking, I would bet that he doesn't. On the other hand, based on the expression on my mother's face, I would bet that *she does*. I wonder how he would take it if he knew that our sweet Sophia was the newest member of the Mason Library. More importantly, what would he say about her having boyfriends he never knew about. At this point, I just don't know what he would be more outraged about.

In between conversations, I take a seat next to Aunt Ersella. She puts her arm over me, leans me in toward her chest, and gives me a tight squeeze. In her usual form, she wastes no time and lectures me about "allowing" Alessia to drink so much, and how I must be a better influence over her. As if anyone could influence or control her daughter. I quickly distract her by mentioning her old friend Father Gabriel. She tells me she had spoken to him last night and was very happy we had the opportunity to spend time with him. She then quietly whispers in my ear how grateful she is that I am willing to keep their "little secret," and how Alessia could not have a better sister in life.

Having her say that makes me somehow feel less alone in this big world. Loneliness is something I've struggled with since I can remember. Not because I grew up alone as an only child; there were always plenty of friends and family around. It feels more like . . . something I inherited. I suppose some people inherit the color of their mother's eyes or their father's laugh. For me, it's loneliness, and the same kind that I see in my mother's and grandmother's eyes.

My mother hands me a tray with a beignet and tea to bring up to my grandmother's room. Nonna isn't supposed to eat sweets, so she tells me to hurry before the day nurse arrives. It is like fireworks on the Fourth of July when she sees me with her favorite treat. She has me sit at the edge of the bed near her feet with my legs crossed, just like I used to as a child. She asks me about my morning; I mention that I had spoken to Sophia, and that she sends her love, and I that ran into Dwintra near the stream. I explain to her that he is the same person that helped me find the shortcut down the mountain. She seems very happy that he had been so kind to me. She says that he is an expert at all things wilderness, and that he also saved her many times over the years. I can tell that she is very fond of him. I pull the stone he gave me out of my pocket and place it on the tray sitting across her legs. She looks up at me bewildered and asks me where I got it. At the same moment Aunt Ersella comes into the bedroom, eyes wide open, and looking very inquisitive.

"Everything okay, sister?" she asks.

"Ersella, come closer please," Nonna says. My grandmother gestures with her eyes to look at the stone sitting next to her teacup.

"Child, where did you find this?" Aunt Ersella asks me, as she clutches one of her many necklaces. "It is a very ancient stone, impossible to find."

Looks like Dwintra wasn't fibbing about that after all.

"Dwintra gave it to her," Nonna says calmly, before I can answer. "Seems that he has helped Eli recently."

Aunt Ersella's expression softens.

"Well, that's very good. I didn't know he was back in town," she says.

"You must invite him for tea, Ersella," Nonna requests.

"Yes, wonderful suggestion," Aunt Ersella replies.

"Nonna, how did you know Dwintra gave it to me? I didn't tell you that," I ask.

"That's because many years ago, he gave us one too," she says, then gestures to Aunt Ersella to let go of her necklace. And there it is, the same stone hanging around her neck. I've never noticed it before. I suppose it's not easy with all the layers of jewelry she wears. She has the stone placed in a beautiful pendant. It is in the center of an ornate design of silver leaves and branches that intertwine.

"I'm sure he told you what it was for?" Aunt Ersella asks.

"He did, but is it actually true? Does it work? Because you know, I don't believe in that kind of thing."

"Yes, it does work, Eli. I will take it to our family jeweler this afternoon, and have it set in a pendant," she says picking it up. "It's important that you wear it for the remainder of the time you are in Italy. OKAY?" she says forcefully.

"Okay," I reply to her reluctantly, "I'll do it if it means that much to you."

"It would mean that much to *me*," my grandmother interjects. Boy, she really knows my weak spots. I agree to her wishes.

"Now, onto important things," my grandmother says after taking a sip of tea. "Tell Ersella and I about these blackouts you've been having."

"I'm not really sure what to say about it, other than I've never had them before. It's like one minute I feel either sleepy or tipsy, and then I'm completely out. It's really strange."

"Yes, I couldn't agree more," Nonna replies.

"Amelia, what would cause this? You are the medical expert

and healer in this family," Aunt Ersella asks.

"And you Ersella, are you not the singing-potion-maker of this family?" she replies in a witty tone. Allegedly, my aunt sings as she puts together natural remedies she calls "potions."

"Now that just isn't fair, we both know my gifts have limits," she answers, annoyed with her sister.

"I have a solution! How about you both work together?" I say crisscrossing my index fingers at one other. "Sounds like a task 'The Healer' and the 'Singing Potion Maker' can certainly conquer."

"What are you saying, that my potions are no good, Eli?"

"NO Auntie, of course not. But I would refer to them as remedies, not potions. That's a little voodoo-ish."

"There is an irony to this conversation. Don't you agree sister?" Aunt Ersella says, with one eyebrow lifted.

"Yes, quite."

"Dwintra used the same word in almost the same context today. What are you trying to say?" I ask the both of them.

"It means that just because you do not believe, does not make it untrue," my grandmother replies to me softly.

"How did you turn out to be such an *Igni?*" my aunt asks, as they both giggle like children.

"What does that mean?"

"It is a word we made up as children for mortals who do not believe magic exists," my grandmother answers.

"Mortals?" I say dryly. "Very mature Aunt Ersella."

"Well, it's true!" she says, nodding her head. "I've never met anyone so . . . so . . . against magic!"

"This again?" I roll my eyes. She loves to bring this up.

"You would think between Disneyland and Hollywood she would believe in something other than non-fiction," Aunt Ersella continues.

"That's precisely why she doesn't. I think that was the point of her mother taking her there. When you see how it's made, it's hard to believe in the fantasy," Nonna replies.

"Wow, okay, lots of theories, ladies!" I say, shaking my head. "Why do you care so much anyway? It's so silly."

They look at each other silently. My grandmother shakes her head "no" at my Aunt. This is not new to me; they've had their own secret code and language since I can remember. It's like playing charades without using your hands or body. Not very exciting for those not included.

"Per usual, this has been fun, and I am no more educated than I was before this stimulating conversation."

"Eli, please go easy on Luca. He is a good man, he only wants to do right by you," Nonna says to me, taking a hold of my hand as I get off the bed.

"How do you know him?" I ask surprised at hearing his name. I haven't thought of him since yesterday.

"I delivered him. I know a good soul when I see one." She smiles. I don't know how to respond. She's never been wrong about a person's character before. But I just don't know how to feel. I don't think I can trust him again; he's lied and broken his first and last promise to me.

"Give us a few days Eli, we will try to figure out what's really going on with your blackouts," Aunt Ersella says to comfort me. "In the meantime, why don't you take your cousin on that tour Father Gabriel suggested."

I welcome the distraction, but I don't understand why Alessia and I are being so encouraged to take an all-day church tour. I'm not sure if they just want to get us out of the house for a day, or if they are trying to wash their hands of telling us what's really going on. I was prepared to end this conversation on a good note, but I think now is a good time as any to bring IT up.

"Yes, there's the blacking out, but what about the fact that I'm physically changing? Why isn't anyone talking about that, because it is kind of a big deal. Everyone I know looks at me like I'm some kind of science experiment. They would never say anything, but even our own family is perplexed by it," I say with a heavy sigh, as my mother walks into the room.

"When will you finally explain to me what's going on? It's happening to *me* and yet *I'm* the only person not privy to the truth."

My Aunt Ersella proceeds to tell me how right I am and how unjust this may all seem. That there is no intention to keep me in the dark, but that there are a few things they need the answers to first. They seem overwhelmed—judging by the expressions across their faces—and I can tell Aunt Ersella is being sincere. But that doesn't change the fact that this has been going on much too long. I've been promised since the day I arrived that they would explain everything, but it's just been more riddles and stories that make no sense.

"Okay, I get that, but what about your personal stories? Why can't you just tell me those? That seems so basic!" I can feel the frustration I've had buried for too long finally rise. "I don't know what kind of hold you have on people, but everyone refuses to spill your secrets. It's like they have made some kind of sacred vow, and if they don't obey, they will face God's wrath! This is insane, someone speak up!"

"Please Eli, don't be angry with me," Nonna says quietly.

Tears start to pour out of my eyes uncontrollably. "Look at me! All of you, look at me! How is it possible that Nonna and I are both . . . *changing* in almost the same way," I cry out. "WHO am I? And WHO are all these strange new people who I've never met before, that consider you all friends? What the hell is going on!"

My grandmother starts to cry and Aunt Ersella walks over to comfort her.

"Eli, you are my daughter. I love you so much. I'm so sorry, I didn't realize how upset . . . how much pain you are feeling. You're always so good at hiding your emotions," my mother says as she throws her arms around me. "No one thinks you're a science experiment. We may not have told you, but we have been working night and day to figure it out. We just wanted to do everything we could to keep things as normal as possible. I didn't do a good enough job. I've failed you, I'm SO sorry!"

"My beautiful girl come here," my grandmother says, wiping her tears with an old handkerchief that belonged to my grandfather. "This is my fault; your mother has nothing to apologize for. But, we . . . we didn't know. How could we? And now we must make sense of the *why*. I know this is all just more riddles to you, but I ask that you trust me just for a little longer. I promise to tell you every detail and answer every question, in time. I know I don't deserve your patience and love, but I am asking for it. Can you do that please, my love?"

I take a moment to stop my sobbing and compose myself. I walk over to her, get on my knees, and lay my head in her lap. I love her more than life itself and I hate that I've allowed anything I said to hurt her. I fear disappointing her, but I fear losing her even more.

"Yes of course. I'm sorry I allowed my emotions to get the better of me," I say to her.

"I am in awe of you. No one else I know could be as brave and strong as you are. I will never abandon you Eli, I just need a little more time," Nonna Amelia says, caressing my head. "You have nothing to be afraid of, Eli. I know it is jarring, but you are okay. You need not be concerned with the state of your health or well-being. Okay?"

"Okay."

Over the next several days, Alessia and I hibernate and recover from what seems like the longest weekend of our lives. We don't talk about the Vincis or Pretare once. For a moment, things feel as if they're going back to normal. No calls from Sophia, no visits from Luca, no dramatic physical changes and no blackouts. We sleep, go for walks, eat lots of amazing food and spend time with our friends. I almost forget how sick my grandmother actually is; she seems to have more energy these days. She and Aunt Ersella have been actively researching what could be causing my condition. I've been secretly doing my own research through old books at the library and online. I can't help myself; I want to read about all these silly and mysterious stories and see what they're really about. But I'm not getting anywhere, there's little to no documented literature, just small fragments and side notes about legends.

My grandmother has my mother bring down her old books from the attic. I am not able to understand any of them, as they're in a foreign language I can't read. When I ask her what language it is, she says it is an ancient one passed on by the elders before her. It makes me sad to think that there will be no one left that can read it once she is gone, other than my aunt Ersella. Maybe I can talk Auntie into teaching me one day. The pictures are strange and don't make any sense; there are various lines that create shapes I don't recognize. Along the sides of the drawings are numbers, almost like mathematical equations. It gives me relief that there is so much interest in finding answers on my behalf. Between Sophia, my grandmother, my aunt, and my mother, I know I'm in good hands; but I still can't shake this unsettling feeling.

Chapter 10

"SO, WHAT ARE WE DOING to celebrate your birthday? It's a big one! And you're finally going to celebrate it here, with all of us in Italy!" Alessia overly-enthusiastically says, as we are driving to Montegallo. The pick-up for the Seven Church Tour is stationed there.

"Well, it's still a couple of weeks away. A lot can happen in two weeks, let's just wait and see," I reply un-enthusiastically, as it's eight AM and much too early for her excitable energy.

"I suppose you're right," she says, with no less bounce in her step.

"I don't think it's a good idea to plan a party with Nonna the way she is."

"But you're going to be the big 2-5! We can't just do *nothing* either."

"Is it *really* a big deal, Ále? Does anything *really* change?"

"It IS a big deal! I mean, initially it doesn't seem like it does. And then one day you realize that all the brainwashing your parents did, actually worked." I wasn't sure what she was getting at, I must have looked confused because she went on to further explain, "What I mean is, you actually do all the things you're supposed to do . . . " Ále then lays out a laundry list full of things that our parents would nag us about for the rest of the drive. From getting to places on time, to remembering to pay bills before they are due, and always using our manners. Although she is only two years older than me, I admit, she has become more responsible and dependable in the last few years. So maybe I should pay attention to her sound advice.

The conversation makes the drive pass quickly, and before I know it, we have arrived. We park in a designated area of the local travel agency to pick up our tour tickets. Ále and I are both relieved to see that we will be taking the newer bus, which means it will have both air conditioning and a bathroom. Which is very important when on a nine-hour tour. We agreed on the premium tickets because they include unlimited beverages, snacks, and a picnic lunch. We were just too lazy to pack our own lunches this morning.

Our bus is mostly filled with tourists, and to my surprise, it's quite full. I recognize at least one American English-speaking family. They are sitting in the seats to the left of us. It's a couple with their two teenage kids, a boy and a girl. Alessia already has her eye on a handsome English lad traveling alone. She spotted him before we even got on the bus. She's had a thing for English boys and their accents ever since she spent a few years studying in England. She left a string of broken hearts in London. Those poor boys, they had no idea what hit them. I'm sure that is not what my aunt had in mind when she told her to pick a major.

The tourists on the bus are predominantly from France, Switzerland, Germany, Poland, and Spain. Other than the tour guide and driver, I think Alessia is the only native. Our tour guide is a darling woman named Eden. She's in her late fifties, has lived here all her life, and is extremely knowledgeable about all things regarding Italian history. I'm impressed at how well her voice is projecting considering her very petite 5' 1" stature. She has brown eyes, and her brown hair is cut into a chic bob. Her style is more conservative, but very refined. She speaks several languages, and may I add, quite exceptionally; she is very polite and diplomatic in her descriptions. The tour is in Italian, and most of the tourists are using digital headphones for translation, but she informs us that she would be happy to take questions in any language she speaks. We are promptly off at nine o'clock, which is rare, considering Italians are notorious for doing things on their own time.

The Tour of The Seven Churches is dedicated to the Virgin Mary, as are the churches themselves. It became popular after a theory surfaced by an Italian researcher. She discovered that by hypothetically linking the seven churches located in the Sibillini mountains, they mirror the exact position of the stars in the Virgo constellation. They are both divinatory figures, so I suppose there is a syncretism between the two: Mary as the "Virgin" mother of Jesus, and Virgo the "Virgin" carrying wheat and the scales of justice.

I love history, science, and old churches; for someone like me, it's as close to a perfect day as it can get.

Our first stop is the Church of Santa Maria in Pantano. It is about a ten–minute drive from Montegallo's center. The tour is not designed around the way the stars are connected, but by the most convenient way for travel. They call this church the "Spica," which is known to be the central star of the Virgo constellation. On our way there, Eden shares some information about how these churches were constructed: "It is believed that these churches were built by the Soldiers of Christ and of the Temple of Solomon, eventually known as the Knights Templar. As legend would have it, this unique destiny between the Virgin

Mary and Virgo exists because the churches were built over meaningful pagan temples or sites. This was a common practice for the Knights Templar. They were the wealthiest and most powerful Christian military order in the west. They existed for over two centuries."

As she's telling the story, she pulls mini champagne bottles out of a bag, and hands them to each adult on the bus. Once she makes her way back up to the front she asks, "Who likes champagne?!" and pops her little bottle open. We all cheer and join in as we open our own.

Eden continues, "The Knights were started in 1119 by a French nobleman by the name of Hugues de Payens from the Champagne region! He collected eight of his knights and started on a mission to protect pilgrims on their visits to holy places. King Baldwin II of Jerusalem permitted them to set up their headquarters on the Temple Mount, which is assumed to be the site of Solomon's Temple. For nine years they did so peacefully. But as time went on, the Knights became very well known throughout Europe. They fundraised and asked for donations of money, land, or for noblemen's sons to join the order. The implication of these donations was that they would be defending Jerusalem and ensuring the donors' place in Heaven. If only that were true, right everyone?" She lifts up her mini bottle and toasts. "The donations became considerable, and over time they were able to create a three-class, impenetrable infrastructure. They considered themselves warrior monks, which was an extremely powerful combination. They justified war on anyone that wasn't Christian, by saying they were defending the innocent and protecting the Church against violence. Initiation meant swearing to religious vows of obedience, chastity, and poverty. They represented the common class, so individual knights were not permitted to have wealth, land, or even receive something as simple as private letters. This is very important, because the Knights Templar single-handedly destroyed artifacts, books, art, buildings, temples, and anything having to do with knowledge of life before Christianity. Which also means they mercilessly destroyed history and achievements throughout Europe. Pagan life threatened the existence of Christianity, and therefore the Knights cruelly spent more than two hundred years obliterating anything the Church did *not* want us to know, and what they *did* want people to forget. There will be many things that seem un-explainable on this tour. You will see Paganism and Christianity sitting at a crossroads facing one another until the end of time. This is the magic of our story today," Eden says.

Her words shake something deep inside me, I had never imagined that. It gives me great sadness that there are so many things we will never know. I know our history is incomplete, but this takes it to another level for me. An Order destroying the remnants of a pagan world, and our recorded history, all in the name of God. It all seems like the opposite of anything He would want. I don't know Him to know that for sure, but I feel it.

"Andre, hurry and finish your champagne so we don't get left behind," the Polish girl in front of me says to her husband, an American. They are a very cute and stylish young couple. She is wearing a loose floral dress with her hair in a topknot; she has bright blue eyes and a beautiful profile. Her tall, dark, and handsome husband is a cool-looking rocker type.

"Hi! I'm Eli, I couldn't help but notice you speak English," I say, as I extend my hand to meet them.

"Thank GOD!" she says, and she is as beautiful as her profile. "I'm so happy to meet a young, English-speaking person on this tour! I thought it was going to be a bunch of old people. I'm Mika!"

The four of us introduce ourselves. They are both very energetic and have a great sense of humor. They explain to us that they live in Pasadena, California, but that they're here on their honeymoon. They've just come from celebrating their second wedding in Poland with her family. We make small talk about how close we live to one another, hang out in each other's cities, but have never seen one another. People say it's a small world, but if that's true, then Los Angeles is its labyrinth.

"Does anyone know what Pantano means?" Eden asks, but no one replies. "It is the Italian word for 'marsh.' This area is known for their luxuriant sources of natural spring water," she continues on.

"Noticeably, the Church of Santa Maria in Pantano does not sit in a village like most churches. Instead, it is isolated and fused between a pine forest and the bottom slopes of the Sibillini mountains. There are no major roads that lead up to it. So, I hope you've all brought your comfortable shoes today. As noted on the website, we have at least a thirty-minute walk from where we are about to park, to the church."

The roads are narrow and mostly made of gravel and grass. The bus pulls into a designated area and we all set foot on a dirt road. As we begin to walk deeper into a grassy plain, things begin to look like a painting from the childhood storybooks I used to read. The grass is emerald green, and the luscious trees are in such abundance, that even the sun has to work hard to pierce through. I can hear the sounds of the streams coming down from every direction. Hearing the birds chirp and watching the lizards climb up the trees gives me a feeling of peace, just as I feel in the forest of Umito. The air gets cooler as we walk further into the woods, until we break into an open plain once again. Just further ahead I can see one of the streams that echoed into the woods just moments ago. I begin to look around and notice there are several more streams weaving through the plain, and some going directly into the woods. Eden tells us the spring water comes from the highest peak of the Sibillini mountain range referred to as Mount Carrier, technically the highest peak of Monte Vettore. It seems like everywhere I go, I just seem to circle around this mountain.

"There is very little known about this beautiful land, other than it is believed to once have been a place the Cistercian Order settled. It was part of their expansion process for a work-based economy in the fields—the foundation of a real granary farm, and the breeding of animals. The church is along a small path they call 'Path of the Reapers.' This territory was an important reference point for travelers, shepherds, merchants, and anyone else who migrated during those years," she says. "It is a land pregnant with minerals, but it has never been excavated due to it being a protected national forest. In a few hundred feet, we will be reaching Fonte Santa, which means 'blessed water.' It is said that this water is miraculous, so be sure to have a drink of this sacred stream."

My first thought is, how wonderful that the government would respect and protect such splendor. My second thought is *why?* Why haven't they looked into these natural minerals to see what this land could provide and give to those in need. Not that I'd ever want that to happen—I believe in preserving as much of the earth's natural state as possible. But because it seems too progressive . . . for *any* government . . . My political conspiracy thoughts are interrupted by the small, man-made wood bridge that crosses one of the larger streams. Everyone stops to take pictures, and I can't say I blame them. The backdrop is something straight out of a CGI movie; it looks unreal. Alessia and I make our way over to the edge of the stream. I cup my hands in the water to drink from it. It is ice cold and refreshing, and familiar. It tastes exactly like the water from the stream Wasi and

I drank from on our ride. It must come from the same mountain. I haven't thought about him since we left, I miss him. I pour out the remaining drops of water I have in my water bottle and fill it up with fresh spring water to drink on the remainder of our walk. I look around for Alessia who was standing by my side just a moment ago, and I see her speaking to the Englishman.

"Looks like you lost her," Mika says to me.

"Looks like it."

"Can't say I blame her, he is HOT!"

I look up at Andre, he seems to not care or even mind her comment.

"Well he *kind of* is," Andre replies. "I mean, he's not my type," he says playfully, "but I can see why girls would dig that. Don't worry Eli, you can hang out with us."

"Thanks guys," I reply. Looks like cousin-bonding time is over. But like Mika said, you can't blame the girl. And I can't blame him either, I'm surprised it took him an entire twenty minutes to speak to her. Maybe it was the romantic scenery that inspired the moment. I walk with Mika and Andre the remainder of the way.

As we reach the top of the hill, we make our way to the front of the church. Eden urges us to be very careful walking because the church is currently under construction, and there are re-inforcement bars everywhere. The earthquakes of the last few years devastated and brought most of central Italy to its knees. It seems like everywhere we go, there is either restoration, or a complete rebuilding of structures. The church itself isn't very big, but it's very old, isolated, and humble looking.

Within moments of standing there, Alessia walks over with the English fella, and introduces him to the three of us. His name is Liam, and he's even more impressive close up. His features are masculine and striking.

"Do I know you?" I ask Liam, "you feel familiar to me."

"No, I don't think we've ever met, I'm from London. Alessia tells me you live in Los Angeles. I've never been there and it's my very first time in Italy," he replies with that perfect sultry accent every girl lives for.

"What brings you here?" Mika asks. I think I see the glisten from a little drool on the side of her mouth. "Andre and I are on our honeymoon."

"Both work and family," he politely replies.

"Oh, family! Do you have a cousin you can set this one up with?" Mika asks, winking at me. I haven't known the girl thirty minutes, and she's already acting like *my* family. Liam smiles as he tilts his head down. Everything about him seems so familiar, and yet I can't put my finger on it.

Eden gathers us closer and I watch all the tourists put on their translator headphones as she's about to begin.

"The foundation of the church is dated back to 745 AD, but this is neither supported by documentation or historiographical tradition. Just like the land it sits on, we know nothing for sure about its origins. We know for certain that there was an older church under the current one. But without an archaeological investigation of both inside and outside the church, we are surely never to know why Santa Maria in Pantano is the survivor of such an enigmatic and lonely fate. As you can see, it's almost as if the path to this beautiful place is slowly concealing itself." As she says that we all take a moment to look around and observe how isolated it *really* is.

Before the entrance of the church, there is a covered porch with three large bays, and the entrance to the porch is through the middle bay. Above that on the roof are brick blocks holding a bronze bell suspended in its center. To the left side of the bell is the chimney; it sits peculiarly on the edge of the roof right above the left and middle bay. As we step onto the porch, I notice that the chimney is connected to the housing on the upper floor. Eden explains it as "very characteristic" to its structure, and that things were most likely shifted during one of its many remodels throughout the years. Before we step into the church, she also points out the curious nature of the height of the front wall, because it breaks frame with the rest of the wall. She refers to it as a "portal" because it bucks into an ancient wall which then leads to the formation of the wing where the chancel is. I can't say I've ever been interested in the details of architecture, but this is quite extraordinary.

"So, it's like a 'Matrix' church," Andre says out loud, and we all laugh.

"That is an excellent way of putting it, Mr. Andre!" Eden says, humored by his ability to make us understand through sci-fi pop culture. She then turns our attention to the inscription above the door of the portal. Dated 1704, it reads:

O Mary, Mother of God, we gather under your protection.

"Before I give any further explanation, why don't we go into the church. I believe the frescos will reveal a great deal," Eden says with excitement and raised eyebrows.

As we step inside, there is that cool air again; I get a shiver up my spine. I have tingles of familiarity all throughout my body. I feel like I have been here before, but I'm sure I haven't. Is it possible that I've seen so many churches they are looking alike to me? I shrug it off and continue on, as I am distracted by the beautiful frescos throughout. Eden then calls our attention to observe the "Four Scenes from the Life of Mary."

The frescos on the side and back walls were painted by Martino Bonfini, who was a very well know artist around these parts, in the seventeenth century. The right wall and vault are in such poor condition, they are almost completely lost. The first scene is on the back wall: it is a painting of the Eternal Father surrounded by angels in the golden light of Heaven. As I move my eyes to the next scene, I cannot believe it, my mouth falls open. I've never seen such a thing in a Christian church, and before this moment, I never thought it could even co-exist in such a place.

"Miss Eli, I must say the look on your face is priceless. It's the best reaction I have seen yet. You must recognize who they are," Eden smiles at me.

"Well, I'm not totally sure. I don't recognize any of them. Oracles always look so different in every painting I've ever seen." I answer, feeling confused, "because if they are Oracles, wouldn't it be considered blasphemy?"

"Technically, yes," she replies, "but this church is often called the Church of Sibyl. Sibyl is another name for Oracle. This church represents the meeting of Christianity and Pagan culture. This land is sacred to both Mother Earth and Christians. The building, frescos, and sacred treasures once stored here, are of great historical value."

"Sibyl as in Sibyl Apennine, the Queen of Faeries? *That* one?" I ask, skeptically.

"Yes, she is one of twelve," she answers politely. "Apennine as in the Apennine Mountains, the same range that the Sibillini mountain is a part of."

I feel like that floating chimney may have just landed on my head.

"Does anyone want to let us in on this conversation?" the older man from Germany asks.

"Yes, my apologies," Eden addresses the tour. "Here, side by side are the four Prophets from the Old Testament and the four Oracles. The Oracles were all very different and unique in their delivery. Such as Cumaean of Naples, she would either sing or write her prophecies on oak leaves and leave them at the entrance of her cave for the high priest to collect. Her role was to be a kind of *guide* to the Underworld, for those seeking advice from the dead. She is also known to be the one who sold the very coveted Sibylline Books to the last king of Rome. But most importantly, she is the one who prophesied the coming of Jesus. The Sibylline Books were actually attributed to Hellespontine," she points over to her image, "they were a collection of prophecies written in rhyme in the Greek language. Kings were known to consult the books during dangerous times. Hellespontine foretold the Crucifixion of Christ—you will see her most often depicted next to a cross," she pauses. "Next, Agrippa of Egypt, she foretold the flogging, crown of thorns and unimaginable suffering of Jesus . . . and lastly, Delphic of Greece. She was the first to announce the birth of Jesus, and it earned her a place on the Sistine Chapel painted by Michelangelo himself."

I can hear gasps from the older generation, while the younger ones seem to have woken up.

"Oh, I see," replies the German man. "No one has ever made a stink about such a thing being in a Catholic church?"

"No. The pavement of the Siena Cathedral, the library of Pope Julius II, and the Vatican itself, all have images of the Oracles. There is a strong fabric of tradition and beliefs that are very much alive here. It is something that the people want to remember; it is our history, our story."

"Where did she, Sibyl, come from?" asks one of the tourists.

"Although Oracles are only known by legend, it's said that the sacred Temple to Apollo Gergithius gave birth to them. Before they and their prophecies were silenced by Christians in the fourth century, they were known to be the intermediaries between God and man, and the keepers of all secrets. They were the ones that received messages directly from God, and shared them with the leaders, kings, and priests of their time. That was mankind's only way of knowing what God wanted for them, and from them. And since it was the Oracles who told the world of Jesus' coming, it should only be fitting that they are represented in the story as well."

"What role did Sibyl have in the prophecies?" the German man's wife asks.

"I would say the most important one of all. But you will have to wait for her story, I will be telling it this afternoon. There is a beautiful painting of her by Adolfo De Carolis, dated 1907, in the reception hall at the Government Palace of Ascoli Piceno. You absolutely *must* see it! BUT . . . " Eden pauses to make sure we are all paying attention, " . . . as a special treat today, this group will be the first to see a recently discovered painting of Carmentis, or Chemistry Sibyl, as some have called her. It's very exciting!" Eden silently claps her hands together with anticipation.

"Where is this painting?" Liam asks while raising his hand, as if we could miss the tallest man in the room.

"Well, that's a surprise! You will just have to wait, Mr. Liam," Eden replies, with excitement.

She moves to the third scene of "Mary's Life," depicted in the central panels, and called *The Nativity and the Annunciation*. This is by far the best one preserved in the church. And then finally onto the fourth and final scene. On the side of the church's vault, there are two painted red boxes, and a list of names along their left side—probably of those who had commissioned the work to be done. The author's statement with unreadable dates are on the right of the vault. As I look closer at the list of names, there is one that I recognize: *Alessandro Vinci*. Looks like wealth really is hereditary; it must have been one of his ancestors.

"This church once held a much desired and worshiped statue of Pieta. It is approximately thirty-three inches in height and constructed of polychrome terracotta. It was made by an unknown artist in the fifteenth century. Today, this priceless artifact is kept in the Diocesan Museum of Ascoli Piceno. If you have an opportunity, please go to see it. It is a very emotional piece of artwork; the artist truly brings that moment to life. It's almost as if you can feel Jesus in your own arms, and the excruciating pain of what Mary must have felt, watching her child die in her arms," Eden shares.

My mind immediately goes to Nonna Amelia and the image of her baby Mauro dying in her arms. I think about all the women in the world that have suffered in the same way, and I cannot help but pray for their broken hearts. I choke up and start drinking my water to calm my emotions.

Eden gives us a moment to linger about before we all meet outside. Our little group of two has suddenly become a group of five. As usual, I am typically the third, or fifth wheel in this case. It happens so often I barely notice it these days. As we wait for directions, Eden walks by and hands out a piece of paper with a map of our tour today. It has black dots indicating each of our stops without any lines connecting them. Our current location is marked with a star and it says "Spica." She tells us to hold onto it and connect the dots as we travel to each location. She said she will reveal the purpose of it at the end of the tour.

In the meantime, Mika and Andre have started speaking to the American couple, Dr. Nina Matthew and Dr. William Matthew, who are both archeologists. They've brought along their young teenagers, Vanessa 12, and Eric 14. I overhear them talking about attaining more information on this part of Italy, before they petition the Italian government for limited excavation rights. With the recent earthquakes there have been new discoveries, and they are hoping to lead the Italian team, due to their specialties and credentials. I can't help but roll my eyes, I saw that coming. To be honest, I'm surprised there aren't more of them on the tour.

"You don't think that we should learn more about this land?" Liam asks me.

"What?" he catches me off guard.

"I saw your dissatisfied look at the Americans."

"Oh. Sorry, I wasn't trying to be that obvious," I reply. "I just think that if it's been at peace for this long, there must be a reason. Some things are just better left alone."

"Yes, I couldn't agree more," he answers, with that all-to-familiar smile.

"Are you sure we've never—" we are then interrupted by Eden, gathering us around to speak.

"As promised, we will now *begin* to unravel the unique destiny between the Virgin Mary and Virgo."

I'd almost forgotten that's what this tour is about.

"Anyone here of the astrological Virgo sign?" she asks the group. I raise my hand; looks like I am the only one.

"Hey! Aren't you, Aunt Amelia, and my mom the only Virgos in our entire family?" Alessia whispers to me, as if she's just caught onto something. Although Liam's looks were distracting, they were not enough to keep Alessia's wheels from turning.

"Nonna Rosa was too," I reply softly.

"Oh, that's *not* weird *at all*," she says sarcastically back to me.

Her words give me a moment of doubt. When I think about it, how many people really share the same astrological sign in a family?

Eden proceeds by giving us some background on Greek mythology and its connection to astrological signs. After fifteen minutes of this, she can see that we've become restless from her overzealous knowledge of this subject.

"Sorry, onto the main topic!" she says a bit frantically, trying to win our attention back. "The Seven Sisters are the daughters of Atlas and Pleione. They mirror Virgo and are located in the constellation of Taurus. They are some of the closest stars to Earth. Virgo, meaning 'virgin,' is based on the image of the goddess known as Astraea. She was the last immortal god to abandon Earth, after the rest of the gods fled to Mount Olympus. She stayed because she could not imagine being separated from her groom, the man she intended to marry, Talus, or as we know him, Taurus. But he had one last job to do for God before he could leave. Astraea stayed as long as she could for him, but eventually could no longer bear the increasing ignorance and violence among humans; it just became too painful for her. According to legend, Astraea will someday come back to Earth in the utopian Golden Age, bringing peace and heightened consciousness." Let's hope so, I think to myself, this world could really use it.

"What was the job?" asks one of the tourists.

"I will reveal that story to you when we get to our sixth stop, Santa Maria di Casalicchio." Eden has all of our attention once again. "Virgo is often associated with the Virgin Mary, because they are both virgins that represent innocence and purity. In one hand, Virgo holds two sheaves of wheat, and one is marked by the Spica," Eden pauses. "Would you call it coincidence that Santa Maria in Pantano was built under the exact position of the Spica star of the constellation, in a land only ever known to grow wheat? At this very moment, you are standing on the 'Path of Reapers'."

We all shift our bodies and look around; I think the word "reaper" generally makes everyone a little nervous.

Eden continues, "In her other hand, Virgo holds the scales of justice, known to us as Libra; symbolizing balance, truth and justice. Who is bold enough to attempt a connection?" Eden asks us.

For a moment, everyone is silent. Then the American archeologist, Dr. Nina Matthew, raises her hand and says, "Maybe this is where that saying, 'you reap what you sow' comes from."

"Yes, I am so impressed! This is absolutely the most intelligent group I've ever had. I'm really going to have to step it up today," Eden replies ecstatically. "Where there is harvest, there is life. At the center of each life is God's most sacred promise to us—having free will. He gives us life, but whether we are blessed with balance, truth, or justice is based on our decisions. This will be a very important point when we discuss Sibyl's story so be sure to write notes on the paper I gave you."

For a moment, Eden loses her train of thought, and then continues, "Oh yes, back to my original point. The Seven Sisters star cluster mirrors the seven stars that create the Virgo constellation. They are known as Celestial Beings who once roamed the earth. There are several myths and stories of their existence, and why they returned to the Heavens. But the most interesting story of all is that only four of the seven sisters ever returned. And that is why all but three stars are visible to the naked eye. Those three are often referred to as the 'Lost Pleiades. But some would say they are not lost at all, and that they stayed here to live among the mortals all these years."

As everyone laughs at the speculation, Eden tells us that she will give everyone a five-minute break to take photographs before we head back to the bus. Alessia and I exchange glances. She gestures at me to walk over to the side of the church and excuses herself from Liam. We try to speak, but there are still too many people around to have a conversation, so we make our way over to the edge of the forest and pretend to take selfies near the trees.

"Eli, is this for real? I feel like I'm going to have a heart attack," Alessia says calmly, as we fake smile and take photos with her phone.

"I don't know, but I don't believe it. That is impossible, Ále. It would defy nature, science, and all of existence as we know it," I reply, feeling completely unsure of what I'm saying.

"Are you really going to be logical at a time like this?" she says, as she has me pull out my phone for photos to buy a few extra minutes. "Our family could actually be some mythical creatures and you're going to try to downplay it?!"

"It would explain why everyone wanted us to come on this tour. It beats the hell out of them explaining it to us," I respond, surprised by my own admission to this insane possibility.

"Shit, Liam is walking over. I'm going to distract him by having you take photos of us. In the meantime, let's play it cool for the rest of the tour and figure out what else we are supposed to discover about our shady mythological family."

"Yes, okay," I agree.

My mind is spinning as I take photos of Alessia and Liam. She has an amazing poker face; I'm not sure I have the ability to disguise my feelings so well. I feel so distracted that it wouldn't surprise me if I'm chopping their heads off in every picture.

After the very brief photoshoot, I quietly walk alone on the way back to the bus. I stop to refill my water bottle at the stream. I cannot get enough water—it seems the more I drink, the thirstier I become. I pat some of the icy water on my forehead. If I wasn't around so many strangers, I would strip naked and put my entire body in it. I feel flushed and overwhelmed. Stories and voices are playing in a loop in my mind, and I can't quiet them down. If this is only the first stop, what will the other six be like? Can I handle this? There is a part of me that wants to leave before it is too late. But there is an even bigger part of me that needs the truth.

*	*	*

Our second stop is Santa Maria di Lapide.

Within fifteen minutes, we arrive to a quaint town that seems to be built like a fortress. It's isolated from nearby towns and sits higher than usual on a hilltop. At its very peak, I can see the church with two large brass bells on its roof; with a little effort we make our way to it. As we reach the church, the archeologists take notice that it looks much older than the date of reconstruction listed. I hear them say that some of the stones used to rebuild it are much more ancient than 1491, and that there were probably so many additions made to the building over the years, that there are no original pagan elements left. I wonder how they can tell, but I suppose if it's something they do every day, they must have a trained eye.

Santa Maria di Lapide is a very large church; when I first enter, it seems almost unimpressive with not much more than a beautiful Latin cross. The room itself looks like a church hall. There are no aisles, passageways, arches or vaults where the altar should be. Eden tells us that the distinct uniqueness of this church is in exactly what you *cannot* see. This church has many small secret doors. It even has a ninth century crypt designed with several slits and shelves, to hold devices such as weapons. It is a multi-story building that used to house the defense army of the Knights Templar, whose duty it was to control the area. I was right; it was a fortress.

Eden asks if anyone has heard of, or knows about electrum, and about half the room raises their hand. She explains that it is an alloy of silver and gold, and that it means "amber" in Latin. She then goes on to tell us a little about the philosopher Thales of Miletus. His main interests were astronomy, mathematics, ethics, and metaphysics. In 600 BC he stated that if two pieces of amber are rubbed together, they attract bits of straw, which manifest the effects of static electricity.

Before many of our minds can grasp what she is alluding to, Dr. William fixes the glasses on his face and states with extreme enthusiasm—as he and his wife share a glance—"Ms. Eden, are you suggesting that the Knights Templar used alchemy to make silver and gold for their army and church through the use of electricity, before it was actually "created?" That explains why the river runs almost under the building; they would have needed the power from the current!"

"Yes doctor, that's exactly what I was getting to." Eden looks like someone has just taken the wind out of her sail, and also seems upset with his overzealous outburst. "How about you give me a little more time to explain next time? Not everyone here has your extensive knowledge, and we certainly want everyone enjoying themselves today."

"Yes of course, pardon me," he says embarrassed.

"As Dr. William pointed out, we believe that metal alchemy and electricity were in existence long before anyone knew about them. The Knights Templar were their keepers. They used them to become the greatest and fastest growing army of all time. Both the metal alchemy and electricity gave them power and wealth beyond what any one country had ever seen. And that was more than enough reason to keep both a secret. This behavior led her to realize that humans were not ready for this knowledge. She took it away, and it would be nearly a thousand years before she would even consider giving it back."

"Who's 'she'?" asks the German man.

"Electra, of course. Mother of all things that shine bright and one of the Seven Sisters," Eden says in a matter of fact tone, while tilting her head slightly.

"Wasn't God the creator of light?" he replies, confused and uncomfortable with her confidence.

"God is an excellent delegator! You can't possibly imagine how busy He is! So, He gave His celestial creations the imagination to create the things He wanted. And through divine intervention—voila! Wouldn't you say they did incredibly well?" she replies, with a moment of joy and pride.

"I'm not sure I understand, but if you're right, then, yes—very well!" says the German man, laughing at his own admission.

Our tour inside is brief due to Eden's annoyance with Dr. William. I can see he feels bad about it, as his wife pulls him to the side to speak with him. We are not permitted to visit any other parts of the building due to "safety" reasons. But it looks perfectly safe to me. Eden says because of all its secret factors regarding the true birth of electricity and alchemy, the true nature of the building and visiting those rooms would never be permitted to the public by the Church. And since the Church owns them, they will always have the final say. Mika, Andre, and I discuss how we believe there are so many excuses constantly given by the government and the Church to hide things from the public. It occurs to me just then that I may have found my conspiracy soulmates.

Eden leads us outside to a dirt road, next to a stream along the church. We follow the stream, which takes us further into the woods. We stop at a small shrine; it looks like a gravestone of some kind.

"As you can see, this church is quite vigilant and grand. But all its secrets may lie at this very spot. 'Lapide' means tombstone." She gestures toward the shrine, "This was built to mark the point where the Old Road passed to reach the church. Most travelers would be coming in from the forest, the opposite side of where we came in from. This was the indication that they were in the right area."

"What is the Old Road?" someone asks.

"It is a secret road that runs from Rome through central Italy, and as far up as Florence. Travelers followed the Rio River," she points to the stream, "which is a tributary of the Fluvione River, which in turn is the tributary of the Tiber River that flows through the city of Rome. The Tiber River is the second largest river in Italy after the Po River. It extends 406 kilometers long. The river was an integral part of one of the building's fused complexes. Since we are not allowed into the other parts of the church, it is impossible to know which one would have been so important."

Andre nods his head at Mika and I, confirming our suspicions. I pull out my phone and take pictures of the building, and a beautiful glisten reflects off the ground from the sun.

"Any road or wall built with that kind of length, is a tactic to protect land and control borders. Who were they trying to keep out?" the German man asks skeptically.

"It was more like who were they trying to keep *in*," Eden answers. Under my breath I mutter "Sibyl," at the same time she says it to the group.

"While they worked hard to keep Sibyl in, they were working just as hard to keep those seeking her wisdom, out. We are standing at the foot of Monte Vettore. They would have needed to take this path to arrive at the mouth of her cave without having to hike through the other side of the mountain, where they could at times encounter impossible weather conditions. But there were soldiers that searched every inch of these woods, and it would have been very difficult to get past them. A shrine was actually placed here as a mark for Sibyl, to light the path to her cave. But instead, it was turned into a tombstone by the Knights Templar as a symbol to all the travelers, that it would be their destiny should they choose Sibyl's path."

We discuss what an incredible force she must have been to need an entire army to try to control her. As each moment passes, I become more impressed with her. She must have been quite a threat to every empire, including the Christian Church. What were they so afraid of? From all the reading I've done, she is mostly described as beautiful, dignified, and good, and very little portrays her to be wicked and evil. My curiosity has started to become as great as my thirst—I feel so dehydrated. I finish my water from Pantano and refill my bottle at a fountain near the church on our way back to the bus.

*   *   *

I take a much-needed nap on the hour and fifteen-minute drive to our third stop, Santa Maria della Cona. It is located near a small village called Frascaro, about 6 kilometers outside of the city of Norcia. I wake up to Alessia singing in my ear. I always forget how angelic her voice is, she got it from Aunt Ersella. But the way she is singing into my ear is so loud it might burst an eardrum.

"Are you trying to wake the dead?" I ask, as I push her face away while attempting to open my eyes.

"Funny you should say that. This place is next to a cemetery, can't wait to hear this story," Mika says, as she checks her hair and lipstick in a hand mirror. I notice that almost everyone is off the bus. I look to my right and see Andre and Liam outside with their faces pressed up against my window.

"When did *that* happen?" I ask.

"Andre was trying to interrogate him, but instead they just bonded over music. That husband of mine is just too nice, he makes friends with everyone," Mika replies, as she grabs my hand to get me off the seat.

"Of course they did," I answer sarcastically—naps sometimes make me cranky.

"Girl, you need some Chap Stick, are you thirsty? Your lips are so dry," Alessia mocks me. Just as she says it, I can feel the intense dryness in my mouth and in my throat. I finish drinking the rest of the water I have left in my bottle, but it isn't enough, Alessia gives me her water too.

We're in front of a stand-alone, lonely church near a small cemetery with nothing else around. It is salmon-colored on the outside, with a thin, small cross on its roof. It has two doors—one at the front entry and one on the side—and only a few windows. The building is set slightly below ground level; we walk down a few steps before entering the church. It is very simple in its layout, there doesn't seem to be anything unique about its few frescos, altar, or design. I see a beautiful Latin cross, and a painting of the Virgin Mary, as I expected there would be on a such a tour. The church is standard in terms of sixteenth century architecture.

I find myself impolitely eavesdropping on a conversation Eden is having with the archeologists. They are bombarding her with questions, as they were doing when I fell asleep on the bus an hour and a half ago. I admire her; she seems to have an endless amount of patience, or just really loves her job. Something she says catches my attention. "This area has traces of human settlement dating back to Neolithic times, about eighth century BC. But the foundation of Norcia did not begin until fifth century AD."

"That would leave almost 1,300 years unaccounted for," Dr. Nina Matthew says, with an almost euphoric look on her face. Eden excuses herself to begin the tour, as the couple starts scribbling erratically into their notebooks.

"Typical church in an Italian village, right?" Eden asks. But I already know that nothing could possibly be that simple on this tour. "If you said yes, you're right. But," there it is, "faith is not about what we can see with our eyes, it is what we know with our hearts. Sometimes the more typical and basic something can look, the more complicated it turns out to be," Eden smiles and carries on. "Cona is taken from the word, 'Icona,' meaning sacred image, and so here we stand in Our Lady of the Sacred Image. One of the many connecting themes is that there have been apparitions of the Virgin Mary at each of these locations. Keep in mind that there were also Pagan shrines here too. Which might explain the second meaning of Cona: a map maker's name for someone who lived by a roadside shrine. Can anyone take a guess who that would be for a place like this?"

"Grave keeper," voices reply throughout the room.

"Very good!" Eden shouts. It looks like all that talking with the archeologists hasn't slowed her energy down a bit. "Since we are on the subject of meanings; Frascaro, the closest village to this church, is derived from a Latin term meaning 'green branch.' Well, we know that the branch is the limb of a tree, and a tree symbolizes life in many religions."

I start to feel static in my brain, like a television during a thunderstorm.

"And in religious scripture, BRANCH, in all capital letters, has been used to refer to the Messiah. Green is the color that symbolizes balance, nature, fertility, and life," Eden pauses. "Now . . . what would a Pagan shrine, celestial sisters, an apparition of Mary, the Messiah as the limb to the Tree of Life, the color green that symbolizes life, and a cemetery that symbolizes death, all have in common?" The room is quiet.

My mind starts to go crazy with what feels like electricity, then it goes black, and then finally, an image appears.

"T-t-ti . . . " I can't get the word out.

"Eli, you okay?" Alessia touches my shoulder. I look around, everyone is staring at me, waiting for me to say something.

"Ye-es," I clear my throat and try to focus. "Time. That's what they all have in common. Time is God's first creation, 'in the beginning and so it shall be in the end.'" I don't know how I know that verse or where it's from, but it just came out of me.

"That is quite extraordinary," Eden seems speechless. "In all of my years, no one has guessed that correctly . . . Please, a round of applause for Eli."

I am horrified by the attention as everyone applauds. I wait a moment until everyone turns away and their eyes are back on Eden, and then step outside to catch my breath. I start shaking my head and put pressure on my temples with the palms of my hands. Alessia is right behind me.

"Sister, what is going on?" she asks me gently.

"What did I just see in my head Ále? What was that? What did I just say in there? What was that static in my head?" I ramble.

"Let's get you some water, there's a fountain nearby. Just sit here and try to take some deep breaths." She's right, I need to calm down. We are far from home and we still have a long day ahead. Whatever this is, now is not the time to deal with it. I tilt my head back and try to concentrate on mindless things to distract myself.

I feel a nudge at my feet. I look down and there are two huge dogs lying next to my legs. I'm totally startled and quickly pull my legs away. I've never seen dogs this big! They look like some kind of husky breed on steroids. They must have sensed my fear, because one puts its head on top of its paws, and the other rolls over for me to rub its belly. It makes me giggle a bit when I see them do that and after a few moments, I realize that they are harmless and just want to play. Their coats are incredible; so soft, shiny, and a beautiful color. It's a mixture of grays, silvers and whites.

"Oh, my goodness! Where did you find these handsome

fellas?" Alessia hands me the water. As soon as they hear her voice, they both get up and start licking her hands. She kneels down and starts rubbing their faces and gives them compliments.

"They were at my feet when I opened my eyes. I assume they're from the village. They're very well groomed, I'm sure they come from a good home. I have no doubt their owner will be looking for them soon," I reply.

"Big, strong, handsome boys, where's your collar? Wow! They're huge!" she says, as she hugs one of them. They seem completely enamored with her, it's very sweet. I've never thought of Alessia as an animal lover. She pulls out her phone and starts taking pictures with them.

"GET AWAY!!! GET AWAY FROM THE WOLVES!!!" Eden is screaming, as she runs toward us. Liam runs past her, and within seconds he is standing between us and the dogs. He slowly starts to push us back. Eden is yelling at everyone to get on the bus quickly. The dogs start to become angry. Their demeanor completely changes from fun-loving animals to aggressive and savage-like, as they begin to growl, snarl, and salivate. They do not like Liam. Eden then puts herself in front of him.

"Now boys, I don't know what you're doing this far down the mountain. You know you shouldn't be here. Now leave these girls alone! We are going to get on that bus and you're going to let us, now shoo! Get going!" Eden says firmly to the dogs, as if they can understand her. But they don't back down. Liam grabs Alessia's hand, and they start to bark like crazy as if they are about to attack.

"Get on the bus NOW," Eden says with a low and stern voice. We all back up to the bus door quickly and jump in. The door closes without a moment to spare. The canines take a leap and land right outside the doors.

"GO! GO!" Eden yells at the driver. We sit down in our seats almost breathless. Eden walks over and asks us to explain what happened. We tell her that we don't understand how that went so bad so quickly. The dogs were so loving towards us, and we were having a wonderful time playing with them. I explain how I thought they were so well kept; we were sure they weren't wild animals—she seems surprised by our recollection. As the driver pulls out of the driveway, we notice Eden's eyes are locked on something in the distance. I look outside my window and notice a large bird sitting on one of the tombstones in the cemetery.

"What is that?" I ask her.

"A golden eagle, it is a very rare animal . . . even for this area," she says softly. "What the hell is going on . . . " she mutters sharply.

I ask what she means, and she assures me it is nothing for me to trouble myself with. She shakes her head and explains to us that what we thought were dogs were actually the Apennine wolf called Canis Lupus Italicus, and that they are extremely dangerous. They have only ever been reported being seen in small herds high in the mountains. Her demeanor quickly shifts to lecturing me and Alessia on the danger we could have been in, or potentially put Liam in. Catholic guilt works every time.

Once Eden has had enough of us, she gets on the microphone and apologizes to the group for cutting the visit short. She explains that safety is the first priority and that this was a rare, uncommon event. There should be no further disturbances from nature for the rest of the tour. And since we have a forty-minute drive before arriving to Castelluccio, she will review what we missed on the drive.

*   *   *

Before going to the next church, we are making a pit stop at a restaurant in Castelluccio. It is world famous for its lentils! When I was little, I remember my father and grandfather would make it an annual trip and stock up. It was always a big deal around New Year's Eve, because in the Italian tradition, it is said that eating lentils at midnight brings prosperity and good fortune all year long. I've heard a great deal about the beauty of Castelluccio. Unfortunately, it has also been a victim of the earthquakes, and the town was nearly wiped out. When the earthquakes first occurred, there was no way of getting in or out, the roads were completely destroyed. Three hundred residents had to be airlifted to safety. Thirteen souls refused to leave—they were mostly farmers who wanted to stay close to their cattle, sheep, and horses. And good thing they did, or else most people would not have had a livelihood to come back to. Today, locals and tourists are doing everything they can to help the community rebuild; it's also the reason that the visit has been added to the tour. They hope it will help regenerate the economy and bring business back.

On the drive, Mika and Andre tell me stories of their wedding day to help the time pass. It sounds like vodka is to Poland what wine is to Italy. I'm not sure if they really like me or if they just feel sorry for me, but either way I like them, and I love their sense of humor. I welcome the company and desperately need the distraction.

The main road into Castelluccio goes through the lentil fields before reaching town. Harvesting the lentils takes place in July, and by August they are dedicated to threshing the fields. Outside my window I see both workers and machines working hard to clear the land. From what I've heard, the winters here are harsh. But it's the cold climate that keeps the insects away, and therefore the crops do not need to be treated with insecticides and preservatives, making the lentils a truly organic product. Just the thought of them is making my mouth water.

The restaurant is in the newer part of Castelluccio. It's located in one of the many new structures in the area designed to be tourist friendly. They've worked hard to preserve as much of the culture by designing the buildings to have an Old-World feel. On the walk through the restaurant to the terrace, there are many beautiful photos hanging called, "Flowering of Castelluccio." They are various images of the fields as the flowers blossom in June. There is an endless number of mixed flowers of all different colors; tourists flock from all over to enjoy their beauty. In that moment, I remember standing with Luca overlooking the magnificent plains of Pretare. I don't think I will ever see anything that beautiful again.

We are greeted on the terrace with a much-needed glass of wine. There are several tables with umbrellas throughout. Along the railing I can see a buffet area with several trays of lentils and small bowls. We are encouraged to try the many different ways lentils can be prepared.

"This is so awesome, it's like a lentil tasting instead of a wine tasting!" Mika says, as she beelines to the buffet. I can see that she wasn't exaggerating when she called herself a "food enthusiast" on the bus. The five of us sit together as we try the very delicious options. Mika proceeds to tell us that lentils have the second highest ratio of protein after soybeans, and that they have been part of the human diet since the Neolithic times, 3000 BC.

"Babe, you're like Eden part two with all your historical knowledge of lentils," Andre says laughing.

"What? She's on point! I wish I knew half that history. We lucked out having her as a tour guide," she replies.

"She's a little long winded if you ask me," Liam chimes in. "She could do with a little less detail."

"Speaking of details, what's your story? Handsome, single guy on a tour like this . . . not to be rude, but it's weird," Mika says to him. Thank goodness someone finally asked, she took the words right out of my mouth.

"I had a day to myself and I wanted to learn more about this part of Italy. When I was looking through the various tours, this one seemed the most interesting." Hmm, that seemed a bit rehearsed. This guy is no actor and I'm starting to become suspicious.

"What about you, Eli? Your cousin tells me that you wanted to come on this tour, why?" he asks. I give Alessia a glare, and I can see her mouth smirk but her eyes are hiding behind her sunglasses.

"It was suggested to us. I thought it would be a fun way to spend some time together and bond." I add in some Catholic guilt to get back at her for the smirk. I'm sure she's rolling her eyes at me. "What are you enjoying more Liam, the religious or the mystical details of the tour?"

"I quite enjoy both. Who's to say they are not both legitimate?"

"I didn't take you for a believer," Mika says to Liam.

Liam redirects his attention towards me and asks, "Are you a believer, Eli?" Alessia laughs.

"I believe in science, facts, and all things that can be proven. That doesn't mean I don't believe in a higher being; I'm just not sure I completely understand what that is, or what it looks like."

Alessia takes off her sunglasses and gives me a long hard look. I'm sure she must be upset that I am still using this kind of verbiage after having discovered so much. But I hardly know these people, and I am not about to let my guard down. "Back to you Liam, I'd like to know more about you. You said you have family here and you're also here for work, what do you do?"

"Well, it's not your typical job; I'm an antique book dealer."

"A what?" Mika says, as she and Andre lean in.

"It's really not that exciting. People hire me to find rare books, and it's my job to travel around the world to procure them." Alessia assertively puts her sunglasses back on.

"Man, that sounds like the best job in the world, how did you get into that? You look so young, I thought only old people do that kind of thing," Andre asks, as we all nod in agreement.

"Family business. I've been trained to do this since I could read."

"I would ask what kind of books you're looking for and who your clients are, but I'm sure you'll just tell me that they are high profile and you are unable to disclose their identities," I say, as he tilts his head down and smiles, "but since it is such a niche market, I am fairly confident you know our cousin, Stefano Goto."

Mika and Andre pick up their glasses of wine, they can sense it's about to get good.

"Uh-um yes . . . I believe I have met him on occasion." This guy is seriously no actor. I seem to have caught him off guard and he suddenly seems uncomfortable. By Alessia's body language, I can tell she has caught on too.

"Wonderful. That must mean that your last name is . . . *Vinci* . . . that is your family name, correct?" Checkmate—I got him.

Mika and Andre start whispering to each other, trying to figure out who "Vinci" is, and how this is by far, the best part of the tour. Alessia tears off her sunglasses so aggressively they land across the table. She must be fuming inside, that she did not pick up on it first. To be honest, it surprises me too—she's typically the much better detective between the two of us. He freezes up for a moment and doesn't know what to say. I am not a confrontational person by any means. But just a moment ago, when he tilted his head down to smile, I remembered exactly who else does that—Luca. I don't know how I didn't see it before; they look so much alike.

"Yes, how did you know?" Liam asks, as he regains his cool manner. "Do you know them?"

Looks like he wants to continue to play the game. I smile and say, "Only through Stefano. Very nice family, please say hello to them for me."

"Yes, of course. I'm sure they'll be pleased we had an opportunity to meet."

I excuse myself to use the restroom. My hands are shaking, most likely because I never act so boldly. This is a new feeling for me, one that I think I might quickly adapt to. Alessia and Mika follow me in.

"Dude, what was that about! What's a 'Vinci'?" Mika exclaims.

"A very wealthy and complicated family that seems to know way too much about ours. I have a strange feeling in my gut, Ále. Did you notice anything strange about him?" I ask.

"No, I mean other than his phone's always going off. He receives text messages nonstop. I can't believe he's a Vinci! I thought he really liked me," Alessia says sadly.

"Believe me, he does. I'm very good at reading body language, and there isn't any part of that, that isn't real," Mika comforts her.

"Ále, I need you to carry on as you have been. Just tell him that you were pissed initially because it seemed like he was withholding information, but now you can see it was just a coincidence. But you need to figure out if it *is* actually a coincidence," I say. "Mika, can you please continue to read his body language and tell me if you pick up on something unusual?"

"No sweat off my back girl, that man really is lentil-delicious!" And with that, she breaks the tension.

Chapter 11

B Y THE TIME we get to Madonna delle Gee, our fourth stop, Eden seems to have forgotten the situation at Cona. She is back to being her peppy, energetic self. Good thing too, I would not have wanted to be the cause for an upset Eden—she's too lovely.

The church is very pretty but small, off a pebble-strewn cart track. It looks like it is made of white stone. On the right side of the roof sits a brass bell. The door is made of a beautiful antique wood, placed right in the center of the church, with two small windows on either side and another slightly larger window above the door. If you didn't know any better, you'd drive right past it; it is very unassuming. There are no crosses or any indication that it is even a church. The road wouldn't get you far though—the church stands at the beginning of an untouched valley, seemingly endless with lush hills, mountains, and trees.

"The town Vallinfante was originally called 'Valle delle Fate,' which means Valley of the Faeries, due to the legend that they once inhabited this land. Now it is the habitat to the most charming of all the animals, the deer. I do hope we get to see one while we are here today, they are quite magical!" Eden says with her typical enthusiasm. "At the bottom just there," she points over to the side and down to the bottom from where we're standing, "you will hear a stream. It is the Nera river; a tributary of the . . . "

"Tiber River," everyone replies in unison.

"Very good! Now I don't know about you, but I'm starting to see a connection," she teases the group. "According to legend, the Nera river once flowed out of two grottos that were in the shape of an Ox's nostrils."

She walks over to open the door of the church and lets us through. To my surprise, it is a single, empty, square room. It contains only an image of the Virgin Mary painted on the wall.

"This church has also been known as Madonna della Maina. Maina is from *imago*, Latin for "Icon," for the painting on the wall where a miraculous apparition once appeared. Whereas, Madonna delle Gee comes from the German "gebirge" meaning mountain; translating to Our Lady of the Mountain," Eden says, then takes a question from the German tourist.

"Why would they have used the German word for mountain?"

"Yes, well isn't that the right question! If we could only ask those who named it." Everyone giggles. "Very little is known about this church. We don't even know precisely when it was built, but many have assumed it was around the seventeenth century." I can hear the Matthews chuckling under their breaths, saying that it is much, much older.

"Local legend says this church was built at the same point where a child was threatened by a flood but was then rescued by a bear that carried him to safety in a cave. Could that bear have been one of Sibyl's magical creatures? It is said that in her kingdom there are magical creatures of all kind, and that she has a special love for the pure of heart. She would have never allowed an innocent child to die on her land," Eden pauses. "Or maybe it was one of the seven celestial sisters, Taygeta—mistress of the animals. She was known to transform into a deer with golden horns."

Taygeta was my grandmother Rosa's last name—Alessia and I lock eyes. Everything on this tour is starting to feel like more than coincidence. We walk down to the stream at the bottom of the hill, to have a private moment. We take pictures of one another, smile, and speak quietly so that no one will hear us. As we start speaking to one another, I realize that neither one of us is making sense. We can't seem to make heads or tails of the information our minds are trying to process. There are still too many holes in the story for us to be able to see a full picture. We decide that we need to find out what the other six celestial sisters' names are. But we agree not to get ahead of ourselves; we don't want to draw any more attention than we already have. If Eden doesn't mention the names by the end of the day, then we will ask.

Alessia takes a moment to reapply her lipstick before we walk back up the hill. I bend down to refill my bottle with the crystal-clear, ice-cold water from the stream. My thirst has not been quenched, instead it seems to be growing. The lentils must have been saltier than I thought. A shadow appears in the water from the other side of the stream. I look up, but I see no one and nothing around. I feel a chill in my spine.

"Hey, did you see that?" I ask Alessia, as I stand up.

"No, see what?" she asks, as I continue to look into the fullness of the forest and in-between the trees. Still, nothing.

"Come on guys! We're leaving!" Mika waves her arm at us, as she shouts from the hilltop. We make our way back up and onto the bus for the hour and a half drive to Montefortino.

*　　*　　*

Fifth stop, Madonna delle Ambro. The church is about seven kilometers outside of Montefortino. It, like most of the other churches on the tour, stands isolated between slopes and steep cliffs in the Sibillini Mountains, with a river that flows nearby; completely immersed in silence and rare beauty. It is often referred to as the "Little Lourdes of Sibillini," because it resembles the famous Our Lady of Lourdes. Both churches have apparition stories that are very similar.

As I step off the bus, the church is directly in front of me. It looks so familiar . . . I think I've been here before. I remember this beautiful place with snow cascading all around like a perfect winter-wonderland postcard. But I can't recall when or with whom I was here. But wouldn't I remember? Maybe I was a child? Well, with or without snow, the landscape is breathtaking. Within moments I feel so relaxed and at peace. I can feel the earth's soil from under my feet, telling us that we are on *sacred* land. It's a sensation I've never felt before, I don't think any of us have, and yet it is once again familiar, like home.

We have a brief lunch scheduled by the river before the tour of the church. As we make our way over, most people are talking about how full they still are from the lentil tasting. But that's the Italian way—full or not, when it's time to eat, *you eat*. Once we reach the spread, not one more complaint is uttered. It is a spectacular picnic-style layout with large blankets and pillows, right along the river. The buffet table and mini bar are right under very large ancient trees, and we are surrounded by the smell of sweet, summer wildflowers. The accommodations have been made by the local restaurant, and well worth the ticket price. Mika and Andre start kissing like the honeymooners they are, along the riverbed. Even Alessia and Liam take each other's hand for a stroll. I look around and see all the couples get just a little more loving. It warms my heart, and it gives me hope that one day this will exist for me too.

The teenage kids and I are the first to the buffet line for food. We joke about how gross all the romance is, and how I should drink a bottle of wine for them too. We find a perfect little spot next to the river with just the right amount of shade. Eden asks if it's ok to join us; she's probably feeling the same. We finally make proper introductions over paninis. Eric and Vanessa are smart and well-educated, mostly home-schooled due to their parents' travels. Eden and I are very impressed with their ability to maintain an intellectual conversation, and yet they have a very funny teenage sense of humor. They tell us several hysterical stories of their adventures, before their parents make their way over. Before long, Alessia, Liam, Mika, and Andre, all join our picnic spot.

Dr. William and Dr. Nina ask Eden about the Ambro River. The kids simultaneously roll their eyes and lay back on the pillows. I have a feeling they are used to their parents turning social time into learning time.

"Well, it is a tributary of the Tenna River. And as we've learned, all roads, in this case rivers, lead to Rome," Eden says, amused with herself. "The river is best known for the area where the Apparition of the Virgin Mary took place around the year 1000 AD. She appeared to a poor shepherd girl named Santina, in the cavity of a beech tree. Santina had been mute since birth. Our Lady granted her the ability to speak and the original chapel was built in 1037 on that very site. Just right over there," she says, pointing to the back of the church just across from where we are sitting.

"What does 'Ambro' mean?" Vanessa asks.

"Well, that's a long story and frankly there are many interpretations of it." I can see Eden trying to choose her words carefully, but her mouth seems to have gotten the better of her. "But . . . but the truth is that . . . " she pauses and lets out a sigh, "Ambro means 'amber tone,' which IS the color of Mary's skin! And oh, it is splendid and magical! There's never been anything quite like it! And, of course, little Santina was simply enamored by it, so she called her Madonna with Amber Skin. Which is also how the river got its name. The reflection of the sun from the river made her skin and eyes look golden amber . . . quite exquisite really. You see, most people have only ever seen the Madonna in paintings where she is portrayed to have very pale skin with dark eyes. But she was far from it, she had immaculate darker skin . . . " Her mind seems to have drifted in nostalgia for a moment. "Well, they got the dark eyes right, but not the skin, or body, or hair . . ." In between the enthusiastic sighs and her rambling confession, she looks around and catches a glimpse of everyone's surprised faces. Her face becomes flushed.

"Ms. Eden, you speak as if you knew the Madonna herself," Dr. Nina giggles, "and you tell the story as if you were there! You make it so exciting; you're quite a storyteller and the absolute best tour guide! Oh, if they could all be like you! I think you deserve the applause this time." The group echoes the sentiment and instantly begins to applaud. Eden smiles, but seems flustered and fidgets with her blouse. The look on her face seems to be of embarrassment or regret, I can't tell.

Huh . . . Ms. Eden the Storyteller. I'm not buying that. My gut tells me there is more to *her* story. If I didn't have so much to figure out about my own family, she would be a very interesting onion to peel.

"Yes, there's definitely more to this!" Alessia says to me out loud, but her voice is drowned out by the applause, so only I can hear her.

"Huh? I didn't say anything," I reply, as I turn back to look at her in confusion.

"Well then, I guess I just read your thoughts," she says sarcastically, "because I totally agree," as she stares in Eden's direction.

Is she serious, can she really read my thoughts? Or was she just saying that because she knows me well enough to know that we are thinking the same thing? I'm suddenly feeling a bit paranoid, this is a new emotion for me. I think this tour—actually, this entire vacation—is getting the best of me. I seem to be a different person since I've arrived. I don't know who or what to believe anymore. Everything I have been so sure of being fact all my life, I'm now questioning. My mind is going in circles and I tune out the tour as Eden walks us into the beautiful pink church, and begins her lecture about its history and exquisite art.

I'm not able to focus on her words, and I realize I need a moment of detachment from all of this before I go completely mad. I decide to pull out my phone and check my emails. I *need* something to anchor me to reality, to my real life. There are several emails from friends which I read first. They are mostly gossiping about crazy nights out, and new love interests, and their recent sexcapades. It feels wrong reading this kind of thing in a church, but I need something "normal." I hope God understands. Once I get through a handful of them, I start to relax a bit; my thoughts aren't so heavy. In between reading emails about drama and sex, there is a reply from my job that I've been waiting for. I had requested an extension for vacation time. Although it wouldn't be paid, I did not feel that it is the right time to leave my grandmother's side.

DECLINED.

I take a deep breath and look up at the ceiling. I ask God to give me patience to deal with my asshole boss. Cussing and sex talk in church—if He doesn't hear me now, I'm not sure He ever will. I move away from the group and sit in a pew towards the back, and I do something I haven't done in a long time: I pray. There is something about these buildings that holds my feet to the fire and makes me humble. The thoughts in my mind are heavy again. The email indicated that my position would not be held for me if I did not return next week, which is a nice way of saying that I will be fired if I don't get back to work. I'm at my first major crossroad—people said this would happen at twenty-five, but this seems a little premature. I then check my bank account to see how much I have in my savings; I have enough to be unemployed for a few months. So, I begin to reply to the email from my boss; I don't think I've ever typed so fast.

"Hey, we're walking to the original church, come on! What are you doing anyway?" Alessia asks, and I can tell she's completely annoyed with me.

"Replying to my boss' email. I'm sending my letter of resignation," I reply, as I get up and follow her through the church, but never take my eyes off what I'm doing.

"How do you have reception when no one else does? I thought you were playing some stupid game on your phone this entire time, while I was listening to what feels like a repetitive lecture."

"Really? Huh, I don't know," I reply to her, as I focus on finishing the email to send it off, before I change my mind. Alessia stops and crosses her arms as she waits for me to finish.

SEND.

"Ok I'm done!" I say, as I finally look up and simultaneously put my phone back in my bag. "Why are we standing at the altar, I thought we were going to the old church?"

"Well, if you were paying attention, you would have heard that the old church is located in the apse of this church, and we have to go through these two main doors," she tilts her head towards them, "here at the altar, to go inside." Her arms are still crossed.

"I'm sorry, I just needed a moment."

"You look as if the weight of the world has been lifted off your shoulders. I'm proud of you, I'm glad you quit."

"I didn't have a choice. They wouldn't accept my vacation extension."

"I know that was your dream job, I'm sorry. But they don't deserve you. You dedicate your life to them, this is the least they could have done for you," she says, and she leans in to hug me.

"Thank you Ále," I reply, as I feel myself getting emotional. She's right, it was my dream job, but I never felt like I fit in. I never feel like I fit in anywhere, or with anyone. For being such an ordinary person, I don't understand why my mind is so complicated. She takes me by the hand and walks me into the church with the others.

Eden is calling the quadrangular-shaped original church, the Annunciation Chapel. The church was expanded in the 1600s because it had just become too small for the parishioners. I look around the room and the chapel is overwhelmingly filled with various paintings, sculptures, and pictures of hundreds, maybe thousands, of children, families, women, men, and soldiers, who were either sick and in need of healing, or were healed from their visit here. The items are placed around the altar to thank the Madonna for her grace and protection. There are endless votive offerings throughout. And true to the pattern that we've seen throughout this tour, there is a stone sculpture of Mary and Child as its center. Eden points out another very impressive pictorial painted on the ceiling and walls by Martino Bonfini.

"Another recurrence, wouldn't you say?" Alessia snarks. She really must be reading my mind.

"What do you think that's about?" I ask.

"It wouldn't have been uncommon for a local artist to paint in many of the churches in his or her province, during that time," Liam chimes in. That seems like a logical explanation to me, but Alessia isn't buying it.

"But we've seen his work only in the churches that have *both* paintings of the Madonna and the Oracles. That can't be a co-incidence," she insists. I must have missed those paintings in the main church while I was checked out. Liam stays quiet, he must have caught on that when Ále puts her claws into something, she doesn't let up until she's satisfied with the answer.

"If you look closely at the vaulted ceiling, you will notice that Bonfini adorned it with numerous paintings depicting Sibyl. So many have asked time and time again how a 'demonic' image can exist in such a sacred place. But God's history, much like our very own, is intertwined. These Sibyls, or Oracles as they are also known, were once God's messengers. They are His children from a different time, it is right that they are represented in God's house too. It's a silly connotation that they are in any-way demonic or should be forgotten. The messenger may have changed, but the message of God has not," Eden so eloquently explains. There is warmth and comfort in her words.

"Which Sibyl is this? Weren't there twelve or thirteen of them?" the German man asks.

"There are twelve original Oracles. Twelve is the number used in the Bible and throughout history to symbolize God's power and authority. That is why we believe there are twelve Oracles—together they are the voice of God, and their job is to carry His message to humanity," she corrects him. "And the one I am speaking of is the same Sibyl we have mentioned throughout the tour, the Apennine Sibyl."

"What is her story?" Dr. William asks, as Alessia and I are looking up at the ceiling trying to get a clear look at her but can't seem to get a good angle to look at her face.

"Thank you for asking. I find that talking about these things can at times make people uneasy, especially those who are very religious. Should anyone here find this part displeasing, please feel free to go into the main church for a few moments." No one moves.

"Well, that's a first!" She seems excited with the response and continues on, "a precious few Oracles were born when God created the world. Apennine Sibyl was one of those. Some of them chose to teach their gift to humans who showed promise. Today, they are often referred to as intuitives, psychics, or mediums. Descendants of those taught by an Oracle, are the only people that bestow this ancient magic; the rest are just faux. The gift is not guaranteed to manifest itself in every generation. Sometimes it can skip thousands of years, and sometimes it's given to every person in that bloodline. But it is only granted when God calls them to serve." Eden has a moment of reminiscence. "Sibyl served God patiently and unconditionally, spreading his message and wishes to humanity from one generation to the next; throughout every war and evolution. Her initial gifts were like many of the others, to prophesize. Meaning, to read the future, see the past, make predictions, provide answers and—because she was a virgin prophetess—she was able to seduce anyone and anything. Most people think that Oracles were something born out of ancient Greece, but nothing could be further from the truth. The Greeks were just the first to simply document them. Their existence is as old as time itself. We are often led to believe that Adam and Eve were the first two people God created, and that also could not be further from the truth."

"Aren't you Catholic? How are you so certain, don't you believe what the Bible says?" asks the German man, confused by her words.

She smiles at him warmly and says, "I am a servant of God. He's made me a teacher and I share what I know. Saying that God only has one way of doing things is like saying there is only one road to travel on Earth. There is an unlimited amount of knowledge, much of which is not shared by many churches. I'm sure they have their reasons. But having insight into what others may not know, doesn't make me less of a true follower; it actually makes me a more loyal believer. I pray that is the lesson our Church will learn one day."

Silence fills the room. It is definitely a drop-the-mic moment.

"Now, if I may continue?" He nods at her politely, pleased with her response.

"Apennine Sibyl was God's most trusted and loyal Oracle, so He gave her many extended abilities over the years. She was humble and never bragged about what her abilities or 'gifts' were. I suppose we still don't know what they are or what she can do . . . " Eden drifts off for a moment. "Sibyl's story truly begins in Jerusalem shortly before the birth of Jesus. Because she was without a doubt God's favorite of the twelve Oracles, He chose her to deliver the news about the coming of Christ. Upon hearing this news, she begged God to let her be the Mother of Jesus. She wanted it more than anything in the world. Sibyl felt that she had proven her worth and served God well. She had never asked Him for anything before and was certain He would not deny her this request. But then she learned that He had favored a humble virgin instead, and she *rebelled*. She was angered to be disregarded as part of the 'Sibyls of Classic Antiquity,' and not a part of the new world He was creating. She knew that Christianity would make them irrelevant and obscure. She was devastated and felt used and tossed to the side like garbage. You can't imagine how intense she became! That might be where the saying 'Hell on Earth' comes from!" Eden seems very amused with herself and giggles, until she catches on that we aren't laughing. She then clears her throat and carries on with the story.

"God became so angry with her rebellion, that He condemned her to dwell in a cavern within the Sibillini Mountains until Judgement Day. It is said that the last three prophecies were given to her by God. The first was the coming of Christ. The second was the fall of Rome. And the final being, that the *End of the World* takes place in the Central Apennines, in the same area of the Sibillini mountains where Sibyl is said to be in exile. One can't help but wonder what the connection and meaning could be."

"Well two out of the three isn't bad," someone says out loud. Everyone but Eden seems amused by this comment.

"Why there?" Dr. William asks. I can see the excitement in his and Dr. Nina's eyes.

Eden squirms for a moment then replies, "Because all the ancient Oracles claim that there is an entrance to the Underworld there, in that mountain . . . just through that magic realm."

"How fascinating . . . so you're saying if we found her cave, we could find our way to the secrets of the universe," Dr. Nina says, with a glimmer in her eyes.

"Before you get any ideas Dr. Nina, the entrance has been sealed. Anyone who has ever attempted to find, or 'unseal' it if you will, has found it to be an utter failure and a complete waste of resources."

"I don't understand. She was cast to exile because she rebelled against God after a billion years of serving him?" These words somehow fly out of my mouth. Just the idea of that makes me angry.

Eden smiles. "God's word is final. She was made from Him, she knew that."

"Well, we're all allegedly made in His likeness, I mean that's what the Bible says. Then why would God give us free will?" I seem to have no control of my mouth.

"I don't believe God didn't know she would rebel. I think it was always His plan. She was too hurt to see that He was giving her a new purpose in a new world. But the anger overwhelmed her, because she wanted to choose her own fate. She couldn't see it then and she can't see it now."

"*Now?*" Mika asks perturbed.

I glance over at Alessia and Liam; he seems to be glistening sweat. Eden quickly changes the conversation to something she knows we will find even more fascinating.

"Despite the rumors, she is a good and dignified woman. And a *beautiful* woman. She has done anything but dwell; Sibyl has built her own kingdom in these mountains. She is the queen and mother of her own magic—we call them faeries. The peak of Monte Vettore is recognized as her crown. Sibyl is not only a great Oracle, but a great Faerie Mother."

Immense enthusiasm fills the room as everyone bombards Eden with a million questions about Sibyl, faeries, and the Underworld. I take this opportunity to walk around the chapel to get a better look at the paintings. Alessia is right behind me. She begins to inundate me with various connections and theories about how all this could be connected to our family. I reply with several nods of the head and uh-huhs, but I can't concentrate on what she's saying. I keep looking at the "Sibyl"—there is something recognizable about her, but the painting on the ceiling is just too far to really see any detail. I find myself walking in circles with my head tilted up, trying to look at the fresco from different angles.

"Ále, why does she look so familiar? Does she look like someone in our family?" I ask, interrupting her ramble.

"I thought that too, but no." She finally stops talking and looks up with me. Within moments Eden calls everyone back into the circle.

She looks exhausted from the questions but seems happy to move on. She proceeds by sharing that all the areas we visited today are of great importance, not only for their history, but also for their legendary alchemy. Today, it's called "folk medicine," and it's passed down from one generation to the next. This is very familiar to me, because it is the kind of medicine both my grandmothers used. Since there were so few and available doctors, my Nonna Amelia was the town nurse. She has extensive knowledge about this kind of medicine. She built a makeshift apothecary in a shack that was detached from the house, and had various infusions and ointments for diseases, ailments, or minor surgeries. Both of my Nonnas used a collection of roots, flowers, herbs, minerals, vegetables, essential oils, and just about anything that could be useful. I often found that their Old-World ways were better and more effective than modern medicine.

Eden talks about this being a common practice for many centuries for the people of this area. "In past centuries this kind of alchemy was criticized for being magic and used in witchcraft, which of course is mostly not true. Witchcraft was declared a form of heresy by General Inquisitor of Carcassone, Jean Vieneti in 1452. A witch hunt began, and many innocent people lost their lives to such ignorant claims throughout Italy and Europe. The Church was determined to end all Pagan ways, and anything deemed even slightly suspicious was considered witchcraft." She pauses in sadness then clears her throat. "They say this enigmatic land is special and filled with such rich soil, spring sources, and medicinal plants, because Chemistry Sibyl was sent here by God, through prophecy, to discover it and teach others. Thus, it became known as the 'Land of Alchemists,' and people came from all over the world to learn from her. Her mind is a brilliant, endless source of information. She manifested a place where ancient medicine was created and healing could occur. She is credited with formulating many cures for plagues and diseases that ravaged humanity and eliminated civilizations. Devastatingly, during the Holy Inquisition, her precious books that held sacred formulas were taken and destroyed by the Knights. Chemistry Sibyl escaped by the skin of her teeth and nothing would ever be the same again." She pauses in reflection. "I often wonder what our medicinal world would be like today if those books had survived . . . " Eden smiles gently, then places her hands together. "Now, do you remember that surprise I have in store for you? Well, just behind this drape cloth is another fresco painted by Martino Bonfini, of our very own Chemistry Sibyl! Today is the first time it will be seen by the public eye, what a treat!!!"

I blink and the red silk drape is removed from the painting. I gasp for breath as Alessia and I lock hands. This can't be. I've never experienced a panic attack before, but I think it's what I'm feeling. I can hear Eden's voice move further and further away. I put my hand on my heart as I try to calm myself and refocus my eyes on the painting. I want to make sure what I'm seeing is correct. I take a deep breath and blink hard. I open my eyes again and it's her. Julia.

Chapter 12

Yes, that little old darling woman in Luca's kitchen with the sweet husband, Gian Carlo. How is this possible? It looks exactly like her, just slightly younger, but she has the same face, same skin, same profile, she even wears her hair in the same braids around her head like a halo. In the painting, she is wearing a white gown with long sleeves, holding a long tablet with something written in Latin. The dress is similar to what I saw her wear every day at Luca's house—I thought it was just her uniform. Apparently, she's had this look since 1610. How can this be? Could she just be a descendent of Chemistry Sibyl? No. No, I am sure it's her. The long ears, the big eyes, the nose, the full lips, and the distinctive slight hump on her back directly beneath her neck. Just then I remember those remedies she would make . . . no wonder they worked so well. I can't breathe again; I tilt my head back for oxygen.

And if I didn't think I could feel any more insane . . . I catch a glimpse of the ceiling once again. And I see a second woman I recognize. There she is clear as day . . .

Sibyl. *My* Sibyl.

The striking lady I met at the festival. The same one I encountered horse-back riding. I'm sure of it now. It's her, I can see her face clearly as if she suddenly appeared right in front of me. Dear God, how is this possible? It's as if the walls are closing in on me, I need to get out of here. I let go of Alessia's hand and rush out the exit door. I begin to hyperventilate. The moment I step outside the church door, I hunch over and lean against the wall. It feels like my chest is caving in, I hold it tightly with my hand.

"ELI! You're scaring me, breathe. Breathe, Eli!" Alessia stands me upright and hands me a bottle of water.

"Ále, w-what is happening? I don't understand, it's, it's too much," I reply pushing the water bottle away, holding my chest once again.

"I know. I mean, I don't know. Just don't think about that now. Try to slow down your breathing. This hasn't happened since we were children." There's panic in her voice. I know she means well, but it's the last thing I need.

"What?" What is she talking about? I don't ever recall having panic attacks as a child. "Ále, just give me some space. I'm going to the river for some fresh cold water."

"Ok . . . " she replies with a trembling voice. Just then I notice Liam by her side pulling out his cell phone.

"No! Don't call the ambulance!" I shout at him.

"I won't, I promise!" he says to me, slowly putting his cell phone away.

I walk as far as I can to get away from them. But I need water. My thirst is the worst it's been all day and I need to cool down. I stop at a fig tree adjacent to the riverbed. I lean into the river and cup the water in my hands to drink, but it's not enough. My body feels like it's on fire; I start to splash my face, neck, chest and arms. It's still not enough. So, I pull my hair back and put my face completely into the icy cold stream. It is completely silent under the water, and after a few moments I can feel my mind begin to quiet itself in the tranquility of the stream. I sit up, take deep breaths, but I'm still very thirsty so I tilt my head sideways into the stream so I can both breathe and drink. I do that until I can finally feel my heartbeat slow down. My head feels fuzzy, but at least I don't think I'm going to faint anymore. I take off my shoes, roll up my jeans, put my feet in the water and lay with my back against the grass and my head under the fig tree's shadow. Just for that moment, I'm able to close my eyes and block everything out.

Before long, my feet start to feel cold, so I pull them out, sit up, and I pat my face with cold water again. I remember the quiet of the stream and decide to place my head back under water; but this time with my eyes open. I want to see what the perfect crystal ice water looks like from the inside. I feel the water push down-stream from the right side of my face. All I can see are small pebbles at the bottom, other than that everything looks perfectly clear, and the silence is everything I've ever wanted to feel in my mind my entire life. I close my eyes.

"Hello my beautiful girl," I hear a voice and I open my eyes. I see a beautiful woman in the water.

"Darling, I need you to open your mouth. I'm going to blow a bubble into it."

In disbelief, and against my better judgement, I do as she asks and it occurs to me . . . I've officially lost my mind.

She blows the crystal-like bubble into my mouth, and I feel my chest fill up with oxygen. "There that's better. Now you can breathe and speak to me."

"How did you do that? How am I able to do this?"

"Always so many questions," she says, as she smiles back at me and opens her arms for me to look at her. She has long black hair that covers most of her body as it gently sways in the water. She seems to be naked, but I can't tell for sure.

"This water is freezing, aren't you cold?" I ask her.

"No, not at all," she giggles. "Come join me," she says, as she takes me by the hand, and I slip the rest of my body into the stream. I find that my body temperature immediately adjusts and I'm no longer cold. She is exquisite, her body slender and long. She looks a little bit like a very, very young version of my Aunt Ersella. As my eyes move down her body I notice her legs; there seems to be something strange about her legs. As I look closer, I notice several small, soft-blush-colored scales in the shape of abstract seashells from her hips to the bottom of her feet. But her feet are not feet at all, they are fins. OH!

"You're a siren! Of course you are. You look different from the ones I've seen in faerie tales. I must be completely mad. Am I dead? Did I drown in the stream?" I say to what I assume is my hallucination.

"No. And you're not hallucinating either!"

"Oh, so you can read minds too?"

"Well, yes. Kind of. It's more like a connection, a feeling."

"So, I'm sharing feelings with a siren now?" I say, as I close my eyes and shake my head in disbelief of this moment.

"I'm not *just* that. I know today has been very difficult and I can't say it's going to get easier. But Eli, you need to open your mind. If you don't, you might just end up losing it. An open world begins with an open mind. Remember that." We look at one another in silence for a moment, and she caresses my face.

"Eli, Luca will be here in a moment. Please go easy on him, he means well. You will have many difficult moments ahead and you will need him. You will need *everyone*. Be strong, Eli." As she kisses me on the lips, I feel the oxygen leave my chest. And before I know it, Luca is lifting me out of the water.

He slams my back against the grass and starts compressions on my chest; he nearly knocks the wind out of me. I start to cough as I smack his hands away and jump up.

"You lunatic!!! Don't you think you should check if a person is breathing before you start CPR!" I shout at him.

"I'm sorry, I'm so sorry . . . I . . . I just panicked," he says, covering his face with his hands then running them over the top of his head.

"What the *hell* are you doing here anyway?" I ask angrily. In that same moment Alessia, Liam, Mika, and Andre run over to see what's happened.

"That's an excellent question! How did you know where we were?" Alessia asks, shouting.

"Now everyone, take a deep breath," Liam says gently, pushing his hands in a downward motion to calm everyone.

"Who's *this* clown? I mean he's a gorgeous clown, but still . . . clown. Do you guys know him?" Mika asks defensively and with a protective tone. Maybe I have made a real friend in her after all.

"He's a family friend. And a relative of *this* clown," Alessia points to Liam.

"Well then, gorgeous clown number one, the lady asked you a question, you best answer her! And how are you related to gorgeous clown number two?" Mika asks Luca with authority. Andre is standing behind his woman with his arms crossed, looking ready to jump in and protect any of us girls.

Luca locks eyes with Liam, but before Liam can get a word out, Luca stands to his feet to speak.

"Shit you're tall, I didn't see that coming!" Mika shouts, as Andre nods in agreement.

"Liam, let me be the one to explain. This was all my idea and I need to take responsibility," Luca says to him.

"YES, you do," Alessia says, as she walks over to me. I want to believe it is for support, but I think the real reason may be that she wants to put distance between herself and Liam, to keep herself from killing him. Whatever this is, it isn't good, and we can all feel it.

"I . . . I asked Liam to come on this tour when I found out you booked it. I knew you would finally make the connections, and I just wanted someone to be here in case you needed anything. I never meant to intervene, but when I saw you in the water, I panicked."

"Intervene? You mean you've been watching us? Following us?" I'm shouting again. "Why did you have Liam come on this tour if you were going to follow us!"

"Yeah, that's an excellent question," Liam replies, while looking at Luca. I can see he wasn't in on that part of the plan. It is obvious from the look on his face that he is angry Luca didn't completely trust him.

"I wasn't following you guys! I was conducting some business nearby, but I didn't know exactly where you were on the tour because Liam hadn't replied to my recent text message. I was just checking in now and again to make sure things were ok." Luca is interrupted by Alessia physically charging at Liam. She bounces off his solid body like a ball bouncing off of a tree.

"You son of a bitch!!! That's what you were doing on the phone the entire time—texting Luca!?! Telling him our every move? You weren't going to call an ambulance just now, were you? You were going to text him to tell him what happened! Aagghh!!!" Alessia is infuriated and pounding on his chest. I'm sure it feels like a feather to him. Luca grabs her by the waist and lifts her off Liam, she looks like a child in his arms.

"Don't touch me! Get off me!" she shouts at Luca, as she squirms out of his grip.

"Is it weird that this is kind of sexy?" Andre asks.

"YES!" Alessia and I shout at the same moment that Mika shouts, "TOTALLY HOT!"

"I mean yes, no . . . I'm confused, I don't really know what the right answer is anymore," Mika says throwing her arms up, pretending to hit Andre in the arm, as she winks at him.

"Please don't be angry, I was just worried. I didn't know how you would take everything you've learned today. I know this is more than you bargained for. You have every right to be angry with me Eli, I know I'm the last person you want to see. I know I let you down when I broke that promise to you. And I'm just trying to make it right. I may not be doing things the way you want me to, but I have NO choice in the matter. Please believe me." I can see by the look on his face that he is sincere.

"Ok then, let's start with the truth. Who is Liam to you?" I ask demandingly.

"Liam is his middle name. His first name is Dante. Dante Liam Vinci, he is my brother. Son of Victoria Mason and Alessandro Vinci. Brother to Micella Vinci," he says proudly.

"BROTHERS?" Alessia screams. She looks like she might have a meltdown.

"I promise Alessia, nothing else I've said to you today was a lie," Dante says, trying to comfort her, but she pushes him away.

"Man, we thought LA was drama!" Andre says laughing. Mika nudges him and shakes her head.

"Sorry," Andre says to us sheepishly.

"So you had Lia-Dante fly out from England just to go on a tour with us. Don't you think that's a bit *crazy*?" I ask Luca.

"No, he is here on business too. This was just a favor I asked of him."

"See, I didn't lie," Dante pleads with Alessia. She rolls her eyes at him.

"If Dante didn't tell you where we are, then how did you know?" I ask Luca.

"Look at your necklace Eli," he replies, staring at my pendant, "you must have thought of me when you touched it."

I completely forgot that I was wearing the crystal Dwintra had given me, that Aunt Ersella had placed in a pendant on my necklace. Her words echoed in my mind about its meaning and what it does. Like everything else, I chose not to believe her. And like everything else in my life, I was wrong.

"What, does it have GPS? . . . Never mind that, but since we're on the topic of weird shit, how about we address something a little more important. Like the *MERMAID* we all saw swim upstream! ANY thoughts on that, anyone!!! . . . NO? REALLY?" Mika has lost her patience, calling us out on the topic we most wanted to avoid. I see Luca and Dante cringe in the corner of my eye as she says it.

Since no one else will really be able to answer, I decide it is best to tell them what I do know. "Yes, it was a siren. I'm relieved that you all saw her too, I thought I was losing my mind. I have no idea how to explain it . . . I'm not sure I ever will. It *is* weird shit. I'm sorry, I hope you don't regret making friends with us."

"Are you kidding, this is the BEST honeymoon ever!!!" Andre exclaims. "We thought this was going to be a mildly boring tour with a bunch of stinky old people. But instead, we got to make rad friends and see a bunch of supernatural creatures, which is totally nuts! Seriously, other than marrying my wife, this is THE COOLEST thing that's ever happened! I mean no one is going to believe us, but who cares!" Andre says with so much joy.

Thank God for his words, they put me at ease.

"Creatures, as in plural?" Luca asks. I guess he caught that.

"Yeah dude, there was the deer with the golden horns hiding in the forest in Pantano. The girls even got a picture with it."

Alessia and I look at each other and have no idea what Andre is talking about.

"And then there was that amber light that looked like electricity that was bouncing all over the forest in Lapide—"

"Yeah! And then there were those crazy werewolves in Cona. And those other things in Gee that looked like . . . bees maybe? And of course, a MERMAID. Hello! Dang, I can't wait to see what's next!" Mika adds with excitement.

Dante, Alessia, and I all look at each other in disbelief. Other than the wolfdogs we seemed to have completely missed everything else.

"Really guys?" Luca says disapprovingly at our lack of attention. He then reverts back to questioning Mika and Andre.

"Do you know if anyone else noticed or mentioned anything about these 'creatures'?"

"Just the kids, Eric and Vanessa. Other than us, they are the only ones that saw what we saw," Mika answers. "Why?"

"Just curious," Luca says casually.

"Uh-hum," she replies, looking at him up and down.

Our private gathering is interrupted by rapidly approaching footsteps.

"Eli, why are you all wet? Did you fall into the river?" Eden asks frantically walking over to me. She glares at Luca then snaps at him, "Luca *what* are you doing here?"

"You know each other?" I ask her, as she takes off her scarf and starts to dry me off with it. Luckily with today's humidity I should dry off quickly.

"Yes. Luca why are you here?" she asks again, this time with a stronger tone.

"Yes, Ms. Eden is my greatest childhood teacher. We've known each other a long time." Dante says with respect in his voice, before Luca can answer.

"So, I suppose that's *Dante* and NOT *Liam*? He was just a small child the last time I saw him. It's nice to know he turned out to be a manipulator, just like his father. The Vincis and I go back a long way. Let's just say they're not fans of my teaching skills, nor my honesty," she says sternly, helping me dry my hair.

"Ms. Eden, you have a right to be cross with my father and my family. But you know what you mean to me," Luca says to her lovingly.

And in his usual charming form, he wins her back with those sweet words. He leans in and they embrace. She then embraces Dante too and apologizes for taking a cheap shot at him. She tells us that there's no time to catch up now because we need to get to our next stop. She asks if Luca will be joining us for the rest of the tour.

"With your permission, I would like to follow since I have my car with me," Luca replies.

"Yes, that will be fine. But I think your brother should ride with you to Casalicchio. Alessia looks like she could use a breather. Or we might find ourselves with a fatal situation on the bus."

We all agree in unison.

The five of us are the last on the bus. Eden being the true professional doesn't miss a beat. She reports to the tour that the sixth stop to Santa Maria di Casalicchio is less than fourteen kilometers and about twenty minutes away and excites them with some historical details. Meanwhile, Alessia and I sit at the very back of the bus for a little privacy. We check in with one another, but it's obvious that neither one of us are okay. She pulls out her makeup bag and starts to clean up the smeared makeup off my face. I pull out my phone to see what Andre was talking about. I notice several missed calls from my mom, but I'm not going to bother reading or listening to any of the messages, I'm sure Luca has that covered. I begin to look through the photos erratically.

"Shit Ále! Andre was right!" I whisper, "Look! If that's not a deer with golden horns, I don't know what is. How are we so oblivious? Are we really that self-absorbed that we didn't notice this?"

"Well, we were in the middle of trying to figure out who li-ar-liar-Liam-Dante was. Let me see." She gestures and takes the phone from my hand. "I'm speechless—a deer with golden horns and a siren all on the same day! And why do I have a feeling it doesn't end here?"

"That's what she said."

"Who?"

"The siren."

"She spoke to you, Eli? Oh my God, tell me everything!" she whisper-screams. I go through every detail with Alessia, how the siren looked and every word she said, including her warnings to me.

Our conversation then moves onto Dwintra and the crystal. I contemplate taking it off, but Alessia discourages it in case I should need to reach her. Since neither one of us really under-stand how it works, we decide to give it a trial run. I go into the bus's bathroom, close my eyes, and hold the crystal as I think of Alessia. After a few minutes I walk out, and I ask her if she felt anything. She says it is not just a feeling, she could actually hear my voice calling her name in her head. Then she describes an urge to close her eyes, and when she did, she could see exactly where I was, like a satellite that zooms in to an exact location. She's in disbelief about how much detail there was, but she also seems frazzled.

"Was there anything else, Ále?"

"Well . . . It's more than hearing and seeing you, Eli. I could also *feel* you. As in, I could feel what *you* are feeling. Now I un-derstand why Luca was so panicked and blew their cover. Please don't be mad at me for saying that."

"No, of course not."

"Eli, I didn't realize how scared you are. I'm sorry I've been so selfish. I have been so determined to find out the truth, that I wasn't thinking about what kind of impact it would have on *you*. Your mind works in opposition to all of this, I see that now. I can feel how it's shaken you to your core and made you question everything you know. This is totally out of your comfort zone, and I didn't ever think of how out of control and afraid you might be. I've pushed you too hard, I'm sorry. At the next stop, we can ask Luca to take us home and this will all end here. We don't have to keep going. Maybe it's not too late to get your job back; I bet if you hop on that plane and make your case, they'll take you back in a heartbeat."

"You got all that from a stone?" I slightly smile at her, as she grabs my hand.

"Yes. And you've calmed down a lot since the chapel. I can't even imagine the depth of what Luca may have felt from you."

"You make a good point, Ále. But we both know it's too late to stop this now, you can't un-ring a bell. I'm trying to open my mind, but it's hard for me. I'm trying to contemplate and understand why so much has been kept secret from the entire world for so long. I think about all those people out there that are lost and alone. People who are dying to find a purpose and something to believe in, even a little something that will give their life worth. Do you know how many lives can be saved and how much good can come from people knowing the truth? Just to have an answer as simple as to why we are here on Earth. And more importantly, is God real? The idea that an alchemist could have the solution for disease, famine, infertility, war, pain, and maybe even *fucking world peace itself*, blows my mind! Why would anyone deliberately keep that from humanity?" I go silent as my mind starts racing a million miles a minute, thinking about the endless possibilities.

"Fucking world peace . . . " Alessia says as her eyes drift off.

"Do you know what the worst thing of all this is?" I ask Alessia.

"Oh my God, there's a worst thing?" Alessia replies sarcastically.

"Julia is ALIVE. All these years she could have rewritten the books. Why didn't she? Why did she stop helping people?"

"Um, maybe because they tried to kill her!"

"No, I don't believe that. She is the Chemistry Sibyl, you know . . . from God. A little threat isn't going to keep her from doing his will."

"Well, maybe she got another memo from Him to stop."

She has a valid point, He is her boss after all. But something inside me isn't satisfied. I need to see her as soon as possible.

"Are we ever going to talk about sex-vixen Sibyl? I mean the girl has not aged a day! Damn!" Alessia says with her eyes wide open, shaking her head.

"I can't even start that conversation. She was cast into exile because she argued with God about being Jesus' mother. Then she became mother of the faeries. Who are possibly connected to our grandmothers—according to Aunt Silva. So, what's the connection between faeries, Oracles, Virgo, and the Seven Sisters? I mean, what does all of this have to do with one another?" It's all just jumbled in my mind and I'm starting to confuse myself.

"Shut up, Eli! You are making my head hurt!" Alessia snaps at me.

*   *   *

Out of the bus window, on our way to Montemonaco where Santa Maria di Casalicchio is, I see a sign that says Venarotta. It's pointing east from the direction we are traveling in. I remember my Nonna Rosa. I was born in a hospital in Ascoli Piceno, but I was raised and spent the first five and a half years of my life in Venarotta. Before we moved to the United States, I spent every day with my Nonna Rosa. We were best friends and completely inseparable. I could not go anywhere without her; she was my entire world. Both my parents worked long hours—sometimes even in other countries—and I was lucky enough to spend every day with her. She was a patient and kind person, not a bad bone in her body. No one I've ever met had an ill word to say about her. Everything about her was extraordinary; she was unique in her thinking and being. She often saw things differently than others, but never spoke up and never argued. And yet silently, without opening her mouth, she always managed to get her way. She was brave and strong, but not as fearless as her true best friend, Nonna Amelia. Together they seemed to create the perfect human being; they were unstoppable. Looking back, I don't know how they managed to do so much in a day, a week, a lifetime. They would often say that we all live on borrowed time, and we need to make each day count. Being too small to understand the statement, I can recall asking who the time was borrowed from. Nonna Rosa would laugh and tell me I would understand someday, but I still don't completely get what that saying means. Maybe I should ask Nonna Amelia before I lose my chance again.

Luca and Dante arrive before the bus. I can see them leaning up against a black car. Alessia is once again impressed by Luca's choice. But I can't tell the difference between the last four I've seen him drive. They walk over as the bus doors open and help everyone off. I notice a few of the ladies fix their hair before exiting. I can't even imagine what they must think of these rich, chivalrous, handsome lying jerks. When it's my turn to exit the bus, Luca reaches for my hand to help me down the stairs. But I still feel too angry to accept any assistance from him, so I keep my head down without making eye contact and ignore him. I can hear Alessia behind me telling him not to feel bad and to just give me a moment to process.

It's hard to imagine anything bothering Luca; other than that moment in Ambro when he thought I was drowning; he's always so composed. My anger towards him makes me realize that I care, and I don't want to care. I have enough going on without trying to make sense of whatever this entanglement with Luca is about. I know I should feel intimidated by his looks and position in life, maybe even feel like he is my superior, but I don't. I can't make out if I feel this way because *he* makes me feel equal to him, or just because of the many years living in Los Angeles. There is always someone in LA who thinks they are more successful, more beautiful, smarter and richer than you, and they let you know it. The city will chew you up and spit you out if you don't believe in yourself. Sometimes I think that kind of self-worth that I refer to as my dignity, is the very reason why all of my relationships fail. I know I'm still young, but from my point of view, it feels like most men are just too lazy to treat their wives or girlfriends like queens. There seems to be a kind of obstinate mentality in the men of our modern society, because equal rights should not, and do not, dictate less chivalry. Both men and women should never trade one for the other, but instead, create a balance of both. I turn my head to look back at Luca and I wonder what kind of man he truly is inside. As a million thoughts about his character go through my mind, I realize that we have already entered the church, and I have no idea how long Eden has been speaking.

The church is rich with beautiful frescos, but you'd never guess it by its humble and simple exterior. Eden points out its Gothic style and describes its many alterations and radical changes over hundreds of years. Like the other churches we visited today, this one is also built on the ruins of an ancient Pagan temple. It astounds me to see the lengths the Church went to eradicate Paganism.

I raise my hand and Eden calls on me. "Why did they do it?

Why did the Church erase so much of the world's history? We have the right to know what existed here before Jesus."

Eden smiles, "Yes we do. Even though many believed Jesus was the son of God, they also still believed in the Old World and its ways, such as alchemy and magic. But these kinds of things could not be controlled. And the Church sought to control the population and demanded submissive behavior. And the only way to force people into submission, was to take away their control and free will. All Pagan rituals, buildings, and holidays were replaced with Christian ones, attempting to erase the Old World. But much to their dismay, the Old World lives on, and will continue to, until God—not humans—decides differently. I know for many religious people this way of speaking is inappropriate, but right or wrong, this is our history. There is no way of telling it other than honestly."

Her candor is refreshing.

Eden changes the conversation and continues walking us through the church. The natural light shines in from the large windows, allowing us to see the lovely frescos perfectly. There is one in particular on the right side of the wall that catches my eye. It is an image in the lunette of the Virgin Mary ascending into Heaven, as Jesus supports her.

"Dormition of the Virgin," Luca says to me as I transfix on the piece.

"What does that mean?"

"Madonna of Death," he replies.

"Huh, I never thought about her death. Or even how long she lived," I pause. "But from this depiction, she doesn't really die, she's just escorted to Heaven by Jesus."

"Nothing gets past you, Eli," Luca says with a smile.

I look into his eyes.

"That's the problem Luca, everything has gotten past me for

almost twenty-five years. My life used to be safe. Predictable. Now I learn that my life is—*this*. Unexplainable. Illogical. Unsafe." He stays quiet.

"Why did God choose a mortal, normal girl to be Jesus' mother instead of Sibyl? Was she really His favorite?" I ask him, as I turn my attention back to the lunette. "And don't say you don't know. I have a feeling that you absolutely do, since she's your neighbor!" He waits a moment before he answers.

"Yes, she was His favorite. She still is. But she can't see it, because He didn't give her what she wanted. He chose Mary because He wanted the world to know that humans could also be called to do divine work. Up until that point only Oracles, Founding Fathers and Mothers, Celestial Beings, priests, kings, and queens had been permitted to do the work of God. He wanted to change that and show His people that He believed in them, and that they were also in His favor."

"Well, that backfired! Humans have managed to erase and rewrite history. And so many leaders nearly killed civilization time and time again just to become the 'ruler of the world,'" I reply cynically.

"That temperament has always existed, mortal or not. Just not as often. Today it seems to happen in every generation. I think it's because people don't know if God is real."

"Is He?" I lock eyes with Luca.

"Yes," he replies with that beautiful smile. "Let's get back to the group, the best part is coming up."

I roll my eyes as he laughs.

We walk to the outside of the church. I hear water and look around and notice a riverbank nearby. I rub my throat and feel it burn as my thirst returns. I notice a fountain nearby that receives its water from the river. I run over quickly to drink from it.

"Easy. I don't want to have to do CPR again," Luca says jokingly, standing behind me. Looks like the entire gang is watching me closely now. Alessia, Dante, Mika, and Andre are all surrounding him.

"What? Guys, what do you think I'm going to do, jump into the river?" I say sarcastically. They respond by either crossing their arms or raising an eyebrow. I shake my head and make my way back to the group where Eden is waiting for us.

"Now that we're all here, I'd like to share the most interesting part of this church," Eden begins. She draws our attention to the only decorative area on the entire outside of the church. She points to two stars on either side of an installed concrete lancet window. The one on the left is an upright six-point star. And the one on the right is a five-point star, slightly tilted to the left. Eden explains, "The hexagram on the left is often referred to as the 'Star of Creation' in Christianity. Its origin is intended to be a symbol of the perfect balance achieved between God and man, and if maintained, the result would be Nirvana. It IS depicted with similar meanings in various religions around the world, thus showing that we are united under one God, regardless of the name people call Him by. Remember earlier today in Lapide, we learned that if God is the branch, then the tree is life. And so, we see this star pattern within something called the 'Tree of Life' throughout the world." Eden points to it again. "A star within a tree is an image older than *any* known religion."

Her statement startles me, I suddenly recall the painting in the Vincis' home and how the gold of the painting matched perfectly with the necklace Micella was wearing. Eden goes on to say that in Paganism, the hexagram is often seen as the combination of the four elements.

"Fire." With her finger she shows us the upward pointing triangle.

"Air." Also upward pointing triangle, but with a horizontal line going through its center.

"Water." Downward pointing triangle.

"Earth." Downward pointing triangle, but with a horizontal line also through its center. Eden continues to move her fingers through the lines.

"When fire and water are combined it creates a hexagram. When air and earth are combined it also creates a hexagram. Put them together, and it is a double hexagram. And lastly, combining the elements of fire, air, water, and earth is the very thing that creates life. Bringing it back full circle to the 'star' and/or the 'tree of life.'"

She moves our attention over to the left of the tilted pentagram. I know I've seen this image before, but I can't pinpoint exactly where.

"Mr. and Mrs. Matthew, can you tell us the first artifact found with a symbol of the pentagram?" Eden asks the archeologists.

"Well, there are three dated around approximately the same time. The first is a flint scraper in the Israeli Negev desert dated 4500-3100 BC. The second was found in Mesopotamia 3200-300 BC on a spindle and a vase. And the third on an Egyptian hieroglyph dated 3100 BC. This one in particular had a pentagram enclosed in a circle, which symbolizes the Netherworld— the underworld of the dead," Dr. Nina says with joy in her voice, pleased to have been able to share some of her knowledge with the group.

"Excellent Nina, thank you," Eden says with gratitude. "Who can tell me what it means for Christians?"

"The star of Bethlehem and the incarnation of Jesus Christ," says someone in the group.

"Wonderful! And who can tell me what it meant in the Old World?" Eden asks the group. Everyone is quiet until Dante raises his hand.

"The 5 elements. The top point symbolizing the Spirit, and

the other four being Fire, Air, Water and Earth."

"Looks like you were paying attention after all, young man," she smiles at him and he smiles back.

"Why does it tilt to the left?" Alessia asks. Looks like we're back to her reading my mind.

"It is tilting West. We know it to be the way the sun sets, but more importantly, it is the direction the Earth and the moon rotate. If the Earth rotates then we can walk, drive, and live. If the Earth did not rotate, then we best tie ourselves to the Flintstones' bedrock," Eden says, laughing along with Luca and Dante. It must be an inside joke because no one else is laughing.

"Well, we've seen the star used all over the world, in flags and symbols of excellence. It takes on endless meanings in various cultures and religions. You may recognize this particular star shape made famous by the organization associated with Freemasonry, called the Order of the Eastern Star. That history is just much too long, let's just say—" Eden stops abruptly as she looks at Luca. I notice a moment of tension as she sees both boys cross their arms in disapproval of where the conversation is heading.

"Goodness, where was I," Eden says to the group, pretending to have lost her train of thought. But she's just not that good of an actress. "Ah, yes—" she says, then stops abruptly again. This time she pushes her shoulders back, lifts her head up, and moves her body in the opposite direction of the boys without ever taking her eyes off them. Her body language is clearly stating that she will not be told what to do. "On second thought, I will tell a brief story," Eden states, darting one last stare toward the boys before looking away.

"Um-hum, girl it's about to go down. Take out your note pad," Alessia smirks quietly to me.

She's right, this is obviously not a topic Luca and Dante want her to discuss. The conversation with Sophia pops into my mind.

I remember her saying that Victoria Mason was head of the Mason family, making her the leader of the Freemason organization. Although it's unclear what Victoria's true role is, I suppose Luca and Dante don't want mommy's secrets getting out.

"Order of the Eastern Star is a division of the Freemasons open to both men and women. This is important, because Freemasonry is strictly a fraternal organization. There are several ludicrous stories about dates and names of the creators, who their members are, and what purpose they serve. It is safe to say that just about everything you read about them on Wikipedia or in various books, is mostly inaccurate. They are a secret society with a very deceptive public image." I can hear Luca's jaw lock as she says this. "The irony of it being a fraternal organization is that their leader is, and has always been, a woman. I know that because I personally know her and have for many years."

I can hear the groups' interest peak as they generate enthusiasm and begin to ask questions. I look over at the boys who both look like they're about to have a meltdown. I can't help but giggle a bit.

"I wish I could answer all your questions," Eden continues, "but that would mean this tour extending another day. Let's get back to the original point. These men called Master Masons are her messengers, her soldiers, her peacekeepers, and her loyal guardians. She had no choice but to use men for many years because, well, women did not have the same rights for the greater part of history. In the mid 1800s, the Order of the Eastern Star was created for the daughters, widows, wives, sisters, and mothers of the Master Masons, to serve. These women also have titles and serve in unique positions. Both the men and women swear upon the duty of obedience to the will of God. And as we learned today, the will of God was given to His people by His messengers, the Oracles, before the birth of Jesus."

That's it! That's the missing link! This is what Sophia was talking about, the secret she's been trying to unravel. Victoria must be one of the twelve original Oracles—the keeper of the world's secrets. That would explain the Mason Library, the endless artifacts, and extensive global connections. It also might explain why Luca is unable to open up to me.

Eden goes on to explain that character-building lessons are taught in the Order with stories inspired from biblical figures, such as: Adah—daughter; Ruth—widow; Ester—wife; Martha—sister; Electa—mother. As she explains why the ray points downward—something about a manger—I take that moment to hide behind Alessia and pull out my disposable cell phone to text Sophia. When we were children, we would play a game converting numbers in correspondence to the alphabet, to write out the name of the boy we had a crush on. It was our way of keeping others from finding out. If there was ever a time to bring it back, this was it.

TEXT:

*Sophia, I miss that game we used to play when
we were kids. We had so many crushes, so boy crazy!*

22.9.3.20.15.18.9.1	[Victoria]
14.1.19.15.14	[Mason]
9.19	[Is]
1.14	[An]
15.18.1.3.12.5	[Oracle]

SEND.

I quietly slip my phone back into my purse. Alessia whispers that it was a great idea to use code to text Sophia.

"I don't know what I'm more freaked out by, you or a siren reading my mind," I whisper behind her ear.

"You didn't tell me she could read your mind," Alessia responds surprised.

"The fact that I spoke to a siren might have taken precedence. She said it's more like a connection, a feeling," I reply.

"Yes, that's exactly right."

"How long have you been able to do this, Ále?"

"I guess in a way all my life, but the last few hours it's been . . . intense." I've been so caught up with my own emotions that it never occurred to me that Alessia may have been going through changes too. Looks like we are both lacking in some much-needed self-awareness.

"Why didn't you tell me?" I ask her, feeling guilty.

She pulls me under her arm and embraces me. "Didn't seem urgent. Now shut up and pay attention."

Eden moves onto the lancet window in between the stars. She points out that the window is overlooking the Old Road. I suppose it's another thing all the churches have in common. Someone in the group finally asks why a window would be made of solid concrete and wouldn't that defeat its purpose. She explains that it was not always concrete, it had been filled during one of its many alterations. Dr. William suggests that using such material may have been symbolic. Since the lancet name comes from the shape of a pole weapon or spear, it would have shown strength against enemy spies and allegiance to the Church. Eden confirms his theory, adding that during the Holy Inquisition, Santa Maria di Casalicchio became a place of political sanction, and used for the four neighboring "free communes" to come together to pray for peace. Going to war in God's name has always been a difficult concept for me to digest. It's contradictory and hypocritical. I once saw an inscription on a lighter that sums it up best:

Going to war for peace is like fucking for virginity.

"Ms. Eden, we did some research and saw that Lake Pilate is very close to here. Would it be possible to take a small detour or a different route to Foce by way of the lake?" Dr. Nina pleads. "We were hoping and wanting to see it, and the kids are dying to see the faerie shrimp! And I'm certain it would be exciting for the group."

Everyone begins to ask about faerie shrimp and the lake. The doctor sure knows how to stir things up. Eden is trying to explain and regroup everyone's thoughts. "It is close, but it is nearly a six-hour hike to get there and back from the lake. There is no easy way to access the lake by car. Well, actually, there might be one . . . there is a single private road that cuts across the mountains and takes you directly there. It happens to be owned by the family of two of our guests today. Maybe if you ask nicely, they will say yes and allow us to use it." Eden looks at Luca and Dante with a smile. Although her demeanor has changed, it's evident that they are still upset with her.

Everyone turns their attention to the boys and begins to ask for the favor. I'm a bit surprised at how excited everyone is over a lake and some shrimp. I didn't even think they'd want to add anything onto our already extremely long day.

"I don't think that's wise; no one has used the road in some time. And it still requires a thirty-minute walk from the car parking to the lake," Luca replies.

"I hate to ask for so much, but it would really mean the world to us," Dr. Nina is pleading with the boys.

"This is not a good idea," Dante leans in and says sternly to Luca.

Little Vanessa walks up to Luca and Dante and holds out her hand.

"Hi, I'm Vanessa," she says, shaking both of their hands, "and that's my brother Eric," he waves. "My parents lied to us and said that the lake was a part of this tour. They knew that was the only way we'd come. So, if you could please do us this favor, it would make today worth it, and I'll probably talk to them again before I'm 18."

Everyone laughs at her confident charm, and I can see it does the trick. There was no way they could resist sweet Vanessa. The brothers look at each other for a moment, and then Luca turns to address Eden.

"Ok, tell your driver to follow us closely. We will go slow since it's mostly paved in gravel, but we should be there in 15 minutes."

"You are good, kid," Alessia whispers to Vanessa, as she pats her on the shoulder.

"Just keepin' it real," she answers, pleased with herself.

Chapter 13

W̲HEN WE GET BACK on the bus, Eden informs us that we will not be able to stay at the lake for longer than twenty minutes. This impromptu stop will delay our tour by thirty minutes. She urges everyone who is being picked up to call their rides, and let them know we will not be returning to Montegallo until 6:30 instead of 6:00 pm. Even with the delay, everyone seems content and talkative. It's funny how no matter how old you are, inside each person there is a rebellious side that seeks adventure.

As we approach the private road down the street from the church, I see two security guards at a station. Luca stops to explain the situation. They look so serious, for a moment I think they're going to ask for our passports, but instead, they allow us straight through. By the time we reach the bottom of the hill, it doesn't just look like a different country, it looks like a different dimension. I can hear the audible gasps, and my own heart skips a beat. Eden said we were in for a treat, but I could never have imagined *this*. Pastel colors like I've never seen, the heavens look pink, the rocks on the mountains are baby blue and white. The grass is long and a pastel yellow, but the earth is mint green, and together they reflect a chartreuse hue. The trees are sparse, but are absolutely the largest I've ever seen, with millions of bright lavender flowers hanging from them. The trunks are wide with deep roots spreading as far as I can see. There is wildlife everywhere. I find myself captivated by the metallic-silver butterflies. I can see their wings reflect off the sunlight—they sparkle like diamonds. Alessia and I are speechless; our eyes cannot absorb all the details of this beautiful land. It's no wonder the Vincis keep it private. If I owned something this magnificent, I wouldn't share it either, for fear that someone might taint it.

The fifteen-minute ride feels like a flash. We reach the other side of the mountain before we know it. We must have been so caught up with the sights, that when the security guards open the gate and let us through, we're not prepared. Things look different on this side of the mountain. Still beautiful, but ordinarily beautiful, like a world without the magic of rose-colored glasses, if there is such a thing. Half a mile down, the bus pulls into a designated car parking area. As we exit the bus, there is a wave of euphoria in us all, like we'd all shared something truly magical. I can see Eden, Luca, and Dante standing next to each other smiling. I see their mouths moving, but I can't make out what they're saying to one another. I feel so happy and so at peace, that I don't even care. All of today's fears and distress have fallen at my feet and away from my soul.

The thirty-minute walk to the lake is easy, and much needed to stretch our legs. The air here is clean, so clean that I can feel it burning in my chest. I seem to feel it more than the others. They tease me and say it's because I'm from Los Angeles, and I'm used to breathing in pollution and poison. They might be right. We reach the lake and it does not disappoint. Everyone graciously thanks Luca and Dante for allowing us to take the shortcut so we can experience something so special. The ladies do not miss the opportunity to hug them both, even little Vanessa. I see Alessia staring at Dante. They haven't spoken in an hour and a half, which is the longest they have gone without speaking to one other since they've met. Which is now eight hours. The idea of it makes me want to roll my eyes into the back of my head, but what if they really have a special connection? I don't know anything about love at first sight, but I think I may have witnessed it happen today. She seems to gravitate to him in a way I have never seen her do with anyone else. I give her a nudge and tell her to go speak to him. As he sees her walking in his direction, he doesn't hesitate, and takes giant leaps with his stilt-legs until he reaches her. I watch him desperately throw his arms around her small body and embrace her tightly with his eyes closed. It must be all the euphoria still circulating in my mind, because I feel a bit moved by it. I've never wanted anything more than to watch Alessia find true happiness, and I think I just did.

I feel Vanessa taking me by the arm, and walking me over to where her parents, brother, Mika, and Andre are standing. Silently, in a breathtaking valley encompassed by hills and mountains, we look around and take in the surroundings. This is true paradise for nature lovers. There are unusual plants and animals in the area that we've never seen before. Dr. Nina takes several photographs of the curious creatures. She then carefully cuts samples of the plants, as Eric diligently labels them in small, separate bags for her. In the meantime, the rest of us are enraptured by the multi-colored rock formations along the mountainside. They all look so well blended, there is no true solid color. All the colors of the universe living in unison, peacefully together intermixed and layered. There is not one hue trying to overpower the other. Each color blazes with just the right amount of intensity, permitting each one to shine, while simultaneously enhancing the beauty of the other. This collaboration manifests into something so unique, it's nearly indescribable in beauty. If only humanity could find such a way to coexist.

I quietly stand in admiration of some of Mother Nature's greatest work, when I feel a chill down my spine. Although there is nothing tangible or obviously strange to concern me, it is still a place surrounded by an aura of mystery. Dr. William and Dr. Nina tell us about their recent visit to the Sibyl Museum in Villa Curi, Montemonaco. I'm surprised to hear such a museum exists. What could they possibly have on display, faerie dust? They reassure us that it is filled with rich historical artifacts, and countless art pieces and exhibits that include ancient books and scrolls. They were impressed with the curators' ability to marry the charm and history of this land with the myths, magic and legends that surround it. They seemed most enraptured with something they called the "Great Stone." It is thousands of years old and was discovered at the basin of Lake Pilate, with letters scratched into it that look like scars. Scientists and archeologists have been studying what they refer to as "Sand Language" but have not been able to make much progress. There is little understanding of the language and what it could mean, other than it played a very important role during dark times.

The lake is in the middle of this wide valley, and in the heart of the Sibillini Mountains, right under Monte Vettore. It's one of the very few glacial lakes in the Apennines. Water from the rain and melting snow is what fills the lake annually. Of course, even with all the beauty around us, we are most excited about the faerie shrimp. There are thousands of them swimming all around in the crystal-clear water. I lean in and see them perfectly, as their small bodies cast a shadow on the brown and black rocks inside the lake.

"These faerie shrimp are a species of crustacean called *Chirocephalus marchesonii*. They are only found here in this lake, and nowhere else in the world. There are other types of faerie shrimp globally of course, but not like these. Isn't that incredible, kids?" Dr. William says to Vanessa and Eric. Meanwhile, we all respond with fascination to his words. He realizes that we have all become his audience, and proceeds to tell us about the faerie shrimp. He dips his hand in the water as a cluster of them swim over to the palm of his hand. "See how they move around each other, it's like a mesmerizing dance. Amazing, they are almost feather-like!"

Everyone but me puts their hand into the water to experience what he's talking about. I can't believe that less than an hour ago we didn't even know such things existed. We are all in awe of these delicate creatures. They have black eyes and their bodies are a coral color, and they're transparent.

"Both sexes measure anywhere from nine to twelve millimeters. The body is divided into three parts—its face, the thorax that has seven pairs of fins for breathing function, and the abdomen, which holds their reproductive organs. An egg sac for the female and two penises the same size as the sac, for the male."

"Ewww Dad, that's gross!!! Really?" both Eric and Vanessa shout out.

"Babe, that's the dream," Andre says to Mika, smiling from ear to ear.

"For us both, babe," Mika replies tapping his chest, as she and Dr. Nina start laughing. I'm fairly certain the kids and I look disgusted at their sexual innuendos.

"These fascinating creatures adapt to their environment and are subject to long seasonal stress, such as the lake freezing or draining. In order to overcome these difficulties, the *Chirocephalus* produce a form of resistance around the embryo called a 'cyst.' It protects and keeps them vital, until there are ideal conditions for them to hatch. Their life span as adults is only a few months, so, it's important for them to choose the time that will give them the longest span possible. These cysts can be left season after season without hatching, at times even for many years, to ensure survival of their species. Climate change has made it very difficult for these little guys, and they could very well disappear in a few decades if we don't begin to do right by Mother Earth," Dr. William says with admiration and sadness. I start to move my hand closer to the water and before my fingers are wet, I notice that all the shrimp begin to swim in my direction.

"Way to put a damper on it, Dad," Eric says as he takes his hand out of the water and splashes him. This turns into a playful exchange, and I get caught in their crossfire. As I open my mouth to laugh, a huge splash lands on my face and in my mouth. I'm trying to spit out the water when Dr. William reassures me that that water is safe, and there is nothing for me to be concerned about. Good thing, because I accidently swallowed some. I find myself drenched once again.

"Eli, you really need to not make a habit of this," Eden teases me as she hands me her scarf once again to dry off.

"I'm sorry Ms. Eden, I think I owe you a new scarf now," I reply, only partially joking.

"Oh, that's alright. It looks like it was a lot of fun. Are you enjoying yourself today?" she asks me.

"Yes, I think so. It's been a bit of a rollercoaster," I reply.

"I suppose it has. Real history, opposed to perspective history, is always a rollercoaster. Your mind must undo the stories you know, to make room for the truth you don't. And I don't get the impression you want to live blindly."

"You're not *just* a tour guide, are you?" I ask her point blank. She smiles back at me and waits a moment before she replies.

"No. Well, yes and no. Not by the modern definition, but I did well today, wouldn't you agree? Today was a favor for Father

Gabriel. I didn't understand why he asked, until I saw you get onto the bus. I saw your face, and instantly I knew who you were. I must say, you are more *divine* than any of us could have imagined."

"Oh, thank you, but—" I begin to say, as Eden cuts me off.

"No darling, not in that way—but of course you are of superb beauty. Divine as in *divinity*."

My face must have drawn a blank, because I have no idea what she means. So, she tries to further explain. "Proceeding directly from God . . . Heaven-like." This still makes no sense to me, and she can tell. "Eli, at our final stop we are going to wrap things up, and I will answer questions about these churches and the Virgo constellation. It will be the link you will need to make your connections."

"Why can't you just tell me? Why can't anyone tell me? It all feels like a cat–and-mouse game," I say, frustrated once again.

"Well, no one's told the reason. But if I had to speculate based on all parties involved . . . I would say it's because you need to SEE the truth, not hear it. Which means you're a skeptic, an Igni."

"Igni?" I repeat laughing, "So you know my grandmother and aunt?"

"Honey, *everybody* knows your grandmother and aunt!"

"Not everyone. Just those in *that world*," I say, rolling my eyes.

"Yes, you're an Igni alright. And why do you say '*that world*' like it's a bad thing?" Eden says crossing her arms and lifting her eyebrows. "The irony of Amelia and Rosa sharing an Igni grand-child. No one will believe it!"

"I don't mean to be rude, but I don't know what 'that world' is? I haven't been given the language! I don't even know what to call . . . them . . . you . . . *that world*. Or whatever the hell all this is."

"Well, that doesn't seem fair to you now, does it? Your mother and father did a great job keeping all of it from you," she says, pondering her own thoughts.

I remain quiet.

"Now listen, I only have a few minutes to cover the history of the lake. But at the end of the day, if you still have questions, I'd be happy to answer them for you. Everyone knows I don't follow the rules. And Father Gabriel knows I can't keep my mouth shut. He shouldn't have asked me to do this if he expected better from me," Eden says tapping her foot.

"I'm sure that's precisely why he asked you. He doesn't seem like a man who makes many mistakes."

"Maybe you *are* their grandchild after all," she says, with a slight grin while staring at my necklace. "I love that Halledrite, I haven't seen one in so long. Tell Dwintra I say hello, that son-of-a-bitch still owes me."

Eden checks the time on her watch and gathers everyone together quickly. I find Luca standing to my left and Alessia to my right. I can see by the relaxed look on her face that she and Dante have made up.

Eden tells us that Lake Pilate is not just famous because of its beauty and water, but more so for the mysteries and legends that surround it. Dr. William mentions a legend suggesting that from the time of Pontius Pilate's death through the Middle Ages, the lake was a favorite destination of necromancers, wizards, and witches from all over the world. They called it the "Cursed Lake." Eden confirms what he is saying, and adds that there are chronicles with reports that say that various religious people, like priests and the magical community, would all come here at night to make sacrifices. They hoped that it would allow them to speak to the dead or make a request to the Underworld. During the Middle Ages, a wall was built around the lake to prevent these acts that were deemed sacrilegious by the Church.

The lake is originally named after Pontius Pilate, the Roman military leader who gave the order condemning Jesus to his death, for claiming to be King of the Jews. Although he was reluctant and personally found no fault with Jesus, he agreed to execute him in order to appease the public, and then washed his hands of his decision. Once word of Pontius Pilate's reluctance reached the Roman Emperor Tiberius—most famous for the defeat of Anthony and Cleopatra at Actium—he himself condemned Pilate to death. Legend has it that his dead body was put in a sack and tossed on the back of a cow-driven chariot; they didn't care where the chariot ended up. But it rode on until it reached the top of Mount Vettore. There, the cow threw itself and the body into the lake. From that day forth, the lake started being filled with small red shrimp living peacefully in the water.

Eden goes on to tell us that the "cow" leaving Rome was no ordinary cow; it was Talos. He is also known throughout history and various religions under names like the Giant Man of Bronze, the Golden Calf, or the Sacred Bull. In our modern world, he is known as Taurus. Talos was the last Celestial Being on Earth, or so he thought. To keep the Roman soldiers at bay, he did not show his true form until he reached the outskirts of Rome; it would be his last moment on Earth. Eden continues to tell us that when all the Celestial Beings left, God asked Talos to remain on Earth until he fulfilled his destiny. He anxiously waited for thousands of years for that time. He desperately wanted to be in the Heavens with his "daughters," the "Seven Sisters." Until he could be with them once again, Virgo agreed to protect her fellow sisters and she became a mother figure for them. Virgo was in love with Talos, and to his knowledge, she was the last to leave Earth. Virgo's real name is Astraea meaning "star-maiden." She created the Virgo constellation to hide and protect the Seven Sisters until Talos returned. She did this by arranging the stars of the Virgo constellation in almost the same layout as the Seven Sister star cluster, to act as a decoy.

"Ms. Eden, are you suggesting Astraea was in love with her father, Talos?" Dr. William politely asks.

"Oh, you make it sound like a juicy story out of a soap opera, good doctor! No, I'm not suggesting that at all! Let me clear up an important detail; Talos is *not* their real father. God is the only father and mother of ALL Celestial Beings. Talos referred to himself as this endearing term, since he felt they needed the protection because of their vulnerability. You see, the Seven Sisters were both virgins *and* nymphs, so you can only imagine the aggressive courting. If they were created in the world we live in today, they would need an entire army to protect them!" Eden answers lightheartedly, and everyone laughs enjoying a bit of Old-World gossip.

After a few questions, Eden turns our attention back to the original story. She says Talos knew his only way back was to go through the Underworld, but Sibyl would not grant him access. So, he was forced to enter through the lake by tossing himself in with Pilate. He escorted Pilate's body and soul to Hell as God had requested, and he fulfilled his destiny. God kept His promise, and Talos reclaimed his place in the Heavens where Virgo will rest peacefully on his right shoulder until the end of time. When they were finally reunited, he discovered that three of the seven "daughters" were still here on Earth and were with him the entire time he was there. In his devastation, he asked God why this was kept from him. God replied it was because it would have kept him from fulfilling his destiny. Since Talos was so understanding, God thanked him for his sacrifice by allowing the Taurus constellation to be the closest to Earth, so they could all be nearest to the girls that stayed behind.

Someone in the group asks what happened to the other three girls that remained.

"Rumor has it that they live among us like regular people, and you'd never know if you encountered one," she pauses and makes eye contact with me. "But they aren't *just* virginal nymphs, you know! They are also known to have very specific and unique magic that is much desired by humans."

"Like what, Ms. Eden?" Vanessa asks inquisitively

"Vanessa, raise your hand if you have a question," Dr. Nina scolds her. "I'm sorry, she loves *all* magical things."

"Oh, that's alright, I love magical things too!" Eden says to Vanessa. Luca has been rubbing his forehead and is now scratching his arm and chest. I think this conversation is giving him hives.

"Well, they can all do basic magic and potions, of course. But more specifically, what makes them so special is that they are the *mothers* of unique beings . . . such as sirens . . . "

Luca's scratching is becoming increasingly aggressive.

"Are you allergic to this conversation, Luca?" I whisper to him. His leg begins to twitch uncontrollably. Luca never replies to my question, he just gives me a look of stress.

"If you've ever wondered where the notion of magical entities such as healers, sirens, dragons, elves and—well I could go on forever—comes from, they are made by one of God's original creations. You know He's quite imaginative." She winks at Vanessa. "Just as there are Founding Mothers, there are also Founding Fathers. But to go into such detail would take an academic semester. So, how about we leave things off on that note. I think it's time to make our way over to Santa Maria di Foce, where the supposed entrance to Sibyl's Faerie Cave is located!" Eden says with big eyes, and an even bigger smile.

Luca does not look any better, as he announces that we will be taking a back route into Foce to make up for some time that we lost. But if you ask me, he just doesn't want to take us through the "pastel land" again. I don't think he and Dante want to be bombarded with questions about their land. He probably regrets joining the tour.

"Ále, did I drink hell-water today? Am I going to start talking to the dead like a necromancer now?" I ask her, while wiping my tongue with a napkin as we wait our turn to get on the bus.

She starts laughing uncontrollably and says, "I don't know girl, did you make a sacrifice to the dead when no one was looking?"

"It's not funny! So much weird shit keeps happening, I don't know what to think anymore!"

"I didn't see the door to the Underworld open for you, if that's what you mean!"

"Yeah you're right, I need to stop being paranoid," I say reluctantly.

Our drive to Santa Maria di Foce is only fifteen minutes, but it feels like forever. The road is very narrow and mostly uphill; the bus is an inch away from the mountain side almost the entire way. It's a good thing that it's a private road and there are no cars coming from the opposite direction, because there is literally no space for two cars, and barely enough for one, let alone a bus. It's mostly a quiet drive the entire way, but I can sense there is anxiety and concerns about making it in one piece. Eden hands out waters and keeps talking about local myths to distract everyone from looking outside the windows. She's very calm and doesn't seem worried at all; I think this is giving everyone comfort. But the higher we go, the steeper and more narrow the road becomes; I can feel my palms sweat. Everyone starts to move to the side of the bus closest to the mountain, since the side of the cliff has no railing. Just as I feel like we can fall off the road at any moment, we turn a corner into a deep, lime-green valley near a river; Eden calls it the Aso River. It seems to come out of nowhere in the heart of the Sibillini National Park. We park in what seems like a random place in the middle of nowhere. Everyone rushes out the bus doors to get some fresh air and calm their nervousness. Dante walks over to Alessia to see how she's doing, as Luca goes to Eden to speak with her.

"Dante, were you guys trying to kill us? That was *so* scary! I literally thought we were going to fall off the side!" Alessia says with a nervous giggle, while trying to remain serious.

"No of course not, we would never do anything that would put anyone in harm's way," he says, comforting her as he takes her hand. "Besides, that road is protected, no one can fall off it."

"Like, there's a spell to keep cars from falling off?" Alessia jokes with him.

"Yes, you didn't think that bus could make it up here on its own, did you? The tires were like six inches off the road, it was so cool, I even got a video of it!" Dante spouts out, as Luca arrives just in time to smack him on the back of the head.

"What's wrong with you, man? Was it really necessary for you to tell them that!" Luca says, shaking his head at Dante. I feel all the blood leave my head.

"You might want to add a spell that keeps people from having anxiety when going up that hill, while you're at it," I say quietly as my stomach turns. I see Luca reach out for me, but then quickly retreat. I notice that since that weekend at his house in Pretare, he keeps a wide physical distance between us. I haven't thought to question it because I'm still feeling embarrassed about my blackouts. But there was no strange electric-like static feeling between us when he touched me at Ambro. I wonder what that could mean. I almost want to touch him, just to see what would happen.

"I know that ride wasn't the easiest, but I hope you can all see it was worth it," Eden says reassuring everyone. "Because it's a private road and we are standing on private property, no one has ever seen this part of the park. The Vincis are one of the very few families in the world that hold ownership in a National Park, due to agreements made a very long time ago. Consider this our lucky day!" Eden says, throwing her hands up in excitement. "Now, if you remember on your tour information it said we would only be able to visit the village of Foce because the hike to Santa Maria di Foce is six to eight hours?" Everyone nods their heads and replies yes. "Well, thanks to our nearly life ending ride up the very steep mountain, it is only a thirty-minute hike from here! Oh, my goodness, can you believe it?! I'm going to hand it over to Luca, so he can tell us what to expect!"

Everyone applauds him, and he smiles graciously as he addresses the group.

"Ms. Eden tells me everyone's brought their walking shoes, so be sure to put those on. Also, if you've got a jacket or a sweater bring that along too; the temperature will drop once we get higher up the mountain. Please leave your bags and cameras and any personal items here. The hike will require the least amount of weight for you to carry. Also, please leave your phones behind, the signals are jammed and they will not work. The path we are taking is very old, in the past it had great meaning. But like all things, over time it loses its value and slowly starts to disappear. Paths are born, they live, and then they die just like us. The devastating earthquakes in these parts left many landslides and eroded trails, but we were very fortunate that ours remained intact. Many great men and women have walked this path, I hope you will enjoy this very old, but very beautiful walk today."

Just then, in the moment he was speaking, something shifted inside me. I feel as if I am looking at Luca for the first time through everyone else's eyes. In this moment, I can see the admiration, lust, and intimidation. He is handsome and well-spoken. Sincerity and kindness bound to his quiet, gentle soul. He has a way of connecting with everyone despite their age or background; everyone instantly loves him. People see the son, brother, friend, or husband they've always wanted in Luca. He is funny, but serious. Witty and intelligent. Dominant in stature but equal to all those around him. In spite of all these very impressive attributes, what I still cannot see is *who* Luca truly is. I don't even know if he has a favorite food or color, because he never shares any personal details. Most of the guys I know that have half his looks and charm, never seem to be able to stop talking about themselves. I find it refreshing and disarming. He is as much of a mystery to me as the rest of my family. This thought leads me to see that my angst towards him is not just because he keeps secrets from me, but because he shuts me out. It's unfair that he knows everything about me and my family, and I know little to nothing about him and the Vincis. I don't take well to being at a disadvantage in any situation with any person, but this one has a greater sting for me. And with that, the rose-colored lenses drop from my eyes. All I see is wall after wall and distance between us. I don't know if it's something I did or something he did, but it's done. And I don't know if it can be undone.

We are too different, I think, as I find myself glancing at Alessia and Dante. In one day, they've had more chemistry and emotion for each other than I have had with Luca in the last several weeks. But I can't say I've been at my best around him. So far, I've been unimpressed, argumentative, drunk, rude, ungrateful, and then there are the ever-attractive blacking out moments. What a mess; I'm surprised he still talks to me. I may be flawed, but I've worked so hard to be someone I'm proud of and I don't want to lose that. Everyone tells me relationships are a compromise, and anything worth holding onto takes hard work. That might be true. But if it is, then why do so many people look so unhappy together, and why do they remain in marriages disillusioned by broken faerie tales? To be fair, I have seen many beautiful relationships with couples that are perfectly matched. But they don't seem to work "hard" at the relationship; it's more organic—with understanding, balance of power, and respect, before the love that exists between them. I'm not sure if I even believe in marriage. Not because I can't imagine being with one person for the rest of my life. But because I don't want to work so hard and compromise who I am. That all sounds so exhausting and draining. Maybe I feel this way because I have never felt truly safe in love and in life. But in feeling safe, do you truly have to give up so much and work so hard for it? My mind can only imagine sharing a life with someone who complements and encourages me to become a more evolved person, without the anxiety and worry of not being loved for the person *I have yet to become*. In all fairness, they marry the person you are at that moment, and so often they leave because of the person you later become. I don't know if anyone can be blamed for that. But true love is love that never dies, and never changes, regardless of what you do or who you are. And I'm just not convinced that exists.

"Hey, snap out of it! You're going to give yourself a headache thinking about all that," Alessia says, putting her arm around my shoulders, and dragging me onto the path with the others. And into the mountains we go.

Chapter 14

LUCA WAS RIGHT, the temperature drops a lot the further up the mountain we walk. Although the hike is completely uphill, most of it is without difficulty, even for the older tourists. Luca leads the way, and he helps everyone climb rocks and cross the river with ease. Dante remains in the back of the group to ensure no one is left behind or gets lost. Alessia and I remain in the back with him. The path is more beautiful than the way it was described; I think some things just have to be experienced. The land is various shades of emerald green that extends throughout the grass and trees. Some greens are so deep they almost look black, while others so bright, they look nearly neon. I can see the mist on the leaves, slowly dripping onto the flowers that surround the trunks of the massive trees. I can smell the unique but familiar scent wafting from the moss and the flowers. The chirping of the birds is everywhere. I notice a peculiar bird; it is so green I almost can't tell the difference between it and the moss-covered tree. We are all enraptured by the beautiful sound it makes. Luca says they are called Pentwilin; it means "story-bird." They are part of the hummingbird family, which is evident by the shape of their bodies. They are just larger, and their wings move at an even faster speed, which makes it look like they are floating in the air.

"Pentwilins are endemic to these woods specifically, which is why most people have never heard of them. They are often shy around humans and have a tendency to disguise themselves within the trees when they are around. Looks like they are feeling brave today, they must be excited about something," Luca says, as he makes eye contact with me.

"They are my sister's favorite birds, she says their singing gives her comfort," Dante says to Alessia and I.

"How is Micella?" I ask him, genuinely curious.

"She's . . . she is quite busy. She has a large task at hand but has always had a difficult time asking for help," Dante responds lovingly, with a twist of concern in his voice.

"I like her a lot; she was so kind to us. Please let us know if we can do anything to help," I reply.

He smiles and says, "Yes, she feels the same about you, both of you. I will pass on the message, Eli."

"Do they call it a 'story-bird' because they sing their conversations and tell stories?" Alessia asks Dante.

"Yes, how do you know that?" Dante is surprised by her question.

"Oh, because that one is singing about how excited they are to finally see Eli. And that other one is recalling a story about the day she was born," she answers nonchalantly.

"What? You can actually *understand* them?" he asks her, his tone filled with disbelief.

"Yeah, is it weird?" Alessia says calmly with her eyes closed.

I stay quiet. I don't think I really know how to define what's "weird" or not anymore.

"Well, what do you know, I've got a proper Cinderella," Dante says warmly and leans in to kiss her. I go to cover my eyes when we hear frantic shouting.

"Vanessa! VANESSA!!!" Dr. Nina is screaming into the woods.

I see Luca telling Dr. Nina and Dr. William to stay put. Dante flies by me like a bat out of hell, and they both run into the woods from different directions. Alessia and I rush over to find out what's going on. Eden pulls the family aside and is trying to soothe them. I ask Mika what happened; she says that they were all standing around enjoying the birds singing, when Vanessa bolted into the woods out of nowhere. They were about to follow her in, when Luca stopped them. Vanessa seems like an even-tempered kind of kid; I know I haven't known her long, but it seems strange that she would just run into the woods. I ask Alessia what the birds are saying. She furrows her brows in concentration.

"They are saying that someone named Elise is going to be in big trouble today. And that the boys are close to wherever Vanessa is; they'll be back soon."

"You really are Cinderella, or Snow White, or whoever it was that talked to birds. How are you doing that, Ále?" I ask shaking my head in astonishment.

"How is anything we did today possible?" Alessia responds with a big sigh. She has a point.

We walk over to the family to check up on them. Alessia pulls Eden aside to speak with her in private. Dr. William is holding his wife, and Eric is sitting on a large rock; I sit next to him. He seems like a good kid that's shy and sensitive, not one to make trouble. I ask him if he is okay. He nods yes, but I can see by the look on his face that he's angry with his sister's reckless behavior. I know how he feels. Growing up it was always Alessia who was the spontaneous and crazy one. There was always some drama she got into that I had to cover up for. I envied her moments of reckless behavior. I know deep inside Eric does too.

I hear overall sighs of relief from a distance. Eric and I stand up on the rock. Dante and Luca are walking back onto the trail—Luca has Vanessa on his back, giving her the piggyback ride she's surely been dreaming of all day. Her parents rush over to her, and he lets her off. I see Dr. Nina squeezing her small body tightly and kissing her on the head. Before anyone can ask her why she ran into the woods, she peels her mother off her and blurts it out.

"MOM! I *knew* it! I knew it! I saw one. A faerie!!! I saw a real faerie! I knew they were REAL!!!" Vanessa screeches out.

"Honey, what are you talking about?" Dr. Nina asks her, clearly confused by her words. But before Vanessa can answer, she addresses Luca and Dante and asks, "Is she telling the truth? What did you see in there?"

They stay silent.

"MOM, DAD, I'm not lying! You have to believe me! I saw her hiding behind a tree while we were walking. She ran when she realized I saw her, but I couldn't let her get away, so I followed her! She finally stopped and talked to me. Dad you would love her, she's so cool! Her name is Elise." My stomach feels like it is in my throat. "And she's *so* nice, and *so* beautiful; she sparkles! Her dress is so pretty. And her body is like a regular girl except for her feet. She has hooves for feet, like a goat. And her voice is angelic and her singing . . . it's like . . . enchanting. Mom, faeries don't look anything like they do in my books, they're so much better! Like, so much more magical!"

Vanessa is speaking a million miles a minute; I can see her hands shaking as she tries to catch her breath. She has so much to say and wants to say it all at once. After a few moments of this, everyone starts to gasp and whisper among each other. I can hear that some believe her, and others are saying that it's just the imagination of a child, and she made up a story so she won't get in trouble for running into the woods.

"Okay love, just drink some water and take a couple of deep breaths," Eden says, handing her a bottle and rubbing her back. "Why don't we all have a seat. I've laid out some snacks for everyone. How about we take a break and have a bite while Vanessa tells us her story."

We look behind us, and there is a beautiful spread of fresh fruit and a box of cookies. Eden says she picked the blackberries on the side of the road on our hike up. She was in the front and I was in the back the entire walk up, so I have no way to verify what she is saying. And the cookies have been in her side bag that she's been carrying around all day. Without questioning, everyone walks over and starts helping themselves. The blackberries look so delicious and too tempting to resist. They are larger than the ones that grow in Umito but look just as sweet and fresh. I extend my arm to take a few, when Alessia grabs my hand and tells me not to eat anything. I pull back. She tells me to watch and pay attention. Little by little, everyone begins to normalize. They talk about the weather and their favorite parts of the day. Vanessa eventually stops talking about the faerie, and her parents stop lecturing her about her dangerous act of running into the woods. The pastel land with the sparking butterflies has all been forgotten within fifteen minutes. It is as if their memories have been selectively erased, and they can no longer recollect any magical moments the day had gifted us. It makes me feel sad and cheated for them all, especially Vanessa.

I need a moment alone to digest this, so I decide to walk back down to the river to refill my water bottle. My mind is racing with questions. Like, what did the blackberries do to these people? And why would Eden erase so many beautiful memories? It feels so invasive and cruel. I arrive at the river and all I want to do is scream at the top of my lungs. I lean into the river to place my bottle in the stream and watch it fill up. Against my will, tears fall from my eyes into the water. Under my breath I ask God why this is happening. My chest hurts, and I feel a pain piercing through me. It's as if my body, my soul, is being violently torn in two. I try to gasp for air. I hear voices behind me, but I can't make out what they are saying. Everything feels like it is closing in. The harder I try to breathe, the tighter my chest is getting. I try to drink some water in hope that it will help calm me. The coldness feels good dripping down the sides of my mouth and into my throat. But I'm so light-headed and my eyes are heavy, I cannot keep them open any longer, and then there is darkness.

*   *   *

I open my eyes and there she is again, Nonna Rosa. Even still more beautiful, and so young. She greets me with a kiss on the forehead and helps me get up. I look around; we are back in that beautiful, yellow cliffside valley in Umito, where I saw her a few weeks ago in my dream.

"Am I dreaming again, Nonna?" I ask her.

"My love, it's best that you think of it as a dream for now. We only have just a moment together, so I need you to listen to what I'm about to say. Pay close attention to this last part of the tour. You must remember how to get here, and you must remember every detail that Eden shares about it."

"Why is it so important?"

"Because the entrance directly into Sibyl's cave is here. There will come a time very soon, when you will return—you won't have a choice. I've done everything I can, but the tide has turned and destiny has stated its commands," she replies, with sadness in her eyes.

"I don't know what that means. I'm so confused, I feel so lost!"

"I know, and I'm so sorry my darling. I wish I could take that all away. But I need you to focus right now, Eli. Please . . . "

"Ok. How do I get in?" I say.

"You will be guided to it."

"How?" I am confused by her riddle.

"You drank from each of the seven rivers of the seven churches today. That is the key, and the only way to enter the cave without her invitation. Your thirst was not a coincidence. Nothing that happened today was coincidence. But the ability to enter will only last one moon cycle. There are very few people that know this; your grandmother is one of them. But you mustn't tell Amelia or anyone else. She will kill herself trying to prevent the inevitable."

"What's the inevitable?" I ask, but she ignores my question.

"I must also tell you that we think drinking from the seven rivers may break the spell we placed on you before you left Italy as a child."

"The what!"

"Now don't be cross; I promise to explain. You will begin to slowly remember things. Don't be afraid of the memories, embrace them, it's who you are. It's who *we* are," she says smiling gently as she caresses my hair. "It's time to take you back. We'll see each other soon."

I hold my grandmother's hand that she has placed on my head. I don't want to let her go. A bright light flashes and within seconds I find myself opening my eyes slowly, with my head in Alessia's lap. Suddenly I hear everyone exhaling deeply, and Alessia is kissing my forehead, wet from her tears, and thanking God.

"Did I black out again?" I ask with a dry, raspy voice.

"Yes babe, you did," Alessia answers through her tears.

"Why are you crying Ále?" I ask confused, but she just holds me tighter.

"Your heart stopped, Eli. We've been trying to revive you for the last seven minutes," Luca answers in a distraught tone.

"How do you feel, love?" Dante asks gently.

"I feel alright, I think," I answer, sitting up slowly. I see Eden wiping the tears from her eyes as she walks over to me. She hugs me tightly.

Eden pulls out a tiny needle with a small pearl at the top. She tells me she's going to poke my finger to make sure my vitals are alright. I'm not sure how that will help, but I allow her to anyway. She pushes the needle down to my bone, but it still hurts less than donating blood. She then pulls it out and holds the side with the pearl up to the sky. A light appears radiating from the pearl, and it begins to pulse like a heartbeat and then shine like a star. She glances at Luca and Dante—they look relieved and smile. She then takes a drop of my blood from the tip she poked me with and rubs it between her index finger and thumb and smells it. She does this a few more times and seems pleased with the results.

"Right as rain! You gave us quite a scare for the second time today, my dear. I mean it when I say let's not do this again," she says, holding the needle back to the area she poked. I watch my blood transfer slowly like vapor from her fingers and the needle, back into the point of exit. She then turns it around, and with the pearl she seals the opening. Alessia and I look at each other in amazement; Eden has thoroughly impressed us.

"No need to be coy now. I'm like your grandmothers. Different," Eden says, putting the needle away in its case.

"What are you?" Alessia asks.

"I am God's second creation," she says solemnly and definitively. "But no asking questions about it, we've all had enough excitement for one day. I think it's best to wrap this up and take Eli home," Eden says decisively.

"NO, no please," I beg her, hearing my grandmother's words in the back of my mind.

"Has the altitude affected all of your judgements? We need to take Eli to the hospital, immediately. *Her fucking heart STOPPED!!!*" Alessia pauses and looks around furiously at everyone.

"That may not mean anything to you since you're all . . . whatever the hell you are, but to us mere mortals that means *SHE died!* For seven fucking minutes, far past the time required for brain damage! Aren't you all the least bit worried? She needs to be checked out by a physician in a proper hospital!"

"Do not insult us, Alessia," Luca snaps back. I can see she is about to tear his head off, and I step in front of her.

"It's okay, I'm fine, I feel fine! Eden said it herself, I'm right as rain!" I answer, pleading with her as I place her hand on my heart.

"What does *she* know! She stuck your finger with a needle then swirled it around on her finger and smelled it! This is unbelievable coming from you, Eli! You're supposed to be the logical one!"

"Well, I did a little more than that," Eden mutters under her breath.

Alessia directs her hostility at Dante and Luca, and demands that they call for a helicopter to take me to the hospital. She starts screaming obscenities at them when she doesn't see them moving. I've never seen her this hysterical, and she has a fear in her eyes I've never seen before. She's afraid to lose me. She's afraid I'll die. My mother had the same look in her eyes last year when I was in the hospital. I take her hands and pull her close to me, then I whisper in her ear, "We've come so far Ále, I want . . . I *need* to finish it. I want to know how their story ends."

"Whose story, Eli?" she whispers back.

"Sibyl's. The Seven Sisters'. Ours. After everything we've been through today, don't we deserve to know?" I reply.

She stands there just looking at me, hesitating, not knowing what to say.

"I'm sure. Please Ále, let's do this," I say reassuringly.

"Fine," Alessia agrees reluctantly. "Let's hurry up and get this over with. I want to get her home as soon as possible," she says to Eden and the brothers, in the most serious tone I've ever heard her use.

Before we walk back, I apologize and thank them. We agree not speak about this to anyone. Alessia is glued to my side and won't keep her eyes off me. I can tell that she doesn't want to overwhelm me but is conflicted between her worry and curiosity about what I experienced. We make our way back to the others. I see they are clueless about what just happened and are feeling quite happy. I'd completely forgotten about the berries. I ask what was in them, and all Luca will tell me is that nature is Eden's specialty. We are told that the walk to the church is still another ten minutes away.

"Do you think I really died, Ále? That explains how I was able to see Nonna Rosa," I ask her as we are hiking. The shock is wearing off, and it dawns on me that I may have actually died for seven minutes.

"You saw her? What did she say?" Alessia asks, surprised.

"A lot, but I don't want to get into it now," I answer. "Do you think this means that the first time I saw her, you know, when I fell asleep in the yellow field, that I died then too?"

"Shit, Eli. That seems like a lot of dying," she says, trying to ease tensions, while simultaneously imagining that innate possibility.

We agree to put the conversation on hold until we can speak freely. There are too many people around, especially those with bionic hearing. I look up at the sky and see the sun once again trying to fight its way through the long, crossing branches of the elm trees. There are so many beautiful Pentwilin birds around, singing their beautiful songs. Alessia tells me that they had alerted her I was in trouble and told her to get to the river quickly. I mouth "thank you" to them, and then kiss my hand and place it on the tree trunk, in the hope that they can feel my gratitude.

I catch up with Vanessa who is just up ahead, and we chat for a while. I ask her how she is doing; she seems indifferent, but extra sweet. She clearly has no recollection about anything that happened. Mika and Andre are walking ahead of us, they seem to have a deeper connection than they did this morning. I notice Dr. Nina and Dr. William being affectionate; very different from their body language all day. Dante is looking at Alessia like he's going to tear all her clothes off. And Luca has what seems like a lustful look in his eyes, and he won't take them off me. Come to think of it, as I look around, everyone is either being very loving or overtly kind. Either those berries really are something special, or Alessia is right, and the altitude is really affecting them. Maybe it is in the air, because I just kissed birds through a tree, and that is definitely not normal behavior for me.

Eden suddenly stops us and asks if anyone is feeling extra loving, or even euphoric. Everyone raises their hands. Oh my.

She explains that we are standing at the church of Santa Maria di Foce, or as legend has it, the entrance to Sibyl's cave. We are bemused by her words. Where is the church? All we see is the mountainside, rocks, greenery, trees, flowers, and a small stream of water. There is no building, or even remnants of one.

"What happened to the church?" Mika asks.

"It collapsed after a massive earthquake. It shattered into thousands of pieces, and its ruins are now part of the earth under our feet," Eden replies with a sigh.

"So, earthquakes are very common around here, I take it?" asks Andre. "I remember seeing that series of earthquakes on the news that happened here a few years back. Left thousands of people homeless and it almost took out all of Central Italy."

"In our world, we call those earthquakes 'Sibyl.' And I really wish people would stop blaming them on Mother Nature; it really is unfair to *her*," Eden says clearly irked.

Wait, God's second creation was *Earth*. I gasp! It's true, our tour guide is Mother Nature herself! A laugh escapes me, and I quickly cover my mouth.

"Everything alright, Eli?" Eden asks.

"Yes, fine, sorry!" Well, what do you know—Mother Nature is a badass!

"Seriously, you *just now* got that she's Mother Nature?" Alessia whispers in my ear in dismay.

I open my eyes wide, shake my head, and give her a "what?" look. So, I might be a little slow at the moment. I mean, I just died . . . give me a break, woman! My mind is just barely catching up.

"Anyway," Eden carries on, "it is Sibyl's way of trying to break free when she becomes restless or angry."

"Does it work?" Andre asks.

"It does a little. She pushes the boundary that she can access and travel, each time she causes a disturbance in the earth's plates. It's as if she is pushing the line in the sand a little further with each ocean wave."

"Soooo eventually won't she be able to push through enough to get free?" Andre says, making a valid point.

"No, of course not! She'll never be able to be completely free. She's only able to do it because God allows it—although I'm not sure why He does," she says, perplexed by her own thought.

Mika turns to Andre and tells him how smart and sexy he is,

and within seconds they are fully making out. And I think we all agree, they look hot doing it.

"Euphoria is a feeling that the faeries invoke. So, if it feels like this out here, imagine what it feels like in *there*," she says, pointing to the mossy mountainside.

Eden further explains that old church documents legitimize where it once stood. But the last testament of its existence is written in a book by Antoine de La Sale, where he allegedly visited the church on May 18, 1420. He describes it being of Gothic origin with a small rose window on its façade, two bell towers, and two long upright windows separated by stone. Other than that account, there is no evidence that would endorse its existence.

"*Le Paradis de la Reine Sibylle* is preserved in the National Library of Paris. It's a fascinating read; if you have an opportunity to read a copy, I would strongly suggest it," Eden comments. "Now, what most people don't know is that all faeries are nymphs—"

"Just like the Seven Sisters!" someone says interrupting her.

"Very good sir, thank you for remembering," she praises the attentive tourist. "They are the only other magical creatures that possess this characteristic. They are able to seduce and enchant any man or woman, and completely bend them to their will in the name of love or lust . . . As many of you know, love is the most dangerous drug. It can start wars or heal an entire civilization. It has the power to divide families or give birth to all that we hold dear. To build and bring down empires. But most of all, love is the greatest gift ever given to humankind. And with that comes not sanctity, but an endless struggle of power."

Eden then turns her attention to Vanessa and Eric to make her point.

"When you two fight, is it usually about one of you being cross that the other did something to anger or hurt you?" she asks, and they answer "yes" through their laughter. "Well, would you say that is because in that moment you feel like they do not love you, and have put their own needs or wants before your own?" They agree nudging each other in the arm.

"Ms. Eden, you've just identified the core issue of ALL the world's problems. Have you thought about a career with the UN?" Dr. William teases her.

I've got to give it to her, with the example of a sibling quibble she just described, it's no wonder why we won't ever have world peace.

"Thank you, doctor, I'll have to check to see if they have any positions available," she teases back. "This kind of thing is not just true of this world, but all worlds, including the magical world. Our story began today with the Queen of Faeries who was cast out by God and left to spend the remainder of her life here in this place, until Judgement Day. And so, it seems only right that the story should end at her door," she pauses looking intently at the side of the mountain. "I'm sorry I have no church and no door to Sibyl's cave to show you, as you can see that has been sealed also. But what I do have is the story of Sibyl, the Seven Sisters, and the seven churches to tell. I hope that will make up for what we cannot see. Typically, only experienced hikers can make it up this far, so this is quite a treat. This morning I thought I would be telling you this story around a picnic table at the bottom of the mountain in the small town of Foce. I could not be more pleased that this is not the case. Now, if you can all take a seat."

We all take a seat on the surrounding rocks, or the driest patches of the mossy grass we can find, and make ourselves comfortable. I don't know if it is the euphoria or the absolute anticipation of the day, but the moment of truth is finally here. I just hope my heart doesn't stop once again.

Eden pulls out three sheets from her bag. One is white, one is clear, and one is a transparent baby-blue color. The white one is a laminated map of the area with a dot indicating the location of each church. The clear one has a simple line drawing in the shape of the Virgo constellation. And the transparent baby-blue one, has a star for each of the Seven Sisters. First, she holds them up individually, then she takes one at a time, starting with the map of the Seven Churches, and begins to place them on top of each other. The dots, lines, and stars align perfectly. She does it again, this time slower; the syncretism is real.

The others are fascinated. I feel relief. Relief that today was not another goose chase. Relief that for once someone is finally telling me the truth, no matter how unfathomable it may seem.

"The idea of a magical existence hidden behind the Church, hidden behind walls, mountains, and legends, may seem both hypocritical and an absolute farce. I assure you, it's not. Magic is the first language of the world. It was the language before words, before mathematics. Humanity can accept concepts like space travel to other galaxies, and yet magic can only be real in the minds of those who believe it, or in the imagination of children. If you ask me, that is hypocrisy at its best," Eden says passionately. I can feel her speaking directly to me, the Igni. She continues, "Today is not about convincing you that magic is real; it is about opening your mind that it is possible, and that God created it too. Now with that being said, does anyone today have a theory of why these stars would align directly over the Christian churches all named after Mary, the mother of Jesus?"

She pauses and looks around. No one is brave enough to answer, there's just silence.

"Are there any patterns or similarities?" Eden asks the group. Still silence.

"I know you don't have access to your notes since everyone

was asked to leave their personal items behind, but I do believe each person here has his or her own theory about it. Don't be shy! Who would like to give it try?" she says as she looks around. Her eyes stop on Dr. Nina.

"Well," Dr. Nina clears her throat, "as it's already been mentioned, all of the churches were once Pagan temples. Which means they held great significance to the Old World. They are clearly linked to one another by the stars in the sky, the rivers, and the Sibillini Mountains, and more specifically, Sibyl's king, Monte Vettore. It's almost like the outline of the perimeter creates a kind of map."

"It looks like a border," Eric adds.

"Or both!" Dr. Nina replies excitedly. It's as if a light bulb has gone off in her mind. "Oh my goodness, yes! Why didn't I see it before? Of course!"

"Are you going share that thought, Mom?" Eric asks, as she jumps up.

"Yes dear, sorry. The outline of the Virgo constellation, plus each of the stars in the Seven Sisters cluster, shine down creating the border of Sibyl's containment. She cannot leave this confined area," she says using her index finger to show the geographical area she is referring to. Then suddenly, her facial expression changes to sadness, "It's her prison."

"Prison is not what I would call this beautiful place," Eden says tilting her eyebrows up at her.

"No, of course not. I wasn't trying to be rude. It just seems like a relatively small place to spend eternity . . . to be confined and to never again experience total freedom, all because she wanted to be a mom . . . " Dr. Nina says with a daunting look on her face.

Dr. William raises his hand to add to his wife's theory. "If this is her border, the temples must have served as a kind of border patrol. Possibly a way for others to enter or exit her cave."

"That is absolutely correct! Bravo to the Matthew family!" Eden says applauding them. She tells us that even though Sibyl herself is confined, her faeries are not. And she often had many visitors, some magical and some commonplace. She famously hosted politicians and royalty that would come to her for guidance, and she prophesied the future for thousands of years. But once the Holy Inquisition took place, the Pagan temples were turned into Christian churches, and because so many were slaughtered for their beliefs and practices, the knowledge of how to enter her cave was lost.

I look down at my water bottle and think of my grandmother's words again. She said the door would reveal itself, but I can't imagine what she means; I have never seen anything more solid than this mountain. I look around to see if I have missed anything. But as hard as I try, there is nothing that looks like an opening of any kind.

Eden moves onto the second part of the story. She says that once the conversion of the buildings from Pagan to Christian happened, they named them after the Virgin Mary to remind Sibyl of her sins against God. Initially, it was a form of torture and pain for her to bear witness, as thousands would come to her temples and pray to the "Divine Mary," the mortal woman, the simple human that took away the only thing Sibyl had ever asked of God. She heard the people's prayers of worship, and praises to the mother of Jesus Christ. She wept uncontrollably as she heard them giving Mary thanks, and asking her for help and guidance in being as wonderful and understanding a mother as she was. Those words pierced through Sibyl's heart, breaking it over and over each day. All she ever wanted to be was a mother, Jesus' mother.

Every woman sitting here listening to Eden's story cannot hold back their emotions, no matter how much they try. In this moment, we are all Sibyl. We identify with her pain. It would be a lie to say that in one form or another, we have not all mourned for the loss of something we wanted desperately, but never received. We have all been that person that felt abandoned by God, and in our darkest moment, questioned why His will could not be the same as our own. And why His timing was rarely set with the time of our own clocks.

Eden continues on, "The pain made Sibyl angrier and more resentful towards God. But eventually she became numb, and decided it was time to even out the score. She had instructed her faeries to enchant and bring back into her cave artisans such as painters, writers, architects, and sculptors. She refused to be forgotten, so she had the writers write about her magical cave, and the painters paint images of her everywhere, including in government buildings and churches. She requested the architects of that time to add magical details on each of the seven churches. These details are symbols to remind all those who seek her, that passage continues to be open for those she deems worthy. Surprisingly to many, this amused God. He missed her vivacious ways. But unfortunately, this did not just bring the good into her realm. There were also many evils that sought out her expertise."

Sibyl's plan worked. The Christian Inquisition and the Knights Templar failed. I would say she won, and is far from forgotten by the endless books, paintings, stories, and an entire tour dedicated to her. Most of the churches we visited today are not used as a place of worship anymore, because of damage or safety reasons. I can't help but believe the real reason she created the earthquakes, is so the unfixable damage would keep people from coming there to worship Mary. Instead, they built new churches closer to their towns, where she can't hear them pray.

I can't help but wonder if it is truly God's will to have magic banished? If the answer is "yes," then what is his reasoning?

Alessia nods her head at me and says that she's been asking herself that very question all day; I don't think I am ever going to get used to this.

"Are you seriously reading my mind Ále? That is SO rude," I say, pulling her towards me by her jacket sleeve.

"NO, I already told you I can't read minds," she says, pulling her arm away from me. "It's more like a feeling about what you're thinking. And I can't do it all the time, it's like . . . selective. Why are you so paranoid anyway?"

"I'm not paranoid. But I don't like that, it's too invasive," I insist.

"Easy, don't get upset, you just died like five minutes ago. Let's stay relaxed, okay?" she says, pouting her lips and then smiling.

"Fine," I reluctantly agree. "What do you mean 'selective'?"

"Yeah, it's weird. It's like it only comes to me when it wants to." She then grabs me, turns our backs towards Dante, and lowers her voice. "I tried to get a sense of what he was thinking about when he was looking at me earlier, but nothing. I couldn't get anything off him. I've been trying it on different people all day, but it rarely works. My connection is strongest with you."

"Well, I can tell you what he's thinking, he wants to tear your clothes off!" I whisper back.

"Sshhhhhh!" she hushes me nervously. "Wait, do you really think so?"

"Umm-yah. I think you'll be pregnant by dinner if we don't get this aphrodisiac sonic air out of our system."

"Anything happening on your end?" she asks in a hopeful tone.

"I kissed a tree," I say teasingly, trying to avoid what she is alluding to.

"And you liked it?" She just couldn't help herself.

We both start laughing.

"Shut up, come on!" I reply.

While the group is standing around asking Eden their many questions, I convince Alessia to help me look around. We're both confident that the entrance to the cave will not actually look like a door, so we're searching for anything that can be a gateway or opening of some kind. I am also paying attention for any unusual markings. Each of the previous locations had a symbol or indication, so this one should have one as well. I knock, tap, and kick, but there's nothing but solid mass. Luca and Dante seem humored by our amateur investigative skills. They lean against the wide solid trunks of the elm trees and watch as we fail in our efforts. It's obvious they think we're wasting our time.

I feel a tap on my back. I turn around and it's Vanessa; her face has a soft and pleasant expression, but her eyes look foggy. She gestures that she has a secret she wants to whisper in my ear. I lean in and listen.

"Elise has a message for you. She says there are too many people here today—the entrance will not show itself to you. If you want to go inside the cave, you should come back alone. Look for the broken, heart-shaped rock."

I'm confused by her words; I thought the berries erased her memory of Elise. Was she just pretending to forget?

"How do you know about that?" I ask her.

"About what?" she replies, blinking her eyes over and over tightly. I can see the foggy-like glare has passed. "I don't even remember walking over here. What were we talking about?"

"Oh-umm, the broken heart-shaped rock," I reply. I wonder if Elise had buried its location somewhere in her subconscious. I'm right; she says she spotted something that looks kind of like a broken heart-shaped rock just around the corner from where we're standing. I ask her to show me. We walk down what seem to have been stairs at one time. Now they're just covered in greenery and sappy moss. Vanessa points to a boulder with leaves all around it, against the bottom side of the mount everyone was standing on earlier. She pushes the draping leaf branches out of the way. And there it is: a perfectly, un-perfect, beige-colored, heart-shaped rock, no bigger than the size of my hand. I step up to examine it more closely. The cracks in the center are long and deep—they expose its multi-colored layers under the beige, which blends into the boulder. The dark metallic tones look like thousands of sheets of paper all stacked up. Come to think of it, it looks identical to the stone on the mountainside of Lake Pilate. I reach out my hand to touch it, when Vanessa stops me. I ask her if everything is okay, and she says she doesn't know why she just did that, and apologizes. I can see the discomfort in her face as she silently questions her own reasoning. I tell her not to worry, as I place my arm around her and return to the group.

Both Alessia and Luca see me walk back and shoot an inquisitive look my way. To avoid their questions, I turn to Eden for conversation as we make our way back to the bus. I have a sense of both relief and sadness that the tour is finally over. But what I feel the most is exhaustion; my body feels weak and I am very dizzy. Eden takes notice; she says the adrenaline from the day has worn off. And she warns me that I will need a lot of rest the next few days, because today's events will have a hard impact on me physically. She hands me a hard candy from her bag and tells me that it should help for the next hour. My legs go numb, and I can't feel my body. I don't remember the rest of the walk down the mountain.

Before my conscious mind realizes where I am, I find myself sitting in Luca's car. I don't remember closing my eyes, but I must have. In what feels like a blink, I see the winding road back to my grandmother's house. Another blink later I am in my Uncle Giovanni's arms; he is carrying me upstairs and into my bedroom. One final blink, I see the candle in the window. Lights out.

Chapter 15

I HEAR WHISPERING voices above me. My eyes start to open slowly. I feel so tired; my body wants to continue sleeping. But my mouth is so dry, almost worse than it even felt on the tour. I can feel hunger in my stomach as it's turning. I move from my side onto my back and see several shadows around me. My eyes have not yet focused, and I can't make anyone out. I sit up slightly and look around for water. My mother takes a seat by my side, and hands me a glass.

"You must be thirsty," she says gently.

"It feels like I've spent a week in the desert," I reply with an intensely raspy voice. I drink the entire glass of water in nearly one gulp and ask for another. My mother refills it with the pitcher of water that had been placed on my nightstand. She says they added lemon to help with the thirst.

"You must be starving too. Silva has just gone downstairs to get the oatmeal she prepared for you. It has fresh fruit, just how you like it," she says smiling. What I could really use right now is about three large pizzas. Starving is an understatement.

"Alessia, please open the blinds. Let's let some sunshine and fresh air in," my mother points to the window. Once the window is open, I can finally see the faces of the shadows. Other than my mother and Alessia, my Aunt Ersella, Uncle Giovanni, Luca, Dante, Nonna Amelia, and a man I've never seen before, are all in my bedroom. It's like the party I never wanted. I scoot back under the covers and say hello. I feel so embarrassed—I can't imagine how horrible I must look. The mystery gentleman steps over and sits on a chair that has been placed next to my bed. He's tall with white hair and a short white beard, maybe in his mid-sixties. He's well-dressed, slacks with a matching vest, and a crisp shirt with the sleeves partially rolled up.

"Good morning Eli, my name is Dr. Massimo Borga. Luca asked me to visit you. I observed you while you slept, monitored your vitals, and took a blood sample for testing to ensure everything is okay. It's a good thing you finally woke up. We were just speaking about administering an IV."

I look down at the crease of my arm and see a band-aid over my vein.

"So, you're a *real* doctor?" I ask him.

"Yes." He smiles at me with an understanding of my insinuation. "I'm a cardiologist. I practice at a private hospital in Rome."

"He's being quite modest. Dr. Borga is not *just* a cardiologist, he's one of the most renowned doctors in the world. You've been in excellent hands," my mother says confidently. She knows saying that will put my mind at ease, and it does.

"Thank you for taking care of me. How long have I been out?" I ask him.

He looks at his watch and says, "You've been asleep thirty-six hours."

"WHAT!" I shout out loud, sitting up in bed abruptly. As I partially throw off the sheets from my hands, I catch Luca glancing at my chest, and then quickly look away, as he closes his eyes for a moment. I look down and notice I'm not wearing a bra, and my pajama shirt is slightly see-through. I slowly cover myself up with the blanket.

"Darling, don't excite yourself, you'll only get dizzy. You haven't eaten or had fluids in over twenty-four hours," Aunt Silva says, walking in with food. I notice she looks well put together, which isn't unusual for Aunt Silva, but there is a little something extra today. She places the tray down on my lap and insists that everyone give me space to eat and get myself together. Everyone except for her and Dr. Borga leave the room. As I inhale the oatmeal, fresh fruit, and toast, I listen to them speak as if I'm not in the room. They review possible tests and a nutritional diet. They are both quite enthralled with one another, the chemistry is everywhere. Aunt Silva is an RN. That was a very proud moment for my grandmother, since she herself never received formal education, and to have one of her daughters become a nurse was a dream come true for her. I remember hearing that at one time Aunt Silva was working at a hospital where she met and fell in love with a doctor. He broke her heart . . . or maybe she broke his heart? I can't quite remember the details of the story, other than he was much older than her, and therein lay the drama. But I do remember it ended badly like most of her relationships. She's always been a magnet for the wrong men. Watching the sparks fly between them now, I wonder if this is "the one that got away."

Dr. Borga checks his email. He shows it to Aunt Silva and they both look pleased.

"Your blood results just came in, and it looks like everything is normal," Dr. Borga says to me, "but I think we need to do some further testing on your heart. Your doctor in LA emailed me your file. It looks like you've been through a great deal the last few years, Eli, and I'd like to do some follow-ups if that's alright with you."

"Yes, that sounds good," I reply.

"Okay, great. Why don't I give you an hour to get ready, and we'll head down to the hospital here in Ascoli Piceno. I've made some calls to my colleagues, and they've agreed to let me use the facility. I'll be waiting for you downstairs," he says to me, as he opens the door to leave my room. Aunt Silva reminds me to drink the water she placed on the tray as she walks out. I take a sip—ah yes, it's the sweet water they use to give me as a child when I didn't feel well. Aunt Silva always said it was a spoonful of sugar in water that would heal my body. As I drink my water I walk over to the window; my legs are trembling a bit. I stare at the lit candle that never goes out. It looks a bit dimmer since the last time I saw it. After everything I've recently seen, I imagine this is anything but "a candle." I used to want so badly to know its secret, but now I find myself hoping to never know.

I get in the shower, and it's never felt so good. I crack open the shower window to feel the warmth of the sun on my face. As I rinse the shampoo from my hair, I see many more subtle, gold-like strands running through it. It's mostly noticeable when I hold my hair up to the sunlight shining in from the window. A flash of the siren appears in my mind. She is illuminated by a golden aura that is reminiscent of the strands in my hair. Was she real? My mind is running in circles. It feels like a dream still.

*   *   *

I spend all afternoon at the hospital. It's no surprise that Aunt Silva offered to come along. My mother stayed behind; she said there was still a great deal she needed to discuss with "everyone." I feel bad for Alessia, Luca, and Dante. My mother can be very stubborn and difficult when she's angry. I'm sure she hasn't stopped grilling them since the second we returned from the tour.

It is hard not to be distracted by all the oohing and aahing around Dr. Borga. The doctors and nurses at the hospital are clawing over each other just to get a glimpse of him. Everyone offers to be of assistance, but he has his own staff drive in. Every person we encounter treats him like an A-list celebrity, and I am fortunate enough to receive all the benefits. It's an amazing change of pace from all the waiting and ignoring I'm accustomed to from my doctors and their staff in LA. I kind of feel bad for never having heard of him until now. But I shouldn't expect any less from a Vinci family referral. What is surprising is watching my aunt softly flirt and bat her eyes at the good doctor. I can tell that he loves her attention, but you wouldn't know it by his extremely focused and professional attitude.

One of Dr. Borga's staff members walks over to detach the patches throughout my body. I must have been staring at Dr. Borga and Aunt Silva too long, because he looks over and takes notice too.

"I don't think I've ever seen Dr. Borga smile until today," he says to me, "not even when he won the Nobel Peace Prize."

"He's won a Nobel Peace Prize?" I ask, impressed by this news.

"Yes, one of his many achievements. I'm Dr. Notte, by the way," he says introducing himself.

"You're a *doctor*? But you look like you're my age." I'm truly shocked, he looks so young.

"Yep. It even says it on my coat. See . . . ?" He points to the name on his white lab coat. *Dr. David Notte.* Now I'm really impressed.

"Are you one of those geniuses that graduated from medical school at seventeen?" I ask, while he checks my breathing.

He chuckles a little and shakes his head no. "I'm actually not that much older than you. I am one of the very lucky people that was chosen to do a residency with Dr. Borga."

I take another look at him. He's actually handsome, and kind of looks sexy in that lab coat . . . how have I not noticed him all day?

"She hasn't smiled in a long time either," I say, trying to change the conversation so he doesn't notice me checking him out. I look back at my aunt and the doctor.

Then. He. Smiles. Ummm . . . perfect teeth, and a smile so radiant it has its own zip code. Finally, a hot guy, with a normal job, in a real world! Not a hot guy who's magical, secretive and weird, and doesn't touch me *ever*.

"She mentioned that they used to work together a long time ago," Dr. Notte nods towards them. So, it *IS* the one who got away! No wonder she's so smitten.

Dr. Notte looks at his watch. "My goodness, the day has gone by very quickly, it's already seven o'clock."

"Wow, already?" I feel disappointed. After all, it finally got interesting.

"Thank you for being so patient with all of us today. You are an excellent patient. And quite an . . . anomaly," he replies, looking directly at me with his beautiful, deep dark eyes. But it's definitely not the compliment I was hoping for. "Dr. Borga will be coming in in just a second to review today's results."

For a moment, I'd almost forgotten why I was here.

My aunt and Dr. Borga come into the room. They both look serious but not distressed. It must be a teaching moment, because all ten of his staff follow them in. He explains that after looking closely at the 3-D imaging of my heart and an MRI of my brain, among several other tests, they've found nothing unusual or concerning. This sounds like good news to me, but he says this is unheard of after experiencing a trauma such as being without oxygen for seven minutes. And it's impossible not to have any damage, considering this was not the first blackout that's happened. He goes on to say that he went over my medical records and family history carefully with each doctor, and they are all flabbergasted. No one had seen a chart like mine, with the patient having lived to tell about it. I guess that's what Doctor Hottie Notte was talking about when he called me an "anomaly." Dr. Borga says that they will continue to research my case to see what they can find, because as he put it, they "do not believe in miracles."

I catch my aunt smiling just then.

"I told you that you wouldn't find anything, Massimo," Aunt Silva says out loud. I see they are on a first-name basis now. "Come on darling, it's time to get dressed and go home. You've heard it from the doctor yourself now. You're fine."

He smiles back at her and then me.

After I get dressed, I step out of the room, and Dr. Borga is waiting for me. He pulls me aside and asks for permission to undergo genetic testing. I know that this is the future of medicine, and I have nothing to hide. If the answer to what is going on with my body is somewhere in my DNA, then I want to know. In the meantime, Dr. Notte is standing nearby with a wheelchair. Dr. Borga says its hospital policy to be escorted out this way, and Dr. Notte has volunteered. I like that.

The four of us ride down the elevator and head outside together. The skies are dark, but the stars look a little bit brighter tonight. I notice a familiar car right out front. Luca steps out of the driver's side. He looks exhausted, like he hasn't slept in days. His hair is more disheveled than usual, and he has heavy dark circles under his eyes. He gives me a partial smile and walks to the other side of the car to open the passenger door. Alessia and Dante get out from the back of the car.

Dr. Notte takes my hand and helps me out of the wheelchair. My aunt gives me a kiss on the cheek and tells me that "Massimo" will be giving her a ride home, and she'll see me shortly. Before I can take any steps forward, Dr. Notte stops me.

"Eli, I really enjoyed meeting you today," he says, still holding my hand.

"Thank you for everything today, Dr. Notte. I'm very grateful to have been looked after by such great doctors."

"Please call me David." he says smiling. "Would it be okay if I called you sometime just to check in? Make sure you're feeling alright?"

"Yes, I'd like that." I feel my heart flutter just a bit. I've never been asked out by someone with a real job.

"Your aunt gave me your phone number. I hope that's okay." We both laugh a bit.

"Of course she did. Yes, it's fine." I can feel myself smiling from ear to ear.

"Okay, call you soon Eli."

"Good night, David."

Alessia walks up to say hello, takes my handbag, and places it over her shoulder. We walk away arm in arm. She can't even wait until we get to the car before she starts asking questions.

"Who's Dr. Yum Yum?" Alessia says, looking back at him. I can see being in love doesn't mean she's lost her touch. "I wanna play doctor."

"Yeah, me too," I reply smiling mischievously. "Maybe Aunt Silva will let me borrow her nurse's uniform."

"Seriously? We're standing right here!" Dante says in disbelief.

Alessia and I just stand there for a moment staring at them.

"How about we get going?" Luca says, with his hand pointing to the car seat. I step in. As Luca pulls away, Dr. Yum Yum and I wave good-bye at each other.

To my misfortune, Alessia and Dante argue the entire way home. They are really killing my emotional high. I wish I'd just driven home with Dr. Borga and Aunt Silva.

When we arrive home, I notice Luca hasn't said two words the entire time. He opens my car door and escorts me into the house. He isn't there even a minute, before he taps Dante by the arm and excuses them both for the evening. Luca looks like he has the weight of the world on his shoulders; I can see that there is something very important on his mind, something much more significant than me. My mother pleads with him to stay. He says they will be going home and staying the night in Pretare, but that he will call tomorrow to check in. Dante looks confused but doesn't argue. He kisses Alessia and tells her he'll be back in the morning. Once they leave, my mom asks me what I did to Luca. She says he looks distraught. I feel bad. I hadn't even noticed.

"He's probably kicking himself in the ass, because Eli got asked out by a doctor tonight!" Alessia says in a gossipy tone.

Just then Aunt Silva walks in and the floodgates open. She tells the entire family about our day, and how Dr. David Notte had his eyes on me all day—but I almost didn't even notice him— and how she felt compelled to give him my phone number. My grandmother and Aunt Ersella exchange a look. They don't seem pleased with this. I think Aunt Silva notices too, because she changes the conversation to "Massimo." Over dinner she retells the story of when they first met, and their love affair. It was actually quite romantic, with a tragic ending written for the books. We can see that she is on cloud nine with the possibility of a second chance.

Shortly after dinner I feel very tired. I remember Eden saying that I would need a lot of rest for the next few days. Being at the hospital all day didn't help. I make my way around to say goodnight to everyone. When I stop at Nonna Amelia, all of the information I learned on the tour sets in and all the pieces come together. In this moment of clarity, it hits me that this woman I've known my entire life as my grandmother is NOT just a woman . . . she is a *Celestial Being*. And sitting next to her, my Aunt Ersella; also, not just my wild, funny, crazy great-aunt, but a *Celestial Being*. She wasn't lying when she said she was almost five thousand years old. In front of my eyes sit two of the Seven Sisters. Right here on Earth, not in a mythological story but in the flesh. Who would ever believe me? My mind still cannot completely process it, but at least now I am trying.

Nonna Amelia touches my hand and I lean down to kiss her goodnight. We both understand it's been a long day; too long for any conversation.

*   *   *

The next morning, I wake up feeling like I slept hard. I look at the clock and it says one o'clock. I slept fifteen hours. At least it wasn't thirty-six this time. I put on my robe and slippers and walk down the hallway to use the bathroom. I hear my mother, Aunt Silva, Aunt Ersella, and Nonna Amelia arguing in my grandmother's bedroom. My Aunt Ersella is lecturing my Aunt Silva about giving the doctor my phone number, and to stop meddling. My Aunt Silva yells back defending her actions. My mother tells them both to shut up and reminds them that only I can make that decision for myself. My grandmother agrees with my mother. She says that only I can decide what kind of life I want to have, and whatever I choose, everyone must support it.

"What do you mean, Amelia?" Aunt Ersella shouts, "That will be the end of our kind!"

"Well, maybe it's about time! If you only did what you were supposed to do a millennium ago, none of this would've happened!" Aunt Silva replies resentfully.

"You ungrateful child," Aunt Ersella replies back with a low and intensely angry voice. "If we'd done that, you and your siblings would have never been born."

"How could you say that, Silva?" my mother asks, with a sad and disappointed tone in her voice.

"Mama, don't cry! I-I shouldn't have said that, it was stupid, I'm sorry!" Aunt Silva says, pleading with my grandmother after seeing how much her careless words hurt her.

"Maybe you're right, Silva. Maybe I was wrong to want a human life. Look at the pain I've caused," Nonna Amelia cries out.

I push open the door. They're all standing around my grandmother, comforting her. When they hear the screeching of the door, they turn around and gasp.

I walk over to look in the mirror of my grandmother's vanity.

"What? Do I really look that bad? I mean I know I slept heavy . . . " I instantly stop speaking. I don't recognize the image in the mirror.

"Who—what am I looking at? Wha—?" I say, touching what I *think* is my face.

They're just standing there in shock. Unsure of what to say or do.

"Someone say something to me, please! I'm freaking out!" I shout at them.

"Ugh, I thought this week couldn't get any weirder," Aunt Silva says under her breath.

"What do you mean!" I yell back. As they stand there in silence, I realize that my grandmother is still seated in her chair, she never got up. Which is not like her; she is curious and inquisitive by nature. I realize that my mother and aunts are all standing around her, as if they are blocking her from being able to see me.

"What are you doing? She's going to have to see me at some point!" I say, throwing my hands in the air.

"Eli, it's not you. Well, I mean it is now," my mother says widening her eyes. "Just prepare yourself, your grandmother has taken a turn for the worse."

I slowly walk closer as my mother and aunts move out of the way . . . My grandmother looks . . . radiant.

I cannot believe my eyes. I kneel at her feet and hold my hands to her face. Her skin is tighter and there are fewer lines on her face. Her eyes are bigger, her posture is better, her breathing is easier. Her hair is longer and isn't fully silver anymore. I can see she is in less physical pain. She looks like she's gone from ninety to sixty years old.

"Mom, what do you mean? She looks thirty years younger. She looks amazing," I say, feeling afraid and enamored by what I am seeing.

"Look at you my beautiful girl, you look . . . *divine*," my grandmother says to me. Just then I remember Eden using the same descriptive word at Lake Pilate.

"That is the problem, my dear. She is going back to her true form. Just as Rosa did. That's why we kept you from seeing her before she 'died.' We knew you were not yet ready to accept who we are. You see, the death of Amelia's human body is the revival of her Celestial one. Once she makes the full transition, she will no longer be allowed to live in the human world. She will have to go back—" Aunt Ersella stops herself.

"Back where?" I ask her aggressively.

"To our world, my dear. One that you may discover yourself soon enough, by the looks of things this morning," Aunt Ersella says, looking down into her teacup.

"Mama, what's going on?" my mother asks my grandmother.

"Silva, please pour a cup of tea. It's going to be a long day," Aunt Ersella replies. "I wish Alessia was here, she needs to hear this too."

"Where is she?" I ask, just now noticing her absence.

"She drove to Pretare to spend the day with Dante. She assumed you'd be sleeping most of the day. But don't you worry, I'll catch her up in due time," Aunt Ersella reassures me.

While my Aunt Silva pours a cup of tea, my grandmother invites me to sit, and begins to speak with more energy than I've seen her have in years. She tells me that the reason they sent us on that tour, is because she knew simply explaining it wouldn't be enough for us to believe. She insists that they tried to tell me the truth verbally many times, but that I simply wouldn't retain or remember the conversations. It wasn't until my visit to the yellow field that they realized that when I experience something for myself, I am able to recall it better. They told me that each time they tried to tell me the truth, I accused them of lying and making up stories. That would be followed by a complete lapse of memory about a conversation we just had moments earlier.

They asked Father Gabriel to have Eden act as the tour guide, because she is the only one who knows the truth and has the ability to tell it without consequence. I told them it took me a moment, but that I had figured that out on my own. But to Nonna Amelia's credit, she's is absolutely right; I would have NEVER believed it coming from my family.

I ask why they think I am having blackouts and memory loss. She says that they have a theory, but they will not tell me until they are completely certain, to prevent any further disappointment.

"Well, at least now I know why we've never met your other sisters," I say, trying to lighten the mood.

She giggles a bit, "Yes, that would be a difficult introduction, don't you think?"

"I see that now," I reply. "So, there are twelve Oracles and God gave them all jobs. Julia was to be the Alchemist, and Sibyl was to foretell prophecy? And then there are ten more I haven't met yet?" I ask, trying to get the details right.

"All Oracles foretell prophecy. But they also have special and unique powers, just like Celestial Beings," Aunt Ersella says excitedly. "Sibyl is not *just* someone who can predict the future, Eli. She IS the *most powerful* prophetess who has ever existed. Why do you think God locked her up! Today she is known as the benevolent Mother of Faeries. But that is only a third of who she truly is."

"What did you think of Sibyl? A little birdy told me you met her," my grandmother asks with a wink.

"She's breathtaking and ethereal, I couldn't take my eyes off her. She looks and smells like everything that is perfect in the world. Maybe it is just that faerie euphoric vibe, but I didn't feel like that when I met Julia and Eden; they seemed lovely, just more . . . human," I say, trying to translate my feelings into words.

Nonna Amelia and Aunt Ersella look at each other and smile. They know exactly what I mean.

I ask what their roles are in all this, and which of the Seven Sisters they are. I've never seen their eyes light up so brightly. They're like children that have held onto a secret for too long, and they can finally just let it explode out of them. They reveal that The Seven Sisters are comprised of:

Maia: Amelia by her human name, and my maternal grandmother. Her name means "Great One" and she is a healer. She has the ability to heal and/or cure sickness, disease, and pain, which is why she took on the role as a nurse and mid-wife in human form.

Taygeta: Rosa by her human name, and my paternal grandmother. She is the mistress of animals. She can speak, control, and shape-shift into any animal. Her favorite form is a deer with golden horns. That explains the deer in my photos in Pantano.

Boy, she wasn't subtle at all. I now understand why she spent her human life on a farm.

Celaeno: Ersella by her human name, and my great aunt. She is a siren and the Mother of Werewolves. If I wasn't already sitting, I would have fallen over. It was her in Ambro! I was not wrong about the resemblance. That's why she's lived near a body of water all her life. It also explains her beautiful voice, and why she can bend anyone to her will.

Electra: The mistress of light and electricity, who can use both to travel through time.

Alcyone: The mistress of warding off evil in the world. She is also able to control the weather.

Astraea: Also known as Asterope. The mistress of the stars, planets and space. She is the creator of galaxies and Asbgahs. She inspired the image of Virgo and created the Virgo constellation to hide and protect the Seven Sisters.

Merope: The mistress of taking or giving poison, disease, or darkness, by the use of bees. They call her the "Bee-Eater." She both causes and alleviates suffering.

I'm in awe that such strong and powerful women exist. For the first time in my life, I feel empowered. I am proud to know that I, and in some way, *we*, all come from that prodigious lineage. To think of all the thousands of people that had to be born, find one another and fall in love, just for us all to exist in this world, is nothing short of phenomenal. My blood line is strong, and I have no reason to feel so afraid.

All my life I have been sheltered and afraid of the unknown, scared of my own shadow, living day to day with my head down, keeping out of trouble, and obeying every law and rule ever written. Never questioning authority and always respecting my elders. Taking responsibility for every action, and often, even accountability for the actions of others. Being so compliant has made me a doormat most of my life.

I wish Alessia was here. She's going to lose her mind when she finds out she's a siren. My aunt asks me to tell her more about the mind reading that happened during the tour. I ask if the mind reading is a siren thing. She says that sirens are able to manipulate minds of others once they are enraptured. But they cannot actually *read* minds. She explains it just like Alessia did; a feeling or understanding of the person's thoughts.

Aunt Ersella explains that my great-uncle Adolfo was the Father of Werewolves. Any son she conceived with him would be a Lycus and any girl a siren. She confesses that she sent Christopher and Marco in their wolf form to Cona to check up on us, since it was so close to where the Lycus pack congregate. But the surprise was on them when they saw Dante. She said they knew we were in good hands but became territorial when they saw the way he looked at Alessia.

Apparently, Christopher and Marco have been able to transition in and out of werewolf form since they were young. I ask Aunt Ersella if Alessia knows about her brothers. She says they agreed not to tell her unless her siren form revealed itself. They did not want her to feel inferior in any way. She said when it first began Alessia was still a toddler, so she doesn't recall much. But when the boys were first learning to control their temper, Alessia was sent to Umito for her own safety. She stayed with my grandmother and that is when she, Stefano, Sophia, and I became so close. A werewolf and a siren; well if that doesn't make for a story in itself! I can't imagine this was an easy secret to keep.

My grandmother reassures me that both of my grandfathers were human. And the love stories I heard while growing up were true, except they left out the part about being Celestial Beings.

We move on to having lunch. While eating, I ask Nonna Amelia to tell me how they made their way into the human world, and how it was possible for them to exist here outside their celestial form all these years? Aunt Ersella says those are "loaded questions without simple answers." So, in return, I ask them to give me the least complicated version possible, since my mind is still trying to process that my cousins are werewolves. My grandmother tells me that when the last of the Celestial Beings left Earth, she, Nonna Rosa, and my Aunt Ersella did not want to leave. But they knew they could not stay without protection. Humanity had grown cruel, and they knew humans would eventually capture them and turn them into slaves to do their bidding. They went to Sibyl and asked for asylum. The faerie world was by far the one in which they felt the most at home. Sibyl welcomed them with open arms; she was kind and gracious. They lived among the faeries for thousands of years, enjoying their time on Earth. Sibyl would often allow the inhabitants of the faerie world to visit and enjoy themselves with the locals. They would dance, sing, and drink the night away. There were only two rules: the first was that they had to be back in the cave by sunrise, and the second, that they had to enchant the locals not to speak of their visits. Every so often, one of the faeries would drink too much and forget to enchant them. Stories would leak about their visits, and Sibyl would frantically go back to clean up their mistakes. But often it was too late, and the human would have already told several people about their amazing night with the faeries. On one of those nights, my grandfather Alfredo was passing through Pretare on his way home from Rome. He saw my grandmother Amelia and it was love at first sight. On his next visit, he brought his best friend Giuseppe along. One look at my grandmother Rosa, and his fate was sealed as well. The rest, as they say, is history.

"I'm sure you met so many men all those years. What made my grandfathers so special?" I ask Nonna Amelia.

"I don't know . . . Rosa and I discussed that so often. They weren't the best looking. Or the smartest. Or the richest. But it was as if our souls fit together like two pieces of a puzzle. Nothing about our union made sense, but we were a perfect match," she replies, smiling gently.

"And you, Aunt Ersella? How did you and Uncle meet?" I turn my body in her direction.

"Adolfo and I met in the Sixth Asbgah. We couldn't keep our hands off each other," she says daydreaming. "Those were the good old days when we could roam freely."

"What's the Sixth Asbgah?" I ask

"It is the 'Living Creatures Asbgah'; the birthplace of Lycus werewolves. There are fourteen Asbgahs altogether. But let's leave all that for another day. If you think your head hurts now . . . " my mother says, opening her eyes wide while caressing the top of my head.

"Mom, you knew about all of this and you didn't tell me?"

"It wasn't my place, Eli. Your grandmothers asked your father and I not to. We all thought it was best for you to have as normal of an upbringing as possible."

"Do any of my other cousins besides Christopher and Marco know?"

"No one else," Aunt Silva replies. "Well, I suppose now just you, Alessia, and poor Stefano and Sophia got dragged into this mess."

"Does anyone else in our family have . . . you know . . . special things they can do?"

"Seems to have skipped a generation in this house," Aunt Silva replies resentfully.

"Aunt Silva, you seem pretty bitter about all this. Why?" I must have caught her off guard with my question, because she stiffens up. Everyone waits for her to respond.

"Because . . . " she pauses, then confesses, "because, it's not right that magic discriminates! Why are some people in this family chosen and not others!"

My mother holds her hand then turns to me and says, "We all have a little magic in us, but nothing like what we are seeing with your generation. Our generation acquired mostly the human gene. Aunt Ersella and Uncle Adolfo's children are magical because both of their parents are."

"What about Nonna Rosa's children? Is it the same for them?" I ask my grandmother.

"Everyone except the first-born son and the first-born daughter on each side, are non-magical," Nonna Amelia says locking her eyes with mine.

"W-w-wait. Uncle Giovanni and my mother are your surviving first born son and daughter. A-and my father and his sister, Aunt Isabella, are Nonna Rosa's first born . . . Oh my God . . . " I drop the glass of water from my hands as I jump up from my seat in disbelief, and it shatters everywhere.

I feel like my heart is going to stop again. My mother sits me back down on the chair, and my Aunt Silva kneels down to wrap a towel around my foot. I see blood seeping through it. I must have cut my foot when I dropped the glass, but I can't feel anything.

"Y-Y-You lied to me all these years, Mom! All this time, I thought I was a bland and boring person who wasn't good enough or smart enough for anything. Turns out we're all a bunch of *freaks*!" I say, glaring at her. She starts crying and covers her face. My Aunt Silva stands up to console her.

"Eli!" my Aunt Ersella shouts, horrified by my words.

"No, stop. This ends here," my grandmother walks over to stand in front of me. She seems taller.

"Eli, we are NOT freaks. I'm sorry you are having a hard time with this and I'm sorry you feel like we lied to you for so long," she says with a stern tone and look in her eyes. "I bound you, your mother, and your father's magic when you left for America. We made a decision based on what we felt was best for the circumstances at the time, which is not something I am going to explain at the moment. Your magic started to unexpectantly unbind itself. That's when you began to change physically. Rosa and I NEVER anticipated that the grandchild of two Celestial Beings could ever manifest into a *new* Celestial Being. Maybe a magical being, but certainly not a celestial one," she pauses reflecting on her words. "How could we? You're the only one that has come into existence in over five thousand years." Her words begin to feel heavier and heavier.

She goes on, "At first we weren't sure what was happening. Ersella and I read every book we had. We still could not find any answers. But when I saw you this morning, it could not have been more obvious. Rosa and I never could have imagined there would be consequences to having two of our children fall in love and conceive a child of their own. We were just two naive and joyful best friends given the greatest fortune of sharing a grandchild. Do you understand that, Eli?"

"The golden strands in your hair give it away," Aunt Ersella says touching them. "This is a gift bestowed only to the Seven Sisters."

"This is unforeseen—your existence is a miracle. But it is also very alarming," my grandmother says to me. She then turns to my Aunt Ersella. "Sister, why now? Why after all these years?"

"I see what you mean . . . " Aunt Ersella ponders deeply on her words.

"I don't! What are you saying!" I reply, on the verge of hyperventilating.

"The golden strands of your hair hold your power. Exactly

what kind, still remains to be seen," Aunt Ersella tries to explain, but her words sound like insanity to me. It is one thing to accept the stories they tell, it's quite another to fathom that I'm somehow mixed in.

"Who gives a shit about my hair! I have no special qualities, no superpowers . . . you said it *isn't* safe for Celestial Beings to live in the human world. And now your body is dying and you're transitioning again, right? So, does this mean I'm dying too? I-I don't understand!" I shout, desperation taking over my voice. I can't sit still anymore, I have to get up. My mother is trying to calm me down, but I don't want to be touched and I keep pushing her hands away from me.

"Wow, she's really taking this much worse than I imagined," Aunt Silva says with wide eyes and a tilted mouth. "Don't you have some kind of spell or faerie dust to calm her down? She's giving me anxiety."

"*Really* Silva!" my grandmother says, shaking her head.

"Eli, look at me. Come on, look at me," Aunt Ersella demands. "Now take a deep breath. Good. Again. One more time. Now, take a seat." I comply to keep from blacking out.

"We had to surrender our most powerful gifts to become human. But you were born in this world, so it is just as much a part of you as the Celestial World." Nonna Amelia pauses to let her words sink in. "You are not dying, and you don't have to give anything up," she gently explains, "but—there is no way to know what your gift is. It will show itself to you when God chooses . . . I know this is a burden. I'm so sorry, please forgive us. We didn't know, how could we know this would happen?"

"Then how can Julia and Eden live here? Aren't they Celestial?" I ask, trying to understand the difference.

"No. Julia is an Oracle. Eden is Mother Nature herself. You see, Oracles such as Sibyl and Julia, and all other Original

Creators, such as Eden and Alessandro, they are all made of flesh and blood by God. You see, they were made for Earth; they can exist and thrive anywhere. Celestial Beings are made by God to exist in the Heavens."

"What is an Original Creator? I vaguely remember Eden discussing that." I spot a bottle of wine on the table and pour myself a glass. I think I'm going to need the entire bottle to get through this.

"NO, not today. That can wait until tomorrow. Let's just stay focused on one thing at a time, please. This is overwhelming for us all," my mother intervenes.

"Fine, back to us!" Aunt Ersella says, as she helps herself to a glass of wine as well. "Amelia, Rosa, and I traded our powers for a one-hundred-year contract on Earth. We thought that would give us more than enough time to live a full life without overstaying our welcome. We figured by then the kids would be grown, the grandchildren well on their way, and two of the three husbands would be dead. I always assumed my dear Adolfo would return with me. His death was a shock to us all . . . " She pauses for a moment and takes a deep breath, "What we didn't realize—detailed, of course, in the finest print—is that once our one-hundred years was up, we would not be able to retrieve our powers. And without them, we can neither reenter the human world, nor return to the Heavens. The Lost Pleiades will always be that—lost and destined to wander the Asbgahs until Judgement Day."

"Mama is that true? Why didn't you tell us?" my mother asks Nonna Amelia, with a frightened look on her face.

"Ah, I see my darling sister failed to mention it." Aunt Ersella takes a big gulp of wine as Aunt Silva also decides to pour herself a glass. "The deal dictates that we must return to the Asbgah on our 100th human birthday. As you can see, neither of your grandmothers have made it that far. It is still to be seen for me.

But before you decide to bombard us with a million questions about why they didn't make it to their one hundredth birthday, save your energy. You'll never get that out of us. Got it?" I reluctantly nod my head and agree to my Aunt Ersella's demand. I will just have to find out some other way.

"There has been great distress in the Asbgahs. We don't know all the specifics, but Luca has told us about some unimaginable things," my grandmother says.

"Luca?" I ask, wondering what he has to do with any of this.

"Well yes," my mother replies, "he's been bending over backwards trying to please everyone. His family is demanding, and ours is in need of his assistance. But I can see all he wants to be, is near *you*. From a distance, he does everything he can to protect you."

"I don't need protecting. I need him to be honest," I snap back.

"Careful what you ask for," Aunt Silva replies in between sips of her wine.

"I worry for Rosa, she is in there without us," my grandmother says rubbing her forehead. "But now I am more worried to leave you, Eli. The timing of my departure could *not* be worse. You will need me to help with your transition, there will be so many questions. I don't want you to feel alone or abandoned."

"That's enough for today," my mother says, helping my grandmother out of her chair and slowly walking her back to her bed.

I look outside the window and it's dark. I can't believe the entire day has gone by. I look at the clock, it says 9:00 pm. I ask Aunt Ersella if she's heard from Alessia; she says that she received a text from her an hour ago, that said she would be spending the night in Pretare. I slip into bed and reflect on everything I just learned and what it all means. Two days ago, my worst problem was quitting my job; today I look like a different human being who may, or may not, be human. I hear a knock at my door and my mother enters. She asks me if I'm alright. I ask her to define "alright." She says that Luca just called to check in and see how I was doing. I look at my phone but have no missed calls or texts from him. Just one from Alessia and another from a phone number I don't recognize. Alessia sent a picture of herself, trying on more of Micella's gorgeous clothes in that huge department store-sized room. I ask my mother why Luca didn't just call me directly, and she says that's a conversation to have with him. She walks over to the other side of the bed and lies with me. She tells me that she misses my father and hopes he will decide to come soon. I've never seen anyone love each other more than they do.

There's been something in the back of my head that's been bothering me about what my aunt said. She mentioned that they made a one-hundred-year deal, but she never said with whom. I ask my mom if she knows. She says she's tried getting it out of them many times, but they won't say. She thinks it might be because they are either protecting someone, or it was stated in the contract that they could not disclose the identity. But it continues to be a topic that remains off limits.

My mom's phone rings; it's my dad, he's calling on FaceTime. She is so excited. They don't usually spend this much time apart. She tells me not to be nervous because he's aware of the changes. When I see his face, I get emotional—I forgot how much I miss him. He is gentle and wonderful as always. He tells me how much he loves and misses me, and how he can't wait to join us. We speak for a while about nothing in particular. It feels so nice to have a casual conversation about everyday things. My mother must have known I needed a moment to feel safe, in what I am most comfortable with. After almost twenty minutes we say goodnight, and she takes the call to her bedroom. Even though the sight of my father and hearing his voice puts me at ease, I still feel restless. I need to get out of this house, I need some fresh air. I leave a note for my mom on my pillow, put on my jeans and jacket, and exit the front door quietly.

*   *   *

Tonight is a perfect summer night. There are millions of bright stars in the sky. I walk to the bottom of the hill and then down the passageway to the stream. Not far down there's a small bridge where I used to go to watch shooting stars when I was little. Someone once told me it was originally built during World War II to assist soldiers crossing the mountain range. I heard that they rebuilt it, and that now it's sturdy enough to stand on. But back then, not knowing if we would fall through the broken and brittle old bridge and into the stream, was always the real fun of standing on it. Walking through here at night used to scare me, but now the light of the moon and the sound of the stream guiding me, soothes my soul.

Standing on the newly restored and stronger bridge makes me feel sad in a strange way. It reminds me how everything changes so quickly. One minute I'm a kid playing on a broken bridge, and the next I'm a Celestial B-B- . . . Geez I can't even think it, it makes me feel weird. I may not have feared change in the past, but I fear it now. Even *if* it is good, I don't want this. I want to keep being invisible and live a peaceful and unassuming life. It's curious that no matter how many times I pushed it away, there was always something inside me that told me to brace myself for a bigger calling, and to stop being so comfortable in my mediocrity. I always had an innate suspicion that my family's secrets would be the connection to understanding what that calling would be. It may not be fair, but I resent them all for it. All I ever wanted was to be a simple girl living a happy life with no expectations. But I guess I'm not made that way, and I wasn't made for that life. Maybe our calling is stronger than our DNA. Or maybe our DNA is created specifically for our calling.

I lie down with my back against the bridge floor. I close my eyes to clear my head and appreciate the serenity and stillness of the night. I try to use the meditation techniques I learned in yoga to quiet the thoughts in my mind. But it just feels like a monkey is doing a triathlon through it. I open my eyes. There they are in their glory, the stars. Do I consider this my origin now? When people ask me where I'm from do I say, "on my mother's side Taurus, and on my father's side Taurus, but both grandfathers are from Italy." I wonder how long it would take for someone to recommend me a psychiatrist.

I look for Taurus, but the stars are so tightly clustered together I can hardly make any of them out. Just then I smell burning wood. I sit up—is something on fire? No, I don't think so. I can also smell something sweet. I recognize it; it's sweet apple bundt cake. It's one of my favorites, I'd recognize that smell anywhere. But where is it coming from? I'm too far down to smell anything that's baking from the houses in town. The only house I know about within a mile of here, is Old Berta's house. She didn't have any children or family members to leave it to and the house was abandoned after her death. I hastily make my way through the trees. I'd been there so often with my grandmother, that I remember the road perfectly. Within minutes, I can see the outline of the little house, hidden within the surrounding trees. I see some light through the windows and smoke coming from the chimney. The closer I get, the sweeter the smell. I pull out my phone to call the police in case of intruders. No signal. Well, at the very least I might get photos of the intruders and send them to the police department. My father still has many friends at the station; he used to be a policeman when we lived here.

I slowly peek in through the side window. I see Dwintra speaking to what looks like an elderly woman sitting in a rocking chair near the fireplace. There is a large teapot, three cups of tea, plates, silverware, and a freshly baked sweet apple bundt cake on the table. Dwintra walks to the front door and I scoot down the wall and into the bushes to hide.

"Eli!" he shouts from the door. But how does he know I'm here? I'm certain he didn't see me. He calls out my name a few times, but I still don't answer. I hear the door close. I look around, trying to figure out the best way to escape without being seen.

"Hello!" Dwintra says pleasantly from the window above my head. He startles me and I hit my head on the wall. "Well, I tried calling you from the front door, dear. You okay?" he asks.

"Yes, fine," I say, rubbing the back of my head while I stand up sheepishly. He invites me to come inside, and I make my way around the house and step in slowly. It's just as I remember it. Finally, one thing that hasn't changed. It feels very peaceful and brings back a lot of memories of Ms. Berta; she was such a good, gentle soul. I remember she always had my favorite candies on her kitchen table. I apologize for being intrusive, and I explain that I was at the bridge nearby and thought maybe someone had broken in. Dwintra says that there's no need to apologize because they've been waiting for me. I am confused by his reply; I'd only decided to come for a walk an hour ago.

The elderly woman stands up from her chair. But before she has a chance to turn around, Dwintra reminds me that all things are possible now.

"I've missed you so much Eli," the woman says to me. "I can see that the changes are quite becoming, you are exquisite." Dwintra agrees with her and extends his compliments. The shadows from the light are blocking her face, but I know her, her voice is so familiar. From the back of her head I see her silver white hair pulled back in a large bun.

"How can you see me madam, you're not even looking at me. Do I know you?" I ask politely.

"Quite well," she turns around and steps out of the shadow to look at me. It's Berta. She's wearing the exact same dress I saw her in last, and the same small eyeglasses that perfectly frame her petite face. I stand there silently, in dismay.

"You are handling this better than I anticipated, Eli," Dwintra says to me, in a pleasantly surprised tone.

"Apparently I keep dying when I go into shock, so I'm just trying to keep myself from doing that right now," I say slowly, keeping my eyes fixated on Berta.

"Swell idea. I've made your favorite cake. Please sit down, let's have a cup of tea," she says calmly to me.

"You died twenty years ago. How are you here? Are you a—" I stop myself because I realize I have no idea what to call her.

"'Freaks is what I hear *you're* calling us," she replies smiling, and insists I sit down at the table. Dwintra leans to my ear and softly reminds me to blink.

"I'm sorry I said that, I-I was—. Wait . . . how do you know I said that?" I ask baffled. Berta tells me to not worry about that and asks me to catch her up on my Igni life. She hands me a slice of cake and I dig in. It has to be the most delicious one I've ever had. I ask her what her secret ingredient is, because no one can make it the way she does. She tells me she adds honey from her bees. Yes, that's right, her bees; they were her pride and joy! I remember that Berta was both a beekeeper and a scientist. She was always mixing concoctions. Rumor had it that women would go to her when they wanted to poison their husbands or lovers. Allegedly, her stuff was lethal and undetectable. But what I remember most is how squeamish she was about needles. My grandmother would have to give her weekly injections because she was too afraid to do it herself. Once I asked what the injections were for, and my grandmother Amelia told me it was a special formula for Berta's arthritis. Staring at Berta in front of me now, it is evident that she is not human. Whatever that "special formula" in her injections was for—it was not arthritis.

"Well?" I ask with my mouth full of cake. I can't stop eating it. At first, they both stare back at me confused.

"Oh, right! How am I not dead! And what am I, and so on and so forth," she says, pouring our tea as my questions all come back to her.

"Now, I'll give you a quick synopsis, but let's not look too far into the past. I'd rather focus on why I'm here today," she says raising her eyebrows.

I agree.

"Berta is my human name, but my real name is Merope. I am one of the Seven Sisters, but you know we're not really sisters, right?" I nod my head to confirm. "Yes, I'm sure Eden explained. They call me the Bee-Eater because I use my bees to *give* OR *take away* poison, disease, famine, darkness, any number of things you may find are less than . . . pleasant."

"So, you're like, the dark side?" I don't know why but my mouth is watering.

"Well, no. Yes. Oh bugger! Yes! Yes, I am, and I'm proud of it. But I'm really quite tired of continuously getting shamed for it!" Berta pushes her shoulders back and holds her head up high. "You know darkness is not the same as evil, right?"

"It's not?" I ask, unsure of the difference. "Are you maybe in denial?" I probe her.

She rolls her eyes at me.

"So you didn't create the black plague?"

She turns her face and pushes the hair towards the back of her bun.

"What about leprosy?" I persist, but she continues to look

away and ignore me. "Polio? I mean, what did those kids ever do to you?"

"Oh goodness!" she shouts, while she slams her fist down on her leg. "I mean it was just supposed to be one cruel and horrible child! I didn't realize it would spread!"

"HIV?"

"Goodness NEVER! That was disgraceful, I had no part in that! But I certainly punished the one who did!" she says, vindictively pointing her finger in the air.

"Yes, but before she could get the antidote," Dwintra chimes in.

"You hush! You were there too; we both screwed that one up!" she snarls at him. Dwintra puts his hands up and moves away.

"Really Eli, must we? I don't want to do this." Berta gets up and begins pacing.

"Okay, but just one more . . . did you really give women poison to kill their lovers and husbands?" I ask inquisitively.

"Not just women. I also gave it to *men*. And politicians. And world leaders. And Celestial Beings, magical creatures, and Oracles. Even Original Creators; you know they used to call them 'gods.' I prefer that word, but it's not very politically correct, I suppose. You know who *really* didn't like that term . . . God." We both start laughing. I forgot how funny she was.

"I've been wondering what an Original Creator is," I say through my giggles.

"Aagghhh!" both Berta and Dwintra exclaim at the same time looking up and rolling their eyes.

"We'd need an entire decade to explain them!" Berta says, moving her hand side to side.

"Where do you keep your bees?" I ask, not recalling ever seeing a beehive.

"They live inside me. They are like my children," she says,

holding the pit of her stomach. I swallow the bite of cake left in my mouth and put the rest down.

Berta gets back to her original point. She explains that she had no choice other than to fake her death, because she had become so old in her human form. She was afraid she would have made national news as the oldest living woman if she'd stayed. It wouldn't have been wise to draw any more attention than she needed to. She said over the years she would occasionally meet my grandmothers here to catch up. I remember them coming down here to do "maintenance" and to make sure no animals had gotten in. I never questioned it, it made sense to me at the time. Come to think of it, they were very good secret keepers. I ask her if she signed a contract too. She says that because of her gifts, she has always been able to come and go as she pleases. It works the same for the other sisters, but they choose not to come because it has caused too many issues in the past.

I ask if she is with my Nonna Rosa. She takes a hold of my hand.

"No. Rosa had to go back to the Asbgah as stated in her contract. I live up there," she points to the Heavens, "where she should be. Where we should *all* be together."

"Do you ever see her?"

"I see her every chance I get when my services are called upon in the Asbgah, even if it's just for a second. But I must say, not as much as you lately! Rosa has been doing a lot of sneaking around and bending rules to see you," Berta smiles. "My, how she loves you."

"It really was her." My heart fills with warmth and my eyes start watering.

"Darling, I don't mean to be insensitive . . . but I really must get to the point of my visit. I cannot stay for a long time without my injections; they allow me to be on Earth for an extended time. But I've only brought enough formula for a week. I've been watching and listening, trying to see if the rumors about you are really true," Berta says gently. "My injection expires in the next few hours. I have to get back before then."

"Yes, of course, I'm sorry," I say, and wipe my tears away.

"This house will always be a safe-haven, it will protect you. It also serves as a portal, if you will. It is the only way to get in and out of all fourteen Asbgahs from this world. I created it, and it's the only one in existence. Dwintra and I know what it truly is; I never even told your grandmothers." She then hands me an envelope with paperwork and a key. "I left it to you in my will, the deed is in your name. I asked my sisters to let me tell you when the time was right."

"Why me?"

"You see, when you were a child, I knew there was *something* about you, but I could never put my finger on it. I never imagined it could be as wonderful as this."

"Thank you, I'm speechless. I've never received such a gift."

"If I'm honest, I could have never entrusted it to a . . . human. And you are the closest thing I have to family." I think that might have been a polite way of saying she had no one else to leave it to.

"Berta, where . . . how does this portal open?" I ask.

"Well, it doesn't. Not for you. At least not yet, but by the look of things that could change any day now," she says, looking me up and down.

"What does that mean?"

"I mean seriously, have my sisters told you nothing! Must I really do *all* the work!" she shouts in exasperation.

Berta clarifies that my transition will be complete sometime after my twenty-fifth birthday. My heart sinks. She says there is no way to prepare or help me, because other than becoming a Celestial Being, no one has the ability to decipher just what kind

I'll be or what responsibilities I will acquire. Responsibilities? I hadn't even thought of that; I've been too consumed with thoughts about looking like I've been under the knife of the world's best surgeon. I haven't really given any thought to what this actually *means*.

Berta tells me the magical beings that God created in the first fourteen days are called the Divine Coteah. She says that only certain beings within the Divine Coteah are allowed to travel into each Asbgah. The rest, as well as all other creatures, are only permitted to travel from their own Asbgah into the human world. They are forbidden to travel into any other magical realm. She thinks God put in that rule to keep them from being distracted from the work they were created to do. I tell them that doesn't make any sense; couldn't they just assemble here? Berta and Dwintra both look at one another and then back at me. Neither answer my question, but they both assure me that once my transition is complete, she will show me how to travel through the portal.

To help me understand better, Dwintra uses the seven churches to explain. The churches are entrances only to Sibyl's kingdom, in the eleventh Asbgah. Eden described it as cave and magical realm, my grandmothers called it a world, Dwintra and others call it a kingdom; how is it possible that this place is all of these things? He goes on to explain that Sibyl is the only one in all of the Asbgahs who managed to find a way to allow humans in. Berta suggests it's because she's the only one of the rulers who no longer takes orders from God. The rest use something called a *Vellous*. It's used to communicate with those on this side without having to enter. Dwintra explains that anyone who enters the Vellous is not protected. They can be shot, killed, even catch the common cold. It was funny to think that even those so powerful, could be susceptible to basic human illnesses.

Berta describes the Vellous to be like a bubble in a veil between this world and the Asbgahs. A kind of dimension. It's a space where those on this side can connect to those in the Asbgah. They exist all over the world, and they can be anywhere. She explains that the yellow valley in the mountains where I fell asleep, and the wheat valley near my grandmother's farm in Venarotta, are both a Vellous. They were created by Sibyl to communicate with Amelia and Rosa during WWII, and they have not been used in seventy-five years—that is, until just a few weeks ago. Berta says Nonna Rosa put herself at great risk by taking such action but assumes it must have been for an important reason. Berta asks me what my grandmother said to me. I explain that I'd fallen asleep in the meadow and she told me to wake up and go home. Come to think of it, that was the day I met Dwintra; I assume that's not another coincidence. I remember the two elm trees and the "short cut" home he had me take. They were the same kind of elm trees I saw in Foce. The moment my mind wonders back to that day, Berta and Dwintra start whispering something to each other in a strange language. I ask them what they are speaking, and they say it is an ancient dialect. Whatever it is, it's obvious they don't want me to understand.

"I don't think there is any language I can speak in this world that you wouldn't understand, but I hope you can understand how rude you're being!" I say annoyed. "So, which one of you is going to tell me why she would be in danger just for wanting to wake me up?"

They both pause.

"Sibyl created it, so she knows if anyone uses it," Dwintra says.

I shake my head at him in bafflement. "You need to be more specific, Dwintra."

"There is a great deal of unsettlement in the Asbgahs. If your grandmother was seen supporting anyone but Sibyl . . . it would be very . . . bad for her," Berta explains. She puts her hands on my shoulders. "Child, I can't begin to imagine how heavy this must all feel. But whatever it is, whatever is coming, I am here."

"Merope, the sun will be rising. You need to go," Dwintra says in a panicked tone.

Berta kisses me on the forehead and tells Dwintra to walk me back to the main road. We say our good-byes and I leave. My mind might be on overdrive, but my gut tells me I haven't even scratched the surface. I look back and see a blast of crystal lights beaming from the house, and wide into the forest. Good thing NASA isn't watching.

Chapter 16

6:00 AM.
I'm standing at the top of the road. I haven't pulled an all-nighter in a while. The air is crisp and the birds are chirping. I check my cell phone; oddly no messages. My phone indicates a new email, from Dr. Borga. It is an authorization form he needs me to sign to run genetic testing. Good thing I didn't sign it at the hospital. I can't imagine what he'd find. I had a flash in my mind of the government taking me and my family away for experimentation like they do in alien movies. I email him back that I've changed my mind and thank him for his kindness.

I turn on the burner phone—Sophia should be calling soon. There's a text from her, it reads:

19.8.5	[she]
9.19.	[is.]
7am	
13.15.14.4.1.2	[Monday]

She is confirming the time of our call today. I decide to walk into town to get a cup of coffee and a Nutella beignet. Stress brings out my addiction to sugar.

I sit down at a corner table and Lolla walks over to take my order. She's run this place since I can remember. She knows everyone's name and who they're related to. And she knows about this town's history more than anyone else I know, other than Eden. She asks what she can get me, and I tell her "the usual." Lolla looks at me hard and asks for my name.

"Lolla, it's me Eli," I reply, thinking she must be playing with me.

"Oh goodness doll, did you change your hair? I didn't even recognize you! You kids are always changing things up on me! Coffee and Nutella beignet on their way," she says flustered.

I can see her looking at me from the corner of her eye the entire time she's making my coffee. Do I really look so different? I catch my reflection in the window. What are my friends in LA going to say? Who am I kidding, they'll probably just want a referral to the plastic surgeon they think I went to.

"Did you put in some highlights? They look soft and sparkly. I can't keep up with all the trends. What kind of color is that?" Lolla asks, putting the coffee and pastry down.

The morning rush is starting and everyone who is walking in can't resist taking a peek at me. I ask Lolla for my things to go. I know there is no way I can sit here without being gawked at. While she is doing that for me, I put my hair in a bun, and put the hoodie from my jacket over it. I get out of there as fast as I can.

On my way back, the phone finally rings. I miss Sophia's voice so much.

"Cousin, we have seven minutes," she says abruptly, "and we already wasted one missing each other."

"What is it with this seven minutes?"

"The first seven minutes of any new correspondence, thought, or action, is the only free will we actually have before interception from magic, nature, or God."

"God?"

"Yeah, apparently that's how bad shit gets past him all the time," she says matter-of-factly. "So, by now you know that you're the first Celestial born in like a million years, right?"

"More like five thousand," I reply to her exaggeration.

"Yeah, yeah, whatever. So, you're like, super special but no one knows why, right?"

"Umm, okay."

"Cousin, listen to me. The minute your transition is finished they are ALL going to come looking for you. You have to find somewhere safe to hide out until we can figure this out."

Berta's house, or now I guess my house, comes to mind.

"Who's coming?" I ask with a bit of fear in my heart.

"Like gods, Oracles, wizards, unicorns! I don't know, like the entire magical community. But this is what you need to know: there is a war brewing in the Asbgahs."

"You know about the Asbgahs?"

"Yes, I've been studying them night and day. It's exhausting!" She's talking so fast, she must have had have twenty cups of espresso.

"Anyway, Victoria Mason isn't just an Oracle. She is the keeper of all the secrets of the Universe, and all the Universe's history! Hence the library; seriously there's so much cool shit in here, I have so much to tell you! And Alessandro is the father of all magic! Crazy, right? Uh-huh, like abracadabra magic shit! No wonder Luca's trippin'! Remember when we wondered why Micella couldn't enjoy all of those amazing clothes? It's because she's in charge of one of the Asbgahs! You probably met Dante by now—he's so hot! What about our parents being magical, that seriously blew my mind. I mean, if that's the case, couldn't they have been more awesome parents? What can your parents do? My mom, sweet old Elenora, is definitely not what she seems— and you're never going to believe her linage . . . ELVEN! Babe, I'm part Elven!"

"Sophia, slow down please." My heart is beating out of my chest.

"No! We only have a minute left. Listen, Luca is on our side. I know you have your doubts, but he is. He's been working night and day to protect you, to find a way around all this. But in the end, everything is contingent on the decisions that you make in *your* seven minutes that will determine this outcome. Do you understand, Eli?"

"No."

"Be safe, find a place to hide. I'll call you again next week. I'm sending Luca with information today. I love you."

Click.

"Sophia?" I look down at my phone—she hung up. The call log says six minutes and fifty-nine seconds.

I don't even realize I've made it home already. The entire walk is a blur. I enter the house and see my mom at the kitchen table. I kiss her on the head, give her my coffee and pastry, and walk upstairs. I should go to bed, but the adrenaline rushing through my body won't allow it. I take a shower, get dressed, and tell my mom I'm going shopping for a birthday dress in Ascoli Piceno. She offers to come with me, but I tell her I need some time alone. My mother suggests I wear one of Aunt Ersella's long wigs, or hide my hair in a hat. She says I'll start to draw attention soon; little does she know I created quite a stir this morning already. I grab my uncle's beanie and say goodbye to her and my grandmother, and tell them not to wait on me for lunch—I will have a bite in the city. I get into Aunt Silva's car and drive away.

When I reach the bottom of the hill, the sign says Ascoli

Piceno with the arrow pointing to the right, and Pretare with an arrow pointing to the left. I turn left. Ten minutes later, there is another sign pointing to the right that says Foce. I turn right.

Twenty minutes later I pull into the area that our tour was originally supposed to be, at the stop in Foce. I wonder if my life would be any different if I hadn't gone that day. Was it the trigger to all these changes? If I'd chosen to not stay, and instead went back home to LA, could I have saved myself from all of this?

I get out of the car and look around; there are a few people walking their dogs in the park. I pull out my phone to look for the hiking trail to Santa Maria. All the directions I find say that there are no signs, and just to follow the trail, and they give me some indicators to look out for. I tuck my hair in the hat, grab my water bottle and granola bars, and head out. According to the directions, if I walk fast and don't make any stops, I can make it there in six hours. Off I go.

Two and a half hours in. I'm short of breath and I've got to stop. It's more rigorous than I imagined. But it has been good for my stress level, I walked off a lot of frustration. And it's also kept me distracted from the reality of what I'm about to do. My body drops down on a patchy area of grass with some shade. I spread out all my limbs, breathe hard, and try to catch my breath. I know I'm not supposed to stop, but the cold moisture from the grass feels so good on my back. I should have spent more time in my life exercising, my stamina is pathetic. My best friend in LA is always pushing me to go hiking with her. Right about now, I'm regretting not taking her up on one of those offers. I wonder how she's doing. If things were different, I would invite her out to visit, she would love it here. I close my eyes and attempt to even out my breaths.

"Beautiful day, isn't it?" The voice startles me and I open my eyes.

"Dwintra! Are you serious? You scared me half to death!" I yell, jumping up. "How did you know I was here? I didn't tell anyone. And it's kind of creepy that you keep popping up."

"Okay, so time to come clean. I'm not a creep. I am the forest keeper . . . of *all* forests," he says awkwardly. "It may sound strange, but it's actually a very important job. And well, nothing happens in *any* forest without my knowledge."

"So, what, the trees and the animals are all just snitches?"

"Now Eli, be nice. They are your friends, and they're just looking out for you. They may even be willing to help out a girl that could possibly be in need of a . . . favor."

"What would you know about that?"

"I know that if you're here, you've decided to go to Sibyl's cave."

"Is it really a kingdom?" I ask him.

"It is. Every Asbgah is a kingdom. But we can't very well go around announcing that, can we?"

"No, I suppose not."

"And our friends, the trees, can cut your commute from another four hours to four steps. Shall we?" he asks, extending his hand to walk forward. He is not joking. We walk through two trees, and suddenly we're standing in front of the shattered heart stone.

"Does that short cut trick only work with you?" I ask.

"Afraid so."

I look back at him to say something, and I can't believe my eyes.

"Dwintra, you're a young man! How did you do that?" He is suddenly a vibrant man in his twenties.

"It's the faerie air, it shows my true identity. I chose an elder human form, because I figured that it's less alarming to see a simple old man in the woods, than a young one with pointy ears."

"Let me guess, you're from the Elven Asbgah? But you're permitted in the human world because you are the Keeper of the Forests?" I reply, putting the pieces together in my mind.

"Something like that."

"Dwintra, why are you helping me? I assumed you'd be trying to keep me from doing this, since I don't have the slightest idea of what I'm getting myself into."

"Because I'm your friend. And I suppose because I know it's inevitable—" Just then something catches his eye and he stomps over to a bush.

"YOU! What are you doing here?" he yells into it. Slowly, a magnificent creature with beautiful skin, pink cheeks, huge bright blue eyes, a perfect button nose, and short, messy black hair pops out.

"Dwintra," she says sternly, looking at him up and down.

"Elise," he says, returning the steel stare. There is an awkward moment of silence.

"So, you're Elise?" I interrupt, admiring her sweet face. I'm sad for little Vanessa that she will never remember her.

"Yes! Oh, so good to meet you, Eli!" She walks over and gives me a tight hug. "I've been on pins and needles with anticipation." Her scent is intoxicating. I feel like putty in her embrace. Dwintra yanks her off me.

"Don't be enchanted by her illustrious beauty, perfect lips, and mind-altering sex!"

"Huh?" I reply, caught off guard. "Oh, I see. You must have been lovers. That explains the hostility."

"I didn't mean that! It's that darn faerie air—makes me do . . . stupid things!" Dwintra shouts.

I can't help but laugh a little. I can see that he's dying to touch her. And she knows it too.

"I miss you my little 'Tra," she says, batting her long eyelashes at him. Honestly, I don't know how he has any self-control with her. But I think I'm finally starting to understand the nymph part of faeries I hear so much about.

"Eli, I'm sorry you had to witness this. This wretched creature broke my heart long ago. I've been trying to avoid her, but she keeps showing up everywhere."

She smacks him in the arm, crosses her long thin arms, and frowns. She's darling even when she does that.

"Eli," she says in a serious tone, directing all her attention to me and turning her back to Dwintra, "I want to be of service today, if you'll have me. I know how scary it can be going to a new place alone. So, I just want to be here for you, in case you want someone to walk with you."

"That is very sweet of you Elise," I say, trying to clear my thoughts from the euphoric air. "But how did you know I was here?"

She points up to the green, singing Pentwilin birds. I smile and nod. Big-mouthed, hummingbird look-a-likes.

"If I know, *she* knows too. She's waiting for you now," Elise says referring to Sibyl.

"You know she has to make the journey alone, Elise," Dwintra reminds her.

"Yes, I know, but I can at least walk her through the door. She'll be less afraid, won't she?" she says, looking doe-eyed at him. I can tell Dwintra is impressed by her genuine gesture.

"Yes, yes . . . But she is braver than she gives herself credit for," Dwintra smiles gently. "Eli, there is no way to prepare you for what comes next. It is like nothing you've ever seen before; it will be both exhilarating and frightening. The entrance to the kingdom is not directly on the other side of the door. It is, as I said, a journey, but not a long one. Use your common sense and know that nothing in there can physically hurt you. Because your transition is not yet complete, the human side of you will be deeply affected; but because of your bloodline, the side effects of the euphoria will wear off quickly."

Elise grabs a hold of my hand and asks, "Are you ready?"

"Yes." I feel a split second of courage inside me, something I've never felt before.

"Eli—one last thing. Once you're in the kingdom, should you be in need of assistance, hold onto your Halledrite necklace and call for *The Guardian*." I nod reluctantly. Dwintra kisses my hand, "Godspeed."

Elise and I walk up to the shattered heart rock, and I place my right hand over it. An opening in the shape of a perfect door appears. I remove my hand and gently push the door open. We enter into an old cave. Elise and I turn to wave goodbye to Dwintra, but he is already gone. Instead, I see figures racing towards me. It's Luca, Alessia, Dante, and Stefano. I see their lips moving, they are shouting something . . . but I can't hear them. I begin to walk back to the door to exit the cave, when the opening slams shut right in front of me.

I stand there unable to move. Panic sets in. I push and feel my way around the door to see if there is anything there that would make it open. But it's pitch black, I can't see anything.

"What have I done . . . " I mumble to myself.

I close my eyes and try to control my breathing. As fear runs through me, I become acutely aware of a stillness. I don't think I've ever realized that there is a stillness in darkness. It feels as if fear and freedom are the same. I wonder if death holds this kind of infinite silence and solitude.

Lately I seem to have lost touch with reality; standing in this cold cave only makes me realize just how much.

"Eli," I hear Elise's soft voice to the side of me.

"What do I do? How do I get this door open?"

"You cannot, you must move forward. Light will appear in a moment and I will be gone—you must take this journey on your own." I feel her take hold of my hand. "Be brave Eli, I'll see you on the other side."

"What other side?"

Silence.

"Elise? Elise!" I yell out.

Silence.

"I'm not brave," I say out loud in the darkness. I'm more like a petulant child that is insistent on knowing the truth at all costs. What am I doing? This is so stupid of me. What in the world makes me think I can do this on my own? I should have taken the next flight home and gone back to my Igni world. My parents must have had their reasons for keeping all of this a secret all these years.

Lights.

Lining both sides of the corridor in front of me, appear fire-lit lanterns. The passageway looks endless, like mirrors that reflect and stretch on forever. It's a good thing the faerie air makes endorphins feel like they're on steroids, because this view is nothing short of something that triggers panic attacks. There is no end in sight. By the look of things, I'll be walking for years.

I look back at the entryway; it is now a sealed concrete wall with no remnants of where there once was a door. I take a few steps into the cave and look around. It reminds me a bit of the photos I've seen, showing the inside of the Egyptian pyramids. The walls are made of stone, maybe limestone. They're a light color with patches of moss sporadically growing everywhere. I place my hand on one patch and it feels like the softest fur I've ever touched. It has a strong lavender scent; it reminds me of Sibyl. The walls are narrow at the top, wide at the bottom, and the ceiling is flat. It is similar to the shape of a coffin. That can't be a good omen. The floors are a hard, compact dirt with a few pebbles. I begin walking down the passageway; the further I go the narrower it becomes. I begin to feel claustrophobic. I lean my hands against each side of the narrow walls and look around for any windows or doors. I don't see any way of getting out. Before I can panic, a gust of wind comes out of nowhere from my right. I close my eyes and turn my head away from its force. After a moment, it calms. My head is tilting down as I open my eyes. I see many leaves of different shapes, colors, and sizes around my feet. There is one particularly large leaf that catches my eye. It's different from the rest, it looks like a fig leaf. I pick it up; there is something written on it.

Welcome Eli,
I'm so delighted you're finally here.
You must pass through three corridors
before entering my kingdom.
I will be waiting for you
at the end of the third corridor.
The "desire to know truth"
is the key to entry of the first corridor.
No looking back now.
*   -Sibyl*

Sigh.

Chapter 17

I FEEL HEAT—a lot of it, like a sauna—so I look up from reading Sibyl's note to see where it's coming from. The walls that confined me are now gone, and I am standing in a *huge* dome-shaped cave. The dirt that was under my feet is now sand. I'm going to take a wild guess and assume that I've just entered the first corridor. I see a very long bridge just as the sand ends, not too far ahead.

I start walking and continue for what feels like an hour, without reaching the bridge. I've made little to no progress. I look behind me and all I see is endless desert sand. How is this possible? The bridge looks like it's only a few hundred yards away, but the only thing that seems to change is the temperature; it keeps rising. It feels like I'm standing next to an oven set at 1,000 degrees. I look around for water, but there's nothing. My chest and eyes are burning and sweat is dripping off my body like crazy. I see steam coming off the rocks on the walls of the dome. I squeeze my eyes together tightly over and over. I want to sit and rest a moment, but the sand is too hot, it feels like I might burn myself if I try. My thoughts are of random things with no meaning. I try to distract myself with unimportant memories of school, television shows, books, and my friends in the U.S.

Another hour passes.

I can't take this heat anymore! I'm tired and frustrated. I've got to get to that bridge or die trying. I begin to run towards it with all the strength I have left inside me. My heart is pounding harder than I've ever felt before. It beats so loudly; it drowns out everything else around me, and my body goes numb. My breath, my heart, and my feet hitting the sand are all in sync now. And in that moment, I begin to see what look like memories flashing in my mind. But I don't know whose memories they are . . . could they be mine? I don't remember experiencing anything these visions are recalling.

*   *   *

I see myself as a child. I am sitting on my bed holding a doll. It must have been sometime in Italy before we moved away. My mother and father are arguing with all four of my grandparents. They are begging my parents to reconsider. My grandfather Giuseppe tells my father that I will never know, and it is a small price to pay for keeping me safe. My grandmother Rosa reassures my father that I will feel no pain, and it will be just like a dream. My mother asks my grandmother Amelia to explain it to them once more. Nonna Amelia holds her by the hand and tells her that it's a simple ritual, and once we cross the Atlantic Ocean the binding will be complete, and I will be protected from any harm. I see my mother shaking her head "no" and crying. She tells them that she could never abandon everyone, and that she could never have a life so far away from her family. Nonna Amelia holds her in her arms while she cries and tells her she must do it to save her family and keep us together. Nonna Amelia tells my mother that she knows this all comes at a large cost, but she must be brave because it is the only way. She goes on to say that the "woman" will not stop until she has hurt me too, and it is time to bring this to an end.

The next memory is mine. I remember it as if it was yesterday. My father is telling me it is time to go to the airport. I'm crying inconsolably as I am torn out of Nonna Rosa's arms. At five years old I can feel my heart breaking for the first time; she is the love of my life. My grandmother doesn't let go until my grandfather has to tear me out of her arms, and my little hands are still reaching out to her as I scream her name. She runs over to me, and I see tears streaming down her eyes as if they're waterfalls. I can see all her pain. She then touches me on the forehead with her gentle finger and says "dementi." And in that moment, I do just that: forget.

*   *   *

Just as I think I will collapse from running for so long across the scorching sand, I see the bridge extending itself to me. I use the last ounce of energy I have to thrust myself onto it. I fall to my knees and begin to cry with a pain in my soul like I've never felt before. I had suppressed that memory until this moment, and just then, it broke free from the prison I had put it in. And all the hurt returned with a vengeance.

Something nudges me. I let out a scream and fall to my side. Between the pain of the burning of my muscles and the tears in my eyes, I can't see anything. I can only make out a large black blur in front of me. My heart starts racing; I use my hands and arms to drag myself away from the shadow and further onto the bridge. It moves closer to me . . . I hear hooves. Even if the legend about faeries having hooves is true, whatever this creature is, it's much too large to be a faerie.

"Who's there?" I demand. I hear its legs walking closer to me. As I try to rub the blur out of my eyes, I see the shadow sit next to me and hear a thump. I suddenly remember Dwintra saying that nothing here can physically hurt me. That gives me comfort. The large figure leans in and rubs itself on my hand. I know this texture, but from where? I slowly and reluctantly extend my hand to feel more of it. My eyes have vision . . . but it is not my own. It's as if am looking at myself from the outside. And it's not a pretty sight: my shirt is soaked in sweat, my hair is disheveled, I am visibly shaking, and there are tears streaming down my face. As I look closer in the reflection of my own eyes, I see him.

"WASI!!!" I shout, and fiercely throw my arms around his neck. "Is it really you, beautiful boy?" I say, laughing and crying at the same time, hoping that this isn't a hallucination from heat stroke. He leans into me as if he is trying to embrace me back. "Wasi, I don't know what I've done!" I pull away and take a moment to reflect. "Wait . . . how did you get here? How did you even know where I was?"

"He's a horse, dear child! Do you think he's going to talk back? Well, not even in this hellhole!"

"Aunt Ersella?!" I scream, looking around.

"Yes dear, I'm right here next to you in the water. Follow the sound of my voice."

"Water?" I reply. I can hear it flowing now, rushing under the bridge.

"Just a little more to your right," she says directing me. I feel her arms reach up and grab me. She washes my face with the water from the stream, and within moments my vision becomes clear.

"I'm so happy to see you!" I say looking down at her, as she wipes the tears from my eyes once again. "How are you both here?"

"I rode Wasi here silly, how else?" She looks at me as if I'm the one who said something crazy. "We came in through Lake Pilate."

"What—How? I thought that was only the entrance to the Underworld? Am I in Hell?"

"This bridge serves as a crossroad between the human world and Inferno. But for a human to get to Sibyl's kingdom, one must also pass through it."

"That explains why it's so wretched hot. I'm not going to accidentally end up in Hell, am I?" I ask annoyed.

"Of course not. You haven't been granted passage to the Underworld." She continues to use that tone, which makes it seem like I'm the one saying absurd statements.

"Yeah, that's a ticket I'll pass on," I say, then change the subject. "How did you ride Wasi here? Another magic trick?"

"Precisely!" She then lifts herself slightly out of the water, grabs me by the shirt, and pulls me into the water with her. She blows air into my mouth, and within a second, I'm breathing under water. I can't believe how young Aunt Ersella looks. Every scale on her body is delicate and perfect. They are barely noticeable, but I can see them slowly fluttering. She illuminates a radiant light. In this magical moment, I realize that I am in the presence of, and staring straight into, an *actual star*. I feel very entranced and am in complete awe.

"Focus, Eli! I know this is all very enchanting for you, but it's no time to be mesmerized!" she snaps at me like the great-aunt I've known all my life.

"Sorry, it's just—" I so badly want her to know how sorry I am for never believing her. She is the only one who was ever truly honest. I always found myself dismissing her words, and thinking she was over the top and a bit crazy.

"Another time my love—I'm not allowed to be here. I only did it to escort Wasi. No one is permitted to interfere with your journey, doing so has severe consequences. But I'm certain once Sibyl sees him, all will be forgiven."

"Why?" I ask, with a bad feeling in the pit of my stomach.

"Wasi will let you know once he is ready. Your connection with him will grow deeper and you will learn to understand one another without words. He knows you need him, and he did not want you to be alone," Aunt Ersella says with sadness in her eyes.

"Auntie, I don't understand. I thought I was just going to walk straight into Sibyl's cave once I entered. What is the purpose of these three corridors?"

"I know it's not what you expected. It never is. Sibyl designed it this way. I can't answer your question, but when you reach the final corridor, she will give you those answers." She pauses and gives me an encouraging smile, "Don't be afraid my love, you are the granddaughter of two of the most powerful beings this universe has ever known. Everything you need to be, and everything you need to know, already lives inside of you."

But there is one thing I do not know, and it is evident to me that it is important.

"Aunt Ersella, who's 'the woman?' I-I know that you know," I ask, while looking straight into her eyes.

"Oh, Eli . . . " my aunt replies with sadness.

"Please tell me. I know she's the reason we left everything we love behind; I saw it in a memory. I deserve to know the truth," I say demandingly.

Aunt Ersella takes a deep breath. She tells me about a woman who fell in love with my father when they were young. But my father only ever saw her as a friend. She became more and more infatuated with him as the years went on. But no matter how many times he denied her, and said that he did not reciprocate the feelings, the harder she fought for his attention and would not surrender. By the time my father married my mother and had me, her love had turned into a mad obsession. The woman was unable to make peace with the fact that he did not choose her. She knew that she could not cause any harm to me while my mother was pregnant, because my grandmothers had cast a light of protection around me while growing in her womb. But on the day of my birth, she placed a curse on my mother so that she would not be able to have any more children. Aunt Ersella tells me that my grandmothers did everything they could to protect me from that day forward, but that it would not be enough.

She goes on to tell me about something that happened a few weeks after my birth. My mother insisted on getting out of the house—she was tired of all the fussing and hovering. She wanted the both of us to get fresh air. She took me for a walk on the main road in an old stroller that was once hers when she was a baby. She was stopped by an old woman she had never seen before, and by my mother's description of her, it was not someone that my aunt or grandmothers knew. The old woman told my mother that she needed to protect me, watch over me, and to never take her eyes off me. I was in danger, and I would never be safe here. She told my mother that I was very special, and born under a very significant star. Everything would be revealed in time, but for now it would be best to take me away. But my mother took her warnings as the rants of a crazy old woman who'd lost her way. She knew it would only cause my grandmothers and aunt to overreact if she shared what happened, and the last thing she wanted was more hovering. So, it was only after the third attempt on my life, that she told them all about this encounter.

I ask Aunt Ersella to clarify. *What* attempts on my life, wouldn't that be something I'd recall?

She reminds me about the fire, the boiling water, and the knife.

I look down at my arm and touch the small scarring that remains from third degree burns caused by the fire. My back twitches as I remember the boiling hot water being thrown onto it. And yes . . . the knife that somehow flew across the room and missed me by a hair. If my grandfather hadn't walked in when he had and moved me out of the way, it would have landed in my heart.

"Those were attempts on my life?" I ask flabbergasted.

"Yes . . . by that *wretched woman* who was in love with your father," she says, with disdain on her tongue and anger in her voice.

"I thought I was just a clumsy kid," I reply, shaking my head.

"Yes, I suppose that is what we led you to believe. It was the only way to raise you without fear."

"That's ironic, since I'm afraid of everything!" I reply frustrated. "And now that I know it's all my fault—"

"Now you listen to me, Eli! *None* of this is your fault! They were difficult times. Your mother and father were arguing constantly. Your father was traveling extensively for work, and your mother was very lonely—this put a great strain on their marriage. She would never have forgiven herself if something happened to you on her watch. It was the best thing for their marriage, and for your family as a whole, to leave," Aunt Ersella grabs me by the shoulders. "Watching you three leave was the hardest thing we've ever done. The darkness and depression it set on our family . . . I don't think we ever recovered. But believe me Eli, it really was for the best."

I nod my head.

"The bitch is dead now; you have nothing to worry about. She can't hurt you anymore."

I look up at her as I have a startling thought. "Did you kill her?"

"Natural causes," she says, winking at me. I gulp.

"Now, don't you worry yourself with details. I've been here much too long; this is your journey and there are things you will just have to figure out on your own. I must go. Be brave, Eli. I love you."

She takes the air from my lungs and pushes me out of the water. Wasi leans his head down to assist me out—I put my arms around his neck and he lifts me onto the bridge. We look back into the water. Aunt Ersella blows us a kiss, and then swims away at the speed of light.

I caress Wasi's face. "I don't know what I did to deserve your kindness, nor understand why you came. But please know that I am so grateful, I will be forever in your debt. Thank you Wasi."

He leans his head down as if to reply.

"Have you ever been here before?"

He shakes "no."

"Do you have any idea what to expect?"

He shakes his head "no" once more.

"It looks like it's a first for the both of us," I say, as I climb onto his back. I close my eyes and lean down to kiss him. Our vision then becomes one, and I now see the road ahead through his eyes. The parameter of my sight becomes wide and deep, despite my own eyes being closed. The bridge is strong and long, and the water beneath it gives us a comforting sound.

That comfort quickly takes a turn when we realize that the farther we ride, the higher the current becomes, and the narrower the bridge gets. The air and climate are also changing. The heat and humidity are now replaced with no temperature at all; there is a lightness and weightlessness, and less and less oxygen is available.

Wasi syncs the rhythm of our hearts, and we begin to share each breath we take. We ride this way until we are fully immersed under water and can no longer breathe. Wasi is calm and it's helping me not to panic. I feel safe with him. I can tell he is not afraid; he is a warrior and filled with courage.

I feel our hearts slow . . . slower still . . . until there is almost no beat at all . . .

We are surrounded by water. I feel a sense of weightlessness come over me as if I am floating in space, yet we are still held down by gravity. I see the walls of water around and above us, turn into crystals that look like a million stars in the nighttime sky, and just as quickly, begin to evaporate around us. Just as we see the last sparkle of the crystals disappear, oxygen instantly fills our lungs. Breathing under water at this moment is the same sensation I experienced with Aunt Ersella. I begin to choke and gasp for air. Wasi takes deep breath after deep breath, trying to fill his lungs.

Through Wasi's vision I see the water begin to move in a clockwise motion around us. It begins spinning at a violent speed, moving further and further away from our bodies and into a cyclone. I can see it spinning above and below us, we are now in the center of the vortex. The cyclone spins with increased forceful aggression, until it suddenly vanishes. I finally open my own eyes and it is night all around. I can see the midnight blue sky filled with stars above, below, and all around us. It's as if we are walking on the stars.

Images start appearing in the beautiful starry night sky. They are images from every important moment, telling the story of my life. From my birth, to the moment I entered this cave. I witness every precious memory I've treasured, and every person that has had a significant impact on my life. It is both beautiful and painful.

"I bet that was more than you ever wanted to know about me," I say, looking at Wasi.

He neighs.

Wasi jerks his head up a few times to get me to look back up at the sky. There is a star shining brighter than the rest. Could that be the North Star? After learning what I know, I can't help but wonder if it could be someone I'm related to. My mind wanders off as complicated questions fill it. But I become distracted by a blinding light. It is the North Star. It is getting bigger and closer with every blink.

"Wasi," I say nervously. My vision goes blurry, and in an instant is in sync with Wasi. This is the first time I can do this with my eyes still being open. Through his eyes the star looks clearer, with beams shooting out of every angle. He steadies my heart with the beat of his own.

"T-hank you," I whisper, but I'm barely able to get the words out. I am in awe of the star. It does not stop moving towards us until we are fully immersed in its light. Then I feel it again . . . vibrations.

I feel vibrations emulate from the light, it's all around me.

I can feel them penetrate through every layer of my skin.

Then into my veins.

Slowly through my muscles.

And into the fragments of my bones.

A cold chill shoots up through my spine. I shiver.

Everything around me has gone from looking like we are floating in a galaxy, to a pure white light. There are small flakes of a lint-like-molecules floating in the air. The center of the light stops directly in front of my face. I am nearly blinded by its intensity. Its shape is changing from oblong to round and back again in a constant loop. Within the light are what looks like electricity and fire chasing and moving in every direction. It is majestic. They accompany each other like a beautiful melody or indefectible dance. I stare into it . . . I feel a peace I've never known before. I am hypnotized.

I hear a voice muffled in the background. As my consciousness reawakens, a word coming from a familiar voice becomes clear.

"Ridáte."

With that word, *all* peace is gone. My mind is assaulted with memory after memory.

Every unaccounted time lapse.

Every ounce of pain.

Every sensation of pleasure.

Every unsure feeling.

Every foggy thought.

Every blackout.

And so, with that word, I remember EVERYTHING.

Chapter 18

I JUMP OFF WASI onto a hard dirt floor. There is no more starry galaxy and no more majestic light. Once again, I'm in a dimly lit and cold cave. My legs are trembling as I walk towards the figure standing in front of a new door, that has appeared on the far wall of the cave.

And in that same familiar voice I'd just heard, the figure says, "Forgive us, Eli."

It is Nonna Rosa in the flesh. Undead. Young just as she was in her wedding photos, but even more beautiful than I could have dreamed. I have never seen an angel, but she looks like what I imagine one would. But my anger stops me from being enamored by her presence. It's like fire accelerating through my veins, and I have no desire for a loving reunion.

"How could you do that to me!" I shout, unable to hold back.

"Now, don't be upset Eli! We only did it to protect you. We thought the protection spell would break once that horrid woman died."

"What about my memory! Why would you take that away from me? Do you have any idea how horrifying the blackouts have been? Do you know how many doctors I've seen? Didn't one of you *once* think to tell me the truth! What the f—" she cuts me off mid-sentence.

"No cursing. You know how I feel about that," Nonna Rosa says in her calm and gentle voice.

"We are going to have to make an exception here! Do you have even the slightest idea of what I have going on in my head right now? I-I-I'm overwhelmed! I don't know where to put all these things I now know. I don't even think I understand any of it. The timeline is all mixed up!"

"Give it a little time, everything will eventually work itself back into its proper place in your mind and memories."

"How much time? Never mind that! Why did you block my mind and give me the blackouts?"

"We didn't. Well, at least we didn't know we did. The binding spell was stronger than we knew. No one had used it in a least two thousand years, it was a bit . . . well, rusty. It not only blocked magic from hurting you, it actually blocked ALL magic . . . up until recently, that is. We tried telling you the truth so many times, but your mind just . . . "

"Blocked it out? Nonna Amelia mentioned that." I reply sarcastically.

"Yes," she says ashamed. "We realized that with each time you could remember something by experiencing it, there would be a fracture in the spell." This explains A LOT. Like why I don't believe in magic, and why I can't stand supernatural and superstitious things.

I ask her how we are able to talk about it now. She tells me that it has to do with the corridor we are in. She explains that the three corridors were created by Sibyl to protect herself and test anyone who enters her kingdom. She'd been tricked and used too many times by both humans and magical beings throughout her life, so this became Sibyl's way of "getting one's cards on the table," as Nonna Rosa puts it. The first corridor was created to see *Truth*. It's designed to know what event in her visitor's life has brought them to see her.

The second corridor, the one we are standing in, is known as *Purification*. It is designed to purify the body and soul from spells, hexes, malicious intent, and magic. It is also used to prevent outsiders from casting and using magic in her kingdom. Only she, her faeries, and her animals are permitted to use it in her Asbgah.

"Since we used magic to cast the binding spell, it is only in its release that you are free of it," Nonna Rosa says, trying to touch me.

"Will I be free of it forever?" I ask as I pull away, memories still flooding my mind.

"I don't know, Eli," she replies sadly. "No one has ever seen this kind of impact on a binding spell. No one knows what will happen once you return to the human Asbgah. I pleaded with Sibyl to allow me to be here with you. I couldn't bear the thought of you having to do all of this on your own."

"It will cost you, won't it?"

"Yes. But anything is worth being here with you," she says with that I smile only she can give. Just then my anger lessens. I can't imagine what she must do to repay the favor. Once again, she sacrificed everything for me.

I tell her about my encounter with Aunt Ersella in the first corridor, and I introduce her to Wasi. She falls in love with him as quickly as I did. She says she's heard a great deal about him from a special someone in the kingdom. If I didn't know any better, I'd think he's blushing. I'll have to get to the bottom of that later. In the meantime, I apologize to Nonna for being so angry. I know she has her reasons, and to take such a dramatic action she must have been very afraid for my life.

Before I am able to have another thought, my mind takes an aggressive turn.

Visions.

Visions aggressively invade my mind with all things that I intuitively know have not yet happened. Places, events, and people. Some I recognize, but most I've never seen before. I start gasping for air.

"My head!" I shout, as it pounds like a sledgehammer tearing through concrete. My grandmother helps me sit on the ground and leans me up against the cold stone wall. "*What* is this? Make it stop!"

"It will pass in a moment Eli, just breathe," she says, holding me tightly as we both sit there waiting for it to pass. She is right. As soon as I see the last vision, the pounding in my head is gone.

"Is that our . . . *future*?" I ask, after sitting in silence for a few minutes, cradled in her arms.

"I imagine it is. But only you can see it, Eli. Even I don't know what you know. And I suppose because of your connection, Wasi does too," Nonna says. We both look over at him. He locks eyes with me and then looks away.

My grandmother asks me how this could have happened. I tell her that by the fragments of memories that are slowly coming back to me, I remember this information about the future being transferred to me during my interaction with Mr. Vinci. I recall speaking to him in his study after dinner.

We were standing in front of the Tree of Life painting, and he touched my hand. He told me he wanted to know my thoughts and found it peculiar that he could not get a proper read on me. Mr. Vinci asked to take a peek into my mind. I thought he was joking, and I agreed. I didn't know who he really was and what he could do. Somehow instead of him entering mine, I entered *his*. He was not prepared or guarded, so I saw it *all*.

"I *need* to know Eli, I need to know what you saw!" Nonna Rosa says desperately. "You must get through the third corridor as quickly as possible. I will be waiting for you inside the kingdom. But so will Sibyl. She will be as anxious as I am to know what you've seen," Nonna says pacing. "Please tell her nothing of your visions. Only tell her that your memory is returning slowly. She will do whatever she can to get information out of you, it is very important that you do not let her."

"Why do you and Luca not seem to like her? She seems so . . . nice," I ask.

"I suppose her duende is undeniable to us all. But she has her own motives for wanting to know. And those reasons are dangerous. Once you know her story, you will understand."

"How will I know her story?" I ask.

"Eli, no one has ever been in Alessandro's mind. And now that you know *what* he is, more importantly what he's done, she will undoubtedly tell you her story in hopes of gaining your compassion," she says as she stops pacing, and puts both my hands into hers. She looks me right in the eyes. "You understand what I'm saying."

I nod my head in agreement and say, "I do." What I don't tell her is how terrified I am by what I've just seen.

My grandmother goes on to say that Sibyl knows better than to grant entrance to anyone, without first knowing the true intention of their heart. And she believes that the level of a person's sacrifice is often an indication of what they want from her. The third, and final, corridor requires an offering. I look at the clothes I'm wearing—they are filthy and sweaty. I check my pockets for money, but I have none. I'm not wearing anything valuable to offer. I panic and ask my grandmother what do to.

She looks at Wasi, who in turn is looking at me. "He has offered himself to Sibyl's service, as an offering on your behalf.

This is the reason Wasi is here, Eli."

"NO!!!" I scream, as I throw my arms around him. My heart shatters. Tears uncontrollably stream down my face. "WHY WASI? WHY WOULD YOU DO THIS?" I feel his heart beat faster and see sadness wash over his face.

"Sibyl has wanted him for millennia. She has his life partner, Malak, with her in the kingdom." I remember the beautiful white horse she rode in Pretare. It explains why Wasi couldn't take his eyes off her. "They were separated during Sibyl's war with God. Wasi got his freedom, while Malak became imprisoned with Sibyl. He knows this is the only way to be with her again."

"Wasi, I'm so sorry. I can't believe you had to endure that," I say to him while caressing his beautiful face. "But I swear to you, I will do everything in my power to set you both free."

"Eli, it's time."

I get back on Wasi and look around for my grandmother. She is gone. Wasi moves his head from side to side as if he's preparing for the biggest moment of his life. He then takes a few steps forward and pushes the door on the wall of the cave open with his nose. We proceed through and enter.

We find ourselves outdoors, standing before the cliff of a mountain. It is dusk; a sweeping blue sky and cotton candy clouds float above us. I look around—we are standing near a forest. The surrounding mountains and molehills are completely covered with bright green moss, and the tall trees are dripping with blush and soft pink flowers. The tree branches sway in the perfect summer breeze. Flying all around, and in and out of them, are Pentwilin birds. The melody of the Pentwilin is echoing softly throughout the hills. On the ground, I see turtles walking ever so slowly. They have small leafless trees growing out of the tops of their shells. Hanging from some of the branches are cocoons, while other branches are clustered with the beautiful silver butterflies that I first saw in the fields on our way to Foce. All the colors and the vitality of these beautiful creatures are even more astounding when witnessed in their own enchanted forest.

Across the way, on a separate mountain, is the biggest fortress I've ever seen. At its center, a gate that must be at least three hundred stories high. I look around for a bridge to cross: there are none. There is nothing but space and air between us as far as I can see.

I hear a jarring sound above me, and I look up and see something beyond my greatest dreams.

"*My God*," I manage to mutter.

DRAGONS.

Wasi takes a few long steps backward. The legendary beasts glide over our heads in synchronized maneuvers, then land so hard, the entire mountain trembles. There is one on either side of us and I can see them closely; they are the most exquisite creatures I've laid my eyes on. I let out a gasp and laugh at the same time.

They are *huge*; their wingspan extends out at least a least one hundred feet. Their color is a light, muted gray. Their sharp eyes are a deep hazel-green color. They look like they are made of pure muscle; every angle and curve on their bodies looks sculpted. Their scales are hard but have something that looks like peach fuzz over them. Their claws, and the arrow shaped tip at the end of their tails, are glistening in the light, and they look sharp as knives. Their long faces are serious, and their stare is raw. There are no sharp gills or horns protruding off their bodies. Their stature is dignified. I can see from their eyes that they are brave and courageous warriors. I don't feel afraid. I feel safe and completely in awe.

They bow.

"Wasi, what are they doing?" I whisper to him. He begins

to move around in an uneasy manner, I can feel his heartbeat accelerate.

Across the way, the gate begins to open slowly. The dragons next to us rise and shift their bodies to face the fortress. Two black dragons exit first. They stop at either side of the gate once it is fully open. Sibyl follows them out and stops when she is standing between them. As she raises her hand, all four dragons step forward to the edge of the cliffs. And with one deep breath, they push out fire from their mouths to create a unified bridge between the two mountains. I don't know *any* world where a human can walk on fire without getting burned to a crisp. Nevertheless, Wasi steps forward, but I pull back the reins aggressively in fear. Wasi kicks his front legs up until I loosen the restraint. As soon as I do, he puts his front legs back down, and pushes his head forward in a motion as if he's telling me to trust him. My heart begins to race erratically as we approach the fire. As we stand closely to the edge, I look down. There is nothing but infinite space below us. I realize that I have no choice; I must trust Wasi with everything I have inside of me. It's the only way I can do this.

My thoughts are distracted by a smell. It's not a burning one, but more like a mix of pine, cedarwood, and sandalwood. I realize that it's the scent of the dragons.

"Wow, you guys smell amazing," I say to them in a low tone.

"That's because they're tree huggers," a male voice says back. I look around.

"Wasi?"

"Eli, you can hear me?"

"Yes!"

"I've been trying to do this from the moment you first rode me! I can't believe I actually did it!" Wasi's voice is deep and soothing. He has a slight Middle Eastern accent.

"How?" I ask in dismay. As if it isn't astonishing enough that we're about to ride across a bridge literally made of fire.

"It happens only when a true connection between a rider and an Uniequuus is achieved. This means you finally trust me, Eli, the way I trust you. It's important to know that you will be able to hear my replies to you in your head, and no one else will. But I *cannot* hear your thoughts in mine. You must say things out loud for me to hear you. Do you understand?"

"Yes," I say, while a million questions that I'm dying to ask him fill my head. They will just have to wait.

"Are you ready, Eli?"

"No." And with that, Wasi takes off with aberrant strength and power.

I hang onto the leather reins with all my might. I tell myself not to look down. I hear Wasi telling me to let my mind go free, and to close my eyes and see through his. And so, I do. My vision extends wide and I see everything with precise clarity. The fire burns brightly in colors of deep orange and gold. The flames create a moving road, with the sides that ride up slightly and create sparks. I hear Wasi's hooves hit the fire hard as he rides. I can feel the adrenaline in his veins. It's like he was born to do this. I can feel the heat from underneath, and as it rises, more memories and visions saturate my mind. As we approach the end of the fire bridge, I remind Wasi that I will not abandon him. I feel his heart skip a beat.

We slow down as we approach and step on land. Wasi walks carefully and cautiously towards Sibyl. When he comes to a full stop, I climb down. Sibyl looks glorious in her usual fashion. Her hair is down and wavy. She's wearing a stunningly red, silk flowy coat, with a high collar and billowy sleeves, and a simple, long dress underneath to match it. I feel like a complete dirty mess. I'm embarrassed to even shake her hand when she motions.

"Welcome, Elita," she says in a lovely and gentle manner.

"H-hello Sibyl," I say, feeling insecure and out of place. "I'm sorry I don't look presentable. It's been quite the . . . journey."

"Quite the contrary, my dear. It looks like you have almost made the full transformation," she says, looking intently at me. "It seems that the rumors are true . . . but, we have plenty of time to catch up. How about we get you inside to wash up and have a proper meal."

I nod eagerly. That sounds amazing. I didn't realize how hungry I am. And I would give anything for a shower. I hold Wasi closely to me by the strap as we follow her in through the gates. The four dragons saunter in behind us.

Immediately upon entering, I am speechless. And by what I can hear of Wasi's thoughts, he is flabbergasted too. What my eyes are taking in, my mouth will never find the words for. I have never seen so much beauty and grace. It is absolute *perfection*. It is the true definition of a magical kingdom. If only the whole world could see what I'm seeing in this very moment, then creating and never destroying a single thing, would be everyone's only priority.

As we follow behind Sibyl, I can't stop looking around and taking in this enchanted place, but there's more than I can absorb at once. This is what I imagine the Garden of Eden would have looked like. Oh!!! I just realize why it's called the "Garden of Eden"! It must have been Eden's first creation. If I ever see her again, I'm going to have to ask her what the real story is between Adam and Eve.

Everything is so intense; all the colors are colors I've known my entire life—but on steroids. I see different kinds of animals peeking out from behind the bushes, and through the leaves of the trees. Intricate plants are growing all around—some I recognize, but many species I've never seen before. The scientist in me cannot wait to explore this land, and to find out more about these fascinating creatures.

The exquisite faeries are everywhere. They all look very different from one another, and nothing at all like I've seen in any faerie tale book or movie. To my surprise, they have no wings. They do not look evil with sharp teeth. But they also don't look like angels that blow faerie dust. Their bodies are statuesque, long, and slender, just like Sibyl. Their skin tones and eye colors are a mix of all the different ethnicities of the world. They are wearing long dresses that capture their own unique style and personality. One of them, who is sitting on a large rock with her legs crossed, catches my eye. Her dress is pulled up to mid-thigh, and I notice she has hooves for feet too. So, it is true about all faeries having "goat feet," it's not just Elise. The hair on her feet is the same color as her skin. Once my eyes reach her calf, I see that it turns into skin and blends in with the rest of her long and muscular legs.

Standing next to her is an ordinary *human* man. Come to think of it, there are a lot of men everywhere. Glancing around, there must be two men to every one faerie. Under my breath, I ask Wasi what the deal is. He says there were many stories of knights that would set out to see Sibyl, but never return home again. He assumes these are those "lost" men. They must think that we are as peculiar as we think they are, because they are staring and whispering to one another.

After a walk through a seemingly endless garden, we climb up several stairs made of limestone. At the top of those stairs, we arrive at a beautiful wooden door that is framed within the mountain side. It is large and wide, and it has hand-carved engravings throughout. A few of the symbols I recognize from the paintings inside the seven churches, as well as some of the stonework which was showcased outside those same churches that we visited on the tour. One engraving that catches my eye in particular, has what looks exactly like the six-point star and the tilted five-point star, seen at the Church of Casalicchio. The only difference is, instead of having a lancet window in between them, there is a large seven-point star. The other symbols look like something from a primitive language.

I feel Wasi pull away from my grasp. I look over to see where he is going. He is walking over to his long-lost love, Malak. He greets her with a touch of the nose, then a gentle caress as they rub the sides of their faces against one another. Malak looks more radiant than I remember, her coat is so shiny it looks like velvet, and her eyes like steel diamonds. I gasp out loud. I must have been so entranced by the magical surroundings that I missed what was right in front of my face, *something* that I should have seen all along . . . his horn.

Sibyl smiles and says, "They are the last two unicorns in existence. They are meant to be together. And it's time for them to mate. Then, just maybe, a little magic can return into the world."

I smile as my heart fills with joy. I knew Wasi was special, I just didn't realize how much.

The large wooden doors automatically push open and on the other side, impatiently waiting, are Nonna Rosa and Elise. They rush out past Sibyl and embrace me tightly.

"Oh Eli! How wonderful that you're here! You're the best thing that's ever happened to this place in like—EVER!!!" Elise says, giggling joyfully. My grandmother pushes my hair back and out of my face. I can see by the way she's looking at me that even she can hardly believe it. Sibyl calls to us and invites us inside her home. My grandmother and I lock arms as she guides me in. It is nothing short of a palace, and grandiose in every way. Standing in the enormous foyer, I'm once again dumbstruck, but also feeling very displaced.

"Where are we? I mean, where is this place? Are we still on . . . Earth?" I ask Nonna Rosa.

"Yes, of course," she replies with a smile. I can see that she finds my naiveté endearing. "I know the journey through the corridors can be off-putting, but rest assured you're still on Earth. As a matter of fact, we are over 7,000 feet above sea level, on Mount Sibilla."

"It's not your typical cave. Actually, it's *not* a cave at all. This palace is massive!" I say, looking up at the huge vaulted ceiling.

"You'll find it to be more like a small city. I'd be happy to give you a tour tomorrow," Sibyl replies. "For now, why don't you freshen up and we'll enjoy a nice dinner. I'm sure you're famished. Rosa will show you the way to your room."

My grandmother takes me up the stairs, and we enter a hallway with a tall arched ceiling. There are beautiful murals on each side of the wall, and lots of natural light coming in through the windows. She stops at the first door and walks me in. Another large room. What is it with these people and their 2,000 square foot master bedrooms?

"This used to be Amelia's room," Nonna Rosa says nostalgically.

"It's beautiful," I reply. And with those few words from my grandmother, the room suddenly becomes bearable.

"Follow me," she says, as she opens one of the three massive sets of French doors along the side of the wall. We step outside onto a wide balcony made out of some kind of marble. The view is extraordinary. It overlooks a large body of water that drifts far out into the sunset. My grandmother says that it travels down the mountain and supplies the locals with their water, and that it has many healing properties. I ask her if this is the same water that we drink from the fountain next door to Nonna Amelia's house. It is ice cold and delicious, even on the hottest day of the year. She nods yes. I could have never imagined it came from

such a splendorous place. On either side of the water are mountains with unique trees and plants that I cannot wait to explore.
The ground below is sectioned with several beautiful gardens,
some even labyrinth-like. They are filled with unique flowers
and greenery. The scent from the roses is strong; I can smell
them from the balcony.

I lean my back side against the balcony pillar that reaches
above my waist. I look up, then to my right, then my left. There
are several balconies all around. It looks like a huge apartment
building that has been built into a mountain side. I ask my grandmother if they are the rooms of the faeries. She tells me that
the faeries do not sleep in rooms. They prefer to sleep in the
forest, or in the gardens among the flowers, trees, and animals.
I ask her, "Then what is the purpose of all these rooms?" She
explains that Sibyl occupies the entire top floor, and that the rest
are for "guests"—some of them are permanent, and some are just
visitors. Nonna says that before she and Nonna Amelia left the
Faerie Asbgah, Sibyl had allowed others from different Asbgahs
to stay and visit. But since, she has closed the passageways and
no longer permits it.

She distracts me from asking any more questions by pointing
to the side of the balcony. She indicates the stairs that take me
down to the bath house. Nonna tells me each room is equipped
with direct access to it. We then walk down to the entrance. It's
an old-fashioned bath house in every way. There are no showers,
just several shallow pools that vary in size and shape, many of
them are even placed outdoors.

"Does everyone bathe together?" I ask Nonna.

"Not really, most of them do so on their own time. Sibyl has
asked the area to be vacant for the next hour so you can have
some personal time. There is a robe hanging there just for you,"
she points to the wall. "I'll be waiting for you in the room when

you're ready. You've had a difficult day, so take your time."

"Nonna, what do I use for soap?"

"Do you see those small pink and lavender flowers in the baskets on the floor?"

I nod yes. She picks up a bunch and shows me what to do.

"These flowers are called Saponaria. Wet them," she dips them in the water, "then rub your hands together until they foam." They do just that, as bubbles and foam fill her hands. The floral fragrance of the soap radiates and it's so relaxing.

"Wow. Is that a magical plant?" I ask surprised.

"No, don't you remember? We used to pick them when you were little and bathe you with them?"

"No," I reply sadly, as that is not one of the memories that has yet returned.

"They would grow on the side of the road. Most people never pay any mind to them; they just think they're pretty." She pauses a moment in thought, then says, "Silly humans, they'll never realize that everything they'd ever need, God has already given to them through Mother Nature herself."

"You mean Eden? She's lovely and so smart!" I answer, feeling so happy to finally have a conversation without a filter.

"You have no idea just how much. Eden is certainly one of God's best creations," Nonna smiles, then becomes serious. "But you know, she also has quite a temper. It takes a lot to get her going, but once you do . . . well, just be sure to stay on her good side."

"When can we talk?" I ask softly. Nonna looks around.

"We must be *very* careful, Eli. Everyone here, including the animals, tells Sibyl *everything*. She has spies everywhere. There are only a few places we can speak openly, and this isn't one of them," she whispers into my ear. I nod.

"So, I'll see you upstairs in a little bit," I answer back nonchalantly. She nods back smiling, kisses me on the forehead, and leaves me.

I anxiously take off my filthy shoes and clothes. I can't wait to get clean. I take one step into the crystal blue bath—the temperature is perfect. I spread out and let go of all the tension in my body. It feels so good; I don't ever want to get out. After ten minutes of trying to clear my mind and floating in the water, I dip my entire body including my head, underneath the crystal surface. I hold my breath and close my eyes for a moment.

There is an alarming flash in my mind. It's a vision . . . no . . . a memory . . . but it's not mine.

It's Nonna Amelia's.

I see her sitting in the chair next to her window in her bedroom. Alessandro Vinci and Victoria Mason are there with her. They are asking her about the *Rose of Venus*. My grandmother tells them she knows nothing of it, and to let her die in peace. She then turns to me as if I'm standing in front of her and says with panic in her voice, "Eli, warn Rosa. They are coming."

Startled and afraid, I push my head out of the bath, and try to catch my breath. I spit out water that I must have inhaled and begin coughing frantically. I lean my head on the cold crystal around the side of the pool to calm myself.

Someone hands me a glass of water. I look up and scream.

"I'm so sorry I frightened you, madam," the little creature says to me in shame.

"I thought I was alone, you startled me, that's all," I say, unable to blink as I stare. One of his tentacles is holding a glass of water, another my clothes, and yet another, my shoes. From what I can see, he still has several more available. My senses return for a moment, and I unsuccessfully try and cover up my body with my hands and arms. Just then I realize the water has begun to bubble like a Jacuzzi. And the crystal blue water has turned into a murky blue tone.

"Who are you?" I ask, looking up at him. He has a small man's body. He is wearing an old, worn down and faded butler's uniform. His head is one of a jelly fish with very big black eyes, and muted human facial features. His hands and feet are made of several continuously moving tentacles. I wonder who he is and how he ended up here. And how he ended up being a jelly-man.

"My name is Thomas, madam. I am but a humble servant. I didn't mean to startle you. Madam Sibyl asked me to come down to retrieve your clothing and have it washed," he says in a British accent. He speaks slowly and with intent. "She told me not to disturb you, and to be very quiet. But when you began coughing, I was afraid you might be drowning. Are you alright?"

"The water is only three feet. It would be hard to drown in here, Thomas."

"You'd be surprised, madam. Many have fallen asleep here. I hear the waters are very relaxing."

"I'm Eli," I say introducing myself.

"Yes, I know. The entire kingdom is talking about your visit." He looks down. "Other than the return of Madam Rosa, we haven't had a new visitor in quite some time," he pauses. "I suppose Madam Amelia will be returning soon too. I'm sorry about that, Miss Eli."

"Thank you," I say, taking the glass of water that he's been holding out.

"I've been assigned to be your personal servant for the duration of your stay. If you need anything at all, all you need to do is call my name. I'll be able to hear it from anywhere in the kingdom," Thomas says.

He then abruptly excuses himself from our conversation. He walks away quietly and quickly, with a look of a child that has just been scorned. Did I do something? Why did he leave that way?

Well, I better wash up quickly before I receive any more visitors. The flower soap is heavenly; I'm going to need to pick an entire mountain-side's worth before I leave. As I rinse the soap off my body, I notice that all the bruising and cuts I'd had from the last few days are gone. Nonna did say the water here has healing properties, but this is miraculous. I dry off with the fluffiest cotton towel I've ever felt; my hair and skin are so soft and luxurious. It's no wonder these faeries look flawless; it must be the water.

I enter back into my room through the balcony. I seem to be interrupting a deep conversation between my grandmother and Elise. They quickly get up from a long stool at the foot of the bed and make nothing of it. Elise—in her typical enthusiastic manner—bombards me with a million questions about my bath, and comments on my hair and skin. In the meantime, my grandmother slips a dress over my head. She walks me over to the vanity and Elise starts braiding my hair. My grandmother interrupts Elise's nervous babble by saying that the dress belongs to Nonna Amelia. She says it was her favorite, and she knew it would look beautiful on me. I hold it in my hands and take a closer look. It is lovely and simple, just like her.

I take a hold of Nonna Rosa's hand. "It must be very hard for you two to be separated."

"It is. I would say being best friends for 5,000 years is quite a long time. But I will see her soon," she replies with a sad smile, squeezing my hand. "What is very difficult for me, is that I will never see my husband and children again. The pain is often more than I can endure." Her eyes well up. Elise stops braiding my hair for a moment to wipe a tear from her face.

"Nonna, I'm so sorry," I reply, as I feel my own heart break for her. The thought had never occurred to me: her husband was human, and her children are half human. They will all live mortal lives, while she will be here forever.

I ask Elise if she could please get Nonna a tissue, and she scurries off to find one. I need a moment alone with my grandmother and this may be the only chance I will have. I tell Nonna that I received an urgent message from Nonna Amelia while I was under water. She hugs me and tells me to whisper it in her ear while covering my mouth. I do as she says and tell her everything. I can feel her body stiffen. I ask her how it is possible for Nonna Amelia to send me a vision. She says that Nonna Amelia is using the magic of the Halledrite crystal to access the Vellous, to send her a message through me. She explains that each Vellous is a space created between the seconds on the third hand of the clock.

The memory with Nonna Rosa and I—that day in the yellow flower valley—is now becoming clear. I am able to recall those twelve hours completely. We spent the entire day talking about what was happening to my body and my mind. She thought telling me the entire truth about our family while in the Vellous would break the binding spell. But even that did not work. She apologized for bruising me, but I wasn't waking up. And if I stayed in the Vellous for more than twelve hours, I was in danger of never waking up. And she knew that by bruising me, both my Nonna Amelia and Aunt Ersella would know what she attempted to try. She really cut it a little too close that day.

Nonna Rosa places her hand over my Halledrite necklace. I feel time stand still. All the particles in the air are floating. In the corner of my eye I see the doorknob, that had begun turning, suddenly freeze.

Nonna Rosa says, "Amelia, I received the message, thank you." She then lets go of the crystal, and a second later time reverts back to normal.

Elise walks in. We let go of our embrace and change the conversation, once Elise hands her the tissue. This is typical for

Nonna; she does this when she worries about dampening the mood or bringing too much attention to herself. So, I'm sure Elise thinks nothing of it.

They both decide I should know the house rules of Sibyl's kingdom and review them with me:

1.   *No one is permitted on or in Sibyl's living quarters without an invitation.*
2.   *No stealing.*
3.   *No entrance to the Faerie Asbgah without Sibyl's approval.*
4.   *No in and out of the other Asbgahs without Sibyl's approval.*
5.   *No speaking about how delicious meat is. Everyone here is vegetarian and/or vegan. Sibyl doesn't want the animals to know what the other tastes like. She's afraid they'll all end up devouring each other, like they do in the outside world. She has a strict "know not, want not" policy when it comes to food.*

By the time they finish explaining all the rules, Elise has finished the most beautifully intricate and elaborate braid I've ever seen. She says it's called *Beaii*, a unique technique known and used only by faeries, but that she will teach me if I want to learn. My grandmother says it took her six months to master it, so not to be discouraged if I don't learn it in a day.

On our walk to dinner, I ask Elise why we've never seen anything like it in our world. I tell her that I have several hairdresser friends that would give anything to know how to braid so exquisitely. She and my Nonna Rosa look at each other for a moment, and then my grandmother nods her head in a "yes" motion.

Elise opens up her big blue eye widely, leans into me and says, "Well you see, before there was that lovely town you know as Pretare, there used to be a quaint town called Colfiorito. The inhabitants were good, hard working people for the most part, and they lived in harmony. All of us here in the Faerie Asbgah had a wonderful relationship with them for many, many years. We taught the young girls of the town how to spin and weave wool, as well as how to Beaii baskets and garments. They were able to support and provide for their families quite well by learning this trade. Sibyl wanted to be sure the girls were able to provide for themselves and not rely on the men." She stops and looks at Nonna Rosa for her to tell the next part of the story.

"Sibyl became angry when she learned that some of Colfiorito's citizens did not honor her faeries," my grandmother continues. "First, she warned them with a rainfall of stones. But this just angered them, because it caused damage to their properties, merchandise, and even killed some of their animals. So, they retaliated by doing something unspeakable—they killed a gentle faerie by the name of Anna. Sibyl was unable to control her anger and grief, so she set off an earthquake that destroyed the entire town with a landslide. It buried almost everyone alive. She left a few survivors to tell the story of what happened to those in other towns as a warning. But none of those survivors were people who knew how to Beaii. It became a lost art among humans."

"So . . . don't piss her off!" I reply with a little fear.

"It's best not to, dear," Nonna answers.

We reach two huge crystal doors. They're slowly opened by two men who are very handsome. I wish Alessia could see this. Elise teases me and she says I'll get used to the "lustful thoughts." But I don't think I'll ever get used to any of this. We make our way into a beautiful dining room that sparkles and glitters everywhere. It's like I've entered a kaleidoscope of diamonds.

"What happened to a 'nice dinner'?" Nonna says sarcastically.

"Oh, come on, Rosa! We haven't had a ball in nearly one hundred years! You must admit, if Eli isn't a good enough reason, what is?" Elise says, jumping up and down, nearly exploding with joy. I can't believe this is all for me, how amazing!

The evening turns out to be the "who's who" social event of the Faerie Asbgah. I am impressed at what a sophisticated society Sibyl has created for herself. Everyone is dressed exquisitely. There is electrifying energy and joy all around. There is a scent of sweetness in the air—it must be from all the sugar on the endless tables that hold the desserts. The food is incredible! I wish veggies and tofu tasted like this in our world. I try so many unique food creations. The chefs even come out and offer to give me the recipes. I can finally see where my grandmothers learned their hospitality from. As I look at Sibyl from the corner of my eye, I wonder how she can really be the monster everyone warns me about. How can such splendor come from someone who isn't divine herself?

As the night continues, I'm shuffled from arm to arm, meeting everyone. Each individual I meet tells me about who they are, what they do here, and why they came. They are all so charming, kind, well-spoken, and well-mannered, just like Sibyl. With thousands of faces, after the first thirty or so, I really cannot remember all the names or stories—they all jumble together in my mind. However, there is one face I see that stands out; I recognize him from my visions. He is distinguished, but young looking. He is one of the few people who is keeping their distance tonight. I ask Elise who he is, and she says his name is Alec. I ask her what his story is, she replies by saying it's "complicated." She mentions that he's Micella's ex-boyfriend. That's definitely a story I'll want to hear about.

The music and dancing go late into the night; the rumors about faeries dancing all night are absolutely true! They are marvelous dancers and I don't get tired once. It is the best time I've ever had in my entire life. I have never felt more like myself than I do on this very evening. I can see why so many choose to stay in Sibyl's kingdom forever.

Chapter 19

"GOOD MORNING Madam Eli, rise and shine!" I hear a jolly old Englishman say to me.

"Jelly-man?" I reply, clearing my throat and trying to open my eyes.

"I prefer Thomas, Ma'am," he says politely.

"I prefer Eli," I answer back.

"I'm not permitted to use informalities Miss; you'll have to pardon me."

"You weren't at the ball last night, Thomas; it would have been nice to dance with you."

"I'm so pleased you had a wonderful time. I watched you from a distance, you're a very good dancer."

Yeah, I'm not sure where that came from, I typically have two left feet.

"Let me guess, you're not allowed to attend the balls?" I ask, as I get out of bed and walk over to the seating area where he's pouring a cup of coffee. He nods yes.

"What is your story, Thomas?" I ask curiously.

"I *sold* a faerie, Ma'am," he says bluntly, and appears visibly horrified by his words. I nearly spit out the coffee I just drank. "I'm so a-ashamed!" he stutters as he tears up. "I was just a young boy then. I didn't know what I was doing! My family was poor, and all I wanted to do was help them get into a proper home. Buy my mum a proper tea set. Send my brothers to school. You know, give them a good life."

"How did you even find a faerie to *sell*, Thomas?" I ask, rubbing his shoulder to comfort him. It jiggles like a waterbed.

"I was a sailor for the Royal Navy, and we were here in Italy on official duty. One night my crew and I stumbled on a town festival. We thought we'd have ourselves a bit of fun and enjoy a pint of beer. Before we knew it, we were dancing with the most beautiful girls we'd ever seen! My mate lifted one of them off the ground, and I saw her hooved feet. Like everyone else, I'd heard the rumors about faeries on this side of the world. So, I shamelessly kidnapped her and brought her back to England with me, and I sold her." He pauses for a moment to collect his thoughts. "I don't know how, but three days later Sibyl's men found me. They brought me here to face my punishment. And a fair punishment it is, Ma'am. I see the error of my ways; I've had nearly one-hundred years to think on it now. I'm to be a servant until the end of time." Another pause. "I think Madam Sibyl, she showed mercy because I was barely eighteen."

"This is horrible, Thomas! Have you tried to negotiate some kind of release date for yourself? Surely, she understands you were just a stupid kid trying to help your family?" I ask, peeved at his predicament.

"I have. She said that when Francesca is returned, then I will be free. But you see Ma'am, it's been nearly a century now. I don't think my family and my mates are still alive anymore. What would I go back for now?"

"People are living a long time these days Thomas, you never

know. Do you know what ever became of them?" I ask.

"No." He looks down and shakes his head sadly.

"I'm so sorry Thomas," I say as I hug him. He really is quite squishy. Thomas begins crying uncontrollably.

"Oh, Eli! What did you have to go and do that for?" Elise says walking into my room. "No one is allowed to touch him or show him compassion. But it's hard not to, isn't it? He hasn't been touched by anyone since he's arrived. It might take him all day to recover now . . . Is he very squishy?"

Thomas lets out a loud sob. I squeeze him a little tighter, and then slowly let go. He runs out the door as fast as he can on his many tentacle feet. I look back at Elise; she's giving me a scolding look.

"Too many rules," I mutter and roll my eyes. I get ready quickly and head down for breakfast. Sibyl is keeping true to her promise and is personally giving me a tour of the grounds today.

Sitting around a large table set for breakfast in the crystal room, are a few guests from last night's ball. Everyone is making small talk about how wonderful the festivities were. I thank Sibyl profusely for such an incredible time. She seems very pleased with the outcome and says that it was just what the Asbgah needed to lift everyone's spirits, because it's been so quiet since the borders to the other Asbgahs have been closed, and there is restricted access to the human world. Nonna Rosa is sitting next to me, not engaging in our conversation. She is quiet and pensive. I lean my hand over and pretend to hold her hand. Instead I use the alphabet letters of sign language on the inside of her palm to ask her what is wrong. She taught me how to do this when I was a child when we didn't want others to know what we were discussing. We even made up some of our own signs that had special meanings. She replies on the inside of my palm and tells me not to make a fuss about her not joining us today. She says to keep

Sibyl out as long as possible; that she will use her distraction with me to do some research. There is much to discuss and we'll meet up later tonight. I sign back "O.K."

"Eli, you must have a lot of questions for me?" Sibyl asks, returning my attention to the conversation.

"I do," I reply. There is one in particular that is burning a hole in my head. "Last night, most of these men—and wow there are a lot of them—said they were once knights. How did they come to stay? How does that work?" I see Sibyl's eyes light up.

"Well, I hope that's a sign that you are considering staying!" she says excitedly. I stay quiet and smile. "I'm uncertain how much you know Eli, but all those here in my kingdom *choose* to stay. No one is forced. Upon entering, anyone can stay for one year without commitment. But once that year is up, he or she must decide if they want to stay or return to their home."

"And if they choose to stay? What then?" I ask inquisitively.

"Then they sign a contract. And must abide by my rules."

"A contract? What kind?" I press on.

"It states that they claim the Faerie Asbgah as their home until Judgment Day. They will be loyal to only me and abide by my rules as their 'authentic selves,'" Sibyl says very seriously. "It is often said that the faeries bewitch and promise those that come here a lascivious life of lust, extravagances, joy, and a fulfillment of all their desires . . . all but the bewitching part is true. Ask anyone in my kingdom, and they will tell you that they chose to live here of their own free will." She pauses for a moment. "You see, if you ask most people, they would rather have an immortal life of everything they could ever want, rather than a horrible lifetime of struggle and pain in the human world. Which do you think they choose?"

"Probably this one," I answer sincerely.

"Smart girl!" she says, pointing her index finger at me. "You see, I wasn't given the choice. I might not play fair, by having all the endorphins secreted into the air, for instance; but I *am* fair."

"Why do you think they choose to stay?" I ask. "I mean, doesn't God promise all these things in the afterlife?"

Sibyl smiles. "Well then, maybe God should have showed or allowed humans to remember Heaven. Then everyone would know the truth of what's waiting for them. But He didn't, because of some nonsense about 'blind faith.' That makes humans feel uncertain, as if there's something to hide."

"One thing I still don't understand, is why is she here?" I ask Sibyl, gesturing to my grandmother. "And why is Nonna Amelia coming back instead of going home to the Heavens?"

She looks at me in shock. "My girl, you really don't know, do you? I hope those memories start downloading in your mind a little faster. Or we might all be in trouble," Sibyl answers, giving a long glare to Nonna Rosa.

"Please enlighten me, Sibyl," I reply, displeased by the look she just gave Nonna.

Sibyl smirks and indulges my request. "Amelia, Rosa, and Ersella chose to stay on Earth while the rest of the Celestial Beings decided to return home, to the Heavens," Sibyl states.

"Yes, I remember that from the tour," I interject.

"That silly thing!" she says laughing. "At least you got the real story from good ol' Eden. Most of those other suckers spend their hard-earned money hearing nonsense and folktales from an uneducated prat!" She pauses, and then with a sound like seething venom in her teeth, and a wicked look in her eyes, she asks, "How is Father Gabriel doing?"

Nonna gives me the "don't answer that question" sign on my hand. Sibyl can see that I'm afraid of her reaction. She takes a second to compose herself and sits back in her chair.

"Let me tell her," Nonna Rosa says to Sibyl, and she nods

in agreement. "You see my darling Eli, we were very naive; we knew the world was changing but did not realize what a dark place it was really becoming. We roamed freely and happily for thousands of years. Then one day the Knights Templar, during the medieval ages, gave the order to kill all those thought to be magical or Pagan. So many were brutally tortured, murdered, burned to death, and sacrificed. It was the darkest time in our history—until World War II, that is. If they only knew that we were *all* Christians. We saw Jesus being born and die on the cross, *we were there*. We held him at his birth and cried with Mary at his feet in the last moments of his life," Nonna recalls with deep pain on her face. Sibyl looks away, trying to hide her own pain. "We tried to reason with them numerous times, but the people of the Order simply could not understand that just because we respected and loved the old ways, it did *not* mean we did not worship the same God. It was a very confusing time, and the war became increasingly dangerous and brutal. They replaced every temple with a Christian church, destroyed precious art, artifacts, and books, and nearly succeeded in wiping out our entire history. Amelia, Ersella, and I tried to save as many people of magic descent as we could. Everyone in every Asbgah helped until the last moment. And many paid with their lives. That's how we found ourselves here."

Everyone in the room is quiet: you could hear a pin drop. I can sense them trying to hold back tears as they each recall their own painful memories.

"Why don't you tell her why you stayed?" Sibyl says, in a cold and angry tone.

"We tried to go home. But . . . but we were denied," Nonna Rosa says sadly.

"You wouldn't be the first," Sibyl snarls under her breath.

"WHAT! God denied your homecoming after you saved and

rescued all those people?" I shout, unable to control my outrage.

"Please, stay calm Eli. We have never been angry with God," Nonna says in that tone, when she doesn't like to see me get overly excited. "For many, many years we thought we were being punished because we stayed. BUT, it wasn't until recently, that we finally understood that it wasn't the reason at all! We believe that it was all . . . so you could be born, Eli."

I sink into my chair.

"Just imagine how many thousands and thousands of people had to be born, live, and die for you to exist. Imagine all of the beautiful couples that had to find each other and fall in love, in order to create generations, just to make you. That's magic!" Elise says poetically.

"But that's true of every person ever born in this world. That is amazing. Every life really is so precious when you look at it that way," I say, lost with wonder.

"Yes, yes, that's a lovely thought," Sibyl says, bringing us back to the topic at hand. "But, we've seen enough Celestial Beings to know what they look like. It's clear by your transition that you are the first born in five thousand years. Now we just need to know—why *you*?" Sibyl says inquisitively. I look up and everyone is staring at me as if they've all had this exact thought since the moment I arrived.

"We are hoping that once your blackouts clear, and your memories return, we'll have some insight. Maybe the answers are locked away somewhere inside you, Eli," Elise says in her sweet voice.

"I promise you all, none of the small and fragmented memories that I've had return, have given me any indication to the reasoning," I say to the room. That was not a lie. What I fail to mention are the visions I saw in Alessandro Vinci's mind. I'm going to keep those completely to myself, for now.

"This conversation has been upsetting, I would like to lie down. If it's okay with you Eli, I'm going to sit out today's tour of the grounds," Nonna says to me. I kiss her cheek and I tell her that I will be by to check up on her later. I must say, she chose her exit perfectly.

Sibyl stands from the table and proceeds to lead us from the crystal room onto the grounds. Elise accompanies us, and four of Sibyl's men follow at a distance. She introduces them as Victor, George, John, and Alex. They are dressed in a modern version of a traditional knight's uniform. Their armor is a unique black matte metal, but the edges are glossy and very sharp; each piece skillfully fits together. I ask one if they are hot standing around all day in metal, but they don't answer me back. Sibyl replies for them and says that they do not speak to those they serve to protect, because it distracts them from what they are intended to be doing. They will only speak when need be. I whisper to Elise and ask if the security detail is necessary? She tells me that it's not for Sibyl, it's for me. I'm not sure if I should feel flattered or afraid. What is she preparing for, war?

Sibyl overhears Elise's reply and chimes in; she says that news of my presence here has spread like wildfire to the other Asbgahs, and that my safety is her number one priority. As a precaution, she has doubled security throughout the land. I look out onto the grounds, and there is a knight at nearly every corner. When I arrived, I did notice them scattered throughout, but nothing like what I'm seeing now. She assures me that I will be protected from any unwanted visitors. But to be careful, because there may even be some lurking within the borders. I tell her that I don't know anyone here to visit with. She laughs, and says I know more than I think I know. Oh.

We make our way down to the bottom of the grand stairs into a lily garden right below Sibyl's palace. I didn't realize it yesterday because it's built inside a mountain, but nonetheless, this is an actual castle. Behind me I hear a galloping that I've come to know quite well. Wasi and Malak ride towards us. He looks bigger and stronger today. His coat is so shiny and even more healthy-looking now, just like Malak's. His hair has been braided into a beautiful Beaii, while Malak's is down, wavy, and very long. Their horns are thick and look powerful; they're the same color as the rest of their bodies. The pair looks just like a storybook painting; but that might be because before yesterday, that's the only place I've ever seen a unicorn.

"Good morning handsome! You are looking well rested to-day," I say to Wasi as he and Malak stop right in front of me.

"As do you, Eli! How was the ball last night? We heard it was a wonderful time," he replies. I tell him it was absolutely amazing, and that Sibyl has been such a generous and gracious host. Wasi and Malak nod their heads at Sibyl, then Wasi turns his attention back to me.

"Eli, this is the great love of my life, Malak."

"Malak, it is such an honor to officially meet you. You are truly exquisite!" I reply.

He says that I've made her blush, but that the honor is all hers.

"It's weird hearing a one-way conversation, isn't it?" Elise says to Sibyl. I'd completely forgotten that only I can hear Wasi.

"I'm so sorry, I didn't mean to be rude. I-I forgot," I begin to say.

"Make nothing of it, it was just a funny observation!" Elise says interrupting me, so I won't feel bad.

"Careful Eli, Sibyl is jealous of our connection. She has never been able to make one with Malak," Wasi says to me. "Malak made a vow that she would never connect with Sibyl until the day I returned. Now that I am here, she is forced to honor that commitment. And Sibyl will not be in good humor with either Malak or I, until it's happened."

"Okay," I quietly reply, once again with a million questions running through my mind. It is the only word I can think to say to answer both Elise and Wasi. Geez, this is going to be a bit tricky.

"Why don't our very precious Uniequus join us for a walk today?" Sibyl says to them.

"Uniequus? I assume that means unicorn?" I ask.

"Yes, that's exactly right," Sibyl says out loud, as Wasi says it in my head at the same time. Like I said, this is going to be interesting.

"It's a very old word. But we continue to use it out of respect. They are so precious and now nearly extinct. It only feels right to call them by their original name."

"Yes, I suppose that's true. What a horrible thought . . . " I say, as I caress Wasi's face.

He winks at me and tells me not to worry, that Malak isn't the jealous type. I start laughing; I can see he's trying to lighten the mood. But I quickly realize that I'm the only one laughing. I mean, Wasi is too, but I'm sure only Malak and I can hear him. I compose myself by clearing my throat as Sibyl marches ahead.

"You're going to get me in a lot of trouble today, my friend," I say jokingly to Wasi under my breath. He replies in his best trouble-maker voice that this is going to be the most fun he's had in a long time. I roll my eyes.

Sibyl motions with her hand to come to her side. We walk down the zig-zag road to get to the bottom of the hill, where the gardens and the large body of water are; I can see now that it's a seemingly endless, magnificent lake. She asks me what I know about Oracles. I tell her not much, other than what I learned in school, and recently on the tour. She asks what I know about her. I explain that I was told she can see a person's past and prophesize their future. Sibyl asks me if that's all I believe. I tell her by the evidence of this Asbgah, she can obviously do *so* much more. She reflects and says that all the Oracles can do extraordinary things, but history has given them credit for so little. That sounds about right for all women in history books. She says that before she can tell me her truth, I must first learn about the other Oracles. She looks over at Malak and says to her that maybe then, after more than two-thousand years together, her Uniequus will finally trust her. Wow, and I thought I had trust issues.

After a few minutes of silence, Sibyl changes the topic and asks me to tell her what Los Angeles is like. We talk about LA, and what life is like there, the rest of our walk down. She seems genuinely interested and wishes to visit the "New World" and "other discovered land" one day. It's kind of a crazy thought that she hasn't seen the way the world has changed and developed in thousands of years. Before we enter what she calls the Persian Garden, she gives everyone a piece of candy that looks like a small Aloe vera leaf. It tastes like mint, and heavily lubricates my mouth. I ask her what it is. She says it will keep me from getting lightheaded around a certain part of the garden. Elise gives Wasi and I a second piece. She says that since it's our first time here, a second dose as a precaution is best.

We turn a wide corner and there it is, the Persian Garden— and what splendor! It is much larger than it looks from my balcony. Everything here seems to work that way; alluring from a distance, but beyond grandiose up close. In the center of the garden is a large fountain with four walkways leading to it from every direction. The garden is filled with lush greenery, red roses, iris, chrysanthemums, poppies, pittosporum flowers, cactus, Persian pearls, and so many others. Surrounding the garden are bountiful fruit trees.

"There are twelve of us," Sibyl begins, as we walk down a pathway of the garden. "Oracles were born on the eighth day of creation. Our purpose was to be the messengers, the mouthpiece for God. It was our job to give God's messages and ensure that all creatures would stay God's course. We did this by receiving messages through prophecy. Some of us distributed messages orally. And some of us wrote them down on leaves. We would call to people to retrieve their message at the entry of our personal grotto. I always used fig leaves, because they are my favorite fruit," she smiles. "For the most part we spent the beginning of civilization in peace. It was a lovely existence."

"How old is civilization?" Being a science lover, I can't pass up the opportunity to ask.

"Over 300 million years old," she answers.

"H-how old is planet Earth?" I stutter.

"Almost 70 billion years old," she replies nonchalantly.

"So, so, s . . . " I stop myself to control my stuttering, "So. What did God do all those years before he created humanity?"

"Huh, so it's true. Humans do *actually* think that they're the only species in the galaxy?"

"There *are* aliens?!" I've waited my whole life to know this!

"Narcissistic humans," she says, shaking her head. "Don't call them that, I don't think they would appreciate it very much. Just like humans would not want to be called that. Eli, we've gone too far off topic."

"Sorry. It's just kind of a big deal in our world. It's been a subject of huge debate."

"Yes, I've heard the nonsense," she says exasperated. "And don't ask me where God is from. I'm not allowed to answer that. I hear that's a big debatable question with the humans too."

It's like she read my mind.

She gets the conversation back on track by explaining to me that all Oracles are called "Sibyl," and then specified by the area they served in. That's why she's called Apennine Sibyl. But some were given human names by the people they served, who considered them to be high priestesses. Such was the case with Persian Sibyl: she is known by the name Sambethe. Some have even referred to her as "Babylonian Sibyl," because she foretold the acts of Alexander the Great. Apparently, some people even think she was part of Noah's family, as in Old Testament Noah, who built the Arc. They said she allegedly married his son, but Sambethe was not a family member, because none of the Oracles can bear children. They are actually *all* virgins and will be until the end of time. Sambethe did foretell Noah's coming. She was the midwife at his birth and stayed close to look over him as he grew up, until he fulfilled his destiny.

"Why are Oracles required to be virgins?" the inappropriately curious side of me had to ask.

"Why is that always the first thing people want to know about Oracles?" Sibyl says laughing.

"Because, you're like 70 billion years old. Most kids can't make it to sixteen without losing their virginity," I say as politely as I can.

"Valid point," she says, as we sit on a lovely Persian-style bench near the fountain. "Because we were created without that need and desire. And so, those around us also do not have that need and desire towards us."

"So, you're like an anti-lust pill," I say jokingly.

"Yes, I suppose we are!" she jokes back. "But I blame Valentina for all this sex talk."

"Who's Valentina?" I ask. Her eyes look down at a gorgeous set of inverted tulips. One of them is much larger than the others. I lean down; Sibyl warns me not to get too close. The flower slowly begins to lift its head, and it begins glowing. Within its center I see a small face: green eyes, long black eyelashes and pink lips. It seems to be watering itself with crystal-like drops that are pouring out of the petals.

"That's incredible . . . " I say, as I get a whiff of its sensual scent.

"Hello Eli!!! I'm SO excited that you've come to see me!!! Yayyy!!! I've been waiting all day! I've tried to look my very best and I even had Melie water me a little extra so my petals would look refreshed!!! Oh my gosh, I can't believe you're here!!!" The flower is speaking so fast and in such a high-pitched voice, I can hardly understand it. It's starting to pour out those crystal drops like a water faucet on full blast. I jump up.

"Valentina, please slow down love. You're getting very excited and you know what that does. I think you might be making the knights, you know, uneasy . . . " Elise says gently to the flower. Her own face and body look very . . . flushed. She keeps eyeing one of those knights like he's ice cream on a hot day. I can see this little flower affects the faeries' chemistry in a significantly different way than it affects the rest of us.

I suddenly feel very . . . happy. Extreme joy washes over me but not just joy—like joy on steroids. What is this? I ask to see if anyone has water. Sibyl hands me another Aloe mint.

"Ohhhhh Eli, I'm SO sorry!!!" the little voice says, "I'm trying to calm myself, I promise."

"What is going on?" I ask happily, which is confusing, because I'm also very disoriented.

"Eli, meet Valentina. She's the reason all my faeries are nymphs. And why everyone else here is always so enjoyable," Sibyl says, laughing a little herself. "It's impossible to be upset around her, so don't bother. Let's get some distance."

"No! No! Don't leeeave! If you wait just a moment, it will decrease by a lot more! Look how much less secretion!!" Valentina desperately pleads.

"Did this flower just get me high? Is Valentina a talking tulip?" I ask, not sure why I'm surprised by this at all. I mean, my new best friend *is* an in-my-head talking unicorn, and just yesterday I crossed a bridge made of dragon fire.

"Hello, hi there . . . okay . . . okay . . . sorry about that again." I can see she's working very hard to calm herself. "It's just that when I get excited, I release secretions that make the endorphins in the brain feel really . . . umm . . . good. The problem is . . . I'm always excited, sometimes it's just a lot more than other times."

"That's an understatement, Valentina," Wasi says. Malak snorts and shakes her head up and down assertively.

Thomas suddenly appears out of the lake. He gives everyone a glass of water and tells us it should help. He then scurries away back into the water and wishes us a good day. I drink the entire glass; it is helping to clear my mind. Now that Valentina's drops have gone down to one per minute, and everyone else seems to have calmed a bit, Sibyl tells me to be careful not to compliment Valentina. It will make her gush all over again, and we'll have an entirely new episode. I ask how such a unique flower came to be, because we could really use some in LA. Everyone is silent. Sibyl asks me if I remember the conversation we had earlier about the contract people sign when they choose to stay. Well, in that contract it states that they will remain as their *authentic* selves. Which, apparently, indicates that they will become whatever they think they *really* are. Valentina was once a highly sexual and bubbly woman that did everything to make everyone else "happy." She would often pick flowers and give them away to bring people joy, and her favorites were inverted tulips. So, that's what she became—a euphoric tulip. I asked how the knights stayed as knights. She said because that's who they believe they truly are; they were born and raised to be honorable heroes, and so they stayed that way. I ask if the dragons, unicorns, and faeries were also once humans. Sibyl says that most of the ones that were human, can be smaller than the originals, and that should help me to know the difference.

"Do they know this when they sign the contract? Do they know what they will change into?" I ask accusingly, no longer feeling Valentina's effects.

"No. The contract clearly states that they will remain as their 'authentic selves,'" Sibyl says, tilting her head indifferently.

"That's trickery. You're lying to them!" I say in a hostile tone. "You're just playing word games."

Now I finally see why people say not to trust her and her faeries. Her game is becoming clear to me. Everyone begins to move away from us slowly; Valentina goes back into her inverted position.

"You will NOT disrespect me in my own home, Elita. I demand an apology," Sibyl replies in a threatening tone, squinting her eyes and scowling.

"Do you *really* think these people would have chosen to stay if they'd known what was really going to happen to them? How is that fair!"

"They have better lives here as who they *really* are, than they ever would have had in that disgraceful world of yours."

"Yeah, really disgraceful, that must be the reason you're dying to get back into it."

"How dare you?!"

"What's all this rubbish about?" I hear the voice of an English woman that's slightly out of breath. An older, heavy-set woman is walking over in a long dress, an apron, a big floppy hat, and a watering can.

"I was just about to ask the same," says a sophisticated voice with a Middle Eastern accent. An elegant woman in a both modern, yet slightly traditional Persian outfit with a scarf draping over her hair, approaches us.

"Now look what you've done to Valentina!" says the English woman kneeling to pet her. "She's trembling, poor thing."

"Thank you for doing such a great job keeping up the garden, Melie. It looks beautiful," says the graceful woman.

"Lovely to see you, Sambethe. It's been a long stretch this time," Melie says, watering Valentina.

"Sambeeethe?" Valentina says softly, with water blubbering in between her lips.

"Valentina, you are looking more radiant than ever," Sambethe says kindly, trying to pull her out of her wilting position.

"She's the best thing that's ever happened to this place. How about we all show her that now and again?" Melie says scornfully at all of us.

"Well said, Melie," Sambethe agrees.

Melie walks towards me. "Hello, I'm Melie. I'm the caretaker of the gardens around here. They tell me you're special, but I only care about my plants and flowers. I have a hard-enough time keeping up with all the shenanigans that go on around here. So please be kind to them, and we'll get along just fine." I shake her hand and nod respectfully.

"Elita, I am Sambethe. I believe Sibyl has told you about me, the pleasure is mine." She holds my hand in both of hers. They are a bit cold, but very soft. She is wearing several intricate rings on her skinny long fingers. Her hair and eyes are as dark as night, and her lips are full. Her skin is olive-toned; she has very striking features.

"Sibyl, my sister. What is going on here? I hoped to find our guest feeling welcomed." She and Sibyl kiss both cheeks.

She then walks over to Wasi and Malak. She says something to them in a language I don't understand. Wasi seems very surprised to see her. He tells me she's an old but good friend, he's missed her a great deal. Well if he likes her, then there's a good chance I will too. She walks back over to Sibyl and they begin discussing the argument we were having when she arrived. Sibyl is very stubborn and seems stuck on getting an apology from me. Sambethe, in a very cross tone, says something to her in the same language that she was speaking to Wasi. Wasi tells me to take the deal she's about to propose, because it's the only way I'll see the entire picture.

"So Elita," Sambethe says as she smiles trying to put me at ease, "let's make a deal. If by the end of the day everything you've learned warrants an apology, you will provide Sibyl with one. And if you do not feel that it does, then she will apologize to you."

Everyone gasps. Sibyl looks like she'd rather eat glass. I look back at Wasi, he tells me this has never happened before. Sibyl must really need something important from me, but the only way to know is to go along with it.

"Yes, deal," I reply.

"Wonderful, let's continue." Sambethe places her arm under mine, and we walk to the next garden.

On our walk, Sambethe explains that Oracles have been given many different names throughout history. Each regime changed their Oracle's name to something that was suitable to their culture. But she believes it was simply a way to show dominance. Once treated with the utmost respect, Oracles were called "Earth Goddesses." As time went on, they were forced to endure deplorable treatment. In a patriarchal society the world became more sexist, and they were viewed as property because they were women. Too often they became slaves to emperors and kings. These ruthless leaders enjoyed playing the sport of pegging them against one another and seeing who had the wiser and more prophetic Oracle. Sambethe says that some centuries were only survivable because they could see the death of the tyrant, with better days visible ahead. And then other centuries they never wanted to end, because they were so wonderful—and they knew there were terrible times on the brink. I can't imagine what a burden it would be to know so much, and not be able to do anything about it. I ask her how lifetimes work for Oracles. She replies by saying that other than human beings, it is the same for all those given existence in the first two weeks of creation; they are to serve God on Earth until Judgement Day. They inhabit either the human world, one of the Asbgahs, or the Heavens.

I never knew there was a second week of creation until this moment. We've only ever been told about the first seven days. I ask Sambethe to divulge more, but she says it would be best to leave that for my grandmother. She asks where Rosa is. Sibyl explains her absence and says that she'll be joining us for dinner.

We walk into a circular-shaped garden. Lining the outside of the circle are tall palm trees with big leaves that cast a wide shadow. The inner circle has five crescent trapezoids flowerbeds; within them bountiful orange trees bloom. The smell of the orange blossoms is wonderful and inviting. In between the crescent trapezoids are five walkways to the center of the garden. In the center is a very large star with a circle around it, both are made of a gray stone. Within the center of the star, is water shaped as a tree that pushes up from the middle. Floating and hanging off its water branches are endless lotus flowers. It is magnificent.

Elise picks oranges off the trees for us to eat. She calls them Sabos. I see her push herself off the ground with her hooves; she holds herself freely in the air as she picks the oranges. Maybe faeries do fly or float after all? Everyone is very enthusiastic as she hands the giant orbs out—even the knights take part. As I peel the massive orange that's the size of a grapefruit, I hear Melie's voice. This time she arrives with a small white bucket. She lectures us not to make a mess, and to toss all our peels into it. I think we all might be a little afraid of her, because we do as she says without question. I finally take a bite; it's so juicy it squirts out of my mouth. It's both so sweet and a little tart, the taste is truly like nothing else. It's delicious! One of the knights leans against a palm tree while enjoying his orange. A large green pepper falls straight onto his head. He grumbles something at it as we all laugh.

"Should have warned you about that, John!" Melie says in good humor. "It's that time of year." She goes to pick it up. "That's a gorgeous one, ripe and ready!"

"Did a bell pepper just fall from the palm tree?" I ask.

"Well yes, where does it grow where you're from?" Melie asks sarcastically.

"The ground," I reply. Everyone mutters an *oh yeah*, or *that's right*.

"Well, here, it's delicious! Go on, take a bite!" Melie says, shoving it in my face. I take it from her hands; it's a bit heavy. I hesitate. I'm not a fan of bell peppers as is, but I don't want to be rude. And everyone is staring at me.

"Well if you don't, I will," John says, teasing me in his very soothing masculine voice. "It was my noggin after all." I guess they *do* speak.

I take a small bite. It's . . . it's . . . the best thing I've ever had! I dive into it, taking ravenous bites one after another. Everyone laughs.

"This is *not* a bell pepper! What is it?" I ask with my mouth completely full. It tastes like sweet, delicious watermelon, and apples, and strawberries, and chocolate, and yet nothing like any one of those things.

"They are called Dawsacas. It's Phemonoe's own creation. She'll be pleased that you love it so much," Melie says, then flings her eyes wide open. She seems to have remembered something. "Goodbye everyone!" she exclaims, as she scurries off in a hurry.

"Who's Phemonoe?" I ask, still chomping away.

"She is known as Libyan Sibyl; this garden is in her honor," Sibyl says. I guess she's decided to speak to me again. "I created a garden for each of my Oracle sisters. This is my way to honor them. As I look out over my kingdom each day, I think of them. Each garden also serves as a custom portal for them alone. They have unrestricted access into and out of my kingdom . . . they are my sisters after all."

It's a beautiful gesture, but she still has a long way to go before she gets an apology out of me.

Sambethe tells me that Phemonoe has always lived among the people in Egypt. She is brave and has a fearless personality, as well as a beautiful singing voice; she was the first of the Oracles to chant her prophecies. She is also the one that tolerates stupid questions the least, and is the most particular about only answering questions that she finds have value. My kind of girl. I wish we could all live our lives this way; say what you mean, and only ask questions that are worthy of answers. But if we did, we would be viewed as elitist, difficult, and have no friends. Phemonoe also foretold the prophecy of *"the coming of the day, that which is hidden, shall be revealed."*

I ask if there is anything marked on the calendar, so to speak. Sambethe laughs and says that only Phemonoe knows. But the day she speaks those words to the world, it will be bittersweet. I feel chills going up my spine before she can even complete her sentence; it doesn't sound like it will be a happy international event.

Our next stop is at a wide and long garden filled with massive olive trees. The trunks are thick and the roots are deep. There are small flowers throughout, growing sporadically. The walkways that weave in and out, and in-between the trees, are lined with woodchips. Climbing quickly up the trees are what appear to be red and black striped squirrels. At least I think that's what they are. Their bodies are shaped more like a skunk's body, but with the same squirrel bushy tail. Their heads are a little big for their bodies, and they have a round face that looks a bit smashed in, and pointy ears. They are chasing all the Pentwilin birds off the trees. The ones that aren't harassing the birds are hoarding olives. Elise says they call them Scapegraces, because that's what they are: incorrigible rascals. I ask her where they're from; she says a squirrel and a ginger owl mated, and now they're all over the kingdom. She warns us to not be fooled by their adorable faces—they might look cute, but they love to eat, and they'll snatch food right out of your hand. Good thing I finished my "bell pepper."

As we get closer to the center of the garden, the olive trees start to come together creating a pergola. Under the pergola is a river, but I can't tell if I'm standing at the beginning or end of it. It looks like it goes on forever and reminds me of the tunnel in the first corridor that never seemed to end. At the mouth of the river is a fallen tree trunk, we sit on it to rest. Wasi and Malak stop to drink the water from the river. Wasi points out the fish that are swimming around and asks me if I think the Scapegraces secretly eat them too. I laugh. Sambethe asks me what Wasi said.

"How did you know?" I ask her.

"The connection between the two of you is like nothing I've ever seen." She looks at him admiringly.

"He's asking about the fish and if the Scapegraces eat them too."

"There are two species swimming together: one is called Acanthobrama Hulenis and the other Tristramella Intermedia. They are both extinct; it's a good thing that none of Sibyl's creatures have the desire to eat meat," she says smiling. "You will find every extinct and endangered creature living and thriving in every Asbgah. It is our responsibility to ensure their return someday. There are many lands both undiscovered and hidden from humans on Earth. That was a deliberate act by God to protect some of his creations," Sambethe explains.

"Like, they're invisible to us?" I ask.

"Yes, invisible is a good word. But it's more like non-existent to humans," she says, pushing her eyebrows up. "So, you can fly over it, sail through it, or walk on it, and you will never know."

"*What?*" I'm dumbfounded by the idea. It makes me feel melancholic and sorrowful that humanity gets it so wrong, so often. We shouldn't have the ability to exterminate and destroy anything.

"Narcissists," Sibyl mutters under her breath, while picking olives off a branch.

Sambethe puts her arm around me, surely in empathy of my small mind that is trying to understand her words. I stay quiet, afraid to say something stupid or "narcissistic," as Sibyl likes to remind me. Are we humans really so engulfed in our own belief of reality, that we think there's really nothing left to discover except for other galaxies? . . . Right now, I'm really looking forward to Phemonoe's day of understanding.

"Don't let this get to you, Eli. There is so much they don't know, that you do. What else do you think all this courting is about?" Wasi says encouragingly to me.

Hummm.

"So, let me tell you about Hebrew Sibyl, also known as Helrea," Sambethe says continuing on. "Can you believe that people thought, and some still do, that she and I are the same Oracle?"

"That's not a difficult leap with so little literature about you all," I reply.

"Valid point, Eli," Elise says with her thumb in the air and a wink.

"Well, Helrea is brilliant! She is the prophetess and writer of the *Sibylline Oracles*; not to be confused with the *Sibylline Books*," Sambethe says, as she gets up and leads the way out of the garden.

She clarifies the difference by having me think of them as two halves, like a "part one" and a "part two." The twelve books from the Sibylline Oracles can be thought of as a kind-of Old Testament. And then the twelve Sibylline Books as a kind-of New Testament, before there were such things as Old and New Testaments. The Sibylline Oracles are a collection from all the Sibyls of what we call "classical mythology." They just call it history. It also contains the early millennium of the Gnostic, Hellenistic Jewish, and Christian beliefs. There is even some apocalyptic literature about how God will carry out judgement to the world for acts against Him and His People. And of course, the coming of the Messiah.

The Sibylline Books, or part two, are a collection of Sibylline prophecies about the destiny of the world and were written by Hellespontine. Suddenly, Sibyl interrupts Sambethe to tell a story. Sibyl says a week before Hellespontine began to write the books, each of the Sibyls had a dream in which God visited them. They were told that soon the world would receive a *great gift*. They were each shown a part of a young man's life. They knew this information was of utmost importance, and so the Oracles chose to meet three days later. When they gathered, they each shared their vision one by one, and it wasn't until the very end they realized that the gift was the son of God, and they called him "Savior." Hellespontine began to write down all their prophecies until they could see no more.

By the time Sibyl finishes her story, we arrive at Hellespontine's garden. We enter through a hand-carved ornate door. Closing off the garden to give it privacy, are very tall hedges in a long rectangular shape. There are many kinds of bright flowers and greenery. Laid throughout the grounds are beautiful and lavish tile floors, with chairs and benches that have the same ornate craftsmanship as the door. On the north wall from where we entered, is a faucet fountain that is continuously running water. We take a seat next to it.

Sambethe tells me that Hellespontine foretold the crucifixion of Christ. She had the most difficult of the visions to endure. Because they could not only see, but *feel* the vision God had given them, it took some time to calm her from the pain and agony she felt from His death. For a moment, both Sambethe and Sibyl sit in silence as if they're reliving those moments.

"Hellespontine is from Turkey, but currently resides in London," Elise says, trying to lift the mood. "And who knows, she might even end up being your mother-in-law one day!"

"ELISE!" both Sambethe and Sibyl shout at the same time.

"What have I said to you a *million* times!" Sibyl continues to yell. Elise quickly hides behind John.

"Elise, what do you mean?" I ask, puzzled. "Please step out from behind John and explain."

Sambethe tries to jump in to rectify the situation, but I stop her and ask Elise to come out again. I know she is the only one here that will tell me the truth. Wasi, very loudly, asks me to not do it this way, he asks me to wait for Luca.

"Luca?" I say out loud.

"WASI!" Sambethe and Sibyl shout again. He hides his face behind Malak's.

I call out to Elise once more. Sibyl finally tells her to come out and get it over with. She walks out from around John slowly with her head down and apologizes to everyone for speaking out of turn.

"Go on," I say anxiously.

"Eli . . . Hellespontine now goes by the name of . . . Victoria Mason," she says gently, while tilting her head.

"Oh," I take a deep breath, I haven't thought about this since my conversation with Sophia. "I-I assumed since Oracles don't have children and they are virgins, that they wouldn't have families"

"They can't have their own children. But marriage has many meanings, to many people. Sex is not always a factor. Victoria and Alessandro had an . . . understanding," Sibyl pauses. "Let's just say Luca is a child of an . . . indiscretion. And Dante is "adopted" . . . if you will," Sibyl says. My heart hurts for Luca. "The boys know the truth. Victoria has taken them as her own. She is the only mother they have ever known."

"Enough about personal things that are none of our business. If you want to know more, you'll have to ask Luca," Sambethe says. I agree; finding out this way feels wrong.

I try to push it to the back of my mind while Sambethe continues, but I'm finding it hard to concentrate. I try to focus in on things I saw in Alessandro's mind. But there are so many faces and so many events, it's hard for me still to distinguish. I hear Sambethe say that it became Victoria's life mission to preserve as much literature and historical artifacts as possible, because humans and their leaders tend to destroy things and keep important information they do not like from being passed on. She entrusted fifteen custodians she called Quindecimviri Sacris Faciundis. Their only responsibility was keeping the books in safety and secrecy. They held these positions for life and were exempt from any other duty. Over the years, the literature and artifacts grew to such a great quantity, that she eventually created a secret society with thousands of members. Their New World name is The Freemasons. They oversee precious things that are scattered all over the world. The ones higher in rank have great wealth and political influence, and they are called the Illuminati. They are responsible for protecting the most important pieces of information.

They say Victoria has made something wonderful of her life. And without her, the world would have less than one thousand years of history at its access. I must say, she's impressive—when she's not threatening my grandmother.

"Are all these Sibylline Oracles and Books in the Mason Library?" I interrupt. They ask me how I know about it. I tell them that Sophia has just become the hundred-and-first member. It's their turn to gasp. They begin speaking to one another in a different language. I look at Wasi and shrug my shoulders. He tells me that they are trying to understand why Victoria would allow it. That there must be something she's not telling them. Secrets among Oracles. Well, this is a turn of events.

"Pardon us Eli, we don't mean to be rude. Our sister's actions have taken us by . . . surprise," Sambethe says, regaining her composure.

"I know how that feels," I reply. I've been in the dark all my life, and lately I'm sideswiped at every turn.

"Yes, I'm sure you do," she says sympathetically. She then stands up and says to the group that it's best we get a change of scenery. She tells the knights to lead the way to Phrygian's Garden.

We exit through a door adjacent to the one we came in, then walk down a flight of stairs and into a huge oval garden, facing three plant covered tiers. It looks like a lush, overgrown amphitheater. Wasi and Malak jump down, bypassing the stairs. The bottom of the stairs is where the third level and the largest of three tiers is. Each tier gets smaller going uphill; it looks like we're going for a small hike. There are various trees and plants of all kinds along the three tiers. But almost no flowers, just a few that grow on the trees; I ask why that is. Sibyl tells me that Phrygian, whom she calls Cassandra, has seen the darker side of the world's history. She says that flowers always die, but trees live on, and that gives her hope. So, Sibyl planted as many trees from all over the world and planted them in Cassandra's honor. Sibyl and Sambethe talk about their favorite rendering of her drawn by Rafael. Sambethe says she recently went to see it at the British Museum. Sibyl looks down. Sambethe takes her by the hand and tells her that she longs for the day they will see the world together again. Even in such a place of enchantment and extraordinary beauty, I cannot imagine having my freedom taken away. I may find myself in discord with Sibyl, but for this, she will always have my compassion.

We reach the top. There is a small pond with four weeping willow trees surrounding it. There is a plaque near the pond, it reads:

> *When the dread trumpet resounds,*
> *the deepest earth will yawn open.*
> *Kings will be set before the throne of God.*
> *He will deliver the final judgement*
> *on the good and the wicked,*
> *For the latter, fire, for the rest, eternal delights.*

Sambethe says that Cassandra uttered those words into an artist's ear in 1575 and they remain the only written words she's ever said.

"Oh really? So, she didn't write the *entire* Book of Revelation?" Sibyl says rolling her eyes. "It was her prophecy to tell about the *end* of time. But instead they call her John. What a hoax. All that just not to credit a woman."

"At least she got to choose her male name," Elise replies in her optimistic voice. Sibyl gives her a look. "Okay, I'll stay quiet."

"Is this true?" I look at Sambethe and Wasi.

"I'm afraid it is," Sambethe replies.

My legs feel weak. I lean up against the tree. Feeling heart-break and anger, I slide to the ground. All because she's a woman, she was not allowed to have a place in the Bible? It occurs to me that even if any of it was written by a woman, she would have had no choice but to choose a male pseudonym to write under.

"Like a good soldier, she still continues to warn people every day. Trying to find ways to get through to them. Whispering in their ears, trying to get them to do the right things to prevent the inevitable. But they just go on living their lives, ignoring her as they always have," Sibyl adds.

"Why John? Why did she choose the name John?" I demand of Sibyl.

"It was once considered blasphemous to utter the name of God; it was only written and never spoken. Over the years the pronunciation of His true name was forgotten. Many began to call him Yahweh. John is derived from the name Yahweh. She couldn't very well use the name Yahweh or the tetragrammaton of His name. So, she thought it wise to choose John; it is a ver-sion of His name after all. But even so, the world acts as if it's "John the Christian prophet." Or they just carry on about absurd possibilities."

"So, God's true name, is the most common name used to de-scribe a man with no identity?" I reply. They look at one another and back at me, fully grasping the irony of what I've said.

This one is going to take some time for me to find peace with.

"Come on!" Sambethe lifts me up off the ground. "Cassandra would want me to tell you about Albunea next. She is an import-ant part of the prophecy she tells. And she likes her a whole lot. Tiburtine Sibyl, is what they call her."

We walk back down to the bottom of the garden and then across a foot bridge. Nearby, walking out of a labyrinth garden, is a faerie wearing a long, multi-layered white chiffon dress. The dress is blowing in the air like a dream, and on her head is a wide brim hat with ostrich feathers sticking out of it. She smiles and tilts her head "hello." In her hands, she's holding a wide ivory rope. The rope is tied around the neck of a very large Phoenix. It is nearly her same height, but much, much wider. Elise walks over to say hello, but we keep walking. I ask why we aren't stopping at the labyrinth garden, but Sibyl just quickens her pace.

Sambethe pulls me back from the group to tell me that the garden was made not in honor, but as a precautionary tale of trusting someone too much. It's a labyrinth in-spite-of Herophile, or Cumaean Sibyl. She says there's a lot of bad blood between them, and it would be best if I didn't bring her up. As we pass the very intricate garden, I notice there is no water anywhere near or around it, unlike all the other gardens we've visited. In this garden, I can see a tall tower at its center, with a spiral staircase leading up to the top. It's very peculiar. Without trying to be overly invasive, I ask Sambethe what Cumaean Sibyl is like. She says that Herophile once prophesied in Cumae, near Naples. She was the most beautiful, and certainly the most famous of them all. There was something about her that enchanted everyone. She put her long brown hair into two braids and nearly every day she'd make herself a crown of fresh flowers to wear on her head. She loved being naked—she found clothes to be restrictive and disparaging. She was a wild and free spirit. I notice Sambethe keeps using the past tense when describing her. This is confusing to me because I know Oracles are on Earth until Judgement Day, so she can't be dead. I want to be careful of not being overly invasive, and shut her down all together, so I ask what she is known for. She says that Herophile was the first to prophesize the coming of Jesus, even before the dream when God came to them. Herophile called him "Savior." She foretold the story of the rise and fall of the Roman Empire, but history mostly remembers her for selling the Sibylline Books to Tarquinius Superbus, the last king of Rome. As the story goes, these books were an invaluable source of power and knowledge and foretold the future of Rome. In 500 BC, Herophile made them available to the king for an ostentatious amount of money, but he refused. So, she burned three of the nine books. She then offered the six remaining at the original price, but he refused once more. So, she burned three more. Then, she offered the last three at the original price; finally, he accepted.

I ask why she only made nine of the twelve books available to the king. Sambethe says the other three held information that was much too advanced for the king's taste; he would have found no value in them. But Herophile was very clever, she knew exactly what she was doing. She and Victoria created a plan using the magic of a Phoenix; the very same Phoenix we just walked past, she adds. Every time the ashes from a book fell, they would rise again into their original form, in Victoria's hands. So, the originals were never destroyed; they've been safely guarded by the Quindecimviri Sacris Faciundis ever since. The three remaining books were stored in the Capital Hill of Rome until 82 BC. They were destroyed in the burning of the Temple of Jupiter. The fire gave Victoria the perfect opportunity she needed; once again she used the magic of the Phoenix to retrieve them. Roman leaders had envoys from around the world brought in to help rewrite the books. They did the best they could from memory and notes, and the new books managed to make it until the end of the Roman empire around 405 AD.

Sambethe says that of all the beautiful paintings and literature Herophile appears in, and there are many, there is only *one* story she has ever wanted told, but it has remained unspoken to this day.

Chapter 20

ALBUNEA, aka Tiburtine Sibyl, lives near Tivoli, Rome. This explains the Etruscan architectural courtyard and the terracotta decorations in the garden. There is plush, vibrant green grass under my feet, I can't help but bend down to feel its velvety texture. There is an intoxicating scent of roses coming at me from every direction. It reminds me of the red roses Nonna Rosa would grow outside of her stairway leading up to the front door. Throughout the garden there is a collection of various rose types in every color you can imagine. There are even colors I've never seen before. At its center is a traditional simple fountain. Albunea's garden is heavenly, and from what Elise says, because of the scent, it is one of the faeries' favorite gardens.

I learn that Albunea prophesied about the Emperor Constantine. But even more importantly, she prophesied about a detail that was not disclosed to Cassandra. It is about the man who will be known as the world's final emperor, called Constans. She saw that he would unite the world by doing things that were different and unique to the actions of the ones before him. He would vanquish all the adversaries of Christianity, end the worship of false gods, and stop the conversion of the Jews. But by doing so, he would make way for the Antichrist. Only, in Albunea's vision was it revealed that the name Constans is an acrostic, a detail deliberately left out of the books. At this point, even though I'm dying to know what the acrostic is, I know better than to ask.

I see something I thought was a statue move from the corner of my eye. I jump in between two of the knights; they seem to be amused by my fear. The statue walks over to one of the lanterns, whose fire was blown out by the wind, it opens its mouth, and spits out a stream of fire to relight it.

"Is that a real Chimera?" I ask, with a slightly trembling voice.

"It's just about time for their shift change. Don't worry, despite what you may have heard, they are very peaceful, unless provoked," John says.

"Are you kidding? I haven't heard anything. They are supposed to be mythical creatures!" I reply, mouthing a silent scream. The knights all laugh.

We all watch as the chimeras get up to stretch, blow fire in unison and change positions. They peacefully rotate the corners of their guard. For having the front of a lion, middle of a goat and back side of a snake, they really do move gracefully.

"What a treat Eli, they rarely do that in anyone's presence. They must want to get a glimpse of you." Elise grabs me from between the knights, "Don't be rude," and nudges me to the front of the group.

To exit Albunea's garden we must walk through a gate that's a giant bronze statue of a chimera's mouth. As we do, the chimeras rise to attention. They push out their fire at least three stories high. My heart starts beating so fast, I walk as quickly and politely as I can past them. Once I get inside of the "mouth" I just run through it, afraid it too might come to life. Before I can stop myself on the other side, I find myself going headfirst into a lake.

I feel a swift pull of something hard against my waist. Its grip is so strong, it nearly knocks the wind out of me.

"Careful Eli, not so fast," a gentle voice says to me. It all happens so fast I don't even know who caught me.

"Thank you, Matthew, Mark, Luke or John. Whoever you are. I appreciate you catching me," I say trying to get myself together, without bothering to look up to see which knight it was.

"Uh, my name is Phillip. And I'm *definitely* not an apostle. Those guys were cool, but also pretty stuffy," the voice replies. I look up and notice something floating in the water.

"WHAT THE F-" I shout, jumping backwards, this time right into the arms of a knight. Damn, these guys feel like robots. I rub the sting out of my arm.

"Phillipthropolus!!!" Elise screeches as she climbs on top of him. "I miss you my favorite hippocampus!"

"I miss you too, my favorite faerie!" he replies in a jolly tone. He sounds young, like a teenager.

"So, I see you've met our youngest Hippocampus," Sibyl says rubbing his head. "Where are the others?"

"They'll be coming up any minute now!"

"I see your swimming speed is getting better," Sibyl praises him.

"Yes, I practice every day. I hope to win the tournament this year!" he says with excitement.

"Well, you keep this up, and you'll win every year!" Elise says as he swims around in circles.

"Where are Wasi and Malak?" I ask, as I look around and see everyone but them.

"Uniequus do *not* want a ride from a hippocampus, dear, I'm sure you can understand why," Sambethe replies. "This is the fastest way to get to the forest; they will meet us there shortly."

The rest of the hippocampi arrive to the landing. They are

large and majestic creatures. The upper half of their body is a horse, and the lower half is a fish. They vary in color but for the most part, they are emerald green with pewter reflections. Their eyes are a honey-brown color. Their two front legs are the same as a horse, but their feet are part hooves and part fins. Their tails are strong and long, and covered with large scales. At end of their tail is a wide fin that splits in two. If I'm not mistaken, there are several small blades that protrude from the tip of the split fins.

Everyone climbs on quickly except for me. I feel like I've just now learned how to ride a horse, how am I expected to know how to ride a *seahorse*?

A very large one approaches me.

"Hi Eli, my name is Martha, I'm Phillip's mother," the gentle creature says to me. "You'll be riding with me. I promise not to go fast and not to make any abrupt movements. It's a smooth ride . . . I promise."

I nod my head and climb on her as I would Wasi. It takes a little more maneuvering than I expected. Then off we go. Martha starts off slow and smooth just like she promised, but I can see the others far ahead of us, so I tell her she can go faster and boy, does she ever. Smooth as a twelve-hundred-foot cruise ship on perfect water, she picks up speed and doesn't stop until she passes them all up. Other than riding Wasi, it's the most exhilarating experience of my life. I don't know what I was afraid of.

Before I know it, and much too soon, we arrive where the water meets the edge of a forest. Wasi and Malak are waiting for us. I climb off Martha and onto the deck. I thank her for such an amazing experience, and for being so kind to me. She tells me that she's available anytime I need her, should Wasi be unavailable. I look over at him and see a twinge of jealousy in his eyes. Martha looks over her shoulder to see how far the others are from reaching us. She then leans in and whispers to me that she has access to the entire kingdom and knows secret paths into the other Asbgahs. I ask how this is possible, with the borders being closed. She says that she has her ways, and winks. She makes me promise her that this will remain our secret. Even her own family does not know; she is afraid that it will put them in danger. Martha tells me that there have been whispers of change, a kind of shift. She thought it was best to create an exit plan in case those in the kingdom should ever need it. I smile. She really is just a mother. My mom once told me that all mothers should follow their instincts. And so, I agree to keep her secret.

The others arrive. We set out into the forest and don't slow down until we are standing in, what I think is, the middle of the forest that I've been dying to explore. It's better than I could have imagined! There is moss growing all along the ground and at the base of the grand elm trees. They have got to be the tallest ones in the entire world. The trees and their branches are a dark brown, but the cracks of the bark expose a kind of honey color. The leaves alternate in different shades of green, from nearly florescent to deep emerald colors. We stop in an intimate field filled with yellow flowers that look like the ones in Umito, but these are far more vibrant. They make it look like the sun is shining from the ground up. The trunks of the trees closest to the field have exposed roots with a hard, outer layer. The roots are enormous and they go in every direction. They stretch out so far that they interlock with their neighboring trees, creating a kind of circle. I don't see water, but I can hear it; we must be near a different part of the lake.

"Not that I don't love hiking through an enchanted forest, but why weren't we just dropped off here?" I ask, pointing to the sound of the nearby water.

"Oh, that's just a small replica of Lake Avernus I had made for

Carmentis," Sibyl says to me, as if I'm supposed to know who that is. "Cimmerian Sibyl," she then adds, after a moment of staring into my unresponsive face. As if that was going to provide me with a light bulb moment. "Oh, for heaven's sake, you really don't know anything, do you!"

"Sibyl . . . " Sambethe says with a calm tone and a cold stare.

She turns her attention to me. "Eli, you must forgive my sister's temperament today. She was under the impression that you would know more about us, than you actually do. Your grandmothers did a very good job of protecting you. I don't fault them. I would have done the same."

"Are you serious, Sambethe? She doesn't even know our names!" Sibyl exclaims, with an offended tone.

"And, why would she?" Sambethe replies to Sibyl, squinting her eyes.

"Isn't today's entire point to teach her about our history; so she can then understand her own?" Sambethe pauses, then says, "She needs to know that we are not the enemy!"

Those words calm Sibyl.

"Bravo! Someone give this lady a drink," Wasi says facetiously. I find his dry sense of humor very funny. I try to hide my smirk, but Sibyl catches me, and her death stare discourages me from any further reaction. Behind Sibyl's back, Elise motions at Wasi to cut it out. She's one to talk.

Sambethe picks one of the yellow flowers from the ground and hands it to me. It does look like the ones in the yellow valley! She calls them Silphium; they went extinct in the human world around 1BC. She explains it was once used as a medicine, seasoning, and even for perfume.

"The plant is an aphrodisiac. But the Greeks and Romans used it for contraception." Sambethe adds.

"Wow, so it makes you horny while preventing you from getting pregnant? No wonder it's extinct!" I blurt out. I think Alessia may have just possessed my body for a moment. I can hear Wasi and Malak laughing at my candor. There may have even been a smile from the ice queen herself.

"That's a fair point," Sambethe chuckles. "Look closely at the seeds. What shape do you see?"

I do as she says and run my fingers across them.

"A heart!" I reply looking up at her. "They are like tiny little hearts."

"Yes. It is because of the shape of these seeds that your world identifies the heart shape with love. It is a plant of great natural resource and great hope." Sambethe smiles.

That is incredible, why don't they teach us these kinds of things in school? Maybe we'd all pay closer attention and be a better and more well-rounded society if we learned about a more truthful history.

"They are Carmentis' favorite, and she makes wonderful tea blends, as well as her famous drops with them." Sambethe says with warmth.

I ask if she still lives close to Lake Avernus. Sambethe explains that though she lived most of her life in a small cave located underground close to the lake, she moved to Colfiorito in the first century, or what is now known as Pretare. I remember learning in my mythology class that Lake Avernus was considered the entrance to Hades. I ask if it's the same one. Sibyl makes a snarky remark that at least I paid attention in school.

"Yes, exactly! The same one!" Elise says nodding her head excitedly.

"But I thought the entrance to the Underworld is Lake Pilate?" I ask.

"Now we're getting somewhere, schoolgirl!" Sibyl says, in a perked up but still condescending tone. "Think of Lake Pilate as the side entrance, and Lake Avernus as the front door."

"So, what did Carmentis do, hold the door to the Underworld open?" I sarcastically reply to Sibyl. I'm getting very tired of her tone.

"Now . . . " Sibyl says with a wicked smile on her face, "what would *Julia* think if she heard you say such rude things about her?"

"J-J-Julia? Underworld?" I mumble. My visons and memories are awoken by that revelation and begin to come together slowly. I sit on a nearby boulder. Could it be true that my gentle Julia is the gatekeeper of the Underworld? Sibyl's right, I really *don't* know anything.

Sambethe suggests that we take a little break. Wasi walks over and nudges me to climb on, and so I do. Sambethe tells us that it's best to meet at the next stop; she instructs Malak to show us the way. We do as she says; I think she can sense that I need some time away from everyone.

Malak leads Wasi and I out of the forest. They are both riding nearly parallel and very fast. Wasi is apologizing to me. He says he wishes he could have told me about Julia, but we have only been able to communicate for a day, and there's been so little time to catch up. I feel tears streaming down my face. I can't believe how dumb I am. No one is who I think they are, not even me. I knew Julia was an Oracle, I knew she was a healer, but *this*? I begin to wonder how many people, friends, boyfriends, professors or employers are even who they say they are? Were they planted in my life for alternative reasons? Whatever I am, whoever I am, I don't want to be her anymore.

"Wasi stop! Stop!" I lean in and shout into his ear. But I lean too far and lose my balance. I fall off hard and straight onto my back. There is a shooting pain like I've never felt before all the way down my back and into my brain. Everything looks fuzzy.

Wasi tells me to be still because my head is bleeding. Malak comes closer to me; I can see her horn radiate light through the cloudiness of my vision. She touches my head with her horn. I feel a warmth and then a burst of energy, followed by a bright intense light. I know this light; I've seen it before . . .

Flashes of memories begin to play in my mind:

The moment he first saw me, watching me, following me. The elevator in his father's house, the soft touch of his hand . . . his strong kiss . . . I'm on top of him, I begin to unbutton his shirt and lean in to kiss him again. The same white light appears. I can see his life . . . the face of the woman that gave birth to him. His childhood, adulthood, schooling, travels, hobbies, friends and lovers. I see all his pain and so little joy.

Flashes of faces, both men and women that are important to him; some I know, but most I don't recognize. I see not only his brother, but others that seem to be part of his blood line. I see Julia and Dwintra, he shows me their story through his eyes. And then . . . thousands of Elves in an emerald land. And finally, Micella standing next to a magnificent tree.

The shock of it all startles me awake. I blink until I can refocus my sight.

"Eli, are you okay?" Wasi sounds like he might be going into shock himself.

"Yes, yes . . . I'm okay."

"What just happened?"

"I don't know, I think I just lost my balance . . . " I say sitting up slowly.

"No, I mean, just now. What happened to you?"

"I-I had a memory," I touch my head to see where I've injured myself. "There's no blood?" I ask.

Wasi explains that Malak means "Angel" in Arabic, and that's what she is. She has the ability to heal. He says to a certain extent all Uniequus do, but she is special. She can heal in a way other Uniequus cannot.

"Thank you, Malak, please let me know if there is anything I can do to repay you. I know I don't have any special gifts, but if there's ever a favor you may need, please know you can count on me," I say to her.

She looks over to Wasi, I can tell that they are exchanging words, but cannot make anything out in Wasi's mind. He turns to me nervously and says that bringing him back to her has been payment enough. I suspect that's not at all what she said, but to avoid any further issues, I nod and she nods back. I just hope she did not actually ask for something that he's hiding from me.

I see her assertively pushing him to say something to me.

"What is it Wasi?"

"She wants to know about your memory, what did you see?"

"Uh . . . well . . . mostly Luca. But I also saw something else . . . I guess with the Sibyls' having so many damn names, no one thought to mention that Carmentis, Cimmerian Sibyl, and Chemistry Sibyl are all the *same* person; the gatekeeper to the Underworld! Whom by the way, I happen to know *as* sweet little old Julia!" I say sitting up, feeling annoyed about my vision. "But you see, that's simply NOT enough. Nope!" I am now pacing back and forth, going quickly from annoyed to angry. "Julia, through all the fires of Hell, sought to create a better world filled with remedies and medicine to help humanity. But of course, she couldn't very well leave behind the responsibility. So, what did she do, you ask? Well, in all her wisdom, she created an army to protect IT. *IT* of course being the Tree of Life. Uh-huh! That tree is the one and ONLY way into Heaven, Purgatory, and Hell. Uh-huh, all three places! I saw a . . . guide, he or she was wearing a cape with a hood so I couldn't see their face—I have no idea who it was. But yep, I saw that in Alessandro's mind! And guess what she not only created, *but* also made her army, y'all?! Yep, ELVES! And are you ready for the best part Malak! MICELLA, Luca's gorgeous half-sister, is their QUEEN! You got it! Julia left Micella in charge of protecting the Tree and the Emerald Land." I've now gone into full hysterical mode. "And no one gets in or out of the forsaken Underworld without her knowing about it . . . Except for Sibyl. Who somehow gets in and out ALL the time. And from what I saw, it's something Micella is seriously pissed off about. Mostly because she A: doesn't know how Sibyl does it. And B: she can't catch her!" I take a deep breath from my rambling. "How's that for an Oracle soap-opera!!!"

Wasi and Malak exchange words as I continue pacing, trying to make sense of it manifesting in my mind all at once. When they finish, I look over and find them staring at me.

"What!" I ask, walking in circles like a lunatic.

"Well, I want to know if this is what a human nervous break-down looks like? And Malak wants to know what a soap-opera is? Other than that, sounds like you got it correct," Wasi replies.

"I think I just need to let out the crazy. This is all just more . . . than I'm used to. But since we're at it, what else haven't you told me, Wasi!" I demand.

"A lot," he mumbles, "It's been a few thousand-millennia." I roll my eyes at him.

I then climb on his back. I'm sure if we don't show up to our next stop soon, they will send the knights to come looking for us.

"Luca. What about Luca? Umm, Malak wants to know," Wasi asks inquisitively.

"Are you sure it's not *you* that wants to know?" I reply, hu-mored by his attempt not to look nosy. Malak makes a sound similar to a human giggle. The sound makes me giggle too, and I tell them to stop gossiping.

*   *   *

We encounter the others at a temple fit for the Greek gods. It reminds me of renderings that I once saw of the Temple of Apollo. It sits up against the hillside of the mountain, surrounded by very tall thin trees, as well as round bushy ones. Circling above us are several dragons and there are also a few napping under the trees, with their tails wrapped around the tree trunks. That must be why Wasi calls them "tree huggers."

Straight ahead are several stairs leading up to vertical columns, being used as pillars for this *very* grand building. Past the marble foyer are two enormous doors up against a beautifully decorated wall. The knights push the heavy doors open and we enter. On both sides of the interior there are many more pillars going all the way down the long building. In-between each column are large statues; some figures I recognize from mythology, and others from ancient and modern history. Everything is built from mixed stone, limestone or marble. I look up and see the entire ceiling is painted with an image of a galaxy. It looks both familiar and different from ours. I see every planet and star that's ever been named, and then some I'm not familiar with. I notice a peculiarity—there is a tenth planet. And many additional dominant stars that I *don't* remember learning about in astronomy.

As we reach the end of the cavernous room, the knights open another set of double doors; they lead us into a garden. It is very similar to the front, but with a fountain the size of a pool in the middle. At its center, is a large statue of a woman. She has a snake coiled around her feet with its head moving up her leg. She has large wings protruding from her back; but they're not like angel wings, they look more like an animal's. I take a seat on the edge of the fountain to get a closer look at the statue's face. She looks strong and proud.

"Faerie shrimp!" I say with excitement, as I look down into the water of the fountain. I'm thrilled to see something I recognize!

Sibyl, in a kind tone, says she created them just for Lake Pilate. She seems to have gotten over whatever was bothering her. She puts her hand in the water and they all swim to her; it's like they recognize her. She calls them her "sweet protectors." But I'm not sure what she means by that, these little guys seem to be anything but dangerous.

"Did Eden tell you about the Great Stone in Lake Pilate?" Sibyl asks.

"She did. She says it has symbols on it that no one can decipher; and no one can figure out what purpose the stone is intended for. I believe it just sits in a museum that's dedicated to you in Montemonaco."

That makes Sibyl smile. She seems to enjoy the idea of an entire museum dedicated to her myth.

"Did you see that same stone in Alessandro's mind, Eli?" Sibyl asks. Although I wish to tell her nothing, I don't see how this one can hurt.

"Yes, I did." Everyone's attention peaks. "The one in the museum is not the original stone. Alessandro and Victoria have replaced it with a replica. The original is buried far beneath the water. Are the faerie shrimp supposed to look after it? Is that what you mean when you call them protectors?"

"Yes. But no, that's not entirely what I mean," Sibyl says dismissively, as she sits next to me. "What else did you see?"

"Oh okay, umm . . . I saw the stone being placed and the symbols being etched with a sharp object." I pause, choosing what else I reveal very carefully. "Then I saw land appear, and landscape begin to form. It was so beautiful, it's as if I was watching the world being born," I reply, recalling the utter peace of that moment.

"That's because you did, Eli. The stone represents the center of the Earth. The stone was placed in the exact location where creation began. It is meant to stay there in that exact spot until the end of time. But the humans didn't know," Sibyl says with a sigh, "And let's just say, when they moved it, it created a very big mess."

"What happened?" I ask, curiously. I did not see that part in any of my visions.

"The dinosaurs went extinct," Sibyl gives me a crooked smile.

"Oh, that small mess," I say shaking my head, trying to wrap my mind around the coexistence of humans and dinosaurs. Meanwhile, I'm still in total awe and I keep replaying the moment of creation over and over again in my mind.

"The real stone is now hidden deep in Lake Pilate, far from anyone's sight. I wish you could have seen it; it is marvelous. One would become mesmerized just looking at it." Sibyl sighs, "A poor man's replacement was put in the original place in Lake Pilate, to remind us of where it once perpetuated all its wonder. Of course, that was until the humans discovered it for the second time and placed it in the museum . . . It's a good thing what they found the second time is a fake. You know, the stone also fuels great magic!" Sibyl says with a glimmer in her eyes. "That's why necromancers, wizards, witches, and sorcerers would visit Lake Pilate. Not because it was the entrance to the Underworld. But because, if they could harness life itself, their powers would grow to immeasurable strength."

"Why did Talos take Pilate's body into Hell through there if there's a 'front door'?" I can't imagine why he would choose such a place.

'OH!' Sibyl and Sambethe both exclaim at the same time and throw their hands in the air. The reaction seems a little dramatic for Oracles. They say that since it contains the Great Stone, what is now known as Lake Pilate is absolutely the worst and most painful way to enter into Hell. The Great Stone shows you the story of life, peace, magic and love. To see and feel it in its purist form is like meeting God himself. To know true divinity and then to never have it, is the greatest suffering any soul can endure. Sambethe says that only Lucifer could dictate Pontius Pilate's redemption. And since only Pilate could have changed the fate of Jesus' death, Lucifer's punishment would not have been swift or compassionate. The condemnation would be brutal.

I need to change the subject. Hell, and anything having to do with it, seriously freaks me out. I'm terrified that such a place could exist.

"What do the symbols on the stone mean?" I ask the two of them.

"Eli, whose hand did you see making those symbols?" Sibyl asks, avoiding my question entirely.

"They look familiar to me, but I can't quite figure it out," I say. Sibyl has a look on her face like she's trying to decide whether or not I'm lying to her.

"I swear it!" I say, holding up my right hand.

"Fine," she replies. I think she might actually believe me.

"The symbols are words in a language by people we can't even begin to explain to you right now. The words will only be spoken once more, by the person who wrote them. And in that moment life will end . . . for the world . . . for all of us," Sambethe says, coming clean to me.

"Oh my God! You want to know how much longer you will be alive! Or exist . . . or whatever you do," I say, shocked at the realization. "So even *you* don't know when this will all be a wrap! But that only seems right; I mean, if we don't get to know our life span, then, why should you?"

"Because you know your life is within a one-hundred-year span. Ours is infinite," Sambethe says. She has a good point.

"Many of us are tired," Sibyl says quietly, looking down.

"The problem is, Eli, there are others who want to prevent the end of the world from happening all together," Sambethe adds.

It just occurs to me that so much of the fighting I saw in Alessandro's mind was not just on the "human" part of Earth. There are many divisions within the Asbgahs and they don't all live in harmony.

"That's where I come in!" says a strong female voice to my right. I look around and don't see anyone new standing nearby. I make eye contact with Elise. She points her finger up to the sky. Coming down at a rapid speed, I see the mother of all dragons heading straight for me. I jump up and mumble a few profanities. The dragon quickly turns into a white light. It is bursting and coming towards me until it suddenly evaporates. The dragon has manifested itself into a warrior woman—a perfect specimen. She has muscles in places that I didn't know a body could have. And she's walking right towards me.

"Call me Krisa," she says holding out her arm, towering more than a foot over me. "I'm also known as Delphic Sibyl. And Pythia. And no matter what the rumor, I go by all those names. And a few others."

I introduce myself. I feel a bit taken aback by her stature. "I read somewhere I'm not to confuse you with Pythia."

"Nonsense! Humans are so easily confused!" Krisa says laughing. "So, you're Rosa and Amelia's granddaughter. You know, of all the Celestial Beings, those girls are my favorites."

"Mine too," I happily agree.

Krisa asks me to take a walk with her around her garden. I can't help but gawk at what phenomenal physical shape she is in. It's no wonder Michelangelo painted her as the most beautiful Oracle in the Sistine Chapel. Damn, I really need to get to the gym.

She tells me a little of her story. She was the Oracle that presided over the area I know as Ancient Greece. She then became the guardian of the Great Stone. The humans that discovered it in Lake Pilate were loyal servants of Zeus, and so they brought it to his attention. He sent his two most lethal eagles to retrieve what he referred to as the "navel" of the world. He believed that finding such a place filled with so much knowledge held geo-political power, thus making it the most important place in the world. But the Oracles knew they couldn't allow this to happen. They each did what they could to interfere with Zeus' plan. Sibyl created the faerie shrimp to protect the stone; she says they turn poisonous and attack any person or animal who tries to steal it. Huh, they always say the sweetest are the deadliest.

Krisa says she knew how ruthless Zeus' eagles were. She knew the faerie shrimp would not be enough to defeat both eagles. So, she asked a sorceress by the name of Gaia to temporarily turn her into a snake that had the ability to swim in the water and hide under the faerie shrimp. They hatched a plan that all the faerie shrimp would attack one eagle, and she, as the snake, would attack the second, and the eagles would never see it coming. Krisa and the faerie shrimp succeeded. The magic of the Great Stone blessed her with a gift for her bravery. It gave her the ability to become half snake, half bird, and the power to turn the snake's venom into fire. At will, she's able to become the first dragon.

It was at this time that she became acquainted with Nonna Rosa, or Taygeta as she calls her. She says that it was known throughout the lands that Nonna Rosa was the mistress of animals, and Krisa needed her expertise. She requested that Nonna ask a handful of snakes and larger birds to mate near the Great Stone. She explains that this was an act of desperation, as she needed dragons to help protect against the unruliness the humans were perpetrating. Zeus and the other gods were near the end of their reign. Stealing the Great Stone was Zeus' last act of attaining power, but he failed. The people were angry, they hated the gods and stopped praying to them. They had started praying directly to God himself.

God directed Krisa to use dragons to keep humanity from hurting each other with war and carnage. And so, my grandmother complied with her request, and the stone granted her several dragons that multiplied for many generations. The dragons kept peace among humans for thousands of years. But in the medieval era, powerful kingdoms turned on them. The dragons were captured and held as slaves; they were forced to do horrible things to please their kings or masters. The dragons that survived the abuse were brought into the Asbgahs for protection. And the world would never really know of their existence.

I ask Krisa why there were never fossils found; that would certainly prove dragons existed. She says they have been found all over the world but have been labeled as various dinosaurs. She says that even though humans see what is clearly in front of them, they choose to not comprehend anything outside what they are capable of understanding.

I think she may have just said that either our brain is too small, or we don't use enough of it.

"Are you the only one that can transform into something else?" I ask Krisa.

"I'm the only *Oracle* that can. But there are many beings throughout the Asbgahs that can transform too. Be careful when you visit them, Eli. Remember, for all the good, there is also bad. Your skeptical mind and strong instinct will serve you well in your travels," she says, staring into the distance.

"My travels? No, I've decided to go home tomorrow," I answer.

"Oh," she replies. I'm not exactly sure what she means, but I don't get the chance to ask her. Our walk has come full circle and we've arrived back to where the others are waiting.

"Eli, I will see you at dinner tonight," Krisa says, holding onto my forearm.

"Dinner?" I ask.

"Yes, I am hosting a dinner in your honor this evening. There are a few people that want to meet you," Sibyl answers.

"Sibyl, did you know that Eli has decided to leave tomorrow?" Krisa asks her, with a look I can't read.

"I did not," Sibyl says surprised.

"I'm very grateful for the hospitality, really. But I've been away from my family way too long, they must be worried sick," I say, feeling a pain in my chest. My mother must be climbing the walls by now.

"When we get back, I can have my secretary Delilah send your family an email to let them know that you're alright," Sibyl offers.

"You have wi-fi here?!" I say, floored.

"Oh dear, how primitive do you think we are?" Sambethe says in a disappointed tone.

"I-I'm sorry. I didn't mean to offend you. It's just that my cell phone doesn't work here, so I just assumed . . . " I say, trying to explain myself.

"This is going to be more fun than I thought!" Krisa laughs. She excuses herself and says she must go; she has things to attend to. She leaves in the same dramatic way she came in. I watch her dragon body soar into the sky.

Wow . . . I won't ever get tired of seeing that.

"Speaking of wi-fi, would you like to know who invented it?" Sambethe says, putting her arm around me as we walk to the next garden.

Chapter 21

AFTER A VERY STEEP WALK down the side of the mountain, we arrive to what resembles a small, private beach. I take off my shoes and bury my feet in the white sand. Wasi and Malak make their way over to the crystal blue water. Watching unicorns stroll near the water is the only time I have ever thought "walks on the beach" looked romantic. I put my head up towards the sun, it feels so good on my face. I might live in LA, but I can't remember the last time I was on a beach. Here, because the water is so close to the mountain range, there are trees sporadically growing out of the sand; their shape reminds me of bonsai trees, leaning and winding into many shapes.

"Well she didn't exactly *invent* wi-fi. But she's definitely responsible for putting clever ideas in people's minds," Sambethe says, sitting on a leaning trunk that's very close to the sand.

"Who?" I ask.

"Phyto; many know her as Samian Sibyl," Sambethe answers.

Sibyl walks away from my and Sambethe's conversation. I watch as she puts her feet in the water and walks out to a sitting on an isolated boulder, about two-hundred feet out. The knight who always follows her closely, stands where the sand and water meet, watching her from a distance. Sambethe tells me not to mind her. All this talk about who they are; she's never had to tell the story of their history—it's like reopening an old wound by cutting through scar tissue. She chose to enshrine herself in the Faerie World and never wanted to deal with her emotions.

I ask her about the knight. It's always the same one standing just an arm's reach away from her. Sambethe says that one is Victor, he's been silently and madly in love with Sibyl since he laid eyes on her. He doesn't care about her stubbornness or her flaws; he sees her as unequivocally perfect. He is loyal, supports her, and protects her at all costs. His life has no meaning without her. And yet, he asks nothing of her, and wants nothing more than to serve her.

I tell her that sounds like bondage role play and ask if people in the Asbgahs are intimate. She giggles and reminds me that I am speaking to a virgin. But the rumor is that there's a lot of activity. That makes me think of our conversation from earlier, and I ask what it means for "it" to be impossible for them. She explains that it is like wanting different DNA than the one you are born with. In the end, we must all accept who we are and what our purpose is.

"What about Alessandro and Victoria? And Julia and Gian Carlo? Why can't the rest of you have companionship without the intimacy?" I ask.

"Julia and Gian Carlo are best of friends and have always been so. They only call each other husband and wife in the human world, because for many years it was frowned upon for men and women to be so close without the union of marriage. So, they just made it up to prevent harassment." She takes a deep breath, "Many of us have loved at least once. But it just becomes impossible—it's not worth the disparity that follows. We all thought

Alessandro and Victoria found a way; it gave the rest of us a glimmer of hope. But in the end, even they, with all that magic at their disposal, could not make it work."

"I'm sorry, I didn't mean to upset you." I reach for her hand and decide it's best to change the subject. "Please tell me about Phyto."

"Yes, y-yes." She squeezes my hand and clears her throat, "She's the cleverest of us all! And I dare say, quite the genius. Her name comes from the word Foito, which means 'wandering.'"

Sambethe goes on to say that Phyto likes to wander in people's minds; she's a mind reader. It first began by whispering prophecies to those intended to know them. And then throughout the years it evolved to going into minds, and whispering advice and guidance to help rectify problems, solve equations or complete plans. Apparently, she unblocks writers, whispers music notes to musicians, advises on war plans to leaders, puts the correct materials in front of inventors and artists, and presents formidable information to scientists. And she does it all by looking into a person's mind to find what part of the puzzle they still need. Sambethe says that Phyto spent most of her life in Samos, Greece. It's the only place she felt peace and where her mind was quiet. Now you can find her in just about any quiet beach town in the world. Sibyl created her garden to be a replica of Samos, so she can always escape if she needs to. Being in people's minds has caused her to seek isolation more times than not.

I ask if she can see everything in a person's mind. Sambethe explains that she can only see into the minds of those that need her; and she can only tune into what she is required to help with.

That's a pretty fancy trick.

"Is that what you meant about inventing wi-fi? She went into that person's mind, and told them what they needed to do?"

"Yes, in so many words. It was the beginning of WWII. The

allies were in need of better technology against the Germans. Phyto whispered how to develop it into the ear of Hedy Lamarr, who then shared it with George Antheil. Together they developed a better radio guidance system that was meant to help the Allies improve their communication. Now that very same technology is used in many things, such as wi-fi. I told you she is clever."

That's one hell of a talent, I wish I could do it.

"Here's our ride," Sambethe says, picking up her shoes from the sand. Around the corner coming towards us are four small fishing boats with no one in them.

"It's the fish in the water that are steering them, in case you are wondering," Sambethe says, reading my mind. Nothing should surprise me anymore, but somehow it always does.

As we are waiting for the boats to come close to shore, something occurs to me. "Sambethe, what was Phyto's prophecy about Jesus? You said you all had one. Come to think of it, I don't know what Krisa's was either, she didn't mention it."

"Krisa saw His second coming. But she won't dare mention it. The only thing we know for certain is that she has been chosen to slay the Antichrist in God's final war. In the Bible, they name Michael the Archangel to be the one to perform this act. But she's no Michael, and she certainly is no Archangel. She's very secretive about it, and she should be. I'm sure there are many that would be very upset to find out that it will be a woman. But goodness, will they be surprised . . . And Phyto, well, she prophesied that Jesus would be born in a stable in the month of March. It really pisses her off that everyone celebrates in December."

"Then why do we do that?" I ask.

"December 25th was the most important Pagan holiday. The Church saw it fit to replace it with Christianity's biggest holiday. It was just another way for them to eliminate the Old World."

The boats arrive. Wasi and Malak go back up the mountain and take the land route to meet us. Sibyl, Sambethe, Elise, and I each step into our own small boat. A knight joins each one of us to paddle and steer them. The water is calm, and the weather could not be more perfect. I can see why Phyto loves it here, the silence and tranquility are unlike anything I've ever felt, even in Umito. I close my eyes for a moment. The more I relax, the better I can see the memories and visions in my head begin to take shape. Timelines are becoming more cohesive. As those become clear, new visions surface.

We pull into what I think is the most unique landscape yet. The land is barren with scarce greenery and mostly dirt. The mountains are jaw dropping. They seem to be made completely out of rock. Pointy at the top, but their shape is in the form of deep ripples and soft ridges, like waves. The surface color is a pale blush or salmon.

"Wow . . . What *is* this?" I ask in awe.

"They are Erymanthe's caves," Sibyl responds proudly, as we get off the boats. "Come. I'll show you inside."

There is a disguised entrance within the largest and deepest crevasse. As we enter, I feel a cold chill. It is dark and dusty.

"Erymanthe really needs to air this place out every now and again," Elise comments, as she covers her mouth.

"Elise, will you please?" Sibyl asks politely, gesturing towards her.

"Oh! Yes, of course!" she replies joyfully as she steps away from us. She extends her arms far and wide, then leans back and then forward. There is a kind of illuminating light coming from behind her. It starts to expand and expand.

"Oh my . . . " I say, as two beautiful golden wings project out of her spine. They are more magical than anything I can ever imagine. "Elise, you're *so* beautiful. Your wings . . . why are you all hiding them? They are magnificent . . . "

"Have you ever heard of faerie gold?" Sibyl asks me.

"Vaguely. I've heard of Faerie Dust."

"The dust is made up of specs that radiate from the gold. Its proper name is Adaturatem, but we call it Ada. It is the unique mixture of carbons that make diamonds, and chemical elements that make gold. It is very unique and extremely valuable."

"What does it do?" I ask.

"*Anything* you want it to, and that's the issue. Some of its powers are permanent and others temporary. It only has one limitation: it cannot bring any person back to life," Sibyl says. "The Egyptians used to call it the 'Breath of God.' But in typical human nature, everyone began abusing its power," Sibyl pauses, "Did you know the third pharaoh of Egypt was a woman?"

"I had no idea." I am pleasantly surprised.

"Her name was Hatshepsut, I loved and admired her very much. She undertook ambitious architectural projects and orchestrated vast trading expeditions. She was undoubtedly one of Egypt's finest leaders. And still, her successor attempted to erase her from history because she was a woman. She saw what her people were doing with the Ada, so she sent out her army to confiscate and destroy every ounce of it. Whatever little she had left of it in her possession, she turned over to me for safe keeping should the world ever need it again. Many, many years later, I used the last of its magic in the darkest . . . days of my life, to create my precious faeries," Sibyl says, smiling at Elise.

But the melancholic tone in her voice carries pain. She goes on to say that a thousand years later, somehow the humans figured it out again. They hunted and slaughtered the faeries for their wings. They would cut them off their bodies and leave them for dead; no faerie can survive without them. The wings cannot be mended, nor do they regrow once they are removed. So, Sibyl forbade them to ever use their wings again without her permission and presence.

She tells Elise to proceed. Elise arches her back and stretches out her wings as far as they will reach. And then with one full swing, she flings them forward. It causes a strong gust of wind. I close my eyes. The wind settles and I open them back up; Elise is engulfed in her wings like a cocoon. All around us are sparkles—this must be the "faerie dust." I watch the sparkles fall onto the hundreds of candles around the cave and light each one. I realize I'm standing in a library.

"TA-DA!!!" Elise exclaims as she pushes her wings open and throws up her hands to the sky.

I applaud her and giggle uncontrollably. This place has to be my dream come true!

"Elise, that was brilliant!" I shout.

"That's nothing, Eli! Maybe Sibyl will really let me show you what I've got later!" she says, so pleased by my response.

"Maybe. Come on show-off, guide the way," Sibyl smiles.

Elise guides us further into the cave; it expands into the largest library I've ever seen in my life. I'm in paradise.

"Well it's not as big as Victoria's, but Erymanthe really gave her a run for her money," Sambethe comments.

"Bigger? How can any library be bigger than this?" I ask, unable to fathom such a thing. They all laugh.

"You don't know Victoria," Elise says teasingly.

"The cave operates as a school for the faerie children throughout the school year. But since it's summer, no one's really been in here for a few months," Sibyl adds, as she looks at the dust that's collected on the tips of her fingers, after gliding them across one of the furniture pieces.

"Faerie children? I haven't seen a child since I've arrived," I inquisitively ask.

"That's because they are at Faerie Camp. Every year I send all the children to the Pink Forest. It is the only place where they can truly learn how to spread their wings and learn to control their faerie magic."

"Oh, it's marvelous Eli! We must take you there, they would love to meet you! Don't you think Sibyl?" Elise adds with an overzealous tone.

"But isn't it dangerous for them to spread their wings?" I interrupt Elise.

"The Pink Forest is the protector of all children. The magic of the forest cloaks the Ada Gold. Should anyone see them, they just look like normal children playing in day camp," Sibyl answers. "They are completely safe. I've made sure of it."

"Do all of the Asbgahs have children and schools?" I ask.

"Yes, almost all the Asbgahs do. It's a shame the children of the different Asbgahs have never been able to meet," Sibyl answers with the same melancholic tone, yet her lips are smiling. "Children are so inquisitive and so charming, aren't they?"

I nod in empathy for her sadness.

As Sibyl's eyes drift away, Sambethe begins to tell me about Erymanthe. She describes her as a brilliant writer and says that she is certain I will have a great deal to discuss with her. She loves literature and she loves teasing people with her innovative rhetoric even more. All her prophecies were written on leaves until she became comfortable with books. She was the first to ever use an acrostic in her writing. She prophesied about the Trojan War, the Redemption of Jesus, and even wrote about the Chaldean people. She was the keeper of both the Sibylline Books and the Sibylline Oracles, until she was instructed to pass them on.

They tell me not to bring those up though, it's a sore subject.

Although the originals were never really destroyed, she can't get past how irresponsible humans were with them. They told the story of creation, answering all the questions we would give *anything* to know today. Such as, how did we get here? Who is

God? And they foretold all the things to come, to help guide us for a better future. And yet, they were treated like outdated encyclopedias.

Sambethe says Erymanthe laughs at the television every time philosophical conversations about God are on. She shouts things like, 'well, it's not like He didn't tell you *everything*! It's not a mystery!' and 'if your asshole ancestors didn't destroy them, you would know, you big jerks!' She especially loves messing with scientists and atheists. She talks about how she wants to get a photo of their faces when they die. She wishes she could scream 'BIG BANG, HUH!' at them, while she takes it. I already like her.

The best part about the thirty-minute walk to get through to the opposite end of the library, is watching Elise do fancy tricks and fly across the air. But before John opens the back door, Sibyl gives her a look. Elise's eyes well up with tears and she pouts her bottom lip. Sibyl reminds her that it would be very rude, and the others would be jealous if they knew. She reluctantly and slowly puts her beautiful wings away. There is still a bit of sparkle dust around her. I put out my finger and wait for one speck to land on it. When it finally does, nothing happens.

"The magic is in the gold, not the dust. The dust just illuminates. It's the most precious metal in the world you know. Of course, only second to the Celestial Gold woven into your hair," Elise says, as she touches my hair.

"Huh? I don't have gold in my hair," I reply, looking at the tips.

"What do you think those 'highlights' are, dear girl?" Sambethe states.

John finally opens the door. It opens into the lily garden that faces Sibyl's kingdom.

"We've come full circle! I hope you've enjoyed seeing our fabulous Asbgah. Welcome to *my* garden," Sibyl says, happy to be back. "Now, let's have some tea!"

We sit under two large oak trees in the center of all the lilies. The table is beautifully set up for traditional teatime. We make small talk as I enjoy plum tarts with my tea. They are even better than the ones from the night before. I look around. It amazes me that such a place and so many others exist here on Earth. Undiscovered areas with the same weather, landscapes and time zones as their shared communities. If people only knew.

A ray of reflective light from my hair catches my eye. I grab a handful of it and examine it. Do I have more "highlights," or is it just the daylight on my hair that makes it more intense? How will I hide this when I get home? Maybe I really do need to invest in some wigs.

"Eli?" Sambethe breaks my train of thought.

"What does it do? Faerie gold does everything. So, *what* does Celestial Gold do?" I ask, feeling irked that I still don't know. "And before you ask, no, I didn't see anything about it in Mr. Vinci's mind. He was in disbelief when he touched me, like he didn't see it coming. The only thing I know, is that the gold in the painting of the tree in his library, is exactly like the gold in my hair. How?"

Sibyl and Sambethe look *very* happy about my admission.

"Thank you for your honesty, Eli," Sambethe says, closing her eyes tightly for a second. "The truth is . . . we don't know. Celestial Gold is so precious, so rare, and individually unique. Yours will not be the same or do the same things as your grandmothers' or any other Celestial Beings'. Your purpose has not yet been revealed."

"But by the look of your hair and eyes today, you are close," Sibyl adds.

"What does that mean? Am I going to live forever like you

guys? Like my grandmothers?" I inquire, panicked at the thought.

"No. You have human blood in your veins. That means that you cannot live forever . . . But! You may be able to live longer than most humans," Sibyl answers.

"What about my grandmothers? Why can't I see their Celestial Gold? I mean, is it cloaked somehow?"

They look at one another and do not answer me.

"Eli, I think you need to ask your grandmothers about that. It's personal," Wasi says to me. He's been so quiet the last part of the day, I almost forgot he was here.

I ask what time it is. I've had no concept of time since I've arrived, and I want to go inside and speak to my grandmother about this.

"It's 5 pm!" says the voice of a young boy, "Same time as the rest of Italy!"

I find myself face to face with a butterfly-winged mouse. He is standing in the corner on my side of the table.

"Peter, why didn't you wait for me!" shouts another, huffing and puffing, flapping his wings as hard as he can. As he gets closer, he loses his balance and crashes into the other upon landing, knocking them both over.

"Really Jacob? Get it together!" Peter says, trying to push Jacob off him. He's struggling a bit, as Jacob is much rounder than Peter.

They both stand about four inches tall; Peter is much lighter on his feet than Jacob. They have furry and fluffy tails unlike traditional mice. Peter has light brown hair all over, except for his center which is a white patch. He has big brown eyes and short whiskers. His wings take up seventy percent of his body and are nearly twice his size in width. Jacob, on the other hand, has a very expressive and curious face with long whiskers, and his eyes are big and bright blue. His hair is darker than Peter's, but with the same white patch going down his center. His wings are half the size of Peter's, but much prettier. The area of the wings closest to his body is baby-blue and bursts into various shades of orange, brown, and white. They sit up on their hind legs and brush themselves off.

"Hi! I'm Jacob!" he waves his little hand at me.

"And I'm Peter! I was trying to say 'hi' before my brother crashed into me!" he says, elbowing Jacob.

"Ouch! I said I was sorry, Peter. I'm not good with landing!"

"Then maybe you should stop eating so many crème puffs!" Peter says, poking his belly.

"Boys, act like gentlemen in front of our guest!" Elise scolds them.

"Sorry," they say at the same time.

"I really like crème puffs too," I reply, touching their tiny hands with my finger. "Nice to meet you both."

"I really wanted to ask you to dance last night at the ball, but there were so many people. Every time I tried to reach you, you had already moved to the other side of the room. I kept running out of breath," Jacob confesses.

"Someone has a crush on you!" Wasi teases.

"She's not going to dance with a fat butterfly-mouse! Which we would never be, if it wasn't for you. I could have been a knight or a dragon! But instead, we're *this*!" Peter says, smacking Jacob on the back of the head. Jacob puts his head down.

"Boys!" Elise shouts, "I said use your manners."

"I'm so sorry about that Jacob. Maybe I can make it up to you tonight. How about you come to my room before dinner?" I say.

"Really?" he says slowly raising his head, "That would be amazing! Yes! Yes! I will be there!"

"Ok boys that's enough," Sibyl says, "It's time for us to go inside. It will be time for dinner soon."

The boys excuse themselves as they shove and push each other, until they fall off the table and onto the grass. But before I have a chance to pick them off the ground, they fly right past me, Jacob falling far behind Peter's lead. I walk over to Wasi and Malak. He tells me that he will be by to pick Nonna and me up for dinner. It is taking place at the cove of the lake that faces my room; he's offered to ride us down. I thank them both for today, and they gallop off.

Sibyl, Sambethe, Elise, and I walk up the grand staircase to the front door together and find Nonna Rosa anxiously waiting for us. She runs to me and embraces me tightly. She then extends one of her arms to Sambethe to greet her, while never taking the other off me. I can see that Nonna has a great deal of affection for her. Sambethe compliments her on raising such a delightful granddaughter, while Sibyl asks me if I would like to send that email to my mother while Rosa and Sambethe take a moment to catch up. My grandmother and I agree to meet in her room once I'm finished.

Since it's been such a long day of walking, Sibyl suggests we take the elevator up to her quarters. We get in. I see there is only one button. I ask her if it only goes to her floor.

She giggles and says, "Alfred, my room please."

"Of course, madam," the deep voice replies.

"That's Alfred, he's our elevator. He can drop you off in any part of the Faerie Asbgah, in any direction. When you get in, simply push the button and tell Alfred where you'd like to go. Isn't that right?" Sibyl asks Alfred.

"My accuracy and time of arrival is unparalleled," Alfred says proudly.

"It's true. He's very efficient," Sibyl leans in to say.

"I wish that stupid voice on my phone could do that. Most of the time it just aggravates me and doesn't give me any of the information I want from it."

"Oh, don't you worry. That will soon improve a great deal," Sibyl says knowingly.

"That reminds me of a question I meant to ask you earlier. Since you're Oracles, can you all see *all* of the future?"

The doors open.

"Yes, but not like we used to. The more time we spend in the human world, the stronger our visions become. But after spending so much time here, I only see minor things every now and again. Your arrival was the first real vision I've had in many years," Sibyl says walking out.

I continue to stand in the same place with my mouth open. Her room, if you can even call it that, makes the Vinci's villa look like a hut.

"Please get out of Alfred, I'm sure he has others to service," Sibyl says gesturing for me to come to her.

"Oh . . . right. Sorry Alfred," I say, as I step off and into a room the size of a small city.

"It was my pleasure, Miss Eli," he says in that very polite and deep voice of his. "Madam Sibyl, I will be back to retrieve you in one hour. Will that do?"

"That will be perfect Alfred, thank you," Sibyl replies, and then turns her attention to me. "Eli, I wish I could show you around but there just isn't enough time. Please follow me into my personal study," Sibyl says, guiding me.

Her home is very decadent. The architecture and interior design, from the walls, to the ceiling, to the furniture, is all from the Art Deco era. It's never been my favorite look, but the way she has things displayed feels classic and it is very impressive.

She pushes open the double doors to her personal study. It feels somehow both intimate and extensive. There is riveting artwork, polished statues, and ancient artifacts from all over the world adorning the bookshelves, walls, her piano, the side tables, and the fireplace mantle. Sibyl takes off her shoes and removes a piece of her clothing one by one, throwing them on the ground. She steps behind a divider, puts on a robe, and steps out. She pours us both a cup of tea then takes a sip and tells me to take a seat next to her on a crimson, velvet sofa. All the while, she hasn't stopped speaking about all the particular pieces in her home that she loves the most. She even shares where she got them or who they were a gift from. Her list is nothing less than extraordinary. As she speaks, I notice that she is stirring her tea with a silver spoon that appears to have a handle made of silver thorns. They look incredibly sharp, and yet they seem to give her no discomfort whatsoever.

"Eli?" Sibyl says, and I look up at her. "Would you like to see my spoon? I can see you're curious."

"It doesn't hurt?" I ask and reach over to take it from her hand.

"Not at all. It looks more masochistic than it actually is."

She is right. I hold it between my fingers, and it doesn't puncture my skin or cause me pain. How peculiar. I instantly feel a vibration coming off the spoon. Within seconds, the rose shaped pendant that Nonna Rosa gave me, which I wear on my necklace, starts to have the same vibration under my shirt.

"You have a good eye, Eli. Do you want to know what it is? If I tell you, can you keep a secret?" Sibyl asks me, completely unaware of the tremor between her spoon and my pendant.

"Y-yes . . . " I reply, trying to keep a calm expression.

"It is the branch of thorns those *animals* used to make Jesus' crown," she says with a deep sadness. "I used a spell to solidify it into this spoon. It's the only thing I could think to turn it into, that wouldn't be obvious."

"What?!! THIS is the crown he wore?!" I ask in dismay.

"Yes. It is said that the thorns were taken from a rose bush with a single rose on it. And whoever possesses that rose, holds great power. It is referred to as the Solomon Rose."

"What kind of power?" I ask, as the vibration becomes more intense. It's as if the spoon and my pendant are trying to connect together like a magnet.

"The kind that leaders go to war for. The kind that destroys humanity," she says with a heavy tone. "More importantly, the rose and the thorns must never reunite. I am the keeper of the thorns and have been for all time. I'm proud to say it's *never* left my sight. But . . . no one knows what happened to the Solomon Rose. Its whereabouts have been a mystery since 1945."

"O-oh, I see. Thank you for allowing me to hold it, I feel honored," I say, handing it back. She smiles as she takes it from me. The vibrations stop.

We have small talk for a while before my eyes make their way over to a massive vintage typewriter. It's facing away from the large bay window and sits on a beautifully carved wooden desk. It reminds me of an old Underwood from the 20's or 30's. I approach it and gently touch it with my fingers.

"Aaaaaaaa!!!" I scream, as eight long octopus arms come jumping out of the typewriter. I hold my chest to make sure my heart hasn't jumped out if it.

"Delilah, what did I tell you about doing that to humans?!" Sibyl shouts.

Her arms are blue hues in an ombré blend going from darkest to lightest, and the center of her suckers are black. I see her tentacle tips moving wildly across the keyboard, typing so fast all I hear are the sound of the keys going 'click, click'!

I read what she has typed: "Hi Eli! I'm so sorry, I didn't mean to scare you. I was trying to clean up my mess before you walked in. I was inside the drawers organizing my things when you touched me. Oh goodness, I'm so ticklish! And all my arms just jumped right out at you! Hahaha . . . "

"H-hello," I say loudly, leaning into the keyboard.

"OUCH!" she types out. "Love, not so close please. I might be old, but I'm not deaf."

I step back slowly.

"She won't bite!" Sibyl says, as she takes my teacup and hands me a glass of whiskey. "Just tell her what you want her to type, and she'll send it to your mother."

"How?" I don't want to offend her, but she is a typewriter and not a computer, after all.

"Oh, she's quite competent. And can be trusted with any-thing," Sibyl says going back to the sofa, "Aren't you Delilah?"

Ding! She sounds, moving her barrel all the way to the left.

"Ummm . . . okay . . . Hi Mama, I'm sorry I left without saying anything the other day. I just needed to figure out a few things on my own. But please don't worry, I'm fine. I'll be home tomorrow. I love you, Eli." Delilah quickly types it out, then presses the button labeled **SEND** on the far right. The words disappear off the page.

"Where did it go?" I ask.

"The cloud," Delilah types. "Just kidding, I've always wanted to say that. In your mother's inbox, of course. By the way, what's the cloud?"

"Great question, no one really knows what 'the cloud' is," I reply sincerely.

"Eli, you need to get to your grandmother's room." Delilah coils one of her arms around my wrist while typing with the oth-ers. "She has some important information to share before to-night's dinner. Don't waste any more time here."

"Oh, is she still going on about that ridiculous cloud? Really Delilah, you're so obsessed," Sibyl says from the sofa. Delilah's words disappear off the page before Sibyl can see.

"Yes, I agree. Thank you for all your help," I say to her.

I thank Sibyl for her hospitality and put down my drink. I tell her that I'm very tired and I'd like to take a nap before dinner. She says she might do the same after such a long day. She escorts me out to the elevator doors and calls for Alfred. He promptly takes me down to the floor of my room. I wait for the doors to close and go straight to Nonna Rosa's room. I gently knock on the door and let myself in.

Her room is nothing like I'd imagined. It is an exact replica of the bedroom she shared with my grandfather at their home in Venarotta. The iron bed, the old dresser with pictures of them on their wedding day and of her children when they were small, and even her pearls laid out next to the frames, they are all there. I can smell the scent of the roses that used to grow outside her bedroom window coming in with the breeze.

"It's not what you expected, is it?" she says, standing behind me.

"No," I say honestly, "Why do you want to torture yourself for eternity, Nonna?"

"It's not torture, they were the best years of my entire existence. My family is everything to me. And the place where you sleep should be the place where you feel the most peace, right?" I nod in agreement. "Well, in that house, with all of you . . . it's been the best gift of my life. I got to be a wife, a mother and a grandmother. That is my idea of bliss."

I put my arms around her and hold her tightly and say, "I've decided to go home tomorrow, Nonna."

"I heard," she says, holding my face in her hands.

"How?" I ask. "Wait let me guess, a Pentwilin bird. I saw them following us all day. Gossipy buggers."

"I asked a few of them to keep a close eye on you. I just wanted to be sure everything was okay."

"You're not mad, are you?" I ask, feeling guilty about not telling her first.

"No. You *must* go back, so I was very glad to hear it," Nonna says, pulling me into her closet.

We walk in and it's no closet; it's a crystal cave. The reflection of the crystals gives off a dim light. It feels like we are standing under twinkling stars on a perfectly clear night. Nonna explains that before her human body died, Dwintra came to see her. He gave her a protective shield crystal called a Bline, to bring with her into the Asbgah. He told her to put it in a corner of her closet and it would multiply until it turned into a crystal cave. He told her it would protect her from danger, and one day, when Nonna Amelia arrives, they will be able to have private conversations without anyone ever being able to hear them. Nonna tells me the added benefit is that when she wants to be alone, she comes here and no one can find her. Should anyone other than her open the door, they will just see an empty closet. I've got to ask Dwintra for one of these crystals, I could really use it in my apartment.

Nonna tells me that today, while we were out, she snuck inside Sibyl's study. This surprises me, she's always been such a rule follower and I'm pretty sure she just broke a big one. She goes on to explain that although Delilah is very loyal to Sibyl, she's got a bad feeling in her suckers. I ask her to explain this "bad feeling." She says no one can explain it; but they can all sense a shift and have been able to for some time. Nonna Rosa and Delilah went through some of Sibyl's personal letters and recorded visions. Apparently, it's Delilah's job to record every single prophecy and event that happens, which explains her magnificent typing skills. Those notes are then taken to Erymanthe's library for safe keeping. Delilah, having a photographic memory, is able to pull up anything she's ever recorded. They found notes about my birth, my transformation, and even my current visit here long before my conception. Nonna says, based on what she read, it's best that I go home as soon as possible. Although we haven't been able to have a conversation about what I saw in Alessandro Vinci's mind, she says she will soon visit me in the Vellous, and we can talk about it then. In the meantime, Nonna has a very important task for me to take care of. She hands me a sealed letter and tells me to hide it carefully on my body. She says she wrote all the details in it and instructs me to follow it carefully.

I ask her if she ever figured out what Nonna Amelia meant by the *Rose of Venus*. She says she's explained what she can in the letter, but that we don't have the time to talk about it now. She can hear Thomas knocking on her door and it's best that we answer, before he makes a fuss looking for me all over the kingdom. He has a flare for the dramatics.

"Hello Thomas. What do you need?" my grandmother says, as she opens her door. I can tell that she's annoyed by his incessant knocking.

"I'm sorry for the interruption, Madam Rosa. I don't mean to disturb your time together, but Madam Sibyl and Madam Sambethe have requested to see Miss Eli before dinner. And I must get her ready first," Thomas responds flustered.

"Well, we wouldn't want to get you all excited, Thomas," she says shaking her head at him. "Why don't you get Eli's things and we'll get ready together here."

"Very well," he says, and darts to my room.

We take each other's hands, worried about why I would be called back up to Sibyl's room again. Nonna tells me not to worry, it's most likely in preparation for tonight. But I feel anxious, I can't imagine what she would want to prepare me for. Just then, Thomas storms back into the room holding garments and shoes in one tentacle, and Jacob in the other.

He holds the little fella up to my face and in a disgusted tone says, "This *thing* says you promised him a dance, but I told him he was mistaken. I had to run all over the room to catch him, until he finally ran out of breath!" He then drops Jacob into my hands.

"Thank you for bringing by my guest, Thomas," I say graciously. Thomas' eyes grow wide in disbelief. "Hello Jacob! I'm so sorry for running behind, but I'm ready for our dance now."

Nonna claps and takes a seat to watch us dance. She knows Jacob well and is very fond of him. Thomas on the other hand is less than amused. I hold Jacob in my hand, and like a true gentleman, he bows. He begins to hum a sweet tune as we twirl and sway. Thomas entertains us for a few minutes, before he loses his patience and starts getting me ready. But Jacob and I don't stop, he flies around me as Thomas raises my hands to replace what I'm wearing with a lovely dress. With the tentacles on his feet, he changes my shoes. And with the ones on his hands he simultaneously fixes my hair, puts a little make-up on my face, and adorns me with the most beautiful jewelry I've ever worn.

Our dance ends right as Thomas finishes getting me ready.

"Oh, Miss Eli, you look gorgeous!" Jacob says. I kiss his little head.

"You really do," Nonna says adoringly.

"Yes, you really do—" Thomas utters, as he drops to the floor from exhaustion. His body lands half on and half off the evening cape that goes with my lovely dress.

"Don't worry, I'll have him bring it to you at dinner," Nonna giggles.

*   *   *

Sibyl's butler escorts me into her formal living room. He pours me a cup of tea and tells me that she will be in shortly. I look around, debating on whether or not I should take a page out of Nonna Rosa's book and snoop around. But instead, my mind drifts as I stare out the glass doors that overlook the water. I can hear all the fuss below as they set up for tonight's dinner. I think about how often I've heard Oracles discarded as myths and legends. And yet, they are depicted in the Bible, books, as well as various paintings and statues, all over the world. It's strange to me that the world has worked so hard to erase their knowledge and influence, when all the Oracles have ever done is sacrifice for it. They have stood by and guided every walk of life, in every generation, for all mankind. Their words have inspired so many to seek wisdom. And their activities must have saved us from infinite global disasters and wars. Their advice set leaders on the right path.

Their words are sent from Heaven, then whispered in the ears of endless innovators, scientists and artists to help bring forth evolution. And yet, all modern history tells us that they are "not real." How did this happen? When did the world start working under the pretense that seers do the work of evil, and conclude that no good can come of their unique gifts? And why would the Bible see them as both essential prophets, while simultaneously doing the work of the devil? If God created them and trusted them to tell the story of His own son, then how can they be anything other than favored? It feels like the epitome of leaving women out of history, and people getting so many things wrong.

My thoughts shift focus as I am warmly greeted by Sibyl and Sambethe as they enter the room in all their Oracle glory, spectacularly dressed. Sibyl apologizes for having to call me back up so soon and hopes that she did not interrupt my nap. Sambethe cuts to the chase; she is insistent that we settle today's argument before the others arrive. She believes the animosity will prevent us from moving forward. It's time for one of us to apologize. I'd almost forgotten about this, but it's not going to be me.

"No," I say.

"What do you mean?" Sambethe is surprised by my reaction.

"No, I won't apologize," I continue, "I didn't see anything today that explains why you keep these souls hostage here."

"Do you really think I force them to stay?" Sibyl says, raising her eyebrows at me.

"I think you trick them into staying. Once they realize what they have to be in order to live in paradise, it's too late to turn back!"

"You really think I'm a monster, don't you?" she says in a cold tone.

"I don't know *what* you are," I reply matching her tone. "I learned about everyone but you today. Your story is the only one you didn't tell. Why! What are you afraid of?"

"LADIES!" Sambethe intervenes. "This is not going to help. And it is not what I'd hoped for." She turns to me, "Eli, I swear on everything that is holy, no one here is a slave. They all serve as they choose to. What you see them as, is only what they ever wanted to be in life."

"I find that hard to believe," I roll my eyes, thinking about all the things I'd seen today.

"It's true," says a small voice in the background.

"Elise?" I turn around. She is standing there in her Sunday best.

"Yes, Eli. We are all who we want to be. I know that must be strange to you because there are so many peculiar creatures here. Each of them had a year to decide if they wanted to stay in their authentic form; once they did, it was final. Those that chose to leave, went back peacefully into the human world with no recollection of this place. It's that simple," she says softly.

She's right; I guess it is hard for me to understand why someone else would choose to be what they are. I mean, why would you choose to be a typewriter and not a princess, or a million other things.

"I know what you're thinking, Eli. But that's the beauty of this place; you can be whoever you are in your heart, without judgement. So *please*, don't judge us. That's why no one spoke up today, it's always the humans that are the cruelest about our choices. And no one wants to be laughed at," Elise says with sadness.

I put my arms around her and ask for her forgiveness. She's right, I've been a jerk.

"Oh! So, she gets one and I don't?" Sibyl says, annoyed, "Why?"

Sambethe thanks Elise and asks her to give us a moment in private.

"Why does everyone call you Sibyl? All the other Oracles dropped that name. They all chose to go by one of the many, *many* names they were given. Why don't you?" I ask abruptly.

"Because it's *what. I. Am.* Unworthy of more. My only merit. A reminder to myself and to the other Oracles, so we never forget. What. We. Are." Sibyl says so close to my face I can feel her breath.

"Why are you so angry?" I say looking into her eyes.

"Do you *really* want to know my story, child?" she asks slowly and intently.

"I do," I answer without hesitation.

I watch her eyes turn white as snow.

"SIBYL, NO!" is the last thing I hear.

Chapter 22

SYBIL

"WHERE AM I?!" Eli shouts, looking around frightened. She doesn't see that I'm standing behind her.

"Jerusalem. But technically, you're inside a fragment of my memories," I answer while walking away from her. "Come."

I lead her down the hallway to the bedroom of my former palace. She scurries to catch up with me.

"When? Wait, what? How?" she asks, completely overwhelmed.

"One year before the birth of Christ," I say, opening the door to my old bedroom. "This was my former home. I was once referred to as the Queen of Jerusalem."

"Queen . . . huh. That explains your attitude," Eli snarls at me.

I think I will take more pleasure in this than I anticipated. We stand along the side of the bed and look down upon my sleeping body.

"Eli, what are you feeling right now?" I ask, knowing exactly what the emotions are. She focuses and says, "Anxiety. Disappointment. Sadness. No, anger. No not anger, rage! What is happening? Where is this coming from? I've never felt anything like this."

"From this moment on, your thoughts and emotions will not be your own. They will be synced with mine as if we are one person. It seems that is the only way to make you truly understand. You will not be able to talk or think for yourself until you've seen it *all*. Brace yourself, Elita."

I take her into my dream. It is impossible for me to show her God's true form; I will have to manipulate the form to look like a light. If I remember correctly, that's how humans like to portray God. It might shatter their damn brains to know God is both male *and* female. He is actually *They*. And more importantly, "They" are a single entity. I don't think humans have the ability to understand such concepts. Sad really, all these years and still no evolution of their brains.

I suppose the Trinity has made it easier for mortals to call God "Him," as opposed to "Anima Animus," which is the more accurate description.

C'est la vie . . . introduction day is sure to be fracturing.

This moment has stayed in the forefront of my mind, every day of my life. I have wondered so often what would have become of me if I'd responded differently? Not that I could have . . . but what if I had? Would I have been happy and free? Maybe free, but not happy. The faeries are my children now, they give me purpose. But even before them, all I've ever wanted to be is a mother. I wanted it more than anything else in my life. Even more so, I wanted to be the mother of Jesus, ever since we were foretold of His coming. That day, I opened my heart and soul to God and begged for this honor. I felt it in the core of my being, that this was my true calling.

June, 3 BC

Here we are, all twelve Oracles, summoned by God, standing around the light. They tell us that Jesus will be born in exactly 40 weeks. That we, the twelve Oracles who make up the North Star, will have a very important role to play. We will be guiding His human parents, as well as various kings, queens, angels and many other special visitors, to the location of his birth. My heart begins to race. I place my hands on my stomach but feel no child inside of me. God and I had spoken so many times, surely he will choose me. I cannot imagine another creature in the galaxy or on Earth, better suited for this task.

"When will the conception happen, my Lord?" I ask, as my heart beats out of my chest with excitement.

"It's already happened, my child," They say, "I have chosen a humble virgin from Jerusalem to be His mother."

"WHAT DO YOU MEAN!" I demand, as my mood quickly turns. "We had a deal. *I* am to be His mother!"

"There was never a deal," They respond pragmatically. "You requested it and I considered it. But I have chosen Mary; that is my final decision," They say.

"How could you!" I feel the blood boiling in my veins. "You betrayed me!"

"Sibyl, stay calm. *Please.* This is God's will, we *must* abide," Herophile says, while grabbing hold of my hand.

"NO! I will not stay calm!" I shout and pull my hand away.

"Sister, please!" Sambethe pleads with me.

"NO." I turn toward God. "You know I want this more than anything! I was born to be a mother! This was my *one* chance; how could you take this away from me?" I say, holding my chest with both of my hands because the pain is unbearable. It feels as though my heart has been ripped out of my body, the insides gutted, and my skin removed with a scorching blade.

"You were born to be an Oracle," They reply sternly.

"What does a poor, simple girl know about being the mother of *God*? She will suffer in a way that is unfathomable . . . this is too much of a burden for any human to bear! It is cruel." I try to understand the reasoning behind this treacherous act with my last second of clarity.

"She is more than a simple girl. I have chosen her for a reason," God says without emotion. "All humans, until the end of time, will be able to identify with the love and suffering of a human mother."

"I have served you my *entire life* without question. And let me tell you, there has been a lot to question. And I have NEVER asked for a single thing in return. All I want is a child . . . I *need* a child. Why would you take this away from me?"

"ENOUGH. You will have to find peace with my decision!" They exclaim, with ultimate force.

"Or else?" I scream back. "What are you going to do to me that can hurt more than this?"

"Sibyl, please stop!" Phyto pleads with me. She must be in my head.

"I'm not Their pawn." I can feel venom seeping through my teeth. For the first time I can feel a rage growing inside of me that I have never felt before.

"Do you defy me?" They demand.

"What happened to 'ask and you shall receive'? Or what about, 'help yourself and I will help you'? Is it all a farce?"

"Sibyl . . . " Phyto says with tears streaming down her face. She is shaking her head "no" in a slow motion, attempting to stop me from what she knows I will say next.

"I. REJECT. YOU." I say, staring right into God's eyes with

a fire burning so hot inside of me, that even Lucifer would be afraid to touch me. "I reject your *every request* from this day on. I reject your commands! I reject your prophecies! NEVER forget, this is on *your* head. It is *you* that rejected *me* first. You chose to deny me the only thing I've ever wanted and prayed for."

"I have never rejected you. I love you. Sibyl, this is for your own good," They say softly with pain in Their voice.

"YOU dare to say that *you* love *me*?! This is NOT love. This is unimaginable torture. A master and servant deal that you created to serve yourself." I cannot control the pain I feel inside. Even the tears coming down my face hurt. I am everything and anything but numb. "And why not? You are *God* after all . . . So, what's the status quo? Did you find that we *all* love you back the way you had hoped? Have you ever asked yourself, who are *you*, without our love? Maybe I'll tell the world your big dark secret . . . What if they knew that the world will end if they *all stop* believing in you. AND sacrificing for you. AND praying to you. AND starting bloody wars for you?! And that one right there," I point to Pythia, "has to clean up your mess! All because you didn't answer their simple prayers. Because you allowed disease to roam the earth, your people to starve, your women to be raped, your destitute children to be sold like cattle! You allow the good to come last, the wicked to prosper, the brave to die, the courageous to know defeat, and the innocent to suffer the most. And you have the guts to say that you love the crippled, the disabled, the poor and abused the most?! How could you? You knew what free will would bring, we all told you not to do it. But it became like a game, an experiment to you. And what will you do when they turn their back on you and worship false prophets because you can't answer their simplest prayers? You will *end the world*. What kind of God are you?!"

Everyone in the room is jolted by my words. They don't know

what to say or what to do. Even if they may have had the same thoughts a million times, no Original Creature has ever attempted to say such blasphemous things and turn their back on God.

I am the first, but I will not be the last.

*　　　*　　　*

I spend the next nine months roaming the world, visiting all the places I'd only ever dreamt of seeing. I freed myself from the chains that had been placed on me all those years ago. I would no longer help the priests, priestesses, or leaders of Jerusalem with my prophecies. I belong only to myself; property and slave to no one. I ignored every attempt that God made to reach out to me. I would not let my sisters enter my dreams or my thoughts. Not because I was afraid that they could influence me in any way, but because I knew it was their only way of tracking my whereabouts. I wanted to be left alone. Wanted to be free. I needed time. I had to figure out who I was, if I was no longer an Oracle of God.

In each city and town I went to, total strangers looked kindly upon me. They must have taken pity when they saw an abandoned woman traveling alone. I found the poorest to be the most generous. They allowed me into their homes, offered me food, water, and a safe place to sleep. I knew I wouldn't ever be able to stop seeing the future, how it shifts and the several outcomes any choice can bring. So, to repay their compassion, I used my abilities as a seer to provide them information and knowledge for a better life. I showed them which were the right decisions, suggested better ways to serve their communities, and for some, I removed their pain and suffering. I told them about new resources to provide for their families. For many, it prevented them from starving and becoming homeless. Over the course of those months, I saw how much peace and joy my words gave the people. The true gift was seeing their situations improve. With each deed, I felt a little less pain. It was my only comfort.

March, 2 BC

I am walking in the shopping market of Cairo, smelling its many spices and looking at the beautiful garments. From the corner of my eye I see a small child fall and scrape his knee. He cries as he pushes the skin together, trying to get the small pebbles out of his wound. I look around for his parents but see no one coming to his aid. I walk over and introduce myself to him. I can't make out anything he's saying in between his sobs. I pull out an ointment from my bag. It's only my lip balm, but I tell him it's medicine. I put it on his wound and place my hand over it. After a moment, I lift it up and his wound is healed. It's a little trick I've learned to do; if people were to believe I am a healer, I'd never have a day of peace. So, I learned to tell them it's a special medication I brought from Jerusalem. And somehow, they believe.

The little boy throws his arms around me and thanks me for my kindness. He gets up and grabs me by the hand and pulls me away from the market. He tells me he would like me to meet his parents and stay for lunch. I follow him into a small home in an alley behind the market. He pushes the door open and I follow in, and we both freeze in our tracks. He hides behind me. I can feel his little body shaking against my leg.

"What are you doing here?" I say, infuriated by the visit. All the peace I've been trying to feel goes out the door in a second.

Sambethe tells the little boy not to be afraid; she is a friend of his parents. They are waiting for him upstairs, in his grandparents' house for lunch. He bolts out the door and up the stairs. I'm sure she designed that poor boy's fall on purpose just to lure me in here. Her trickery knows no bounds.

"How did you find me?" I ask, as all eleven Oracles crowd around me.

"I must say you've done an excellent job at hiding from us sister. But you know that," she points up, "always knows everyone's coordinates," Phemonoe says, smiling. I can tell by the look in her eyes that she misses me. In all the years of our existence, we have never been apart this long.

"I'm certain I've made my position clear," I answer back, squinting as I try to understand the motive for their visit.

"No games, ladies," Cassandra says, getting to the point. "We are here to take you back to Jerusalem with us. Together we are the North Star, and we have been assigned to the most important task. Ever."

"Or have you conveniently forgotten the event?" Albunea snaps. I can see she's angry with me.

"I have not. I can see you have no qualms about adding salt to my wound," I snap back, shooting a dirty look around the room at them all. "The North Star shines every night without us being together. As long as we are alive it will shine! What is the point of this intrusion?"

"We shine our brightest and guide most efficiently when we're together. You know that," Pythia says calmly.

"Do it without me. So what if you're a little dimmer . . . Why do you need me to do this? I certainly won't do it for God," I reply coldly.

"What about the child you once called yours? Will you do it for Him, Sibyl?" Carmentis pleads with her sweet voice. She has always been the one I can never stay angry with.

"Please, I beg you, if you have any love for me. Do not ask me to do the *one* thing that is impossible for me," I beg Carmentis.

"I'm afraid you don't have a choice this time." I hear Hellespontine's voice behind me.

And all goes black.

*   *   *

I wake up in my old bedroom in Jerusalem feeling very dehydrated. I sit up and Carmentis hands me a glass of water. It feels like I never left. I see Hellespontine and Herophile lounging around, writing and reading prophecies.

"What did she do to me?" I ask Carmentis, as I take a drink of water. It tastes extremely bitter; it must be one of her remedies.

"Finish the glass, it will help you to feel better," she replies quietly, not answering my question.

Hellespontine and Herophile notice I have woken up and join Carmentis and I on the bed.

"I see you ladies have made yourselves at home," I say, clearing my throat.

"This palace is incredible, Sibyl! Sure beats the caves we've been living in. I can't believe you chose to leave this place!" Herophile says, jumping naked on my bed.

"Please, for the hundredth time, put some clothes on!" Hellespontine says closing her eyes.

"You're just jealous!" Herophile says, laughing as she jumps off the bed and looks around for a robe. She chooses the one made of the best silk. It is blue-silver, with hand-painted birds and flowers on it.

"I can see you've helped yourself to my wardrobe too." I notice they are all wearing my clothes. I imagine the other eight are too.

"Oh yes!" Carmentis says joyfully. "You have the finest garments. We have never seen such beautiful things. I hope you don't mind. We wanted to ask, but you were sleeping."

"Yes, I suppose I'm lucky you didn't poison me!" I say, rubbing my forehead. "How did you transport me on such a long journey, unconscious?"

"Private accommodations," Hellespontine says, pointing up.

I roll my eyes. Figures.

"So, what are the big plans? How long do I have to be tortured here?" I ask reluctantly.

"Two weeks. Our job starts tonight. The bir—" Herophile stops herself,

"The event itself takes place one week from tonight. But there will be many who will follow the second week. Something about three kings."

"Great, I'm stuck with all of you for three weeks. Just wonderful," I say sarcastically.

"What did we do to you? Why are you so angry with us too?" Hellespontine asks, annoyed.

"It's not what you did. It's what you *didn't* do," I lay back down, turning away from them.

*　　　*　　　*

The girls and I spend the week talking, reminiscing about the past, gossiping about the future, laughing, writing, painting, singing, and playing music. It is very rare that we are all together physically. We mostly visit each other in our dreams or communicate through letters. The only time we are together is when a monumental global event occurs, and the North Star is required to shine at its brightest. The girls enjoy every indulgence the palace has to give. Many venture into town, talk to the locals, and explore the magical city that is filled with so much history. I can't blame them, it really is so beautiful. We see the world in our dreams and through our visions. But traveling the world freely has not been a privilege we have been given.

Most of the time we are isolated in our stationed city. We are required to prophesize God's words and requests day after day for millennia, sometimes for more than a hundred thousand millennia. It can be grinding and exhausting, especially during times when monstrous priests and dictators have abused us. They have done everything from drugging us, to chaining us to walls like dogs, until they have heard what they want. They call it "motivation." Herophile has had it the worst of us all. Because of her beauty, she is sought after the most. Endless men have hunted her down like prey. And one day not so long ago, the priests of the old gods trapped her. They chained her to a wall in the deep caves of Naples for 150 years. Wealthy men and leaders came from all over the world to have their prophecies read by her.

She was drugged every single day by the priests in order to "expand her thinking." The drugs had a strange effect on her, they made her speak in the original language of the world to tell the prophecies. But the priests couldn't care less about what she was really saying, they just wanted it for show. They claimed to be her interpreters but could not understand one word of it. It was their way of manipulating the powerful, and of getting them to do whatever the old gods wanted. A captured Oracle at their disposal was not something any of these people could pass up. And for those who paid a hefty sum, she would be forced to connect with those in the Underworld, so they could once again see and speak to their beloveds who'd passed on. But every day and night we heard her cries. To see and feel everything she was put through, was more than any of us could bear. And to not be able to do anything to save her was worse. We were helpless and not permitted to intervene. So, we visited her every night in our dreams to remind her that she was not alone. It was all we could do to give her some comfort. In true form, when God intervened to release Herophile, it was only to be indebted to Them. We knew all of our freedom would eventually be granted after the death of Christ, but we also saw at what great cost. And we feared it would be our demise.

*   *   *

Today is the birth of Jesus. It's all been bittersweet; I love being with my sisters but I hate why I am here. Tonight, and the rest of the coming weeks, will not be easy for me. I just want it to be over. There is anxiousness and excitement in the air. Everyone is pacing around the palace trying to find a little distraction, because it's going to be a long day. We know He will be born at night and in a stable, per Phyto's prophecy.

9 pm.

"Really Phyto, how much longer now! I don't think I can take much more of this!" Helrea says, nearly rubbing her knuckles to the bone.

"It's any moment now. Why don't we gather round and pray for Mary's labor," Phyto says, calling everyone into a circle.

I refuse. I continue to sit in my lounge chair looking out the window while drinking Julia's calming tonic. The anxiety in my chest feels like it might do me in permanently.

I'm not quite sure exactly how much time has gone by, when a strange sensation enters our bodies. I drop the glass I'm holding in my hand. Our heads tilt to Heaven and our eyes fill with white snow. Our bodies transport to witness His birth.

The stable is humble and small. I am in dismay that no one was gracious enough to help a pregnant woman. What deplorable people. I look at Mary and Joseph who are so young and so lovely, they are almost children themselves. My heart goes out to them, to be mortal and to deal with such complexities.

Carmentis looks around and asks if there is anyone here to help her deliver. Hellespontine, eyes open wide, points out that there have just been twelve women sent here to do it. Carmentis blushes, looking embarrassed for not realizing such an obvious fact. The girls roll up their sleeves and walk over to the young couple. I stay back.

"I see that you are still acting like a spoiled child," I hear Gabriel's voice say behind me.

"Ah, Gabriel . . . when did God's most conceited angel arrive?" I reply sarcastically.

"I've been here all day. Watching. Protecting," he says, smiling.

"And a stable is really the best you could do? You really are so cheap!" I roll my eyes at him.

"What? It was free," he says, shrugging his shoulders.

"You're gross, get away from me. Go blow your trumpet or whatever you're here to do!" I say, flicking my wrist at him to leave.

He gently takes hold of my hand and slowly walks me towards them.

"Gabriel, do you know what they will call us in history?" I ask him, as we walk. "Nothing. The ones who served as her midwives will be left out of this story completely. But do you know who will be remembered? The three kings, the shepherd, even the damn animals. But not us . . . not a single word. *We* are invisible, unworthy of recognition. Can you believe that? The kings won't even be here for nearly another week. No one will. But I guess that doesn't matter either." I pause to wipe the one tear that escapes my eye. "Don't worry your silly little ego, Angel Gabriel; you will be recorded in history too."

"Sibyl, I'm sorry, you're right. But I beg of you, don't miss this," he says softly, leaving me at the edge of the stable.

I see him walk over to Joseph to comfort him, and the girls are working hard to make Mary as comfortable as possible and prepare her for the final pushes. As I stand there watching this all happen, I examine her face. There's something about her that feels so familiar to me, something about her that I recognize.

I don't even know if that's possible because I've never seen her before. I just can't put my finger on it.

An hour later Carmentis delivers Him. She is the most experienced of us all to do this. His birth is the most beautiful and magical thing I've ever seen, and surely will ever see. I've experienced many births, but none so miraculous. I wonder if every mother feels that way about the birth of their own child?

We fall to our knees at His arrival. I am overcome by emotion. I'd never let Gabriel know it, but he was right. There are tears of joy all around. I've never seen my sisters so happy. There is still a part of me that feels jealousy and sadness. But looking upon His face, even I recognize that all that matters is that He is here. Everyone takes a turn holding him and fussing over every finger and toe. I remain withdrawn on my knees with my head down, trying to control my own selfish emotions.

"Sibyl," I hear a gentle voice say, "Come and hold Him."

I lift my head up. It's Mary, she's calling me over.

"You're the only one who hasn't held him yet. It's important to me that he is blessed by each one of you," she continues on.

I see my sisters smiling at me in favor of it.

"Are you sure?" I ask.

"Yes, please," she replies, and holds Him out to me.

I walk over to her and she places Him in my arms. I've never seen anything so perfect. He smells like heaven and feels like sunshine. I cry from joy; I can feel His love and what that love will do for the world. I smile at Him and He smiles back. He has olive-tone skin, dark hair, and brown eyes with already so much depth, that they pierce right through me. I run my hand through his delicate hair, and it feels like the hair of a lamb. That seems both cruel and appropriate, because the world will one day slaughter him like one, as they do with all things that are truly innocent. I don't know if I can ever forgive God for not making

Him my son. But I will pledge my life to protecting His. He *is* magic.

I slowly hand Him back to Mary. I wish I could keep Him in my arms forever. I would give anything to hear Him call me mother . . . I place Him in her arms and look deeply into her eyes. A jolt tears through me like lightening. I get up quickly and walk away; I need to get out of here.

"Sibyl! Sibyl!" Gabriel shouts, as he reaches for my arm.

"Don't touch me!" I shout, pulling my arm away. "I know who she is, Gabriel! God lied to me AGAIN! Did you know?!"

"God never lied to you, Sibyl. They told you They had Their reasons. Mary doesn't know—" he begins to explain, but I shut him down.

"Don't you think I know that? I saw it in her eyes! This is un-forgivable Gabriel, and you know it! You tell God, the next move is mine," I say, seething through my words.

"Sibyl, don't do this. There are severe consequences. YOU. WILL. LOSE," Gabriel says, grabbing my shoulders and look-ing into my eyes, trying to show me something, but I pull away.

"I need to be alone."

I run and run until I reach the palace. With every step, I feel the rage inside me grow. It gets stronger and deeper. It's com-ing from a place inside of me I didn't even know existed. I walk into my library and begin tearing and burning pages and pag-es of prophesies, documents and books. I break every item and piece of furniture in the room. And when that doesn't make me feel better, I destroy the next room, and the next, and the next. My mind is foggy, I can't think anymore. I just feel. I want to stop feeling. I want to be numb but the rage multiplies with each thing I destroy. It's like a hunger in the pit of my stomach that I can't fill.

I hear a voice behind me scream my name; it's Pythia. I tell her not to come near me. She tells me to calm down, but that only makes me angrier. I begin to throw anything in my way at her.

"Who do you think you are to tell me to calm down?" I scream.

"Sibyl I'm sorry. I'm *so* sorry!" she responds, trying to duck the things flying at her head.

"But YOU KNEW! You were all closer to her before I was. You SAW it in her eyes, and you said nothing! And like fools you encouraged me to get close to her!" I say, throwing a dagger.

"Oracle, have you LOST your mind?!" Sambethe exclaims, ducking behind Pythia.

"ME?? WHY YES, I HAVE!!!" I laugh, throwing another dagger.

"Sibyl, I swear it to you on my dragons. We did not know! We saw it only through your eyes, when you looked into hers. We all found out at the same time. PLEASE stop throwing daggers at me!"

"How about a sword?!" I smile and swing at them. Even if I can't kill them, it feels good to try.

Phemonoe puts her arm around my neck from behind me and tells me to put down the sword slowly. I drop it on her foot and break free of her arm lock. I step away and the pain sets in again. Tears come slowly streaming down.

"They reincarnated her again! How could God do that to me?" I can't feel my legs anymore and drop to the ground. Saying it out loud makes it real. "Mary has no idea. She just thinks she's a normal girl, that can give b-birth to God's son . . . "

Phemonoe sits next to me.

"Well, you always said it would be impossible for a mortal soul," she says, pushing my hair aside.

"How does that bitch always manage?" Pythia says, shaking her head.

"That 'B' is now the mother of Jesus, so how about we don't

call her that anymore?" Sambethe states abruptly.

"NO! She's right! The Egyptians called her Hathor. The Greeks, Aphrodite. The Romans, Venus. And now the Christians will call her Madonna. How does she do it? How does she always manage to reinvent herself?!" I shout.

"Because she IS Love. And only Love can be the mother of Christ. Only Love is forever," Sambethe says gently. "You know this Sibyl. I don't know how any of us didn't *see* it."

"And what are we? Trash? Disposable? Unworthy of our own children?!" I cry out uncontrollably through my pain. "So, we will ALL just become a footnote in history! Is that right! Is that what you *all* want? The greatest sorcerer and alchemist whose powers can match Theirs, was born today. And you're telling me you are okay with Him not coming from one of us?! He will manifest the greatest magic the world has ever seen. Those stupid Ignis will call his work "miracles," but it doesn't change what it is—what He is—pure magic . . . After all our loyalty, servitude, and being used and abused day after day by humans, this is what we get! I *know* you have *seen*, what *I've* seen, you dumb cunts! We will be forgotten . . . they won't know who we are or what we've done! They won't even know how to pronounce our fucking names! There won't be ONE single book written about us . . . actually, there won't even be a full page in any book about us . . . being his mother was our one chance to *not* be a lost sentence in their stories! It was our *only* chance!!! And I, more than anything . . . I desperately want to be a mother . . . is it really so much to ask for?!!"

I start screaming again through the uncontrollable sobbing of my tears, and this time the anguish finally tears me apart. The pain eviscerates my desire to exist. I have lost my dignity, my soul, and my God.

My mind goes dark—I feel it detach from the rest of me. I no longer have control.

I only have brief moments of clarity after that. And in one of these moments I recognize that I'm locked up in my palace's jail cell. I shake all day, toss and turn at night, and rock back and forth to soothe myself. I can't eat or drink. All I can do is recall random prophecies all day long. I say them out loud but I don't know to who. I can't remember if anyone has come to see me. I don't know what day it is. My scalp feels itchy and my eyes hurt. A lady comes to see me—who is she? She tells me to smell the pretty flower, and I do.

I wake up with a horrible headache. All the girls are standing over me.

"What happened?" I ask, feeling a wicked hunger in my stomach and in desperate need of water.

"Thank goodness it worked!" Carmentis says elated. "Well, you went into short term psychosis."

"How many days have I been down here?" I ask.

"Five days, Oracle," Pythia says, helping me to sit up. "I'm sorry we had to do that, but we had no other option. You were out of control."

"I came down here every day to try to make you drink the cure, but you would just knock it out of my hands or spit it up. So, this morning I had to poison you with Belladonna and force-feed the liquid down your throat," Carmentis says nonchalantly.

"Did you really have to poison me?" I ask, rubbing my temples.

"Yes, it was the only way to knock you out. Nothing else we tried worked," Carmentis says shrugging her shoulders. "Belladonna gives a brutal hangover, sorry about that."

"Oh, I see. Well, thank you. I guess," I say with a half-smile. Carmentis winks at me.

They help me get upstairs where there's a running bath waiting for me. I soak in it until my body becomes a prune. I don't think I've ever been so dirty. After the bath, we sit together and have lunch. No one brings up the elephant in the room. I'm grateful because I don't think I can deal with it. The fire I felt the other day is still sitting very strongly inside of me. All I want to do is eat and sleep for the next few days. And that's exactly what I do. While I recover, the girls continue to put my house back together and do their best to restore the things I'd broken. They show me more love and kindness than I deserve.

After nearly a month passes, it is time for the girls to go back to their homes. I will miss them. The last two to leave are Herophile and Pythia. Herophile tells me that she is on her way to visit the Great Stone at Lake Pilate. She tells me that it's time to re-center herself and figure out the next phase of her life. She pleads with me to join her. The idea sounds quite nice, it might be exactly what I need. The next day, the three of us set out on our journey. I decide to take Malak with me because she is my best and strongest Uniequus. Pythia travels with us until it is time for Herophile and I to cross the ocean. She sets her horse free and completes the rest of her journey back to Greece as a dragon. It's always her preference, she only traveled by horse to keep us company.

The rest of our voyage is pleasant and we make it to Italy with great timing. On our way to Lake Pilate we stop at a small town called Colfiorito. Herophile says Gabriel is in town on a mission and it would be rude of us not to stop just for a moment. I reluctantly agree; I haven't seen him since that night. We meet him at the traveler's stop. He greets me as if nothing happened and makes no mention of it. I'm grateful for it, but I can't help but feel animosity towards him. The sooner I can get away from him, the better. No such luck. He insists on showing us a short cut to the lake, by going through the Apennine Mountain range. I do my best to discourage him, but Herophile insists he be our guide.

Halfway up the mountain, Malak becomes restless. Since we have never connected, I don't understand what she wants. A Uniequus can only connect with the purest of souls. I try to stop for water and food, but nothing seems to settle her. Gabriel suggests we stop to rest behind an abandoned temple in the forest for a while. I agree, it might be just what Malak needs. He finds a plush green area on the hillside of the mountain. I go to pick fresh blackberries near a great big boulder. I notice a rock in the shape of a heart within the boulder itself. I point it out to the others. How peculiar, a rock within a rock. Something in the shape of a thing so soft, made of the hardest texture. I ask them what they think it means, they say they don't know. Gabriel asks me if it does anything. I touch it and try moving it around. Suddenly the boulder opens as if it had a door. Malak begins to kick her front legs up. I calm her and hold her by the reigns.

"What is this?" I ask.

"Why don't we go in and look around," Gabriel suggests.

Malak is being stubborn and pulling away. I become frustrated with her and force her inside with me. In that moment I realize that Gabriel and Herophile haven't followed me in.

"Aren't you coming?" I ask.

"No Sibyl." Herophile's face is very serious but she avoids eye contact.

"What is this?" I try to exit. But I cannot, I am blocked in. I start pounding on an invisible wall, demanding they let me out.

In a wide swoop, I see Pythia flying towards the hillside. Within seconds of landing she also demands to know what's going on. Gabriel tells her everyone will soon understand. She begins to choke him. Herophile screams at her to stop, reminding her of the consequence of killing an angel. Pythia reluctantly backs down.

"Sibyl, I, we . . . none of us except for this *traitor* knows what's going on! I SWEAR IT!" Pythia says, pulling Herophile by the hair. "But I've had a horrible feeling about this since she first suggested it in Jerusalem. When did this selfish trout ever care about anyone but herself!"

"Pythia PLEASE get me out! I'm scared! What is happening!" I cry out.

The invisible wall starts to darken.

"Sibyl, I'm going to find a way to get you out if it's the last thing I do! I'll tell everyone—" but her voice fades as the wall grows darker. I see her shadow pounding on it until the wall is solid rock, and I am engulfed in darkness.

*   *   *

A dim light appears as a wall sconce lights up with flame. I call out to see if anyone is here. No one answers. Malak stands close to me, I can hear her heartbeat, she is afraid too. We walk in a little further, and with each step a new sconce lights up. When we reach the end of the corridor, we find another door. I push it open. I hear running water.

The moment we step into the space, all the wall sconces along the large oval room light up one after the other, until they are all completely lit. We find ourselves standing in a gray, cold, misty cave with a stream running through the center. There is no natural light, no other doors and no windows. I am startled by a sound behind me and turn around to see what it is.

"I was wondering when you'd get here." I don't know if I feel relieved or infuriated. "Where am I?"

"That should be obvious Sibyl, you're in a cave in the middle of nowhere," my Maker says to me.

"Why? What kind of game is this?"

"This is no game and it's time you take this seriously. I will no longer allow you to hurt yourself, or me," God says. "I see every-thing in your mind, and I do not trust you. I can see it's your life's mission to destroy me. And I can see that you will do everything in your power to stop my son's destiny. You defied me Sibyl, and because you have chosen to continue to do so, this will be your life punishment."

"I don't understand what you're saying," I say shaking my head, "Because I wanted to be Jesus' mother? Because I wanted more for him? And for myself! Because I don't want to follow all your dreadful rules?"

"There's not following rules. And then there's changing peo-ple's destiny, disobeying, mocking and revolting against me. I will not have it!" They say in an angry tone.

"Yes . . . how dare I . . . How long am I to be here?"

"You still don't understand, do you? I banish you *here* for the rest of existence. You will sit in solitude to reflect on your sins until Judgement Day. Do you understand now?" I can see by Their eyes that They are serious.

"You wouldn't do that to me! You can't be that cruel. How will I survive without food and daylight? This cave is so small. How am I to live? How will Malak survive? Please I beg of you, release her—she's done no wrong! Do not do this to us!!!" I kneel and beg at God's feet.

"Now you beg for mercy? It's too late, my decision is final. I will not have you interrupting my plans."

"PLEASE!!! NO!!! DO NOT LEAVE ME HERE!!!"

"I will send food, but nothing more."

"NO PLEASE, PLEASE, I WILL DO ANYTHING. I SWEAR IT! I PROMISE!"

"Find your redemption." These are the last words I hear.

It's too late, God is gone. All that is left in the room is Malak and me. If my mind had gone mad before, it is sure to go mad again. I curl up in a ball and cry myself to sleep.

I don't know how many days I lay there freezing before I get up. Malak won't come near me. She's very angry with me. I do not blame her, but I have nothing to comfort her with. I have never felt so alone. I can no longer hear or see my sisters in my dreams. God has blocked us from having any communication. When I close my eyes, all I see are prophecies and people I can no longer help.

Each morning and every night the current brings in two leaves. One with berries or some kind of fruit for me, and the other, food for Malak. We drink the fresh water from the stream. By its taste I can tell it's coming in from Lake Pilate. Over time, I accumulate enough leaves to make beds for Malak and me, so we don't have to sleep on the hard floor anymore. I save the seeds from the fruit that arrives and plant them in the ground. I wait months and months for something to blossom, but there is nothing. No life will grow in this place. In time, fish begin to swim through our stream. I close my eyes and place my hand in the water when they travel through the cave. By doing this I am able to see their journey and a bit of the outside world. I put my other hand on Malak so she can see it too. Now and again I manage to catch one with my hands and cook it over the fire. I feel guilty doing this, because they are my only visitors. Malak receives plenty of hay and treats. But I often go hungry, I am rarely sent a slice of bread. Most of the food I receive is seasonal fruit or some kind of nut. It has become my indication of what time of the year it is. Each time something different arrives, I take a stone and mark the cave wall with a line. It is my only form of a calendar.

15 AD

The darkness weighs heavy on us. It's been fifteen years without the sun, the moon, and stars. Fifteen years in misery and cold. I am very depressed, nearly emaciated. Malak is healthy and strong. We mostly stay in separate rooms now, I in the narrow front corridor where we first entered, while she is in the larger oval cave, where she can run laps and stretch her legs daily. She is angrier with me than ever and offers no affection. I pray for death each day. I cannot spend another moment here. Malak and I have tried every prayer, spell, and ounce of magic we know. Nothing works. Visions and information come in, but nothing penetrates out of these walls. That gives me an idea.

I kneel over the stream with a sharp stone over my wrist. Malak looks at me and does something I'd never imagined she would; she gives me her approval. I cut my wrists open and bleed into the stream until I am barely conscious.

"That's a good parlor trick, Sibyl," a man's voice says to me.

He sits me up by placing my back against his chest. He then places his thumbs on my wounds to heal them. Little by little I regain consciousness.

"Lucifer!" I turn to embrace him.

"You must be really desperate if you're happy to see me," he says, smiling his beautiful smile.

I laugh as tears come down my face. I haven't been touched for so long that even the devil will do.

"You came," I say, touching his face in disbelief.

"Oracle blood is like heroin to me; how could I resist you?" he replies. "Why do you call upon me, Sibyl?"

"We can't be here anymore, I am begging you, *please* take us to the Underworld. I'll do anything, I just can't take this anymore.

I can't live, I can't die. I-I . . . "

"I watched as you tried to commit suicide over and over again. I never imagined seeing you in such a state," he says, looking sadly at my condition. "You have always been the most beautiful to me."

"Then you will take us?" I ask pleading.

"I want nothing more than to have the first Oracle and the first Uniequus to run the Underworld with. Surely that would make me king!" he pauses enjoying the idea. "Let me tell you my darling, you have wreaked havoc in the Asbgahs and on Earth. You have started a firestorm of rebellion! And you know, there's nothing I quite love more than rebels against God. There are hundreds maybe *thousands* singing your name in glory. And well, I'm a glutton for praise—"

"What?" I stand up and cut off his words. I need to look at him better to understand his words more clearly. "Are they condemned too?" I ask, surprised to hear such news.

"Umm . . . that's the thing . . . they are not. Now, before you get upset, remember that the uprising happened so fast, there was really no way to control it. You made history, darling! I, myself, got drunker than a sailor on his birthday, when I heard what you said—what a true poet. Saying all the things so many of us have always wanted to say. And you, you had the guts to say it to *Their* face. Brava . . . "

He caresses my face.

"Are you serious?" I ask, shaking my head. "I never wanted that. I never wanted others to turn on Them. That was never my intention. I-I just wanted to be Jesus' mother."

"Yes, but instead They chose Lust or Love; or whichever one mothered the little brat," he says, as he flicks his wrist.

"Lucifer, he's your brother. Don't speak that way," I scold him.

"Logistics." He shrugs his shoulders. "Yes, I know, you adore the bugger and swore your undivided love to him. Which leads me to the answer to your question. No, I can't take you."

"But why!" I ask, I can feel the anger rising again.

"Because, you may have rejected God, but then you swore allegiance to Jesus. And hello, they are the same person. So once again, and may I add for the second time, *you sold your soul to God*, and really that is your only crime. But now my precious, even I don't want you."

"You bastard!!!" I scream.

"See you on Judgement Day, darling." Lucifer blows me a kiss and disappears.

I feel like I'm about to implode. I begin screaming at the top of my lungs like a hyena. The anger is rising inside me, I'm losing all self-control. How dare he!

I'm sick of these men who pretend to know my heart or what's good for me. But all they want is to control me. I can feel my nails digging into my skin and my fists get tighter and tighter.

"I HATE YOU BOTH!" And with these words the ground under me begins to shake. It grows stronger with every ounce of loathing I feel in my heart.

SNAP! Dirt crumbles onto my head from the ceiling.

I look up. I see a small crack in the ceiling of the cave. A small ray of the moonlight shines in. I can feel the crystal energy from the moon absorbing into my skin. I look straight into it and can just barely see the North Star. This is the first ounce of hope I feel in years. Hope is the worst emotion an abandoned person can feel.

The next morning, we wake up to a small ray of sunshine beaming in. Malak and I feel it will blind us—it's been so long. We lay in that small sliver of sunlight all day, soaking it in. The day after, to our surprise, we wake up to plants growing all around us. All the seeds I had planted began blossoming. I guess all they needed was a little sun to shine in. I notice a different kind of plant growing in the corner. I touch and smell its leaves to try to identify it. Water fills my eyes. It is not just a plant, it is my favorite flower—calla lily. This must be a gift from my sisters, they must have felt me somehow. I am sure they will come to help us soon.

33 AD

It's been eighteen years since my visit from Lucifer, and no one else has come. My only distraction has been the beautiful plants, flowers, vegetables and fruit trees that I've been growing all these years. Malak has her days—on some she shows me kindness and mercy, while other days, she avoids me completely. She resents me for putting her in a position to make a deal with the devil. Because of it, her soul is now tainted and she will never be the same. This also means that, because both our souls are tainted, we can now connect and speak, but she refuses. She would rather sit in silence all her life than speak to me. We'll see if she still feels that way in a millennium.

I am washing my hands in the river and hear a voice that gives me shivers to my core. It is God, and suddenly I feel myself transported to Jerusalem. As the fog lifts from my eyes, I am standing in an old temple. There I am finally reconnected with my sisters. We hold each other tightly and become overwhelmed with emotion. They tell me that they have come looking for me a million times, and could not find a way in. I can see that they are genuine. They say they have tried everything in their power to connect with me, but are blocked each time. I know this is true, because it has been the same for me. The only thing that distracts me from their beautiful faces is a *very* human and severely aged Herophile, hiding in the corner.

I lunge at her while screaming obscenities about her betrayal.

It takes four of them to get me off her. They place us in separate areas of the room, but I cannot take my eyes off her, fantasizing about choking her while she takes her last breath. Herophile falls to her knees and rocks back and forth, with her head down, crying and begging me for my forgiveness. I am surprised at this reaction. They explain to me that although I cannot see them, they can see and feel everything I've been through. It is God's way of reminding them of their fate should they choose to take the same path as I did. I feel embarrassed and look away.

"STOP IT! You have nothing to be ashamed of. It is us that should feel shame! With all the knowledge and power we have obtained over the years, we could not find a way to save you. I'm so sorry Sibyl," Pythia says, holding my hands, "That day haunts me every day of my life. I see it over and over again in my mind . . . watching you disappear behind that boulder. I . . . "

"It's true. She shares the memory with us every day, so we never forget to stop looking for a way in," Carmentis says, placing her small hand over both of ours.

"T-thank you," I say softly, holding back my emotions.

"Aren't you going to ask about what happened to our very own Judas?" Hellespontine asks, sarcastically.

"Who's Judas?" I ask.

"You will find out the day after tomorrow," Hellespontine replies.

"You're the one that foretold His crucifixion Hellespontine, is that why we are here? Has the time really come?"

"It has," she says, clearing her throat.

"I was able to see him grow up, you know . . . it has been my only peace. Even in that brazen cave, it brought me joy to watch him learn his craft, perform magic, stand up for injustices, feed the poor, help the sick and, well, a million other things. He is so brave, and *so* good. I love Him more every day," I say, looking down.

"God actually lets you see that? How inconceivable!" Albunea shouts.

"Actually, it was my only joy." I pause, reflecting on those visions for a moment. "Yes, I see everything that is happening in the world, I see it changing."

The girls look away in sorrow.

"Herophile, would you like to tell Sibyl what happened to you on your way back to Cumae from Colfiorito, or shall I?"

Hellespontine asks her.

Herophile looks out the window and directs Hellespontine to tell the story.

Hellespontine tells me that upon leaving me in the cave, Herophile felt proud of herself for being able to outsmart me, and deliver on God's request. She stopped by the travel station we had just been to a few hours earlier, to have a celebratory drink.

I feel my blood start to boil.

There, Herophile encountered an old friend, Gaia the sorceress. She bragged to her about what she'd done. Gaia said she should be rewarded for such an act, so she granted her a wish. Herophile made a wish to live for 700 years as a human. But she made a fatal mistake; she did not ask for eternal beauty, she forgot that humans age. Gaia transformed Herophile into a young, eighteen-year-old woman, and much to her surprise she began aging from that day forth. So here she is now at nearly fifty-one, alone and in hiding for another 667 years.

"I don't think she got half of what she deserves," Cassandra snaps.

"I agree," Herophile replies, looking back at me.

I feel no commiseration for her, only spite and repulsion.

"I hear there are others that have made the same rebellious decisions as I. And yet they roam free. Why?" I ask.

"Because they don't know all of God's secrets, Sibyl," Cassandra says,

"And we all know you are Their favorite, and for that reason your punishment is the most severe."

"Was. I *was* God's favorite, but even that is subjective." I sigh. "His favorite . . . it makes me laugh, really. Would you put *your* favorite child in darkness until the end of time?"

"Possibly, yes," Cassandra answers. "They are allowing Their only son to be murdered on a cross. So, definitely yes."

"The next seven days will be long and difficult. We must brace ourselves," Victoria says, shifting the subject. "We have each been assigned a room here in the temple and will not be allowed to leave. We must rest at night, because the days will be filled with visions and prayer. This is our last and final act as Oracles until Judgement Day."

"And who will I pray *to*?" I ask her.

"Just pray *for* Jesus, don't trouble yourself with who you are praying *to*. Okay?" Hellespontine says with empathy. I nod in agreement.

We do just that. Each day we pray morning, noon, and night—but can hardly eat or sleep. Hellespontine's visions are each coming true one by one. Watching them unfold in the exact moment that it happens is more than any of us are capable of dealing with. We feel, see and experience EVERYTHING Jesus does the entire week. And on the day of His death, we feel the weight of the cross. We hear all the mockery. Feel every fall, every whip lashing, every nail hammered into his body and every cut that makes him bleed. And through it all, I love Him more, and still wish with everything inside of me that I was His mother. I wish I could walk alongside Him to give Him courage and hold Him as they bring Him down from the cross. There is nothing in this life or the next that will ever make me change my mind or ask for forgiveness for these desires.

Somewhere in the back of my mind I can't help but think about Their words . . . And maybe, just maybe, They had a point. I would have interfered. I would have not allowed for such a destiny to unfold for my son. Not even for the benefit of human salvation.

We each do our part as we promised, no matter how hard or painful. On the day of Ascension, we say our goodbyes. Even though I know I will see my sisters again at the end of time, it still feels like forever. They have all been given their freedom to go out to do all the things we once dreamed of. They tell me that they will teach many how to become *seers*, so those people can help others in the world. They are determined to create a legacy of those with the "gift." I do not feel envious of their freedom; with the death of Jesus I feel as if I have nothing to live for. I don't care to travel or teach or anything else. He was my only purpose. Now even the darkness can have me.

Before I am transported back, I thank my sisters for the calla lilies. I tell them how much comfort they are to me. They have no idea what I am talking about. But, if it isn't them, then it can only be from one other . . .

I arrive back to the dark cave. I don't bother to look or speak to Malak and walk straight over to the calla lilies. They have doubled in size in my absence. On one of the flowers I see a note hanging. I recognize the ancient language, it's from God:

> *I hope today you have understood*
> *my reason for the choice I made.*
> *I love you infinitely regardless*
> *of your loathing towards me.*
> *Until we meet again.*

I crush the note and stomp on it. I pull out every lily from the root until every flower is destroyed. And I cry and I cry and I cry, until I fall to the ground with my palms down. I feel a rumble, it grows louder and stronger as does the pain in my chest. I begin screaming until the earth shakes so hard, the small crack in the ceiling above us breaks wide open. I run over to Malak, to move her away from the downpour of the ceiling and wall. After a few minutes, the earth stops shaking and we find ourselves standing under the great big sky.

I let out a scream as hard as I can, I can't help but laugh and cry from joy. I walk over to where the edge of the cave meets unchartered land. I look over at Malak before I take the first step. She nudges me with her head and pushes me over the threshold. I can feel the perfect spring air all around us as the heavy winds blow. The birds are chirping, and the first flowers of the season are blossoming. I never envisioned this day could be possible. And just for a moment I feel *peace* again.

Over the next few months Malak and I explore the land. Being outdoors has improved her mood vastly and she has allowed me to ride her again. She persists on not connecting with me, but I'll take what I can get. It seems that we are still in Italy and in the same Apennine Mountain range I was first brought to. We travel as far out as we can, but I am limited by a boundary I cannot see. I realize soon enough that the Seven Temples of Virgo are used as borders to hold us in. This is a very old kind of magic, one that only few still know how to do. God must have known I would eventually figure out how to break free and took preventative measures. The Seven Temples were built in the exact location underneath Virgo's stars. Because this area is known for its agriculture, the people in the ancient times built them to honor her. They would come to the temples to pray and offer sacrifice in exchange for good harvest. And who better than to pay homage to than Virgo, Goddess of the Harvest.

There is almost no one living in this area. Now and again,

Malak and I will get a glimpse of a passing farmer or shepherd. Living under the stars is nearly as lonely as living inside the cave.

Almost a year later, Malak and I find ourselves standing outside the dreadful place where I'd been deceived so many years ago. I stare at the heart-shaped stone in the mountain that I had touched to seal my fate. My heart begins beating quickly. I pick up a rock from the ground and throw it as hard as I can at the heart-shaped stone. The stone shatters. It looks like a heart broken into a million pieces, just as my own has. I can't stand the sight of this place. But before I climb back onto Malak, I notice the strap of a satchel under ivy leaves that have grown over it.

I gasp.

It's *my* satchel, the one I had with me on that day. I don't remember it falling off me, but it must have. I thought about it a million times when I was trapped in the cave, but I just assumed Herophile or Gabriel had taken it. They must have not noticed it either. I open it quickly; everything I left in it is still here. I start laughing and shouting with joy. Clutched in my hand is Ada Gold. If those fools had only known what I carried.

*   *   *

I use most of the Ada Gold to create my faeries. They are my children, created by my blood and Ada magic. And the rest, I use to shift the lands into the most ethereal landscape in existence on Earth. Within a few days I run out of gold, but I still have a kingdom to build. Then one of the faeries has an idea. She says, since the faeries have no geographical limits and can go just about anywhere, they will bring people to me. I can then read their fortunes, and in exchange they will bring me whatever I need. What a splendid idea it is! Little by little, word begins to spread and people come to visit me from the nearby towns. Soon enough, they start coming from outside provinces, and then, from all of Italy. The news finally reaches my sisters and we reunite shortly after. My home is now their home. Since Oracles have no Asbgah of their own, I create one for us. The Faerie Asbgah.

I begin to use the Seven Temples as gateways into my kingdom; and as the only way in or out, as a means to keep order. People are arriving night and day. I need knights to protect my kingdom, so the faeries start bringing me the bravest and the strongest among them. We lure them, entice them, and make their every lustful fantasy come true. I do not deny that the more people want from me, the greedier I become. I do not answer to Heaven or Hell, and therefore I begin to create my own rules of right and wrong. I use every trick in my book to get what I want, and give those that want to stay in my kingdom the most indulgent and blissful life they could ever imagine. Countless leaders, royals, and politicians come to my door with the best fabrics, spices, riches, money, gold, and jewels. The more money they have, the more I take. I lie, cheat, steal and start wars if it suits me. Even those from the other Asbgahs come for my help and guidance. I comply for a piece of their magic. I now become both Oracle and Original Creator, and the only one of my kind; completely unstoppable.

Throughout these years my only challenge has become the Catholic Church, which grows more and more powerful. Their laws have become the laws of the world, and their wealth becomes limitless. I always wonder what their followers would say if they knew that those in the highest positions of the Church seek advice from little old me. Even so, the Church becomes less tolerant of the Old Ways, and begins destroying all remnants of it. They claim to know Jesus' word and write it in something they call the "New Testament." I ask one of the Church's leaders to bring me a copy of a book they call the Bible on his next visit.

I read it and tell them many, many times that they've left out so much. And that so much of the truth is not being represented. I demand to know why so many of the accounts written are not translated properly and not credited to the rightful authors. Their answer is always the same: "It is God's will." I become so angry; I stop allowing them to enter my kingdom.

In retaliation, they change Virgo's ancient temples into new Catholic churches. But no matter how hard they try, there are always remnants of our existence. They begin holding something called 'mass'; a barbaric man they call a priest scolds humans and makes them feel shame for every action and every desire in their hearts. I try to listen in on a few of them, but I can't bear the hypocrisy. In the name of Jesus, they begin killing all creatures that do not fall into line with Christian values.

It is around this time when our beautiful Taygeta, Maia, and Celaeno request sanctuary on behalf of the dragons that they saved from being tortured and were intended to be killed the following day. It isn't the weakness or wounds of the dragons that convinces me, it is the girls' kind eyes and their pure souls. They are hypnotizing; I cannot help but agree to their selfless requests. I'd never known Celestial Beings like them before. Their illuminating skin, ethereal beauty, and unconditional love and kindness for all living things is unmatched. It really is like looking right into a star. To experience it makes one feel almost . . . unworthy.

The girls stay the night. It is the first real rest they've had in months. Carmentis and Pythia stay up all night with the dragons, nursing their wounds and feeding them. The dragons look emaciated, I can tell they have been starved for months. Starving them is the only way to make them weak enough to kill. They cry from pain, and Pythia cries with them; they are her children after all. Her greatest fear is coming true, dragons are closer than ever to becoming extinct. That night she lets out a savage cry, calling all the dragons into hiding. She tells them it is time to permanently leave the human world, and retreat to the Faerie Kingdom. By morning the dragons arrive, all twenty of them. It shakes me to my core. I didn't realize things had gotten so bad. The alpha dragon, Vladimir, tells Pythia where another dozen are being held captive. The next day my knights assist nine Oracles, as well as Taygeta, Maia, and Celaeno in retrieving them. There is nothing more infuriating than having to sit on my hands and wait. When they return, they look exhausted and defeated. I don't understand why, all twelve dragons have been recovered and everyone is home safe. The knights explain to me they have never seen so many magical creatures killed with such brutality. John, one of our most seasoned knights, mentions the gruesome scene of thousands of Uniequus decapitated for their horns and drained of their blood. Malak starts to panic, and John tries to calm her by insisting he didn't see Wasi among the dead Uniequus. John tells us that he heard from a sorcerer they encountered along the way, that Alessandro has cast a spell, making all Uniequus look like regular horses to the human eye, to prevent more deaths. I can see this does not give Malak much comfort.

All of this is the opposite of anything Jesus would have wanted to be done in His name. And completely contrary to what He stands for. This is all for the Church's own gain and power, nothing more. I have seen this reoccur in every religion throughout history. They are not the first and will not be the last. The Church's rituals, garments and eccentricities are beautiful, but their greed is worse than my own. From the fifth to the fifteenth century, my faeries and knights had to be very clever about getting people in and out of the kingdom. Anyone who wasn't deemed to behave like a Christian was hunted down and slaughtered, just as they had done to our fellow magical creatures.

*   *   *

Eli, you see, Taygeta, Maia, and Celaeno were the only non-Oracles I have ever *invited* into my kingdom. I offered for them to take refuge here. They were delighted to find a place that they loved so much and felt safe in. It was their idea to become a permanent part of my family. But I had my own reasons for hoping they would stay. It wasn't because they had special powers, or because they were the last three Celestial Beings on Earth and I wanted to help them. No . . . It was because they are *so* forgiving. Forgiving of all crimes, pain, suffering, injustices, ill-will—I could go on forever . . . I wanted to know how they are able to do it. In all my years of existence, I've never encountered anyone or anything so unjaded, so untainted, so *good*. I wanted to observe them, know them deeply, and learn how to be less angry by understanding the way they think. I'd grown tired of my hatred. Their trust and belief in God, Jesus Christ, and even the imperfect Catholic Church is impenetrable. There is nothing that could ever happen to take them away from their devout beliefs. Whether they were in the Asbgah or in the human world, they walked to church every Sunday. Sometimes they even attended mass two to three times a week. They read the Bible and prayed the rosary daily. Whatever the reason that God did not allow them back into the Heavens, did not matter to them. They believed it was right to be punished, and to pay their penance for not leaving Earth when they were told to. But after meeting their husbands, they truly believed there was a greater purpose all along. Now with you, Eli, that may be more true than ever. To have that kind of undying faith is something I have searched for all my life; but it's hard to grasp and even harder to hold onto when you've seen as much as I have. But they do it so naturally, it's like second nature, like breathing. I'd hoped having them around would show me what the secret to being devout is. And maybe, just maybe, I could even learn how to forgive.

In all the centuries they have been with me, the girls have had limitless freedom, no contracts and no obligations. They come and go as they please, into the human world and the other Asbgahs. But with the invention of photography, their visits into the human world became less frequent. They were very hard to miss. My kingdom remained open to those I deemed worthy up until 1945, that is until you, Eli. You are the first outsider to set foot here in more than seventy-five years. And I'm afraid you've given us hope once again. This is not a compliment—it is a dangerous word and an even more dangerous emotion. I don't know if I should protect or abandon you.

Eli, I do not need your apology, your forgiveness, or your permission. What I need is for you to know *who I am* and what I've lived through. That is all.

"It's time to open your eyes, Eli," I say out loud, easing her back into the present.

"Call her grandmother up," Sambethe says to my servant.

Eli opens her eyes slowly; I watch as the white snow deteriorates from the reflection in her eyes. She is frozen and unresponsive. Her skin has lost all color and her breathing is so low, I check her pulse to make sure I didn't break her. Taking someone human into my memories usually has the opposite effect: their hearts race so quickly that they are on the verge of cardiac arrest. But nothing about this girl is traditional. It is clear from the way she carries herself, that she does not see what the rest of us see. It is obvious that she thinks of herself as "normal," uninteresting and less than attractive—which could not be further from the truth. Her eyes are haunting, they pull you in just as her grandmothers' eyes do. The first time she looked at me at the festival in Pretare, I thought she could see through my soul. Like her grandmothers, she is charming, smart as a whip, and possesses a refreshingly uncommon beauty. She thinks people take little notice of her, and that she's just another face that is lost in the crowd. And that men don't approach her because she's "ordinary." If she only knew that they don't approach her because she is *extraordinary*.

She doesn't see that she is the true aggressor. She allows herself to be pushed around and told what to do, never asks questions and allows others to believe they can manipulate her. But between the spider and the butterfly, she is the spider, trapping only those she wants in her web, and silently devouring the rest. She comes across as fragile and afraid of her own shadow. That is the furthest thing from who she really is. Her sharp mind, and her calculated and well-thought-out words, will make her a fair rival to anyone in the other Asbgahs. Her bloodline is unlike any other; she is the first celestial/human hybrid. And since she is an only child, there is no other DNA like hers in *any* world.

Although we await anxiously to see what her gifts will be and what her purpose is, I worry for her transition. Once it's complete, she will be hunted down by every eternally damned soul from the Asbgahs, the Perdition. She doesn't understand the power of the Celestial Gold that glistens in her hair. She has even less of an idea how incredibly precious and rare it is. It is a million times more valuable than the Ada Gold my faeries carry. I assume her grandmothers haven't told her what it is in order to protect her, but they need to do it soon. Time is running out. We thought the last of it on Earth was taken from Taygeta, Maia, and Celaeno all those years ago. I still think of their sacrifice as the bravest and stupidest thing I've ever witnessed. But here it is, Celestial Gold reappearing on Earth almost five thousand years later, on a young girl who thinks her life is a footnote. I wonder, with a name that carries the promise of a great destiny, how can Elita believe she is of no significance. When Taygeta first arrived here after her human form passed, I asked her why such a name was chosen for the child, since it was unbeknownst to anyone other than the Oracles to be consequential? Despite our visions, even our knowledge of her was limited. To this day, we cannot see what the intention of her existence is. There is a blind spot where there should be a prophecy. Taygeta swore to me that Eli's mother Elizabetta, just heard the name one day and fell in love with it. She simply thought it was a perfect symbolic name for the grandchild of two Celestial Beings. I believe Taygeta because she's never lied to me, not that Celestial Beings can lie, but I also think she's holding something back. I know she has her reasons not to trust me; they all do.

I am doing all I can to slow down Eli's transition, but the magic of the Asbgahs is accelerating the process. There is so much to discuss with her, so much to say . . . I'd hope for her to stay a little longer, but I realize now it is for the best that she leaves early. I'm relieved she's leaving tomorrow; it should buy us some time. When my sisters arrive tonight, they will see and feel what I do, and we will put our minds together to find a solution to stop this from moving any faster, until we understand what she's here for.

"Blessed be, what have you done, Sibyl!" Rosa shouts at me, as she embraces her granddaughter.

Eli collapses in her arms, and Rosa lays her down on the sofa.

"Really Taygeta, don't be so dramatic," I reply, putting Eli's legs on the cushion.

Eli pulls away from the touch of my hand.

"Dramatic, huh?" Rosa pushes my hand away. "And I've told you a million times, stop calling me Taygeta! I go by Rosa now!"

"Why does everyone but me feel the need to change their names every two-thousand years? I mean really, it's silly!" I say, throwing up my hands and sitting in the chair next to Sambethe.

"Rosa is the only name I have ever chosen. You should try it, it's very liberating." Rosa pours water on a napkin that is sitting on the side table and pats Eli's head with it. "She's cold as ice Sibyl, what is happening? I've never seen this kind of reaction." Rosa frowns with concern.

"Yes, I know. I was thinking the same just a moment ago," I reply to her.

Sambethe gets up and pulls a blanket that's laying on the arm of the sofa over Eli, then sits at her feet.

"She must think we're all monsters . . . " Sambethe says in a whisper.

"I didn't show her *that*. Are you mad, woman?" I answer back.

"What *did* you show her?" Sambethe presses.

I can see that she's quite cross with me.

"Just my story, that's all sister. No need to be paranoid," I say, looking out the balcony from my seat.

It's nearly night now, the others will be arriving shortly. I stand and tell Sambethe it's time to go and remind Rosa that I will be expecting her and Eli at the cove in exactly thirty minutes. She darts an angry glare at me and then returns to nursing her granddaughter. That's very unlike Rosa, I've never seen her react that way. Her disposition is always so lovely and peaceful, no matter the circumstances.

Sambethe and I take Alfred down. The entire time she lectures me about how reckless I am for allowing Eli into my mind. That I should have known better and I could have put them all in danger. She always worries too much, so I decide to put her at ease. Before they can open, I tell Alfred to hold the elevator doors.

I put my finger in the palm of her hand and replay in fast motion what I showed Eli.

"It's only *my* story," I say confidently, to reassure her.

"You say she has a gift for seeing people for who they really are, right?" Sambethe asks me.

I can see that my efforts to comfort her have been for nothing.

"Well, what if that is true? What if once she's in someone's mind she can see *everything*! Isn't that what she did with Alessandro?" she continues on. "She's done what no one else can do, she has seen the inside of the mind of the second most powerful person in existence. And she has no idea that this information has made her *the* most powerful person."

I shiver at the thought.

"She doesn't remember half of what she saw. You know this from spending the day with her!" I say, suddenly feeling insecure.

"Sibyl, she's nothing if not clever! And she's half human. She knows how to lie," Sambethe reminds me.

"Yes . . . I suppose you're right about that . . . "

I wave my hand at Alfred and instruct the elevator doors to open. We walk out onto the open grassy knoll, that sits at the base of the mountain before the cove. Everyone has done such a splendid job decorating with beautiful summer flowers, candles and endless tables filled with everyone's favorite foods. Although my sisters are in and out and I see them often, it's been so long since we've all been together. I want everything to be perfect. I'm sure they are as anxious to be together, as they are to meet Eli.

*　　　*　　　*

All the inhabitants in my kingdom have joined me on the grassy knoll for the arrival of my sisters. The sun has set, they should be arriving any moment now. Rosa finally arrives, but she is without Eli. I ask her if the honoree has decided to not attend her own dinner. Before she can answer, I hear the sounds of dragons above my head and look up. Well, well, well, our honoree has decided to make an entrance of her own. Eli is riding Vladimir, and Pythia in her dragon form, is riding along, side by side. If she didn't spit fire, I would kill Pythia! She's always showing off, trying to make a scene. For once, I wish she would just do as she's told.

They do a few tricks in the sky that are much too dangerous for someone who's never ridden a dragon. And when they finally land, the crowd applauds like it's a firework show on New Year's Eve. I cross my arms as Pythia and Eli walk over to me.

"They love it! Listen to that excitement! They haven't been this happy in a hundred years!" Pythia says, trying to make me feel guilty.

I scowl at her.

Eli is smiling from ear to ear. The color is back in her cheeks and her eyes are lively and sparkling. It looks like I didn't break her after all. She's usually so guarded and serious around me, I don't think I've ever seen her *happy*. She has a beautiful and contagious smile; it completely disarms me.

"Sibyl, thank you for the dragon ride! That was *the best*!" I'm not sure what she means. I look over at Pythia.

"Yes, I mentioned to Eli how you thought it would be a great experience for her to have before she leaves," Pythia says, winking at me.

"Y-yes . . . you're welcome . . . but we could have done without a few of those twirls and the nosedive, couldn't we Pythia?" I scold, while smiling.

"It was perfect!" Eli exclaims.

Her joy prevents me from saying anything further at the moment, but Pythia and I will have a conversation about this later.

"Does this mean you're not upset with me anymore, Eli?" I ask.

"I didn't mean to be rude earlier. I-I was just . . . it was a lot to take in," she says, with immense joy still across her face.

"I should have prepared you better. I let my emotions get the best of me, I apologize," I say honestly.

"That's okay, I'm not sure you could have prepared me for something like that anyway."

The girl has a fair point. Eli is about to say something else when we hear the ah-ing from everyone around us. Thousands of Lufatas fill the sky over the lake, softly coming towards us. They are guiding the way for the Oracles, who are each standing on very large lotus leaves as the water gently brings them in closer.

"What are those in the sky? Fireflies?" Eli asks, with a wondrous look in her big eyes.

"They are called Lufatas. From far away they look like fireflies, but they are actually the same height as a regular person, just part faerie and part lantern," Rosa says.

I can tell by Rosa's expression that Lufatas are something she missed while she was in the human world.

"I guess they are a kind of Faerie-Fly!" Pythia giggles.

Sambethe and I giggle too. I suppose she's right. They are albino faeries, not one bit of color on them, not even in their eyes. Their hair doesn't lay flat, it is in the shape of an 'S' form, pointy at the top. The bottom half of a Lufata's body is a large, round lantern that illuminates soft light. The top of their bodies is human. They are the most delicate and sensitive of all my wonderful creatures. They do not have legs, and therefore cannot walk. One by one they arrive, floating just above the grass.

The lotus leaves stop fifty yards from the shore. My knights go out on fishing boats to retrieve my Oracle sisters. Watching them paddle in with Lufatas floating all around is an unimaginable sight to witness, it takes my breath away. I look over at Eli—she is enchanted, in complete awe, holding her grandmother tightly. I imagine what that moment would be like, to hold my own granddaughter in my arms, sharing such a moment with her. I envy them. Eli catches me staring. She extends her hand. I'm not certain what she wants from me. She extends it further and takes my hand and pulls me close to her. I'm not sure what is happening, my heart skips a beat. Rosa smiles. Sambethe takes my other hand. And for a brief moment, *I* feel *happy*.

All eight sisters step onto the shore, and we walk over to greet them. One by one I introduce Eli to them. When we reach Julia, I can see that Eli does not recognize her, possibly because Julia's true form is young and vibrant. I hear in the human world she's an old woman who bakes. How strange . . . I can never imagine her like that. When I say Julia's name, they nearly devour each other with love. Rosa thanks Julia for taking such good care of her granddaughter when she was visiting the Vincis.

"But of course. She is the granddaughter of my very best pupil," Julia replies.

"She is speaking about Amelia," Rosa explains to Eli. "I remember the early years when Amelia and Julia where inseparable, Julia teaching her everything she knew. Amelia's mind was like a sponge, taking in and writing down every little thing."

"Eli, please allow me to introduce someone very special to Luca, this is his mother Victoria," Julia says, holding Eli's waist and holding out the other hand in Victoria's direction.

Eli has a strange reaction; she stiffens and does not extend her hand. She keeps them together in front of her. Victoria perceives Eli's body language, and they both politely say hello without making any effort of physical contact. Julia and I are very surprised by this, we thought for sure Eli intended to make a good impression on Luca's mother. We are not off to a good start. Based on this reaction, I can't help but be intensely curious as to what Eli saw in Alessandro's mind about Victoria.

After their salutations, my sisters take a moment to walk up through the labyrinth garden and into the tower.

"Where are they going?" Eli asks, confused.

"To see Herophile. They must know by now how much that irritates me. Yet, they do it every time they come here."

"Do you mean she lives in *there*?" Eli continues on, "Does she ever come out?"

"Yes, she lives there. My faeries tell me that sometimes she comes out in the middle of the night. When she thinks everyone is asleep, she walks the gardens. On warm nights, I hear she goes for a swim in the lake," I pause. "She needs for nothing. The faeries do everything for her, they feel sorry for her."

"How long has she been there?" Eli asks, looking at the tower in astonishment.

"Not long enough," I answer.

She raises her eyebrows at me. She really does take so much after her grandmothers; it's starting to annoy me.

"Two thousand years now, I think . . . " I reply, while trying to do the math in my head.

"Are you *kidding* Sibyl? I mean, that's nuts! Why! When will she come out?" Eli shouts.

Come to think of it, I suppose it has been a while.

"When I forgive her. That was the deal. She stays in there in solitude until then."

"I know she betrayed you, Sibyl. But at least she's had the decency to be haunted by the decisions of her past, every day of her life. Do you know how many people would never look back? Never care. Most people I know just let pride stand in the way of making things right." Eli touches my arm. "She's paid her dues, don't you think?"

I reflect on her words, and we look up at the small window in the tower. I can see a sliver of Herophile's profile. It's a strange feeling to loathe someone and miss them. And love her still. I never imagined she would last two thousand years here. Two thousand years in isolation, I suppose that is quite an apology.

"Come on, everyone! Let the celebration begin!" I shout. I need a distraction from these thoughts.

I instruct the musicians to start playing music. And with that, everyone begins to dance, eat, drink and socialize. It really is the perfect evening for such an occasion. Watching everyone enjoy themselves is really one of my favorite things in life. My sisters finally join us and when they do, they surround Eli. I can tell they are very impressed with her. My sisters and Eli ask each other questions and speak openly, as if they have known one another forever. Eli wins the hearts of everyone she speaks to; well, everyone but Victoria it seems. Speaking of, where is she? I look around. I see her and Rosa having an intense conversation near the Night-Blooming Cereus. They are beautiful plants that only bloom one night a year, and tonight is that night; but they are not known for their diplomacy. I walk over to Rosa and Victoria and place my hands over their mouths. It's clear to me they don't realize what they are standing next to.

"Hello Queen of the Night," I say to the Night-Blooming Cereus. "How was your year-long nap?"

"Ohhhh . . . quite refreshing, Queen Sibyl. But I'm afraid you've just interrupted a spectacularly juicy conversation between these two," she answers.

"You don't think you would be able to forget whatever it is that you just heard?" I ask politely.

"*They* hear what *I* hear. You know this. If you didn't want them to know, you shouldn't have had this decadent party on such a night!" she replies, with a chuckle.

"Well, you enjoy the party," I reply abruptly, as I pull Rosa and Victoria away.

Rosa immediately apologizes; as I suspected, she didn't realize who she was standing next to. Victoria, on the other hand, knew exactly what she was doing.

"Someone explain to me what you were talking about," I say, trying to get to the point.

I don't have a good feeling about this.

"She . . . " Rosa begins to say, and then realizes she's being loud and brings it to a whisper, "She and Alessandro went to Amelia, knowing very well that she is dying, and were harassing her about the Rose of Venus!"

"Not this again, Victoria," I cross my arms, "And since when are you and Alessandro on speaking terms?"

"I believe the more appropriate question is, how does she even know that I visited Amelia?" Victoria points out.

"Yes, that's a valid question, but not one as stupid as asking about the Rose of Venus," I both whisper and yell. "Look, it doesn't even matter right now. The Night-Blooming Cereus heard whatever you two were saying. Which means within an hour, *every* night creature will know too. So, what *exactly* was said?"

"If you're so worried, then why did you have this event on the only night of the year the Cereus blooms?" Victoria asks, perturbed.

"Because I wanted the other Asbgahs, and especially the Perdition, to know that we are united, that we are one. They cannot see us divided! They think we know what's coming, but we don't. For the *first time*, we don't. It's a level playing field, putting us at a disadvantage. Do you not see that? Or do you not care because your husband is the Father of Magic?"

It just occurs to me that Victoria may not be here for the right reasons. Is that why Eli reacted the way she did?

"For you, that means no matter which way the coin flips, you will land on your feet," Rosa states. "Are you here to spy on us? To find out what Eli knows?"

It looks like Rosa and I have come to the same realization at the same moment.

"Really, you two are absurd! You know I don't trust him! And by the way you're both acting, maybe I shouldn't trust you either!" Victoria responds in an angry tone. "Of course I want to know what Eli knows, don't we all! I would pay a million stars to see half of what that girl has seen. Has she told you anything?"

We both stand in silence.

"What has Alessandro said to you, Victoria?" I finally ask.

"Nothing. But I can tell he's afraid, even though he'd never admit it. The only thing that is keeping that girl safe is her blackouts. Can she still not recall things?"

I don't know what to do. Rosa pushes herself up against me and squeezes my hand tightly.

"Eli hasn't told us any details," Rosa says, looking Victoria in the eyes.

Clever girl.

"Can we please go back to what's important here? Answer my damn question, what were you two talking about next to the bloody Cereus!" I ask again, eager to change the conversation.

Rosa releases my hand. It'll take me an hour before I have feeling in it again.

"I was telling her how upset I am about their visit to Amelia. And she was going on about the Rose of Venus, and something about a Castle of Sorrow. Oh, I don't know Sibyl, I am so confused. My mind is still with my family in the human world. I'm trying to acclimate and catch up with all that's happening here. But I don't know what's important anymore," Rosa replies.

"Don't be daft, Rosa!" Victoria snaps at her. "Sibyl, listen to me. It isn't anything that can hurt the Oracles. Just a warning shot to the night creatures, is all."

"Next time, use your husband's Asbgah to do your dirty work," I say between my teeth.

We return to the party and join the others.

"Your mood is quite splenetic. Can't imagine what brought that on," Pythia says sarcastically. I can see she's already had too much to drink from the faerie well.

"Go to hell," I reply.

"Not until Wednesday!" she says, lifting up her glass as I walk away.

*   *   *

I see Eli sitting alone on a swing made of silk rope and faerie roses, that faces the lake from the cove. It hangs right above the lake on the largest tree in the kingdom; it's my absolute favorite. We call it the Star Tree because actual fireflies live in it and illuminate it every night. I walk up behind her and to her side. I ask if everything is alright. She confesses that she's not comfortable with so much attention, but that's been something quite obvious to me since I met her. I ask her how she likes the *pixie dust water* from the faerie well.

"If it's just water, why do I feel a little drunk?" she asks, with one eye closed.

"Because the magic of the well turns it into either your favorite drink or whatever tickles your fancy at the moment." I take the drink out of her hand to taste it.

"Oh, so you favor expensive champagne?" She has finer taste than I imagined.

"I have a small champagne fridge at home. It's my favorite thing in that entire crappy apartment," Eli says, and looks down at my feet. "Woooow, you're like, walking on water! Hey, did you know that Jesus could do that too?"

She's funnier than I thought. It's nice to see her relaxed, even if it does take champagne to get her there.

"Do you think you'll go back to Los Angeles?" I hand her glass back.

"I don't know. I don't think I've ever felt so lost," she sighs heavily. "You would think this is what everyone wants—to live in a *magical* world. But it's not . . . it's not . . . "

"A faerie tale?" I finish her sentence.

"Thanks, I couldn't think of the word," she smiles coyly.

"No, it's not. But neither are real faerie tales."

"The North Star is so bright tonight, it's the same size as the moon. I've never seen it so big!" Eli says, pointing at it.

"That only happens when all the Oracles are all together. We can be quite the force you know," I answer playfully.

She agrees by nodding her head assertively.

After a moment of silence, Eli turns to me and asks, "What's Victoria really like?"

"Huh . . . well, she's like . . . " I pause searching for the right words, "Like whiskey in a teacup!"

I don't know if it is the champagne or Valentina's secretions in the air, but we both begin laughing uncontrollably. In that moment, I feel a connection to Eli. Maybe because I shared the most intimate and painful moments in my life. Or maybe it's because she is now the only person that can understand the decisions I've made. And I am overwhelmed with a tangible emotion that has eluded me for so long—gratitude. It's unexpected. And even though I don't welcome it because it makes me feel vulnerable, it also makes me feel alive.

"You really like Luca, don't you?" I ask, knowing what's really behind her question about Victoria.

"You can't like someone you can't touch." She closes her eyes.

"What do you mean—" Before I can finish my question, I am

interrupted by Victor's abrupt presence. I've seen that look before, this is not good.

"Madam, Queen Micella and her Elven army are at our border. She says it's *very* urgent. She needs to speak to you immediately," Victor says, standing at the water's edge. Julia rushes up behind him, she can feel the presence of her Elves.

"I will go with you Sibyl," Julia says, with an indescribable look on her face. I can see she is as surprised as I am by their visit. "Micella would never break the rules to come here if it wasn't serious. She knows I'm here."

"We have our differences, but yes I agree, she would never be so bold." I walk off the water and onto land.

"I'm coming too!" Eli jumps off the swing and lands in the water.

"Victor, carry her." I direct him to fetch her from the water. "John, get the horses ready!"

"No need, madam. The horses, Wasi, Malak, and the knights are already waiting at the bottom gate. We need to hurry." Victor gives me a stern look. I can tell by the tone in his voice that we don't have much time.

*   *   *

There is a sudden chill in the air. I have an unsettling feeling inside the pit of my soul. No one has ever had the courage to take on a woman mad enough to be without allegiance to either God or Lucifer. It's always made me unstable and dangerous in the eyes of others. They are about to find out, that is the absolute truth. I climb onto Malak and tell Elise to prepare the others, we are going to have visitors tonight. With no time to create a plan, my sisters do not hesitate—they each straddle a horse and join us. As we ride to the border, our eyes turn to snow as my sisters and I receive the same vision:

A flashback to earlier today when we visited Erymanthe's library cave; Elise expands her wings, Ada Gold dust particles everywhere. One small fragmented speck escapes the cave and floats into the air. It drifts into the dark forest where it catches the eye of a Perdition. To confirm what he has found, he takes it to Tygon, a wicked Lord among the Perdition. They immediately gather their army and are headed to my kingdom, at this very moment. The Dark Forest and Elven Asbgah are adjacent; word spreads quickly of the Perdition's plans, and the Elven Army waste no time to travel here to warn us.

When our eyes re-focus, we see the Elves gathered at the border. Pythia instantly transitions into her dragon form and calls on every dragon to begin circling and patrolling. My kingdom has never been invaded before. It looks like tonight, that is about to change.

"Julia, tell Micella and her army to ride in *now*. I will instruct my faeries to take down the protective barrier where they are waiting. The Perdition will be here soon, we have no time to waste! NOW JULIA, NOW!" I shout at the top of my lungs, riding Malak as hard as I can.

"My God, what have I done?" I say out loud to myself. This is my fault, I should have never allowed Elise to open her wings. Now everyone, in every Asbgah, will know I lied about Ada Gold being extinct. They will come hunting for my faeries again. Tears well up in my eyes. I can't handle losing my children, I can't watch them being slaughtered again.

"Be brave, Sibyl. Be brave. We will do everything necessary to protect the faeries. But first, you need to get Eli out of here. They *cannot* see her under any circumstance—you know why." I finally hear Malak's gentle but strong voice say to me.

If these were different circumstances, this would have been one of the best moments of my life. She's exactly as I had imagined her to be. Malak could not have picked a more perfect *and* unfavorable moment to connect to me.

"Yes, you are right." I feel my heartbeat sync with hers and it feels like it's going to burst. "Thank you, Malak. Thank you."

I am finally forgiven.

My eyes turn to snow and I call out to my sisters once more. I can see to truly be free, I must do the same.

"Herophile," I call out.

"Y-yes sister."

I am overcome with emotion, as I hear her voice for the first time in two millennia. I can hear the tears of joy in her voice.

"*I forgive you.*" And with those words **I am free**, there is no longer anger in my heart.

I can hear my sisters weep with joy.

"Herophile, we are sending Eli back to you. You must get her to Martha, she will know how to get her out of here safely. Quickly sister!" Pythia interjects.

"Wasi get her out of here NOW! Go back! Martha will be waiting for her. Vladimir will follow you!" I shout at Wasi, as we ride side by side to the border.

Wasi and Malak make eye contact. Wasi begins to slow down, then turns in the opposite direction.

* * *

We reach the border.

"Micella." I find myself looking upon a queen, she is no longer a child. The similarities between her and her mother are undeniable.

"Sibyl," she replies, "We are ready to fight alongside you and your people, for our Elven Mother Julia."

I see Julia beaming with pride as she looks upon her creation of strong and fearless Elves. As she should. I am impressed; her army has grown to ten times what it once was, their training and skills are unmatched by any in the other Asbgahs.

"It is our honor, and we thank you," I reply genuinely.

"You and I still have a score to settle. I'll make sure no one can kill you before I have the chance myself," Micella jests.

"Sounds only fair," I reply, amused by her words. "And so, it will be another day then."

Julia smirks, knowing that underneath the dry humor, there is truth to Micella's desire to end my life.

Micella nods, instructing her army to move forward to fight.

Chapter 23

"WASI, WHAT ARE YOU DOING! Since when do you take orders from Sibyl?" I shout, pulling on Wasi's reins, trying to slow him down so I can get him to turn around. But he is fighting me.

I look back. I see Micella and Sibyl speaking. To Micella's right is my Aunt Elenora. I've never seen my aunt look this way, Stefano and Sophia will be happy to know that their mom is a badass. She is next to a man I've only seen in my visions. To Micella's left a woman I also recognize from my visions. Both are fearless fighters. I'm not sure what these Perdition can do, but through my visons I've seen the Elves in action, and they are *warriors*.

"Since the moment it has to do with your safety!" Wasi shouts back. "Eli, you don't understand how dangerous and evil the Perdition are. Their acts of brutality are without limits, and their lords are even worse. It is dark out here, but I don't want to take any chances that they should see a shimmer of your hair. They *cannot* know there is Celestial Gold on Earth, they will not hesitate to decapitate you. All this is happening because of one spec of Ada Gold . . . imagine . . . " I can hear Wasi's voice straining. "STOP fighting me Eli, I have to get you out of here, even if it's the last thing I do!"

I turn my head one last time before releasing Wasi's reins. Fear encroaches on my soul as I see Micella fly into the air with her bow and arrow. She releases it, and it lands into the chest of a shadowy figure who is floating towards her. His features are phantom-like and his head is covered by the hood of his armor. When he lands on the ground his body solidifies—I see no face, there is only darkness. It is the vision I had of Micella, come to life.

I look around, and everyone is fighting, the battle has begun.

Wasi pulls forward so hard he releases my grip, and we ride back to the cove as fast as we can.

When we arrive, I can see the Perdition are gaining pace and are not far behind.

"You must be Eli?" a breathtaking woman says to me as I climb off Wasi. "I'm Herophile. I'm sorry we didn't meet under better circumstances. Please hurry along."

We quickly climb into a fishing boat in the dark waters. Elise and Thomas are there to take me to Martha. Thomas quickly puts the cape he's holding over my shoulders and tucks my hair into the hood to hide it. I look out and see Wasi and my grandmother standing there looking at me.

"Wasi, Nonna, are you meeting us there?" I shout from the boat.

"Eli, you must go! Save yourself and do not think of me. I have to stay to help, this is my home now. I love you and will visit you soon. Do you still have the letter?" Nonna asks. I put my hand over my chest where I can feel it under my clothes, to indicate I have been carrying it at all times, as she requested.

"Malak and the others are waiting for us. We have a long and difficult battle ahead. I do not know what will happen but know that it has been the honor of my life serving you. I will miss you every day Eli, good-bye," Wasi's voice cracks as he says these final words to me.

"I love you." Nonna blows me a kiss. She climbs onto Wasi and they ride away, not once looking back.

"NOOOOOOOO!!!" I scream with everything I have inside, as I watch them disappear into the battle of swords, magic, and dark forces.

They pull me down and slam me against the bottom of the boat, Herophile covers my mouth with her hands, and Elise begs me to quiet down so no one will hear my cries. But it is too late, I've caught the ear of the Perdition. I see two dark figures coming down straight at us. One of them extends his whip, its tip wraps itself around Elise's throat. I see her skin burning around it, she is trying to remove it from her neck. She can't breathe, it's suffocating her.

Herophile punches holes in the boat, water begins to enter and it floods quickly. She tells Thomas to take me and swim as fast as he can. As we enter the water, he has my waist with one tentacle and is pushing down with the others. As we descend further into the water, I see Herophile standing above me on the surface of the lake. With one hand, she is blocking a Perdition from getting close to her with her magic, and with the other, she is releasing a jolt of electricity over and over again, striking the whip to try to release Elise from its grasp. But I can't see what is happening for very long, the water is too dark.

In a flash, Thomas takes off and we are gone. As we take a sharp turn, Thomas' body lights up just a little, so he can better see where we're going. We swim up to the top so I can get a breath of air. He only gives me about five seconds before he pulls me back under. The faster we go, the more his body lights up.

It feels like we are swimming at the speed of light and in thirty seconds time, we reach the other side of the lake where Martha is waiting for us. We crawl onto the shore, trying to catch our breath.

"Thomas, place yourself between those rocks, you're lit up like a Christmas tree! They mustn't see you," Martha whispers from the water, "Come on Eli, there is no time to waste, we have to go now."

Thomas scurries to the rocks and hides his body. I follow him.

"Eli, darling, we really must go, what are you doing?" Martha insists.

"I know Martha, I'm sorry. I just don't know how I'm supposed to leave everyone and not stay and fight with them. I'm just supposed to abandon them? It's wrong and selfish. And my grandmother, what will she do? I can't stand the thought that she's in there fighting for her life and I'm just running away." I cannot come to terms with this.

"Selfish is *staying* here," she says, with an upset tone, "do you know how many creatures will die trying to protect you? At least this way they have a fighting chance. But they will have *no* chance if they are all looking after you. And as for your grandmother, one star beam and she'll either blind them all or burn them to a crisp. Don't you worry about her, she can handle herself."

"She's right Eli," I hear Thomas' little voice saying from in between the rocks, "you need to get out of here."

"Do you understand? Now get on," Martha tells me.

"I'm sorry Thomas. I'm so sorry, I don't want to put anyone in danger. I just want to help. But I'll leave now." I try to hold back, but I can feel the tears start to pour down my face.

I feel a tentacle grab hold of my wrist as I walk away. "We are going to be okay, I promise. Many from the Magic Asbgah are on their way to help too. But if the evil creatures see you, it will never end until they . . . no point in finishing that. You have a life that is waiting to be lived, until we meet again," Thomas says with courage in his voice.

"I don't understand what that means Thomas."

"But you will," he says, releasing my wrist.

I grab his tentacle before he can pull away completely and lean in to kiss it. "Thank you, Thomas."

I walk back into the water, and Martha lowers herself enough for me to climb on. Before we pull away, I see Thomas' little tentacle diminishing in light, waving at me from between the rocks.

"Where are we off to, Martha?" I ask. "Can you get to the human side from here?"

"I can, but that's not where we're going. I have been given specific coordinates, and I believe it is the far east-side of the Elven Asbgah," she whispers, "but it's best if we don't speak until we arrive, we wouldn't want our voices to carry."

"No, we wouldn't want that," I answer, in a defeated tone. Being left to my own thoughts about what I'd just walked away from, is the last thing I need.

Martha is a fast and stealthy swimmer. It explains how she's able to get around in the secret passageways without ever getting caught. About fifteen minutes later, we arrive at a dock at the Elven Forest with elm trees. I recognize these tall, ancient trees, they always seem to be nearby when Dwintra is around.

"Here we are, I was told someone would be here to retrieve you," Martha says.

She pulls up to the dock and I climb off her. I look at her eyes and I'm afraid for her. I touch her face; she is a marvel. I didn't appreciate her the first time I saw her as I do right now. Come to think of it, did I appreciate anything? Now that the most enchanted place in existence is in danger of being decimated, I recognize what a treasure it truly is. Maybe I am one of those disgusting humans that thinks everything will last forever, and don't see the value until it's in danger of no longer existing.

"I don't know what you're thinking, but it seems terrifying," someone says in a delicate voice.

"Lilith, I'm so happy to see that you're alright," Martha replies to the young girl.

"I'm only fourteen, they say I'm too young to fight. I was designated to pick up the package from the Faerie Asbgah. I had no idea it was a human, and a very beautiful and tormented one at that," Lilith says, looking at me.

"Always so observant," Martha compliments her.

"When this situation is over, I would love for us to continue our rides, Martha. Though, I imagine that will be some time," Lilith says.

"Yes, of course. But now that I know Eli is in such good hands, I really must go back. The others are trying to get as many faeries in hiding as possible." Martha tips her head at both of us as she backs up. "Eli, if you need me, Dwintra knows how to find me."

She picks up speed, leaps into the air and does a perfectly elegant dive back into the lake.

"She won't come back up, Hippocampi swim much faster under water," Lilith states.

Lilith is very poised for her age. She has great posture and a lovely disposition. Her hair is bright red and very long; she is wearing it half up in braids, and the other half down and wavy. Her eyes are as bright as the blue sky on a clear day. Her lips and cheeks are naturally blush pink. She is wearing the same style garments that I saw the other Elves wearing at the border: a dark green and black tweed coat with three buttons along the side. Under the coat is a simple black dress, with fitted pants tucked into flat, lace-up black boots. Carved onto each of the buttons is an elm tree. But this one looks very similar to the painting hanging in Alessandro's house.

"Come, he's expecting you. He's been worried sick," Lilith says, "We should get you inside. It's not safe where everyone can see you."

I look around, all I see are the trees and a lake.

"Who's expecting me?" I must sound crazy asking a teenager so many questions. "And who can see me? I don't see anyone."

"Christopher, of course."

"Christopher who?" She looks at me in a peculiar way. Her doll-like face gives me no clues as to whom she's speaking of.

"In the Asbgahs, everything and everyone can see and hear everything." Lilith moves on to answer my next question. "These days, it's hard to know who to trust, especially with the Dark Forest being adjacent to ours."

"What's the Dark Forest?" I ask.

Just as I thought we would take the stairs on the side of the lakeshore up to the land where all the trees are, Lilith goes the opposite direction. She opens a round, wood door in the wall of the cliff under the trees. We walk into a tunnel completely made of branches. Although we are underground and under the trees, the light of the moon from above shines in gently. In the center of the tunnel are old railroad tracks that we are walking over. But I can't imagine what they were once used for, or what they lead to, because outside the door is the lake.

"It's where the Judgement Trees are. If you journey through the forest with a pure heart and good intention, the Judgement Trees will allow you to go anywhere, in any timeline. But if your heart is tainted, the trees will tear you from limb from limb, and suck your soul into the Underworld."

"How do the Perdition live there, aren't they all tainted?"

"Ah, well they live on the outskirts of the forest. You see, the forest is dead, and so it is the only land they can survive on." She stops and looks at me for a moment. "Do you know what the Perdition are?"

"To be honest, I only discovered that they existed a little while ago," I confess. "I've been told that they are evil and brutal creatures. I recognize the word from the Bible. Isn't the Anti-Christ supposed to be the Son of Perdition?"

"Yes, that's exactly right." She seems pleased that I'm not totally incompetent. "They are a group of beings that are in a state of eternal damnation. They believe that punishment should go on forever and ever, and pain should be invoked on those who believe in good works, especially those who believe in God, in love, in joy, in peace and . . . well you get the point. Above all, they believe that all worlds should come to an end, so everyone's souls can finally become nothingness . . . They believe *that alone* can bring the ultimate peace."

"That's mad," I respond.

"Yes. You know, there's a belief that becoming a Perdition happens after people die. That's not accurate; it begins with the choices that are made by the human while they are still alive. All the evil you see in your world, well, those people, those actions become these creatures in ours. Every day they do their best to imprecate evil upon all existence. There is no way to change or convert them."

Cold chills run through my entire body. I always thought that was Lucifer's job.

"Why do they want the Ada Gold?"

"I'm sure they'd find yours much more valuable," she says looking at my hair. "Yours has real power after all. Ada Gold is just magic."

"There's a difference?" I would give anything to take whatever this is out of my hair.

"Quite. I'm surprised no one has explained this to you," she replies puzzled.

"There wasn't a lot a time." My heart hurts as I say it, thinking about what kind of hell everyone must be going through while I am in safety.

"There's that look again," she says, as we arrive to the second round, wooden door, "This should help."

She pushes the door open and steps to the side. The door opens to a small round room.

"Luca?"

The door behind him flies open. A Perdition walks through it.

"Tygon," Lilith's lips are trembling.

"Women are so predictable. You don't think I know who you are, boy?" he says charging at Luca.

"Lilith, *now*," Luca says calmly.

Lilith takes hold of my hand, rushes me over to the other side of the room and opens a third door. While facing me, she pushes me through it with all her might. I feel someone behind me grab me by the arms and pull me through the doorway.

Tygon's attention shifts to me, and he begins to walk in my direction. Luca steps in his path to block him from reaching me.

We lock eyes, as a burning blade passes through Luca's heart.

Darkness.

THE END

Appendix

The following words, terms, characters, definitions, and pro-
nunciations have been created specifically for *The Lost Pleiades*
series (and all affiliated works), and are the unique product of the
author's imagination. Any similarities or resemblances to existing terms, titles, and persons, are purely coincidental.

FAMILY TREE

GOTO
TESANI
Amelia Goto (née Maia)
Alfredo Goto
Rosa Tesani (née Taygeta)
Giuseppi Tesani
Elenora Goto (née ?)
Giovanni
Mauro (d.) (+ 6 siblings, yet to be introduced)
Silva
Elizabeta Tesani (née Goto)
Leonardo
(+ 5 siblings, yet to be introduced)
Isabella
Stefano
Sophia
Elita "Eli" Tesani
LYCUS
VINCI
Ersella Lycus (née Calaeno)
Adolfo Lycus
Tariess Vinci (1st wife)
Alessandro Vinci
Victoria Mason (2nd wife)*
Christopher
Marco
Alessia "Ále"
Micella
Luca
Dante
*Victoria is is the stepmother of Alessandro's children, not their biological mother.

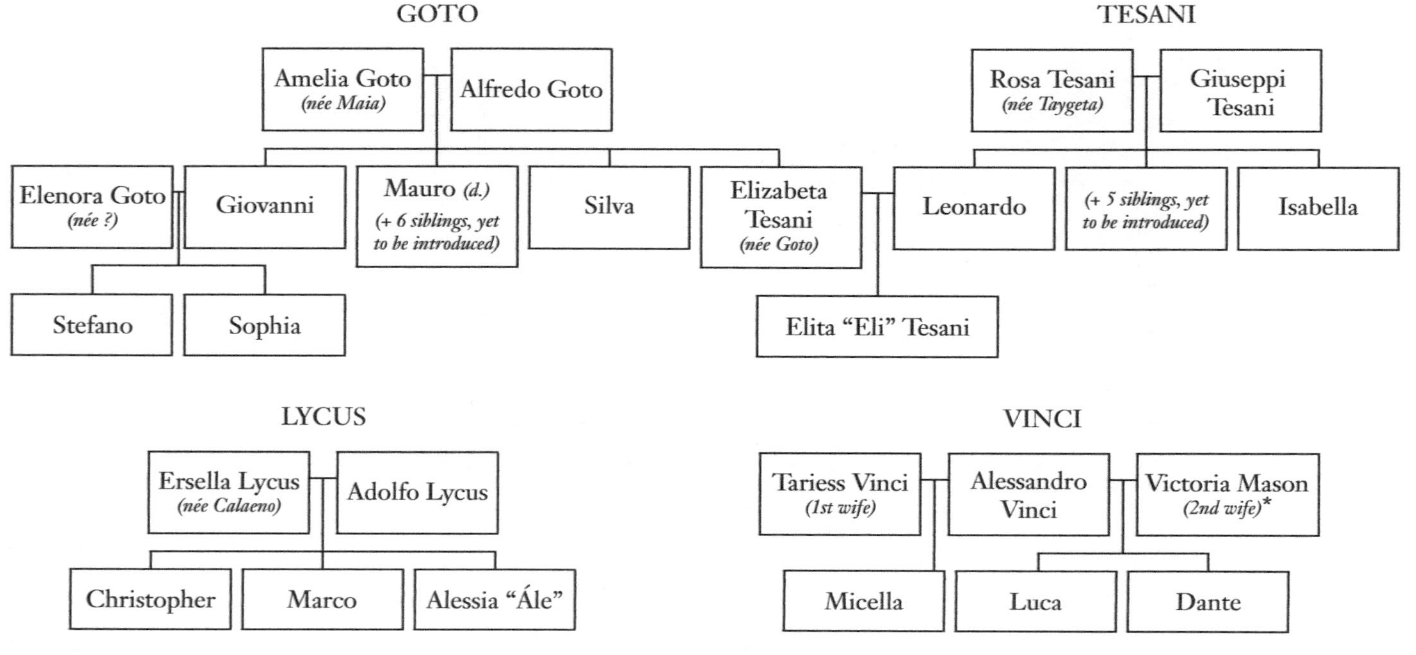

THE PLEIADES
(THE SEVEN SISTERS)

1. MAIA: Amelia by her human name. Her name means "Great One" and she is a healer. She has the ability to heal and/or cure sickness, disease, and pain.

2. TAYGETA: Rosa by her human name. She is the mistress of animals. She can speak, control, and shape-shift into any animal.

3. CELAENO: Ersella by her human name. Siren and Mother of Werewolves.

4. ELECTRA: The mistress of light and electricity, who can use both to travel through time.

5. ALCYONE: The mistress of warding off evil in the world. She is also able to control the weather.

6. ASTRAEA: Also known as Asterope. The mistress of the stars, planets and space. She is the creator of galaxies and Asbgahs. She inspired the image of Virgo and created the Virgo constellation to hide and protect the Seven Sisters.

7. MEROPE: The mistress of taking or giving poison, disease, or darkness, by the use of bees. They call her the "Bee-eater." She both causes and alleviates suffering.

THE SIBYLS

1. SIBYL OF APENNINE, APENNINE SIBYL : Original Creator and Queen of the Faeries, and God's favorite Oracle.

2. PERSIAN SIBYL, BABYLONIAN SIBYL, SAMBETHE : Foretold Noah's destiny and the acts of Alexander the Great. Featured in the Sistine Chapel painted by Michelangelo.

3. LIBYAN SIBYL, EGYPTIAN SIBYL, AGRIPPA OF EGYPT, PHEMONOE : The first of the Oracles to chant her prophecies. She foretold *the coming of the day, that which is hidden, shall be revealed.* Featured in the Sistine Chapel painted by Michelangelo.

4. HEBREW SIBYL, HELREA : Prophetess and writer of the Sibylline Oracles (not to be confused with the Sibylline Books).

5. HELLESPONTINE, VICTORIA MASON : Originally from Turkey, wrote the Sibylline Books, a collection of prophecies written in rhyme in the Greek language. They were used to consult kings during dangerous times. Foretold the Crucifixion of Christ. Stepmother of Luca, Dante, and Micella Vinci. Creator of the Mason Library and founder of the Freemasons.

6. PHRYGIAN SIBYL, CASSANDRA : From an ancient region of Turkey. She has seen a darker side of the world's history. Uncredited author of the Book of Revelation.

7.　CUMAEAN SIBYL OF NAPLES, HEROPHILE : Sang or
　　wrote her prophecies on oak leaves, was a guide to the
　　Underworld for those seeking advice from the dead,
　　sold the very coveted Sibylline Books to the last king
　　of Rome, prophesied the coming of Jesus. Featured in
　　the Sistine Chapel painted by Michelangelo.

8.　TIBURTINE SIBYL, ALBUNEA : FromTivoli, Rome. She
　　prophesied about the Emperor Constantine, as well
　　as the world's final ruler, Emperor Constans, who is
　　foretold to make way for the antichrist.

9.　CIMMERIAN SIBYL, JULIA, CARMENTIS, CHEMISTRY SIBYL
　　: From Lake Avernus. She is the Original Creator of
　　the Elven Asbgah. She is the world's first alchemist
　　and healer.

10.　DELPHIC ORACLE OF ANCIENT GREECE, PYTHIA, KRISA :
　　Mother of the dragons, protector the Great Stone.
　　She was first to announce the birth of Jesus and has
　　been chosen to slay the antichrist. Featured in the
　　Sistine Chapel painted by Michelangelo.

11.　SAMIAN SIBYL, PHYTO : From Samos, Greece.
　　Prophesied the birth of Jesus in March. Responsible
　　for various technological advancements in history.

12.　ERYTHRAEAN SIBYL, ERYMANTHE : From Erythraean,
　　she oversaw the Mediterranean, Aegean and Red
　　Seas. Keeper of the Sibylline Books and the Sibylline
　　Oracles. Prophesied the Trojan War and the redemp-
　　tion of Jesus. Featured in the Sistine Chapel painted
　　by Michelangelo.

GLOSSARY

Ada (Adaturatem) Gold ['æ-d' ('æ-də-tər-a-təm) 'gōld] | *ah-dah (ah-dah-too-rah-tem) gohld* : A powerful metal that bestows extended powers to a magical being. It is a mixture of both the carbons that make diamonds, and the chemical elements that make gold—a very unique and extremely valuable combination. It is the essential element in the golden wings of the faeries, and its only limitation is that it cannot bring anyone back to life. Ada gold is sometimes referred to as "Faerie Gold," because the last of it was used to create these magical creatures.

Asbgah ['æs-bä] | *as-bah* : A kingdom which exists parallel to the human world, and is home to various magical creatures. It is invisible to humans, and discoverable only to a select few. The entrances to the Asbgahs are hidden, and only show themselves to those who are granted access. There are fourteen Asbgahs in total, and they all represent a different faction of the magical, supernatural, and divine.

Apennine Mountains ['a-pə-nēn 'maün-təns] | *ah-peh-neen moun-tns* : Home to Sibyl of Apennine and her Faerie Asbgah, the Apennines are a mountain range that stretches across the Italian peninsula, connecting the southern coast to the northern Italian Alps.

APENNINE WOLF ['a-pə-nēn 'wu̇lf] | *ah-peh-neen woolf* : *Canis lupus italicus*, a threatened subspecies of gray wolf that is endemic to the Apennine Mountains and the Western Alps, and which has been protected in order to encourage repopulation from its vulnerable status. The Apennine wolf is also the final form of the Lycus Werewolf after transition.

BEAII ['bā-ī] | *bey-ai* : A unique braiding/weaving technique known, used, and taught only by faeries. This craft can be applied to braiding hair, as well as weaving intricate baskets, garments, and various textiles.

BLINE [blīn] | *blahyn* : A protective shield crystal that has the ability to multiply and transform into a crystal cave, which provides shelter from danger, and serves as a safe place for private conversations.

CELESTIAL BEING [sə-'les-chəl 'bē(-i)ŋ] | *suh-les-chuhl bee-ing* : A star-borne entity that is part of the Divine Coteah. Celestial Beings are made by God to exist in the heavens, but are able to reside on earth if born here. Each Celestial Being has individual magical powers, which eventually reveal their purpose and full capacity when the chosen time presents itself.

CELESTIAL GOLD [sə-'les-chəl 'gōld] | *suh-les-chuhl gohld* : A precious and sought-after metal, a source of great power for all Celestial Beings. Its magical abilities are individually unique to each Celestial Being who wields it. Similar to Ada Gold, it can grant the power of creation to those who possess or acquire it.

CHIMERA [kī-'mir-ə] | *kai-mee-ruh* : A mythical and magical fire-breathing hybrid creature, with the front of a lion, middle of a goat, and back side of a snake. Long believed to be a monstrous being, chimeras are actually very peaceful unless provoked.

(THE) DARK FOREST ['därk 'fȯr-əst] | *dahrk fohr-ist* : A dead and decaying forest whose outskirts are home to Lord Tygon and the Perdition. It is also where the Judgement Trees are located.

DAWSACAS [dä-'sȯ-kəz] | *dah-saw-cas* : A large, heavy, green fruit-vegetable hybrid resembling a bell pepper, which grows on the palm trees in the Faerie Asbgah, specifically in the garden of Phemonoe (Libyan Sibyl). Ripe and ready to eat in the late summer, it tastes similar to a complex blend of sweet watermelon, apples, strawberries, and chocolate. It is one of Phemonoe's creations.

(THE) DIVINE COTEAH [də-'vīn kō-'tā-yaə] | *dih-vahyn koh-teh-aah* : A pantheon consisting of magical beings created by God in the first fourteen days. This includes heavenly creatures such as Celestial Beings, Original Creators such as Oracles and Mother Nature, as well as holy entities such as angels and Jesus. Also known as the Founding Mothers and Founding Fathers.

ELVES ['elvz] | *elvz* : Strong and fearless magical creatures who reside in the Elven Asbgah, also known as the Emerald Land. They were created by Julia (Cimmerian Sibyl/Chemistry Sibyl) in order to guard the Tree of Life. Their leader is Micella, Queen of the Elves, a valiant warrior, and daughter of Alessandro Vinci.

ERYMANTHE'S CAVES [er-ə-'mænth's 'kāvs] | *er-yh-manth's keyvs* : A series of caverns located in a mountainous landscape of the Faerie Asbgah, made almost completely out of blush-colored rock. The entrance is disguised within the largest and deepest crevasse of the pointy peaks. The caves house Erymanthe's Library, and operate as a school for the faerie children throughout the school year.

ERYMANTHE'S LIBRARY [er-ə-'mænth's 'lī-brer-ē] | *er-yh-manth's lahy-brer-ee* : The hidden library of Erymanthe (Erythraean Sibyl) is a large collection of books and manuscripts, located in Erymanthe's Caves, in the Faerie Asbgah. Although not as massive as the Mason Library, it is still larger than any compilation of literary works that exists in the human world.

FAERIES ['fer-ēs] | *fair-ees* : Magical creatures created by Sibyl of Apennine, using Ada Gold. They have magnificent wings made out of the gold, which makes them vulnerable to those who want to hunt them down for the precious metal. They are nymphs by design, and have been known to lure humans into the Asbgah, in order to expand it. Their bodies are long, slender, and statuesque, and they have hooves for feet. They all vary vastly from one another in appearance, and simultaneously encompass all of the ethnicities of the world.

FAERIE SHRIMP ['fer-ē shrɪmp] | *fair-ee shrimp* : *Chirocephalus marchesonii*, a species of crustacean endemic to Lake Pilate. Feather-like and coral-colored, the shrimp possess numerous fins that give them the appearance of having "faerie wings." They were created by Sibyl of Apennine, and are protectors of the Great Stone.

FREEMASONS ['frē-'mā-səns] | *free-mey-suhns* : A secret organization with lifelong membership, formed in order to protect and preserve the sacred documents and manuscripts within the Mason Library, and tasked with overseeing other precious artifacts scattered all over the world. They are responsible for protecting the most important pieces of information. The leader of the Freemasons is Victoria Mason, otherwise known as the Oracle, Hellespontine.

FOUNDING MOTHERS AND FATHERS ['faυndɪŋ 'fä-<u>th</u>ərs ænd 'mə-<u>th</u>ərs] | *found-ing fah-thers uhnd muhth-ers* : The powerful and magical beings designed and conceived by God in the first fourteen days of creation. Otherwise known as the Divine Coteah.

(THE) GREAT STONE ['grāt 'stōn] | *greyt stohn* : A stone hidden in the depths of Lake Pilate which represents the center of the Earth. It was placed in the exact location where creation began, and it is meant to stay there until the end of time—moving it results in dire consequences. Covered in ancient, etched symbols which foretell the end of humanity, it is also the entrance to the Underworld. Pythia (Krisa, Delphic of Greece) is the protector of the Great Stone, as are the faerie shrimp of Lake Pilate.

HALLEDRITE ['hæ-lə-drīt] | *hal-luh-drahyt* : A magical crystal used since ancient times to both initiate and block conversation. When held tightly while thinking of someone, it will connect to that person. When worn on the body, it causes interference, blocking others from hearing one's thoughts or listening to what one is saying.

HIPPOCAMPUS [hi-pə-'kæm-pəs] | *hip-uh-kam-puhs* : A majestic and aquatic hybrid creature, with the upper half of their body a horse, and the lower half a fish. Avid and agile swimmers, they are the fastest when completely submerged underwater.

IGNI ['ig-nē] | *ig-nee* : Mortals who do not believe that magic exists. It refers to someone who is a skeptic, and needs to see the truth instead of just hearing it.

JUDGEMENT TREES ['jəj-mənt 'trēs] | *juhj-muhnt treez* : Located in the Dark Forest, the Judgement Trees are a portal which allows an individual to travel to any time and any place, but under a very specific stipulation. If one journeys through the forest with a pure heart and good intention, the Judgement Trees will allow them to go anywhere, in any timeline. But if one's heart is tainted, the trees will tear them from limb from limb, and will suck their soul into the Underworld.

KNIGHTS TEMPLAR ['nīts 'tem-plər] | *nahyts tem-pler* : The wealthiest and most powerful Christian military order in the west, founded in 1119 in France. They existed for over two centuries, and were responsible for single-handedly destroying artifacts, books, art, buildings, temples, and anything having to do with knowledge of life before Christianity. These actions were carried out in the name of abolishing Paganism, and preserving only Christian history and legacy.

LAKE PILATE ['lāk 'pī-lət] | *leyk pai-let* : *Lago di Pilato* is a lake located in the heart of the Sibillini Mountains, at the base of the highest peak, Monte Vettore. It's one of the very few glacial lakes in the Apennines. Home to the faerie shrimp and the Great Stone, the lake is also considered the entrance to the Underworld. It has been referred to as the "Cursed Lake," but is originally named after Pontius Pilate.

(THE) LOST PLEIADES ['lȯst 'plē-ə-dēz] | *lawst plee-uh-deez* : Refers to the three of the Pleiades (Seven Sisters) who stayed behind on Earth, while their Celestial Being counterparts all ascended back to the heavens. The three sisters who remained were Maia, Taygeta, and Celaeno. They first took refuge in Sibyl's Faerie Asbgah, and later settled in the human world.

LUFATA [lü-'fə-tə] | *loo-fah-ta* : A luminous, floating creature that is a hybrid between a faerie and a lantern. From far away they look like fireflies, but they are actually the same height as an average human. They are albino faeries. The bottom half of a Lufata's body is a large, round lantern that illuminates soft light, and the top of their bodies is faerie.

LYCUS ['lā-kəs] | *lai-kuhs* : A magical creature that can transition from human form into a wolf, and back again. Colloquially known as werewolves, these Hounds of God are both benevolent beings, as well as fearless protectors of God and the Heavens. Lycus can either be born or created—some are the descendants of original werewolves, and carry their ability to metamorphose through the generations. Others have the gift bestowed upon them when they are called to serve—only Adolfo Lycus, the Father of Werewolves, and those in his direct bloodline, have the power to grant this honor and to manifest a new lycus.

MAGI ['mȯ-jē] | *mah-jee* : An individual who is of a pure magical bloodline.

MASON LIBRARY ['mā-sən 'lī-brer-ē] | *mey-suhn lahy-brer-ee* : The most exclusive and vast library in the world, named for its founder Victoria Mason (the Oracle Hellespontine). The library is the home to thousands of secret documents, lost treasures, and ancient manuscripts, all of which are carefully preserved and fiercely guarded.

MONTE VETTORE ['mȯn-tə 've-tȯr-e] | *mon-teh ve-tor-eh* : The highest peak of the Sibillini massif, a mountain group located in the Apennine Mountain range. Just below the peak there is a small enclosed valley which contains Lake Pilate. Known as the "King of Sibillini," it is the most striking mountain of all the Apennines, and sits over eight thousand feet above sea level.

NERVITUS LIBERUS [nər-'vē-təs 'li-bə-rəs] | *ner-vee-tuhs lyh-beh-ruhs* : Alchemy drops created by Julia (Chemistry Sibyl/Cimmerian Sibyl) which relieve ailments such as nerves, stress, anxiety, and depression.

NIGHT-BLOOMING CEREUS ['nīt 'blü-miŋ 'sir-ē-əs] | *nahyt blu-ming seer-ee-uhs* : A beautiful nocturnal plant which only blooms once a year, for a single night. During that time, the Cereus can hear any conversation that occurs around them, and is able to relay the information to other night creatures.

ORACLES ['ȯr-ə-kəlz] | *or-ah-kulz* : Breathtakingly beautiful, powerful, and immortal prophetesses. Also known as Sibyls, all original oracles are virgins, and are part of the Divine Coteah. Legend says that the sacred Temple to Apollo Gergithius gave birth to them, but they are actually one of God's first creations. Before they and their prophecies were silenced by Christians in the fourth century, they were known to be the intermediaries between God and man, and the keepers of all secrets. For centuries the oracles were sought out by kings, emperors, popes, and various world leaders, to guide them in their quest for

power. There are twelve original oracles, since that is
the number used in the Bible and throughout history,
to symbolize God's power and authority. There also
exist instances of human oracles who were given the
gift of prophecy via divine intervention, and who now-
adays identify themselves as psychics, mediums, seers,
tarot card readers, and intuitives.

ORDER OF THE EASTERN STAR ['ȯr-dər 'əv 'thə 'ē-stərn
'stär] | *awr-der ov theh ee-stern stahr* : A division of
the Freemasons that is open to both men and wom-
en. Founded in the mid 1800s, it was created for the
daughters, widows, wives, sisters, and mothers of the
Master Masons, to serve. Just as their Freemason
counterparts, the women of the Order also have titles,
and serve in unique positions.

ORIGINAL CREATOR [ə-'ri-jə-nəl krē-'ā-tər] | *oh-rij-uh-
nl kree-ey-ter* : A powerful and magical being created
by God, who in turn granted them the sacrosanct ability to create other beings/creatures. Mother Nature,
the Father of Magic, and the twelve Oracles, are all
Original Creators. Since they were formed by God
in the first fourteen days, they are part of the Divine
Coteah/Founding Mothers and Fathers.

PENTWILIN BIRDS ['pent-wəl-ən 'bərds] | *pent-wil-in
burds* : Part of the hummingbird family, these loqua-
cious birds are larger than their well-known cousins,
and their wings move at an even faster speed, which
makes it appear as if they are floating in the air.
Pentwilins are endemic to the woods in the Sibillini
National Forest, which is why they are not common-

ly known nor recognized—they are also shy around humans and have a tendency to disguise themselves. They are as green as forest moss, and their enrapturing songs are known to soothe and comfort the soul. Endearingly called "story-birds," these winged couriers sing their conversations and tell stories, and are Sibyl of Apennine's loyal servants and messengers.

(THE) PERDITION [pər-'di-shən] | *per-dish-uhn* :
A dangerous and evil group of beings that believe in a state of eternal damnation. Their acts of brutality are without limits, and they are led by the ruthless Lord Tygon. They believe that a state of punishment should go on forever, and pain should be invoked on those who believe in God, love, peace, etc. Above all, they believe that all worlds should come to an end, so everyone's souls can finally become nothingness . . . they are convinced that alone can bring the ultimate peace.

PHOENIX ['fē-niks] | *fee-nix* : A mythical creature known for its fiery death, and subsequent reincarnation. This bird with many lives is associated with the sun and fire, and arises from the ashes of its recently deceased previous form.

(THE) PINK FOREST ['piŋk 'for-əst] | *pingk fohr-ist* :
Located in Sibyl of Apennine's Faerie Asbgah, the forest serves as a Faerie Camp for the faerie children, to which they are sent every year when not in school. It is the only place where they can truly learn how to spread their wings with confidence, and control their Faerie magic. As a designated protector of all children, the Pink Forest and its magic cloaks the Ada Gold in

the young faeries' wings, so should anyone see them, they just look like normal children playing in a day camp.

(THE) PLEIADES STAR CLUSTER ['plē-ə-dēz 'stär 'klə-stər] | *plee-uh-deez stahr kluhs-ter* : Otherwise known as the Seven Sisters, the Pleiades star cluster is located in the Taurus constellation, and mirrors the stars that create the Virgo constellation. Only four of the seven stars are visible to the naked eye, since three of the sisters stayed behind on Earth, and became known as the Lost Pleiades.

POTIODAMUS [pō-shə-'dä-məs] | *poh-shuh-dah-muhs* : Alchemy drops created by Julia (Chemistry Sibyl/ Cimmerian Sibyl) which relieve ailments such headaches, nausea, hangovers, dehydration, and boost overall wellness.

SABO ['sa-bō] | *sah-bow* : A gigantic orange fruit which grows in the Faerie Asbgah, specifically in the garden dedicated to Phemonoe (Libyan Sibyl). They are as big as grapefruits, and are extremely juicy and flavorful—they taste both super sweet, and a little tart.

SAPONARIA FLOWERS [sa-pȯ-'ner-ē-ə 'flau̇(-ə)rs] | *sah-poh-ner-ee-ah flou-erz* : Small pink and lavender flowers that turn into a luxurious soap, when dipped in water and rubbed in between one's hands. The result is a foamy, bubbly delight, with an intoxicating and relaxing fragrance. They grow in abundance in both the Faerie Asbgah and the human world surrounding it.

SCAPEGRACES ['skāp-grās-əz] | *skeyp-grey-siz* :
Mischievous and brash little creatures that reside in
the Faerie Asbgah. They resemble a cross between a
ginger owl and a squirrel with red and black markings,
and have a round, squished-in face with pointy ears.
They are incorrigible rascals who hoard olives, chase
Pentwilin birds, and aren't shy about snatching food
away from one's hand.

(THE) SEVEN SISTERS ['se-vən 'si-stərs] | *sev-uhn sis-
terz* : Individually known as Maia, Taygeta, Celaeno,
Electra, Alcyone, Astraea, and Merope. The daughters of Atlas and Pleione, and otherwise known as the
Pleiades, the Seven Sisters are Celestial Beings who
each possess individually specific magical powers.
They form the Pleiades Star Cluster; however, only
four of the seven stars are visible to the naked eye,
since three of the sisters stayed behind on Earth, and
became known as the Lost Pleiades. One of the Seven
Sisters, Astraea, created the Virgo constellation to
hide and protect the other Pleiades. She did this by
arranging the stars of the Virgo constellation in almost
the same layout as the Seven Sister star cluster, to act
as a decoy.

SIBILLINI MOUNTAINS [si-bə-'lē-nē 'maủn-təns] |
syh-buh-lee-nee moun-tns : A massif of the Apennine
mountains, Sibillini is the area of the mountain group
that borders Umbria and Marche. Mostly composed
of limestone, the mountains formed fifty to one hundred million years ago at the bottom of what is now
an extinct sea. The land itself emerged about twenty

million years ago. The highest peak can be reached at Monte Vettore, otherwise known as "King of Sibillini."

SIBYL ['si-bəl] | *syh-buhl* : Also known as Sibyl of Apennine and the Eleventh Sibyl, she is the most gifted and powerful prophetess who has ever existed; a virgin oracle who can foresee into the future, and look back in the past. As God's favorite oracle, she thought she could persuade him to let her become a mother, but after God denied her this wish and she defied him, he condemned her to live in the Apennine mountains until the end of time. Since then, Sibyl has built her own majestic kingdom in the mountains, part of which are now named Sibillini in her honor. She fulfilled her destiny as an Original Creator by using magic to populate her Asbgah with loyal subjects—faeries which she created out of Ada Gold.

SIBYLLINE ORACLES ['si-bə-lēn ȯr-ə-kəlz] | *syh-buh-leen or-ah-kulz* : A collection of detailed Sibylline prophecies from before the birth of Jesus, consisting of 12 tomes, and written by Helrea (Hebrew Sibyl). Not to be confused with the Sibylline Books, the Sibylline Oracles are the first part in the series of the two anthologies, and are a selection of thorough and byzantine narratives from all the Sibyls, of what is now referred to as "classical mythology." The Sibylline Oracles also contain the early millennium of the Gnostic, Hellenistic, Jewish, and Christian beliefs, as well as apocalyptic literature about God carrying out his last judgement, and of course, the coming of the Messiah.

SIBYLLINE BOOKS ['si-bə-lēn 'bŭks] | *syh-buh-leen bookz* : A collection of prophecies written in rhyme in the Greek language, consisting of 12 tomes, and attributed to Hellespontine (Victoria Mason). Not to be confused with the Sibylline Oracles, the Sibylline Books are the second part in the series of the two anthologies, and are a selection of Sibylline prophecies about the destiny of the world. They contain the detailed visions each oracle received about the birth, life, and ultimately the crucifiction, death, and resurrection of their Savior, Jesus Christ. Because of the incredibly meticulous accounts found in the Sibylline Books, kings were often known to consult them during dangerous times.

SILPHIUM ['sil-fē-əm] | *syl-phee-uhm* : A yellow flower with numerous long, thin petals. A relative of the daisy family, it is believed to be extinct. The last human record of its existence was around 1 BC.

SIREN ['sī-rən] | *sahy-ruhn* : A magical, aquatic hybrid creature with the upper-half of their body being human, and the lower-half resembling the bottom of a fish. The scales on their legs resemble abstract seashells, and are the color of soft pastels. Although sirens are able to manipulate the minds of others once they are enraptured, they cannot actually read minds; it's more of a connection to a person, and the feeling and understanding of their thoughts and emotions.

SPICA ['spī-kə] | *spahy-kuh* : The central star of the
Virgo constellation, and one of the brightest stars in
the sky. The name is derived from Latin, and means
"ear of wheat," which the astrological sign of Virgo
carries in her hand. On Eden's Tour of the Seven
Churches, the church at Santa Maria in Pantano is
revealed to have been built under the exact position of
the Spica star of the Virgo constellation, in a land only
ever known to grow wheat.

SYNCRETISM ['siŋ-krə-ti-zəm] | *sing-kri-tiz-uhm* : The
distinct merging of different philosophies, specifically
that of organized religion and pagan beliefs.

TAURUS (TALOS) ['tȯr-əs ('tä-lōs)] | *tawr-uhs*
(*tah-lows*) : A mythical god known throughout history and various religions under names such as the
Giant Man of Bronze, the Golden Calf, or the Sacred
Bull. In our modern world, he is known as Taurus.
Talos was the last Celestial Being on Earth (or so he
thought), and before he could rejoin his love Astrea
(Virgo), and the rest of the Seven Sisters back in the
heavens, he was tasked by God with transporting
the body of Pontius Pilate to the Underworld. After
fulfilling his destiny, Talos reclaimed his place in the
heavens.

(THE) TAURUS CONSTELLATION [tȯr-əs kän(t)-stə-'lā-
shən] | *tawr-uhs kon-stuh-ley-shuhn* : One of the oldest
and most prominent constellations, it dates back to
the Early Bronze Age, and contains thousands of stars,
as well as two open-star clusters. One of those star
clusters are the Pleiades, or the Seven Sisters.

TREE OF LIFE ['trē 'əv 'līf] | *tree ov lahyf* : A magical and sacred tree created by God, that is the root of all life, all existence, and the beginning and end to all things.

UNIEQUUS [yü-'nē-kwis] | *yoo-nee-kwis* : Disguised as magnificent arabian horses in the human world, these magical creatures are able to reveal their true form in the Asbgahs—they are the last of the unicorns in existence. Once hunted, slaughtered, and stripped of their horns by execution orders from the Catholic Church, these majestic beings can only survive outside of the Asbgahs under disguise. Unicorns have a unique ability of connecting with their riders, but only with those who are privileged enough to gain their trust.

VIRGO CONSTELLATION ['vər-gō kän(t)-stə-'lā-shən] | *vur-goh kon-stuh-ley-shuhn* : Created by Virgo to hide and protect the Seven Sisters. She did this by arranging the stars of the Virgo constellation in almost the same layout as the Pleiades/Seven Sister star cluster, to act as a decoy. Virgo's real name is Astraea meaning "star-maiden," and she is one of the Pleiades/Seven Sisters.

VELLOUS [ve-'lüs] | *veh-loos* : A portal used as a communication tool between those in the Asbgahs and the human world. Described as a bubble in the veil between the two worlds, the Vellous is its own micro-dimension. They exist all over the globe, and they can be anywhere, both in a physical and metaphysical sense. One can also access the Vellous using communication crystals, such as the Halledrite. It's imperative to only use the Vellous for short periods of time, as anyone who enters the portal—whether magical or human—is not protected. They can be shot, killed, and even catch the common cold.

GRATITUDE

To my mother and father Marina and Giovanni Testa without whom this book would never be possible. Being your child has been a gift beyond measure. Thank you for sacrificing so much so I could dream. I love you infinitely.

My endless love to my one and only Original Creators Dominika Ossowska, Michelle Footer, and Tabita Padilla. Thank you for giving me your heart and soul with this project. Thank you for the long days and endless hours. Thank you for the insight, passion, laughter, and belief. You have stood by my side and never lost sight of the vision; that has given me the strength to not give up. Your brilliant minds push me to be better and go harder. I wouldn't have wanted to do this with anyone else. Thank you each for your genius and for inspiring me. You have all been a light and compass in my life. You are magnificent. My heart is indebted to you. I love you! It's me and you forever in the Asbgahs!

Thank you to Tabita Padilla and Christy Greenwood for the magical music. To Shannon Marang Cox, Sara Smith, Elise Sherman for proof reading, input and guidance. To Kevin Mills for consulting and sharing all your amazing knowledge of the world of self-publishing. To the Gophers for your friendship and love. To all my friends and family for their love and support throughout this process. To Lizz Lopez for the incredible artwork. You inspire me every day of my life! To Siouxsie Sioux and Depeche Mode for the soundtrack of my life. Your music has been my constant.